THE
RAINS

Voices for American Liberty

Sulayman Clark

LAUREATE HOUSE PRESS

Library of Congress Control Number:
2006907507

ISBN: 978-1-4243-1264-1

Front Cover Design: Michael Sibley and Vincent Bungy

VOICES FOR AMERICAN LIBERTY

"Those who give up essential liberty to purchase a little temporary safety deserve neither *liberty* nor safety."

Benjamin Franklin

"Is life so dear, or peace so sweet, as to be purchased at the price of chains and slavery? Forbid it, Almighty God! I know not what course others may take; but as for me, give me *liberty* or give me death!"

Patrick Henry

"It seems almost incredible that the advocates of *liberty* should conceive of the idea
of selling a fellow creature to slavery."

James Forten

"I would fight for my *liberty* as long as my strength lasted; and if the time came for me to go, the Lord would let them take me."

Harriet Tubman

"Let it be said by our children's children that when we were tested we refused to let this journey end, that we did not turn back nor did we falter; and with eyes fixed on the horizon and God's grace upon us, we carried forth that great gift of freedom and delivered it safely to future generations."

Barack Obama

Dedication

For my mother, Ethel Clark Humphries—
my first teacher, my eternal friend,

My sister, Bahiyyah —
who admirably carries her flame,

and

My closest and best friend —Monette Evans.

By the grace of God, love is a woman. She brings forth life and
is a constant source of renewal—much like the rains.

1. The Dream

"Into each life some rain must fall,
some days must be dark and dreary."
Henry Wadsworth Longfellow

Life rarely if ever, presents us with extended periods of unbroken sunshine. There are many rains – stinging, pelting rains carried by dark clouds that obscure our vision, challenge our faith and separate us from the light.

Chastened by sorrow and unspeakable loss, William Still came to accept such things. Yet he remembered that the rains had also brought him much joy and moments of intense delight. In the twilight of his years, he clung to fond memories of happier days with his first love; a passionate woman who taught him how to love, and surrender himself to her loving embrace and the gentle patter of the rains.

He lived alone now and wrestled with recurring feelings of emptiness and that maddening back and forth between hope and despair. It was a daily struggle not to give in to the latter. She surely would not have approved of such sadness. She would have encouraged him to have faith and look to the future. And as usual, she would be right. He dared not fail her – that special woman who taught him how to find serenity in the soothing sights and sounds of the rains.

Time seemed to collapse in on itself as his days began to run together. Even the years began to fold up against each other like one of those pleated accordions that once spread merriment in the streets of Philadelphia. Many were the days when his tears mingled with the rains and his eyes saw little of the goodness and beauty in the world. His life was slipping away from him and it seemed as though nothing could stop its downward spiral. But that proved not to be the case at all.

It is said that we live in houses constructed from our habitual and innermost thoughts. For a while and much to his detriment, William Still had unconsciously chosen a prison for his dwelling place. It was a seemingly impenetrable fortress without fences or armed guards; a place where happiness would be forever confined, neither let in, nor let out. There he seemed destined to live out the balance of his weary existence. There, but for the grace of God, he would die a despondent and forgotten man, with seldom a skyward glance.

But then came that gray and rainy day in October 1871, when the clouds mercifully parted and he was relieved by a rare occurrence. What first appeared as a tiny glimpse of sunlight, soon gained in strength and intensity as it spread across the dimmed horizon of his troubled soul. Its gentle warmth slowly imposed a spring-like thaw that signaled the end of frozen hope and the beginning of new life. It was then that an emboldened William Still began to patiently hack away at the dense mental thickets that had slowly grown beyond proportion and completely enveloped his mind.

His slow recovery began with a vivid dream that was hatched deep in the inner recesses of his subconscious mind. In it, he wandered through a dense forest where he could barely see the ground beneath his feet. Then came a light beckoning him forward and illuminating a winding path out of the untamed wilderness. He doggedly followed it for a long while. There were indeed moments of hesitancy and indecision. Yet each faithful step added to his confidence and brought him closer and closer to a river—a river whose source was hidden. Following the course of its peaceful flow, he discovered that the mighty river emptied into an ocean of limitless possibilities.

By day's end, the sun had receded, but he could still feel its warm embrace. He paused for rest and reflection at a once familiar place, where the predictable river met the unfathomable expanse—the infinite sea. Lying on his back, he peered at the impressive moon and the canopy of glimmering stars stretched across the evening sky. They seemed to whisper the universe's insistence on order and hint at inescapable realities beyond the realm of common understanding.

A peaceful sleep came just before midnight while a murky fog settled in and lingered through dawn. Hours passed until William Still was awakened in the morning by troublesome bodily pains. And there remained subtle but undeniable psychic wounds that perhaps would never be completely healed. Yet he had survived the long, dark night of uncertainty and disillusionment. It was indeed, a defining moment. He stood erect for the first time in a long time and stared confidently at the far horizon. That day, he took on the unmistakable glow of a spiritual warrior who was at once restored by a benevolent sun and renewed by the healing powers of the rains. It was only a dream. Yet, it seemed so very, very real.

2. Through the Mist of Time: Secrets Kept and Stories Long Forgotten

"Weeping may endure for a night; but joy cometh in the morning."
Psalms 30:5

Joy most certainly came in the morning and born anew was the will to fight back. That dream was only the beginning. In the larger scheme of things, it was but a brief revelatory flash of light. His full recovery took much more time. It surely did not happen all at once. It was more like a season; a season of redemption when he gradually realized new purpose and meaning for his life. It was time for this old warrior to take up new weapons and embrace a new moral assignment. It was a time when he decided to be of all things, a writer – or perhaps more accurately, a storyteller.

William Still had countless stories to tell. For almost three decades, these stories remained untold. That was because they were deposited with him as secrets. Mr. Still was a man who could be relied upon to keep secrets – deeply personal and dangerous secrets. Secrets carefully held and secrets long buried and forgotten—they would be the substance of the incredible stories he would tell.

For many years, it was best that Mr. Still's closely held secrets remained secrets. However, with the passage of time, they could now be set free. Many of his friends had passed on or were safe and beyond the reach of the law. They had endured the long winter of bitter trial and persecution and disclosure could do them no harm. In fact, he came to realize that these secrets could yield much good. That was the inspiration that came to him thirty years ago, on a rainy day in October. It now fell to him and him alone, to tell these stories and to rescue from oblivion those souls who had been written out of history and were all but forgotten. In the end, it was his sincere wish that these stories would somehow uplift others and be a source of inspiration.

Much like the rains, he hoped they would create new life. And, just as the clouds bring forth the rains, he prayed that his humble literary offering would help to replenish the land and reanimate their struggle for a greater America. Like thunderclaps heard from a great distance, he wanted these stories to reverberate across generations, proclaiming again and again an unshakable determination to secure their most sacred liberties.

Baltimore, 1839

Of all the many stories he could recall, Mr. Still never tired of telling this particular tale about two most remarkable people. After five days of strenuous travel, the two had found their way to Baltimore's fashionable Red Rose Inn. The Inn was a well-established hotel and restaurant, popular among wayfarers and local residents. Its crimson shutters, colorful signpost and cobblestone pathway set it apart from the unadorned businesses that lined the dusty thoroughfare known as Chancellor Street. Two days of torrential rain had saturated the city, leaving behind a muddy slush that was difficult to traverse.

The quietness of the street was disrupted by the arrival of a creaky horse-drawn carriage bringing two weary travelers – a diminutive white gentleman of apparent wealth and his Negro manservant. The gentleman was fashionably dressed wearing a well-tailored suit, matching stove top hat and green tinted spectacles. His right hand was in a sling and his face was muffled with a poultice, suggesting a facial distortion or perhaps some inexplicable physical ailment. In stark contrast, his manservant was a tall Negro dressed in dusty brown britches that were held up by a knotted rope. His sleeveless and loosely-stitched burlap shirt revealed his broad shoulders and well-developed biceps, leaving little doubt that he possessed an uncommon muscular strength. His ashen and angular face reflected an intense demeanor that was accentuated by his fixed and disciplined attention to the gentleman's every movement.

Bringing his horses to a slippery halt, the white coachman stopped in front of the Inn and stepped down from the carriage. He was a stocky, unshaven man, with a barrel chest, just slightly wider than his protruding belly. Opening the carriage door and spitting out a well-chewed wad of tobacco, he bellowed,

"Here ya ar sir. Ain't a better place in all of Baltimore. The finest food and drink and the finest wommin folk serving it up…If you know what I mean (wink). I'll be helping you in with your luggage."

"No sir, that won't be necessary, Ol' Henry here attends to all of my needs and he is quite good at it."

As the gentleman stepped down, the coachman gripped his hand. Henry helped him dismount by cupping his two hands together to form a fleshy step into which the gentleman placed his muddy boot.

"Well that'll be five dollars fare from the dock to here. And mind ya, anything else you decide to offer in addition will be greatly appreciated by my wife and six children."

Having reached the solid footing of the cobblestone path, the gentleman reached in his pocket and added an extra fifty cents to the fare.

"Well, I thank you sir for your services and for your fine courtesy. But, that will be all. My very best to you and your family."

Having settled his account, the gentleman walked slowly into the inn with unsure and measured steps. Inspecting his payment, the coachman walked back to the carriage where Henry was unloading a huge trunk.

"Say thar boy, where ya'll headed off to tomorrow?

"We's gwine norf to Pheedadelfee to visit masta's uncle who is a doctor dere."

"A doctor you say? Well I'll be."

"Yessa, I reckon he gonna help cure masta of his rooma-tissum."

"Is that so? I figured something was ailing him. Where'd yaw come from anyway? Virginny?"

"No sa, we done come all the ways from Savanna Joja. We's been trabeling for about five days now – over land and water."

Watching idly as Henry continued his unloading, the coachman pondered the identity of his latest passenger; silently grafting mental assumptions to his careful observations. He concluded that the gentleman must have been some sort of plantation owner. Judging from the softness of his hands, he further surmised that he had probably never done a hard day's work in his life. Irritated by that thought, he continued his crude interrogation.

"I bet he's got a spread as big as the state of Maryland. Yeah, he probably has another two to three hundred other darkies like you working for him, huh?"

"Yessa, I spec he do."

"Now listen up boy, I'll be back here in the morning to take you and your rich master to the train station. I don't suppose you can tell time, but you just remind him to be ready at eight o'clock, ya hear? Those train folk run a tight operation and don't wait for no one; not even a fine, hoity-toity gentleman like your master. Ya hear me?"

"Yessa, I rememba, eight o'clock. Yessa, eight o'clock it is."

Hoisting the huge trunk onto his back, Henry felt himself weighted down; not so much by the trunk, but by the coachman's caustic insults and his flagrant disrespect and disregard for his manhood – his humanity. Inside the hotel lobby, the gentleman rang a small desk bell, summoning a clerk who greeted him with an effervescent smile.

"Good afternoon sir. May I help you?"

"Yes, you may. I'd like a room for the evening."

"Well, I suppose a gentleman of your caliber would be taking our Calvert Suite. It costs more, but I assure you it's the finest room in the house."

"Well that will be just fine sir."

"All right then, that'll be ten dollars. No need for any money now sir. Not likely that a gentleman such as yourself would be skipping out without paying his tab. No sir, you can pay in the morning when you check out."

His cheerful greeting was interrupted by the appearance of Henry effortlessly carrying the huge trunk into the plush hotel lobby. The clerk was momentarily distracted by Henry's imposing stature, but pretended not to notice him. He politely attempted to conclude the transaction by turning the hotel ledger towards the gentleman.

"Now if you'll sign our registry, I'll be glad to show you your room."

"I'm afraid that you have me at a disadvantage sir. As you can see, my writing hand is somewhat out of commission at the moment. But my servant here can sign for me."

The clerk looked on in subtle amusement as Henry lowered the trunk to the floor and grasped the pen in his huge calloused hand.

"Well if that don't beat all. A niggra that can use a pen! That'll be just fine sir. And by the way, we own the stable at the end of this street. Your niggra can stay there for the evening. No extra charge."

Accustomed to such treatment, Henry stood in unflinching silence as his master displayed a restrained but unmistakably bitter reaction.

"Once again, sir we seem to have a problem; one that I hope we can address with the utmost discretion."

"I don't understand."

"You see Henry here is my personal valet. Unfortunately, I need him at every moment to help dress me and fetch my medicine in the wee hours of the night when I have my regrettable fits and spasms. No sir, I can't do without him."

"I perfectly understand your situation sir, but surely you don't expect us to have him sleep under this roof?"

The brief silence of their stalemate was suddenly broken by the gentleman, who pounded his fist on the counter.

"No sir, apparently you *do not* understand my situation at all! I do not wish to give offense to you or your fine guests, but having Henry at my beck and call is the only way I have managed to survive these last few months. And if you can not be more sympathetic to my medical condition, I suppose I must take my business elsewhere!"

"Now see here, of course he can stay with you. Believe me; you can count on my discretion. Yes sir, if nothing else, I can be discreet."

He immediately extended his open palm to suggest his readiness to receive a gratuity. Reaching into his wallet, the gentleman placed a few dollars on the counter.

"I believe you can. Yes, I believe you can. Now if you will be kind enough to show me my room, I would be much obliged. And you can have my assurance that he will sleep on the floor at the foot of my bed, where he is accustomed."

"Why of course sir, of course. Right up those stairs, it's the second room on your right."

"Come along Henry, you mustn't dawdle."

Without further direction, Henry lifted the heavy trunk yet again and followed his master up a long spiral staircase. Opening the door, the gentleman was pleased to observe that the Calvert Suite was every bit as luxurious as the clerk had described it. Once inside, he closed the satin draperies and walked over to a huge four-poster bed. After removing his hat, he sighed and whispered to Henry.

"Did you lock the door?"
Walking towards the bed, Henry softly answered.

"Yes, believe me it is very locked and you are so very, very beautiful."

Henry instantly removed his shirt and the gentleman quickly removed his arm sling, glasses and overcoat. The two of them engaged in a long bodily embrace and fell into bed as their bodies entwined in an intimate ritual of love and celebration.

At this point in the story, Mr. Still would hasten to explain that these travelers were not at all who they appeared to be. The gentleman was actually a beautiful fair-skinned mulatto woman named Ellen Craft who was masquerading as a white man. The servant (known as Henry), was in fact, her devoted husband, William Craft. They were both runaway slaves headed for Pennsylvania, a free state directly to the North. Their stay at the Red Rose Inn was their last stopover, as they prepared to take the train from Baltimore to Philadelphia; the final leg of their long journey to freedom. After their passionate interlude, they lay in bed reflecting in the dimly lit room. William warmly caressed his wife and whispered.

"We did it my angel, we did it."

"No my love, *you* did it. I was so afraid, so shamefully afraid back there."

"Listen to me Ellen, you did just fine. And once we get on the train tomorrow, this nightmare will be over. We can't weaken now. We'll have our whole lives ahead of us."

"You're so right, thank God."

"Ellen, how much money do we have left?"

"Not much I'm afraid. I didn't figure on the cost of this fancy room. That fool clerk pressured me into it; looking suspicious with those beady eyes of his. We barely have enough to cover our carriage ride and buy our train tickets to Philadelphia."

"Now don't be blaming yourself. It couldn't be helped. You did the right thing. But do we at least have enough to buy some breakfast?"

"I suppose, maybe a biscuit or two."

"Well then, that will be our *last supper* as slaves. Yes…it will be our last meal in Hell."

∞∞∞∞∞∞∞∞∞∞

The next morning, William was awakened by a sliver of light that had forced itself passed the thick embroidered curtains of the Calvert suite. He gazed at Ellen who was fast asleep. She was a warm-hearted and strikingly beautiful woman. Edging closer, he smiled at the crude haircut he had given her, compliments of a rusty pair of pruning shears. He had grown accustomed to her flowing chestnut-brown hair and the way it framed her oval face and accentuated her penetrating eyes. He figured that it would probably be months before he could twirl her locks with his fingers again. No matter. That delayed gratification was a very small price for the two of them to pay in order to gain their freedom.

It was much too early to get up. Better to let her sleep as long as possible. Yesterday's tensions had taken her to the brink of emotional collapse. She needed rest and as much of it as possible. Unfortunately, his amorous mood found no distraction. He longed to caress her silky skin again and slowly extended his reach. Then, with a mighty burst of self-discipline, his left arm froze in mid-air as he overpowered the urge to disturb her peaceful slumber.

Ellen Craft in disguise

William tossed and turned and found it impossible to get back to sleep. The week leading up to their escape had been utterly horrific and the painful memories of it constantly agitated his mind. It began with the brutal beating of his best friend, Ned. He and Ned worked the cotton fields and harvested seasonal crops on the sprawling Ferrette plantation in Chatham County, South Carolina. Ned's wife, Matilda, and Ellen were also good friends and worked together as chambermaids in the Ferrette mansion where they attended to Mrs. Ferrette and her two over-demanding children.

It had all happened so quickly. He struggled in vain to stop replaying the events in his mind. On Monday, all of the field hands had been ordered to gather their children and report to the huge storage barn, a distance of two miles away from the slave quarters. When William arrived, he saw Ellen, Matilda, and an additional sixty or so slaves assembled. They were strangely somber and had fear written all over their faces. Mrs. Ferrette and her two sons were there as well, standing motionless with rapt attention.

He followed their gaze to the middle of the cavernous structure where he saw Ned hanging by his wrists from a braided hemp rope that had been hoisted over the center beam. Mr. Ferrette insisted that everyone look straight ahead and form a tight circle as he proceeded to flog Ned unmercifully with a studded cat-o-nine tails. This ghastly spectacle must have taken all of twenty minutes, but it seemed like an eternity. Wringing with perspiration, Mr. Ferrette's arms began to fatigue and he dropped to his knees; but not before he had reduced Ned's back to a soft, mushy pulp. The thrashing was so severe that they had to grease Ned's back just to remove his shirt and tend to his wounds. He died later that night in the arms of his terror-stricken wife.

The circumstances surrounding this brutal exhibition were sketchy at best. Rumors had been circulating in the slave quarters that Ned had been caught stealing a large pork shank from the plantation's smokehouse. Ned was known to be impulsive, quick-tempered and prone to act before thinking things through. But, William knew that if Ned had stolen that meat or anything of an edible nature, he would have surely shared it with him. They were simply that close.

"A true friend wants for his brother what he wants for himself." It was a saying Ned had inherited from his West African ancestors. It was their oath of friendship and pledge of fidelity. Besides, if Ned was really hungry, there were other means at his disposal. Ellen and Matilda were always resourceful enough to secure large quantities of leftover food from the Ferrette dinner table. Despite strict orders to the contrary, they made sure that their family and friends were fed those leftovers ahead of the Ferrettes' herd of prize-winning swine.

Furthermore, William could not understand why Mr. Ferrette had chosen to administer this savage beating himself. He was an extremely cruel man and such acts fit squarely within the range of his sadistic character. In fact, he often bragged about his ingenuity in devising instruments of torture that were used to perform punishments that he dared not mention in polite company. However, in recent years he would usually appoint one of his foremen to dole out these atrocious beatings. Besides, they were all ruthless men who always seemed to take such great pleasure in these assignments. They were well known to inflict tortuous cruelties that would indeed embarrass the fiends of Hell. In William's mind, these inconsistent facts did not add up.

The next day, tragedy struck again. Matilda's lifeless body was found in the shack she had shared with Ned for the past five years. The devastation of it all was too much for Ellen to bear. She was totally withdrawn and refused to speak to her husband. William sensed that she somehow knew more than she was saying about the deaths of both Ned and Matilda. It was a strong hunch that he simply could not suppress. However, given Ellen's edginess, he did not want to upset her further by probing for fuller explanations. Time staggered on and more and more unanswered questions arose and started to haunt him. But, he reluctantly decided to bide his time. A few more days passed but still, his patience was not rewarded. Since that fateful night, she hardly said a word to him about Ned, Matilda or anything else for that matter.

A week later, Ellen broke her silence and unexpectedly came to him with a plan to escape from the Ferrette Plantation. She told him of her recent encounter with a Negro horse-trader whom she met by chance when she accompanied Mrs. Ferrette on one of her frequent trips to the Charleston market. The man whose name was James Evans was one of Charleston's prosperous "free men of color" who made frequent business trips to the North. She told Mr. Evans about her desperate need to flee the Ferrette plantation. Mr. Evans sympathized with her plight and began to suggest a preliminary plan of escape. He told her about a man named Mr. Still in Philadelphia, an important man known to many as "the General". He assured her that the General would assist them. He also offered to serve as an intermediary whenever she and William were ready to escape from Chatham County.

At first, William refused to listen to her. He had never heard of Mr. Still or Mr. Evans. After all, who were they and how did she know they could be trusted? He knew the dangers of such an undertaking and was well aware of the price they would pay for failure. Two months ago Jessup, one of the field hands had been caught trying to escape. He was found hiding in a wagon under a pile of manure that was to be dumped on the edge of the Ferrette property line. As punishment, Mr. Ferrette instructed two of his foremen to submerge Jessup's left arm in a huge cauldron of boiling water. He reasoned that Jessup's mangled limb would serve as a constant and effective reminder to others who might have similar dreams of freedom. Jessup's screams of anguish still echoed in William's mind. That aside, William could not imagine the possibility of two adult slaves safely making their way to Philadelphia without the benefit of money and manumission papers.

His instantaneous objection weakened as she shared with him a complex plan that she had given considerable thought to, right down to the smallest detail. She would begin by obtaining Mrs. Ferrette's permission to visit her sick sister in southwest Chatham County. Next, she would relieve her mistress's upper bureau drawer of all its jewelry and money and find suitable clothing and accessories from Mr. Ferrette's suit closet to complete her masculine disguise.

While the Ferrette family was attending Sunday church services, they would hitch a buggy and ride thirty miles east, just in time to make the eleven o'clock departure of the Palmetto Princess, a popular steamer docked at the confluence of the Savannah River and the mighty Atlantic. From there, they would head north to Baltimore Harbor near Fort McHenry. A coach would take them to the Red Rose Inn where they would lodge for one evening. The final leg would entail a train ride to Philadelphia to rendezvous with the mysterious Mr. Still; a man they knew by reputation only. As agreed, Mr. Evans met them at the docks in South Carolina and gave them some final instructions. He assured them that if they were fortunate enough to reach Philadelphia, they would be in safe and capable hands.

As the creeping sunrise turned darkness into light, William scanned the opulence of the Calvert suite. It reminded him of the inside of the Ferrette mansion. Mrs. Ferrette was a homely looking woman who had a passion for the finer things in life. She liked to make a show of her inordinate wealth and was fond of hosting lavish parties. The mansion was her personal showcase and she spared no expense in acquiring the most exquisite furniture brought from the most exclusive factories of North Carolina. She also had exquisite tapestries from as far away as Turkey (or so it was alleged). She had inherited the mansion from her father, Colonel Jonathan Knight who acquired his wealth through shipping, vast real estate holdings, and a very lucrative slave trading business with outlets extending from New Orleans to Richmond, Virginia.

In contrast, Mr. Ferrette was a handsome man, but a man of limited reputation and meager means. He came from humble stock and was accustomed to pushing and clawing his way upward in the world. Working as a slave auctioneer, he had skillfully managed to worm his way into her life and her family's great fortune. His closest acquaintances knew him to be a cold and mean-spirited man, given to bouts of depression and hard drinking. Perhaps he secretly knew that he was just one of Mrs. Ferrette's human possessions, a walking, talking prop that was allowed to exist in and adorn her rarified world of elegance and ostentatious consumption. In the privacy of his thoughts, he must have known that he did not fit into his wife's social caste. That fact would be repeatedly insinuated whenever the Ferrettes would host one of their grandiose parties. On those occasions, he would be invariably reminded that even though his body was in the room, he was not truly one of them. Those uncomfortable gatherings aside, he rather enjoyed strutting around the place as the aristocratic *lord of the manor*. It was a daily pretense that was apparently not disturbed by the fact that Colonel Knight did in no way approve of his daughter's decision to marry "below her social station".

In a rare display of affection, Mr. Ferrette had given Ellen to his wife as a gift to mark their fifth anniversary. Mrs. Ferrette took an instant liking to Ellen and described her on occasion as being "an uncommonly intelligent negress". Ellen's status as her personal maid afforded her many privileges including the provision of cotton clothing and the right to have her meals indoors and sleep on a pallet in a secluded area of the pantry. She had a relatively pampered existence compared to the grueling poverty and squalor of the slave quarters.

The pantry was where Ellen met William during one of his frequent deliveries of water and fresh vegetables. Over the next six years, it would be their secret rendezvous point. In the early hours before dawn, William would make his way to the pantry where he would be given leftover and stolen foods to take back to the destitute families living in the slave quarters. The pantry also served as a classroom where Ellen taught him how to read and write. On countless winter nights, they were comforted by recitations of the Good Book and the warmth of each other's company.

He soon became her rock and she, the healing balm of his miserable existence. Their love grew strong and deep as their lives took on an unexpected radiance. Theirs was a special relationship born in heaven but precariously situated in an earthly hell. In time, William summoned the courage to ask Ellen for her hand in marriage. But first, they would have to ask for Mrs. Ferrette's permission to set up a household in one of the unoccupied shacks in the slave quarters. Mrs. Ferrette reluctantly gave them her consent on the condition that Ellen would return to the mansion each morning in ample time to prepare breakfast and attend to her customary household chores. A few days later, they jumped the broom and envisioned a life of marital bliss.

But all of that changed the day Ned died at the hands of Mr. Ferrette. Ned was William's closest friend. He was punished for a questionable crime and brutally killed for reasons that were shrouded in mystery – a mystery that tormented William's soul.

∞∞∞∞∞∞∞∞

Restless and fully awake, William's thoughts shifted back to the magnificent woman sleeping peacefully beside him. The few inches separating them seemed as wide as the ocean. Again, he found himself fighting the temptation to cradle her in his arms and experience the tenderness of her reassuring touch. He smiled as he studied her diminutive body, head to toe. Ned used to say that Ellen was half his size and half his age. But those were obvious exaggerations. Ellen was a full foot shorter than he was, and was as best he could tell, only ten years younger. He conjectured that he must be around thirty-five years old although he could never be certain. He and Ned were interstate chattel "property" from Louisiana. No records of their birth existed nor had they ever seen any bills of sale that would attest to their age and value on the open slave market.

Ned would often tease him that Ellen was "too preddy a girl to be hitched to your ugly carcass" and that her attraction to him was nothing less than "da Lawd's doin". Ned joked a lot, but he may have been right on that score. Truth be told, William often wondered what he did to deserve such a woman. However, in time, he came to realize that she loved him equally and immensely for his quiet strength and for being the intelligent and sensitive man that he was.

Ellen had the patience of a saint and the face of an angel. But, little did he know; she also possessed the heart of a lion. Were it not for her unflinching insistence, they would still be in South Carolina, locked in a world of stultifying bondage; trapped in an intolerably violent land abounding in degradation and broken spirits. His reflections about her soon gave way to a sudden wave of guilt about his own shortcomings.

He and Ned had many conversations about escaping but their intentions were never translated into action. For one reason or another, the time was never right for them to assert their wills and take the necessary risks to gain their freedom.

Guilt turned to anger as he thought about his life and how it had been so cruelly diminished by Mr. Ferrette and men like him who held other men in bondage. All slaveholders were soul stealers and *time bandits*. They incessantly striped the Negro of his humanity and robbed him of the one "commodity" he had at his disposal – time, precious time. Mr. Ferrette and the other slaveholders were tyrannical time bandits who trafficked in human flesh and had stolen so much of his irreplaceable time.

William knew all too well about the unbridled greed and barbarism of the time bandits. They were inordinately selfish people who unapologetically trampled on the rights of millions. In addition, they had no moral reservations about stealing any material benefit or asset that was enjoyed by the Negro. They even resorted to murder as an ultimate means to extinguish once and for all, the earthly time of those who challenged them or simply did not fit into their exploitative plans. In the minds of the time bandits, other people's lives were entirely expendable. The world existed for their pleasure and their pleasure alone.

William reasoned that his life was more than half spent. So much time had been lost because he had surrendered hope and failed to reach beyond the fabricated boundaries that had been imposed upon his existence. It was as if he had walked through his life in a crouched position; just waiting to die. The thought sickened him when he realized that he had for so long, cooperated with the time bandits in their blatant robbery. Yet maybe he would have one more opportunity to get it right. Maybe it was possible to reclaim his life and enjoy whatever time he had left, truly living and loving that special woman laying beside him. Suddenly, that train to Philadelphia could not come soon enough.

Outside his opened window, he heard the soothing sound of a steady rain, punctuated by the chirping of a pair of robins perched in a solitary tree adjoining the inn. His mind slipped into a tranquil state. Against the calming backdrop of the rains, the past melted into the present and the future took on the appearance of an uncharted sea.

His earthly cares dissolved and his unburdened soul began to breathe the unmistakable air of Blessed Assurance. This brief sleep filled him with hope and much needed fortification. Two hours later, Ellen awoke refreshed and eager to move on. She kissed her husband's brow gently to awaken him. His eyes twitched, and then squinted as the morning sun pushed through the clouds; slowly filling the room with a warming light.

"We better get going dear," she whispered. "We only have thirty minutes to get dressed."

She leapt to her feet knowing that she would need every minute to transform herself into her travel disguise. William had the latitude to move at a much slower pace. It took him only a few minutes to put on his burlap shirt and tattered trousers which were held up by a knotted rope. His loosely stitched boots completed his gritty ensemble that reflected the subservient role he would play – for only one more day.

His unhurried pace gave him more time for further reflection as he looked at the street below through a space in the curtain. Once again, his thoughts traveled back to Ned. He could hear his muted voice,

"A true friend wants for his brother, what he wants for himself."

That had been their pledge of friendship and fidelity. But Ned was dead now; killed by a heartless time bandit. He did not deserve such an ignoble and brutal death. And now, with every fiber of his being, William wanted justice for Ned and Matilda. He solely needed answers to his questions. Ellen had yet to share with him what she knew about the incident. She was undoubtedly holding something in. But that was not the place for such a discussion. Not there, not then.

His thinking was interrupted by the approaching sound of the coach that had previously delivered them to the Red Rose Inn.

"Better shake a leg Ellen. The coach is here."

"Already? Well I'll say this for him, he may be obnoxious, but he's at least punctual."

After buttoning her coat, she placed a stovetop hat on her head; the final accessory needed to complete her masculine garb. As she reached for the doorknob, William stopped her and drew her close for a long embrace. Kissing the nape of his neck, she whispered,

"I love you William, I love you so much."

"I love you too Ellie, and if you knew how much I loved you, you wouldn't worry so much. You'd know that I wouldn't let anything happen to you."

"I know," she murmured.

He lifted the top hat off her head and kissed her on the cheek. Then with a courtly motion, he doffed her hat and said in his best British accent,

"Now come hither my lady, your chariot awaits."

∞∞∞∞∞∞∞∞∞

The coach rambled down Chancellor Street and onto Pimilco Avenue, the main thoroughfare of the city. William could see Fort McHenry off at a distance and sensed that the train station could not be far away. The left turn onto Druid Street revealed a long row of tobacco mills and slave pens with their unique and distinctively putrid odors. The stench was sharp and unavoidable. Ellen was overwhelmed by the smell and the dismal sight of faceless laborers, perspiring heavily as they lugged huge crates onto the enormous flat bed cars owned and operated by the Baltimore and Ohio Railroad Company. William was no stranger to such scenes. He looked on in silent gratitude that he was at long last, not among them. Ned would certainly approve of this incredible change of fate. *A true friend wants for his brother what he wants for himself.* He could not shake the thought that Ned and Matilda should have been there with them, savoring that moment of joy.

∞∞∞∞∞∞∞∞∞

The Crafts arrived at Baltimore Station with time to spare.

"Well here we are sir and right on time I might add," said the coachman in a self-congratulatory tone.

"I thank you sir for your punctuality. My very best to you and your family," said Ellen.

"Hell, what family? It's just me and old Duke here," said the coachman, petting his overactive bloodhound. Apparently, he had forgotten the lie he had told her the previous day. Somewhat taken aback by his response, Ellen probed further,

"But I thought you said you had a wife and…"

Casting a mean look at the coachman, William interrupted.

"Scuse um me sa, but I reckin we best be gitten on our way. Don't wanna mis dat train."

Ellen completely understood. She immediately paid the fare and walked briskly ahead into the train station.

"Yes, you're quite right Henry," said Ellen.

The coachman was infuriated by William's interjection that had apparently cheated him out of his anticipated gratuity. Grabbing William by the arm, he snorted.

"Looka here boy. Don't be cutting your eyes at me. I don't know how they handle their darkies down in Georgia, but around these here parts, we don't tolerate any uppityness from your kind. You see these calluses on my hands? They're from knocking down no-good, cotton-picking niggers like you all my life. Do you understand me?"

William was seething inside and struggled to gather every ounce of self-control he could muster. The bloodhound assumed an attack posture and began to snarl at his britches. Unbeknownst to the coachman, William had his hand on a small pistol he had concealed in his pocket. On second thought, he visualized himself thrusting his well-sharpened Bowie knife into the coachman's beefy belly; a bloodier but quieter option to be sure.

"Now git on outta here before I get Duke here to pull a patch of flesh outta your leg."

"Yessa, yessa, I's do jest dat."

Meanwhile, Ellen had made her way to the ticket counter and requested two one-way tickets to Philadelphia. Seeing no one with her, the clerk inquired,

"And who will be traveling with you?"

Looking backwards, she spotted William walking through the terminal.

"Aha, there he is, my servant over there with the big brown trunk. He will be accompanying me."

"Well sir, *you* can certainly have a ticket. But a bond has to be issued before I can sell you a ticket for your slave."

"I beg your pardon?"

"I'm sorry sir, but it is the *new* policy of the Baltimore and Ohio Railroad Company to require bonds for all niggers applying for tickets on northbound routes. The policy took effect two days ago."

"But I don't understand."

"I'm really sorry sir. It's my job to enforce the rules, and our new rules strictly forbid any slaves to go through here unless security is given that all is right. You must have a legal bill of sale or get some gentleman who knows you to certify that you have a right to have this particular piece of property travel along with you."

"Why that's perfectly ridiculous! I was led to believe that I had secured clearances in Charleston, South Carolina for this slave and myself straight through to Philadelphia. And as a matter of fact, I am well-acquainted with several upstanding gentlemen in the Carolinas, but I did not know that it was necessary to bring them along with me to certify that I am the rightful owner of my own slave!"

"I'm sorry sir, but those are the rules."

"Well, do you have a stationmaster that I can speak to? This is preposterous! An outrage I tell you, an outrage!"

Ellen's pulse quickened as her blood immediately ran cold. Her palpating heart felt like it was about to burst out of her chest. Tiny beads of sweat surfaced on her brow as she struggled to regain her composure. Perspiration began to force its way through the thick layers of talcum powder that were a part of her elaborate disguise. Her breathing became more constricted as her emotional stress was getting to be unbearable. It appeared as though their well-wrought plan of escape was rapidly beginning to unravel.

Anxious to resolve the matter, the clerk scanned the terminal in search of the stationmaster. He and he alone was the only person authorized to suspend company policy.

"Excuse me for a minute sir. Let me see what I can do."
William used this intermission to try to calm Ellen's fears. She could feel his warm breath on the back of her neck.

"Angel please, let me handle this. Go on over there and sit down. It's going to be okay."

Heartened by his confidence, she took a seat on a nearby bench in the waiting area. It was William's turn to try to find a way out of this unanticipated predicament. A short distance away, he noticed the counter clerk and the stationmaster engaged in an animated dialogue with two police officers who had joined in the conversation. Their brief consultation lasted for only five minutes; but it seemed like five hours to him. The clerk left their huddle and walked slowly back to the counter where William braced himself to receive the results of their deliberation.

"What do *you* want boy?"

"Well sa, as you can see my masta ober thar is mahty sick. He be in mahty bad health. I's afred that he maht not hold out iffen he don't git to Pheedadelfee for his treatment. We gots ta git him on dat dere train."

"Save your breath boy! We're going to let both of you pass, *this time.*"

"Tank ya sir, tank ya fo yo kindness".

∞∞∞∞∞∞∞∞∞∞

This latest encounter had taken a heavy emotional toll on Ellen. She was on the brink of a nervous breakdown as she walked along the platform toward the train. At the entryway of the train, she and William were greeted by a Negro porter who escorted them to their seats. Before leaving them, the porter bent down to pick up a folded piece of paper and handed it to Ellen.

"Ah, excuse me sir, but I think you dropped this."

"Thank you, but I believe you are mistaken. It's not mine," replied Ellen.

"No mistake sir, I'm pretty sure it's yours. Musta fallen out of your pocket", he answered with a wide smile and a wink.

As he left the car, Ellen suspiciously unfolded the piece of paper. It was a commercial handbill that read as follows:

ABRAMS GENERAL STORE

804 Market Street, Philadelphia

Fresh produce, dry goods and confections

Ellen and William were instantly relieved. It was the first time they learned of their specific rendezvous point in Philadelphia.

The train had eight separate cars and they were glad that no one else was sitting in theirs. Ellen was tired and desperately needed some relief from the stress of maintaining her masquerade amidst so many watchful eyes. William was in an entirely different state of mind. His fatigue was of no real concern. His physical energies may have been depleted, but his mind was on fire. Freedom, sweet freedom was at hand. Once again, he became consumed by the thought of God's grace and humbled by His tender mercies. He gulped twice and silently thanked his Creator for their safe passage and their narrow escape from the heartless time bandits.

As the train rolled onward, the urban structures of Baltimore's thriving commercial and residential districts gave way to expansive rural tracts, replete with pastures, cornfields and apple groves. Looking out of their window, the weary twosome could see groups of half-clad male slaves toiling in the early morning sun. Some stood in silence and looked up from their hoes, plows and baskets and stared in a forlorn matter at the northbound train. Off at a distance, a white foreman sat atop his horse with a bullwhip in hand, poised to administer lashes to those who dared to gawk too long.

Ellen drifted off to sleep within ten minutes with her head resting on William's shoulder. Fully awake, William's thoughts roamed between excruciating memories of the past and optimistic visions of their future together. After last night's peaceful sleep, he vowed that memories of the past, however painful, would not rob them of their future. Just beyond the horizon, an ocean of new possibilities laid before him, waiting to be claimed. It was a pivotal moment. He decided then and there, that he would no longer live his life in submissive retreat -- never, ever again.

When the train came to a jerky halt, Ellen was shaken from her sleep. They had arrived at Perryville, a small depot that was a remote outpost for the loading and unloading of fruits and vegetables, more so than passengers. William could scarcely contain his exuberance. He squeezed Ellen's hand and whispered,

"This is the last station stop in Maryland before we cross over the Pennsylvania state line. Our last river to cross, my love."

Suddenly, their conversation was interrupted by an inquisitive white passenger who climbed aboard the train. William wasn't sure, but he appeared to have noticed them holding hands before they had a chance to release their grips. The entire car was empty, but for some strange reason, he chose to take a seat directly across from the Crafts. Perhaps it was Ellen's sickly appearance that drew his attention and aroused his curiosity; or maybe he was just starved for conversation. Ignoring William, he politely introduced himself.

"Good day to you sir. I'm Tom Gorsuch from Christiana. Are you traveling to New York by any chance?"

"No sa, we's gwine to Pheedadelfee. No furder."

Riled by William's unsolicited answer, his pinkish face blushed red as he retorted.

"Now see here boy, I wasn't addressing you! And I strongly suggest you speak to me and any other white man, when you're spoken to!"

"I's sorry sa, its just dat my masta here is hard of hearing and as ya can see, he's mahty sick. I meant no disrespec sa."

Ellen sat speechless as Mr. Gorsuch rose from his seat. He was clearly not satisfied with the feeble apology. He looked at the two of them suspiciously from head to toe, then made his way to the front of the car where he was greeted by the Negro porter making his rounds.

"Top of the morning to ya, Mr. G. Will you be having breakfast with us?"

"Yes, I will. But, I'll be having it in the next car where the air is less foul."

"Yes sa, I'll be right in to serve you. Yes sa, right away sa."

Once again, the Crafts sat alone in total silence until Ellen whispered,

"I could have handled that brutish man."

"I know dear, but you seemed so exhausted."

"I am that. I feel like I could sleep for a month."

"Well Ellen, before you go into any long hibernation, I thought we might work on that son you promised me. I sure would…"

"Not so fast my pet. We're not out of danger yet."

They slid further apart when they heard the voice of the Negro porter approaching their car offering coffee, tea and sweetbread. At that point, William's amorous mood quickly yielded to his hunger.

"Dearest?"

"Now settle down honey. There's plenty of time for that later," Ellen cooed.

She liked to tease and had come to enjoy his romantic innuendos.

"No, not that! I mean do we still have enough money to buy those biscuits you promised me this morning?"

Annoyed by his obvious shift in interest, Ellen responded,

"Is that all you think about… food?"

"No dear, it's all I think about – *when I'm hungry*."

"Well, let me put it to you this way William, my beloved. Do you remember the so-called Last Supper that you were looking forward to?"

"Yeah, what about it?"

"Well your last supper was *the* last supper you're going to have before we reach Philadelphia."

"You're kidding me aren't you?"

"Fraid not. Now close your mouth dear, unless of course you plan to make a meal out of one of these country horseflies."

∞∞∞∞∞∞∞∞∞

As the clouds drifted apart, the sun grew in strength, and eventually burned off the morning haze. Off to the east, a gentle breeze was blowing and a brilliant rainbow graced the sky with its presence. It appeared as though a brighter day was dawning. Ellen peered out of the window and allowed herself a rare moment of silent optimism. Despite their recent ordeals, hope stubbornly reappeared and infused their spirits with the solemn sensation of an open horizon stretched out before them.

And once again, the timeless lesson rang true. One may not know the precise time of their arrival, but just as night follows day; after the rain comes fair weather.

4. The General and His Far-Flung Army

"Thou shalt not deliver unto his master the servant
which is escaped from his master unto thee."
Deuteronomy 23:15

William and Ellen Craft were by no means, typical passengers on Mr. Still's far-flung Underground Railroad or "Liberty Line" as they sometimes called it. Most of his passengers traveled on foot and would arrive in Philadelphia penniless, fatigued and severely malnourished. Many of they came from great distances in the South, slowly making their way north under the cloak of darkness and in constant fear for their lives. Because of their ingenuity and good fortune, the Crafts had no need for the hundreds of relay stations and safe houses the Underground operated throughout the eastern seaboard and in border cities along the Ohio and Mississippi Rivers.

Philadelphia was the natural gateway between the northern and southern states. The city maintained a thriving shipping port and was a central transportation hub. It was also the closest major city to the Mason-Dixon Line, the boundary between Maryland and Pennsylvania. The Line was a geographical designation that separated the so-called free states from the slave states. In Pennsylvania, the Society of Friends (otherwise known as Quakers) led the way by gradually abolishing slavery in 1780 and establishing a strong anti-slavery movement in Philadelphia. In due course, the city became a hotbed for anti-slavery activists and a central hub for the Underground Railroad.

Beginning in the early 1800s, slavery became a bitterly contested moral and political issue. In debating the Missouri Compromise of 1820, the United States Congress voted to forbid slavery in the Louisiana territory north of the 36° 30' parallel. Thus by extension, the Mason-Dixon Line followed the Ohio River from the Pennsylvania border to its mouth, where it flowed into the Mississippi River near Cairo, Illinois. In 1800, there were 893,600 slaves in America. By 1820, that number had grown to about 1,538,000, as slavery became firmly entrenched in the southern slave states as a socially acceptable form of forced labor.

Mr. Still stood at the center of the Underground's mid-Atlantic front. In the north, cities like Boston and New Bedford, Massachusetts had established major abolitionist strongholds. To the west, staunch abolitionist leaders like Levi Coffin helped to create anti-slavery organizations operating in cities such as Cincinnati, Cleveland and Pittsburgh. These interlocking hubs formed the vanguard of a national abolition movement that soon grew in size and political strength.

Together these anti-slavery advocates formed a veritable army comprised of dedicated activists who performed specialized roles. First, there were *the witnesses*. These were men and women of all religious and political persuasions who served as spokespersons for the movement. They lectured and preached and agitated openly for state and federal legislation that would rid the nation of slavery once and for all. They were the public face of the movement – the visible vanguard of a much broader invisible army.

The second type of activists was those who gave financial support to the movement or direct aid to the countless fugitive slaves who were streaming across the Mason-Dixon Line, destined for the northern states and Canada. These kind-hearted men and women supported the fugitives by providing food, safe havens and transportation. They worked underground and were by far, the largest segment of the movement. Mr. Still called them quite simply, *the helpers*—known only to God, the fugitives and one another.

Finally, there was the army's small and "invisible" group of anti-slavery warriors. They organized and led dangerous missions into the slave states to bring fugitive slaves over the Mason-Dixon Line and into the Free states. This work involved the greatest risks and the ever-present danger of death or imprisonment if caught. Some of these men and women were former slaves who fearlessly risked and in some instances, incurred the tragedy of recapture and extreme torture. Using staging grounds in Philadelphia and Cincinnati, these intrepid souls completed countless rescue missions by traveling back and forth into hostile territories to bring thousands of slaves out of bondage. Mr. Still called them his *conductors*—perhaps the bravest of them all.

The witnesses of this movement were bold and outspoken men and women who dared to confront hostile opposition from many citizens who had close commercial ties and sympathies with the pro-slavery south. Until the 1830's, Philadelphia was primarily a money center and financial hub. Later on, the city forged profitable business relations with the southern states, particularly in the areas of shipping, textiles, cotton, tobacco, sugar cane, heavy manufacturing, railroads and the transportation of coal and steel.

Thus many of the city's captains of industry avoided the slavery issue altogether. They were averse to disturbing their business interests and were more inclined to turn a blind eye to the escalating moral debate over slavery and the human misery that it created. Simply put, these businessmen could not hear the plaintive calls for abolition amidst the roar of a society driven by greed and narrow economic self-interest. Slavery was certainly a morally unjust practice. But, as a mechanism for securing free labor, it had emerged as the cornerstone of a brisk economy dominated by the dictates of the time bandits.

∞∞∞∞∞∞∞∞∞∞

William Still came to Philadelphia as a young man at a time when the city was becoming the recognized center of the abolitionist movement. By the grace of God, he had never been a slave to any man, although his parents certainly were. They endured decades of grueling servitude on the eastern shore of Maryland before gaining their freedom in the north. Unfortunately, their liberation did not occur before their firstborn son, Peter was sold to another cotton farmer residing in Alabama. Thus, they were forced to live with the excruciating thought that they would never see him again, never knowing if he was dead or alive. William, was reared under different circumstances. Fortunately, he was raised on the free soil of New Jersey. He later moved to Philadelphia as a young man to become a carpenter's apprentice.

Mr. Still subsequently gained employment as a clerk working in the office of the Pennsylvania Anti-Slavery Society. And, for that work, he was paid a salary of $3.75 a week. However, it proved to be a most rewarding and fortuitous appointment. Working in that capacity, he had the opportunity to meet some of the city's most outspoken white abolitionists. He also came to know many prominent colored citizens who held membership in Mother Bethel African Methodist Episcopal Church and Shiloh Baptist Church, two of the city's oldest and largest colored congregations. Many of their members had close ties with the abolitionist movement and were quite active in the Underground

Railroad. Like most of Philadelphia's Negro population, their parishioners kept abreast of news and events in the southern states and perceived their interests to be inextricably tied to their brethren suffering in slavery. Mother Bethel Church in particular proudly served as the headquarters for the Vigilance Committee, another activist group, comprised mainly of *free men and women of color* who were committed to the abolitionist cause and to Negro spiritual, economic and educational improvement.

Mr. Still soon developed a local reputation as a very competent and but somewhat stoic man. All who encountered him judged him to be a meticulous record keeper who was both conscientious and trustworthy in his dealings. These qualities made him a strong, if not ideal, candidate for recruitment into the more secretive work of the Underground Railroad. In addition, the hard and bitter experiences of his parents had deeply sensitized him to the slavery issue. Thus, it was perhaps only a matter of time before he would be drawn into the orbit of Philadelphia's staunchest freedom fighters.

In the beginning, his temperament for this type of work was not readily apparent. His piercing eyes and gaunt appearance suggested a certain standoffishness and a rather somber persona. Yet those who judged him a sullen and humorless man would soon acknowledge the intense flames of love and human compassion that burned within him. In his heart flowed the blood of a Negro father and mother who endured and overcame the utter horrors of slavery. And in his soul, there were deep reservoirs of strength and an iron will forged by standing up to adversity and Philadelphia's widespread distain for its citizens of a darker hue.

In time, the abolitionist community came to know him as a man of forceful purpose and quiet confidence. Throughout ensuing trials and tribulations, he provided a steadying influence that never failed them in their darkest hours. Amidst swirls of frenetic energy and the crush of constant assaults, William Still sought and found strength in the silence. That is why many of his co-workers came to liken him to the sun – that intense mass of energy that quietly and efficiently accomplishes more than all of man's noisy engines and clamoring machines. But, unlike the sun, his brilliance was not obvious, nor was it ever touted. William Still was a leader who preferred to work in the shadows. He embraced anonymity as an indispensable requirement of his secret world.

∞∞∞∞∞∞∞∞∞

Mr. Still began this volunteer work as a helper. It started with his willingness to offer his small apartment as temporary shelter for transient fugitives. In addition to feeding and housing them, he would often sit with them in the late evenings and listen to them pour out their stories about the horror and heartbreak of slavery and their desperate efforts to escape its iron grip. It was during this time that something quite unexpected occurred. One day, a man who identified himself as Peter Friedman came to visit Philadelphia. He had traveled from Alabama and had gone from state to state working and searching for his family. He had not seen his parents since he was six years old. Yet at the age of forty-eight, he had not abandoned his search. Upon his arrival in Philadelphia, a local minister advised him that Mr. Still might be of some assistance to him as he looked for his parents.

In the course of their extensive conversation, something truly miraculous happened. Mr. Still gradually came to the realization that this visitor was none other than his long lost brother Peter, whom he had heard of, but had never seen before. Peter clearly bore a striking resemblance to his mother. Even more tellingly, Peter could describe his parents and his mother in particular, who had a distinguishing dark mole on her cheek. He explained to Mr. Still that he never knew his *real* last name. He took the last name of Joseph Friedman, a Jewish merchant who had helped him purchase his freedom. At the time, some southern states prohibited slaves from purchasing their freedom. However, with Friedman's assistance, Peter was legally able to execute his "self-purchase" in Cincinnati, Ohio.

The news of the incredible Still family reunion spread like wildfire throughout the city and the greater Delaware Valley region. It was a joyous and moving story that was told and retold to the underground operatives and the countless fugitive slave families that had been torn asunder. That incredible reunion had forever changed the course of Mr. Still's life. From that day forward, he began to write down and collect vital information gleaned from various discussions with fugitives who were placed in his care. He hoped that these written accounts might be useful to similarly displaced and fractured families.

This information included the names of underground passengers, their points of origin and the routes they traveled. It also entailed the names and locations of the various helpers involved in their escape plans and listed the fugitive slaves' final points of destination. Over the next few years, he had amassed tomes of information that he stored in his overstuffed apartment. Later he purchased a home on Philadelphia's South Street and stored them there. At this point, he had become a self-appointed chronicler of untold stories – a keeper of secrets.

Through these efforts, he would joyfully serve as a healer of broken families. Moreover, he would come to know more and more, that the type of forced separation experienced by his family was not at all uncommon. A slave family could be broken up as easy as a price could be negotiated and a piece of paper passed from one slaveholder's hand to another. More than 25% of interstate slave sales entailed the destruction of a first marriage. Over 50% of these sales involved the dissolution of a nuclear family. Many of these transactions separated children under the age of thirteen from their parents. William Still began increasingly outraged by the ruthlessness of these forced separations and the utter heartbreak that they caused.

Thus to no one's surprise, he embraced the cause of abolition with a vengeance. The eradication of slavery soon became an all-consuming passion. Abolition became in essence, the very logic of his life. In his view, slavery was not only a crime against man, but a crime against God Himself. Abolition was for him, a divine calling. He understood that the practice of slavery was deeply entrenched and interwoven with powerful profit interests that drove the national economy. Abolition was not a battle to be easily won, but rather a protracted war that had to be waged on several fronts. Slavery was a multi-headed Hydra, with its long, bloody tentacles stubbornly wrapped around the necks of the defenseless. There would have to be a full-scale campaign to raise social consciousness and turn public opinion against it. Meanwhile, there was the immediate need and the daily struggle to assist fugitive slaves escape until legislatively mandated abolition was achieved at the state and federal level.

Mr. Still vowed to confront these challenges head on. He was now a man with his powers fully awakened. All of his energies and assets were to be channeled into this cause. And for this, he believed himself to be twice blessed; blessed to be born a free man and blessed to help others achieve their freedom. It was a call to service and personal sacrifice that brought him perfect contentment. He would gladly do everything and anything to help his people gain their freedom.

Slavery would most certainly not be defeated overnight and perhaps not any time soon. Yet he drew increasing strength from his resistance to the stubborn and resourceful monster. Slavery may have been condoned by the law of the land. Nevertheless, he found great joy and a deep satisfaction in defying that law at every turn. In his newly forged and radicalized vision, there were now only two types of people – those who were committed to the elimination of slavery and those pathetic souls who condoned it. One chose to be on one or the other side of the ideological ramparts. There was no middle ground, no room for silence, apathy or indifference. All of his social and political relationships, old or new would be assessed on that singular basis.

William Still

The following year, he was unexpectedly offered a position in city government as a recorder of deeds. Fate appeared to be lending a hand. It was as if his life was being directed in a manner that far exceeded his conscious thought and intention. This unsolicited job ideally suited his meticulous nature and his extraordinary organizational skills. More importantly, this work provided him with access to official maps and plats that proved to be quite useful in planning underground expeditions and rescue missions. He had secured this post through the intervention of some of his Quaker friends who were involved in the Pennsylvania Anti-Slavery Society. With their support and cooperation, he widened his circle of acquaintances with some of Philadelphia's leading civic and religious leaders. His reputation grew by leaps and bounds among white and colored organizations involved in the underground movement.

Prior to his arrival in Philadelphia, stalwart advocates for abolition like Lucretia Mott, Robert Purvis, William Lloyd Garrison and William Henry Furness were boldly condemning slavery in the press and from pulpits throughout the city. They were by far, some of the movement's more vocal and visible advocates. Countless others like Thomas Garret, James McKim, Thomas Shipley and William Whipper worked with him "behind the scenes", but were no less effective. Through this work, Mr. Still eventually evolved into a recognized leader and soon became known as "the President" of the Underground Railroad; a title he did not seek and one that might reasonably apply to a number of other freedom fighters. To say the least, Mr. Still was a discreet man who valued obscurity far above titles and public acclaim. He strongly encouraged that humble attitude amongst all who aspired to promote the work of the Underground.

Abolitionist activities were perfectly legal in Pennsylvania and no sensible person would deny the existence of a thriving underground movement throughout the state. However, it was not the authorities that concerned Mr. Still the most. Philadelphia's police force was just beginning to be established and no one was safe from mob violence and the vigilantism perpetrated by those of opposing political and religious views. For these reasons alone, he did not want to draw unnecessary fire from the city's pro-slavery forces. After all, Philadelphia may have been a "northern city", but its residents were very sympathetic towards the South and its business leaders maintained profitable commercial ties with Southern banks, merchants and manufacturers.

His work continued and even accelerated despite countless dangers. At the same time, his sphere of influence was ever widening. In the colored community and especially in the area around South Street, he was called "the General", but never to his face. He was an efficient, but by no means boastful man. He placed the greatest value on careful planning and the disciplined execution of well-conceived plans. This was demanding work. Lives could be lost through carelessness and inattention to detail. This work was not for the indiscreet, the inexact and those unwilling or unable to follow strict instructions.

Careful planning and disciplined execution. That is how he established and maintained his invisible army. That is also how his reputation traveled to South Carolina and all points south of the Mason Dixon line and west of the Mississippi. Mr. Evans had spoken the truth to Ellen when they encountered one another in South Carolina. William Still was far and away, "the man who got things done". And, he was most assuredly, a man you could trust.

Trust was quintessential to his entire operation. It sometimes meant the difference between success and failure; recapture or escape; life or death. However, trust was also difficult to find and hard to maintain on the streets of Philadelphia where loyalties were fragile and sensitive information could be bought and sold at a small price. Like so many cities in the new Republic, Philadelphia was a place where betrayal was quite common and greed had a language and nationality of its own.

5. The Seventh Ward

"Proclaim liberty throughout all the land unto all the inhabitants thereof."
Leviticus 25:10 (Inscription on the Liberty Bell)

The Crafts arrived in Philadelphia amidst the hustle and bustle of afternoon traffic along Market Street, the city's main thoroughfare. Outside the train station, they were overwhelmed by the sheer congestion of people visiting the endless array of specialty shops selling everything from pork to petticoats. Their senses were titillated by the pungent aromas emanating from a phalanx of push carts that lined the street and attracted several stray dogs and cats, feeding on remnants of discarded fish, fruit rinds and rotten vegetables. An endless procession of horse-drawn carriages added to the organized chaos. The steady clop of hooves upon the cobblestone streets blended with the human pulsations of a city brimming with life and producing a rhythm all its own.

Ellen started to look for street signs that might help them establish their bearings. William walked five paces behind her with the huge trunk resting on his shoulder. Walking to the corner, Ellen saw signage indicating that they were at the intersection of Sixth and Market Streets. She knew they were very near Abrams' General Store, their prearranged rendezvous point.

The store was owned and operated by Mr. Solomon Abrams, better known as "Sol" to his friends and steady customers. Mr. Still had chosen the store as a rendezvous point because of its central location and close proximity to the train station. More importantly, he knew that Sol was a man who could be trusted. They had met years ago when Mr. Still was new to the city. Sol had given him upholstering and light carpentry work to do in his home. He also referred him to some of his Jewish friends residing in the city and nearby Merion County.

Sol, like his father before him, was a helper and a member of a small but growing community of Jewish immigrants belonging to the Mikveh Israel congregation. The community was part of an expanding enclave of Jews who were settling in Philadelphia, New York City and Hartford, Connecticut. Sol's father, Jacob was a member of the Pennsylvania Abolition Society and had allowed the Underground to use the store's huge cellar as a temporary refuge and relay station for fugitive slaves destined for the New England states.

∞∞∞∞∞∞∞∞∞

Arriving at the next corner, Ellen could see the sign for Abrams General Store. At that same moment, William noticed a rather large colored man staring directly at them from across the street. The stranger made no effort to disguise his interest in them and his gaze was anything but friendly. William became more apprehensive as the man crossed over to their side of the street. Even though he sensed imminent danger, he chose not to alarm Ellen who was oblivious to the stranger's advances.

Ellen and William entered the store and were still being followed by the stranger. Once inside, William slowly lowered the heavy trunk to the floor and returned a stare of his own at the stranger who began milling around in the rear of the store. Meanwhile, Ellen was greeted by a thin, gray-haired man who was standing behind the counter and bagging apples. She leaned on the counter and whispered to him.

"Moses is dead."

"Yes, I know," said Sol with a warm smile. "And God said to Joshua, it is time to cross the river Jordan and enter the land I promised to the children of Abraham."

His kindly eyes twinkled as he patted the back of her hand. Ellen was apprehensive and nervously tapping her fingers on his countertop. But with that subtle gesture and coded exchange, she breathed a sigh of relief. And Sol knew instantly that his long-awaited "packages" had arrived. Suddenly, William noticed the stranger moving toward them. He quickly placed his hand on the hilt of his Bowie knife and maintained direct eye contact with the stranger as he drew within three feet of Ellen. Before he could pull it from its sheath, Sol offered a friendly interruption.

"Solomon Abrams is my name. And that rather imposing gentleman standing next to you is John Ansar. Mr. Still has sent him to pick the two of you up."

"Pleased to meet you Mr. Abrams, Mr. Ansar," said Ellen. "And this is my husband, William. We are grateful for your assistance."

The menacing stranger's entire demeanor instantly changed and he was now grinning from ear to ear. John stepped closer to shake William's hand and added his own personal greeting.

"Well I'll be switched. Pleased ta meet cha William. We were told yaw would be in disguise, but I never figured on this. Very clever ma'am, very clever. Well, er…we best be going. This area is filled with rats."

Startled by his remark, Ellen scanned the floor beneath her feet.

"Oh my Lord, I've always had a dreadful fear of rats!"

"Not them little rats ma'am. I'm talkin' about the big, two-legged kind. The worst vermin that ever walked the earth. They make their money by snatching colored folk – free or slave; don't matter. Then they send them south to slavery."

"He means bounty hunters dear. They kidnap Negroes and make a living from the capture rewards," added William.

"Good Lord, how can you spot them?"

"You can't", said John. "It's not like the South where they tote their guns and bullwhips out in the open. Up here, they can be in overalls or in fine trousers and top hats. Some of them will be smiling in your face by day and scheming to burn down your house at night. They'd rat out their own mamas if they figure they could make a dollar from it."

Capture of a slave

Judging from her facial expression, it was clear that Ellen was not comforted in the least by John's elaborations.

"I'm sorry ma'am; I didn't mean to upset you."

"No harm done Mr. Ansar. We've come too far to let our guard down now," William responded.

"Yeah, and be careful who you talk to, white or colored; least ways not until you git to know folk. Anyway, let me give you a hand with that trunk William. And by the way, yaw can call me John. John will do just fine."

After saying goodbye to Mr. Abrams, the two men grabbed a handle on opposite sides of the huge trunk that William had been carrying alone since he left Savannah. As they exited the store and walked toward John's wagon, Ellen felt an eerie sensation, a distinctive feeling that they were being watched. Surveying the area, she made eye contact with a sinister pair of white men who seemed to be studying their movements. She instinctively clutched William's arm. John also noticed the two men and politely cautioned her.

"No offense intended ma'am, but I don't think it's a good idea for yaw to be locking arms like that in public; you being dressed the way you are. It's bound to raise some eyebrows."
Ellen immediately realized her mistake and released her grasp.

"Yes John, quite so", she murmured in an apologetic tone.

After hoisting the trunk onto the open wagon, the two men climbed on the buckboard and seated themselves with Ellen in the middle. With a slight tug on the reins, John remarked,

"Well, here we go. Reverend Catto's home is just a little ways from here. He's not in now, but Mrs. Catto will be pleased to receive ya."

"Reverend Catto? We were told that we were to be staying at Mr. Still's home," said Ellen with mild suspicion.

"Change of plan, had to go to an important meeting. It's all right though. He'll be back soon. Reverend Catto and Mr. Still are good friends and members of the Vigilance Committee."

"Vigilance Committee? It that like some sort of political organization?"

"Well I suppose you could say that ma'am. They're a group of hard-working men and women who come together to support one another so we can do away with slavery. A lot of them help us out with the Underground Railroad in one way or another."

In his own simplistic way, John was trying to explain to them that the Vigilance Committee provided the monetary support for the Underground and was the public face or "front" for its clandestine operations. All direct participants in the Underground were members of the Committee, but not all members of the Committee were participants in the Underground. Mr. Still had always believed that this was as it should be, given the nature of the Underground's secretive and exacting work.

"They meet every Tuesday at Mother Bethel Church. Yeah, there's always a lot of food for thought; that's for sure," said John.

"Well er... speaking of food, you don't suppose we could..."

Immediately, Ellen discreetly elbowed her husband.

"I beg your pardon William, what did you say?" asked John.

"Nothing, nothing at all," he replied.

Ellen was pleased by William's restraint and sat silently as the movement of the horses drowned out the rumblings of her husband's stomach that had become embarrassingly audible since they left the opulent confines of the Red Rose Inn.

∞∞∞∞∞∞∞∞∞

William looked around in silent wonder as the wagon rolled down Market Street and turned right onto Sixth Street. Off to his right, a large brick structure with an elegant steeple drew his attention.

"What's that building John?" he asked.

"That's Independence Hall".

"You mean *the* Independence Hall?" asked Ellen.

"Yeah, that's it", John answered nonchalantly.

Ellen was awestruck and well-acquainted with the patriotic legend and lore of the stately landmark.

"Imagine that; the birthplace of freedom and democracy!"

"Not if you're colored," said John in a gruff and dismissive tone.

Ellen sensed that her remark struck a harsh chord with John so she decided to discontinue that particular line of inquiry. Meanwhile, William continued to absorb the sights and sounds of the city and took particular note of the street signs they were passing. There was Chestnut, Walnut, Locust, Spruce and Pine Streets, all in succession. He wondered if all the streets in the downtown area had such fair and sweet-smelling names. He wouldn't be surprised if that were the case. The colorful and exuberant city appeared to his eyes as a glorious, Eden-like dream.

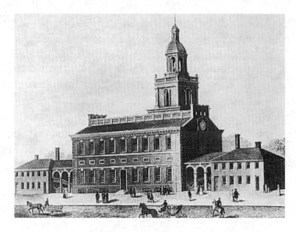

Independence Hall

The Philadelphia skyline was studded with majestic church steeples that filled him with a sense of peace and solemnity. The streets on both sides were lined with spacious, two and three-storied homes that spoke of unmistakable wealth and solidity. Even more remarkably, there were well-dressed colored men and women coming in and out of the front doors of these homes. Was it possible that they were residents or invited guests? William's curiosity finally got the best of him.

"Tell me something John; do colored folk live in some of these houses?"

"Sure do," said John. "That one over there is Reverend Reynolds' house. He's the minister of Mother Bethel Church and the head of the Vigilance Committee."

William gawked at the huge structure with its tall columns and manicured lawn and wondered to himself if John was just kidding him. Ellen had the same thought but decided not to comment. But the fact of the matter was that John Ansar had indeed spoken the truth. Philadelphia had a well-established colored upper and middle class. Men like Reverend Reynolds had ancestral roots in the city that went back before the American Revolution of 1776. Not surprisingly, William knew nothing about affluent colored businessmen like James Forten, Robert Purvis and William Whipper who had amassed considerable fortunes and were respected civic leaders. The city was also populated with highly-skilled colored craftsmen who made a good living for themselves and their families. However, William could hardly be faulted for his incredulity. He saw no wealthy colored people in South Carolina. The only skilled colored craftsmen he observed were the unpaid slaves on the Ferrette plantation whom the time bandits had systematically robbed of the fruits of their labor. In Philadelphia, these same craftsmen were shop owners and entrepreneurs who were prosperous participants in a thriving local economy.

Continuing south on Sixth Street, John Ansar pointed out Mother Bethel African Methodist Episcopal Church, near the corner of Lombard Street. He told them that it was one of the city's most revered Negro sanctuaries and that Mr. Still could be found there at that moment. The Vigilance Committee met regularly on Tuesday's at 7:00 p.m. However, Reverend Reynolds, the Committee's chairman, had called an emergency meeting for reasons John was not willing to discuss. But, judging from the large numbers of carriages and buggies parked outside, it could be reasonably assumed that the meeting was well attended and serious business was at hand.

John assured the Crafts that Mr. Still's failure to meet them at Abrams' store was entirely unavoidable. They would meet him later that evening at Reverend Catto's home. While his explanation was sufficient, it heightened Ellen's nervous anticipation of meeting "the General" at last. She wondered what words she would use to express her profound gratitude for his assistance and thorough planning. William's growing hunger pains placed him on a somewhat different train of thought. He silently wondered if dinner was being prepared at the Catto home and what words he would use to politely solicit a second helping.

∞∞∞∞∞∞∞∞∞∞∞

The wagon turned right again and west onto South Street, where the houses were considerably smaller. John explained that they were entering the Seventh Ward, where he was to make a quick delivery of dry goods to a shut-in widow. As they ventured deeper into the neighborhood, the people outside were all colored and were clearly less prosperous. Here the streets were narrow and spotted with empty lots. There were rows of small band-box houses and jerry-built brick hovels that were all arranged in a haphazard manner.

No longer did the streets have such sweet-smelling names. William's attention was suddenly drawn to crudely made and unpainted street signs indicating "Soapfat Alley", "Razor's Avenue" and "Crow's Place". Off to the left, they saw a long line of tenements framing a flowerless courtyard where unsupervised children were playing in a mud puddle formed by a sizable hole in the ground.

"Up ahead is Bloody Row," John explained. "It ain't the kinda place you want to wander into at night."

William clearly understood his meaning. Ellen nodded in agreement. She clutched her carpet bag and sat in complete silence. John halted the wagon and dismounted.

"I'll be right back."

He walked twenty paces east and disappeared out of sight as Bloody Row made a sharp bend. As William and Ellen sat motionless in the carriage, a group of Negro teenage boys rapidly approached the wagon with predatory glares. For a moment, Ellen had forgotten how she must have appeared to them. William sat motionless like a planted sentinel, poised to meet any threat. He kept his eyes on one of the older boys who appeared to be their leader. On his command, one of them reached for the horse reins and William quickly grabbed him by the wrist. Ellen shrieked as two others quickly climbed aboard the rear of the wagon.

In a flash, John Ansar could be seen quickly headed in their direction. The youths instantly recognized the tall and muscular figure sprinting towards them. His scowling face seemed to freeze them in their tracks. As he got closer, the two intruders who had boarded the carriage immediately dismounted.

"What yaw think yaw doing?" said John belligerently.

"This white man with you Mr. John?" asked their apparent leader.

"And if he is, what business of yours is it?"

'Well, er…er… I'm sorry. I didn't know. We thought…"

"Naw, *you didn't think*! Otherwise you wouldn't have been messing with people who ain't messing with you", shouted John. "Now yaw git out of here before I put my foot where the sun don't shine!"

The nervous group reassembled and slowly walked down Soapfat Alley without uttering a word. Before they got too far away, John yelled for one of the boys who appeared to be much younger than the others.

"Percy, come here!"

The little boy walked back to John while barely lifting his head.

"You know I'm really disappointed in you."

"Yes sir, I'm mighty sorry."

"Well now sorry don't git it. What you doing hanging around with them big boys anyway? And what makes you think you can just take something that don't belong to you?"

"I don't know... I guess I was just going along."

"Going along? I expect better things from you; a whole lot better."

"Yes sir, I'll do better."

"Alright then. And don't let me catch you *going along* again. You hear me?"

"Yes sir."

John hugged the boy and rubbed his uncombed hair. It was a well-received affirmation of forgiveness and renewed trust.

Ellen was visibly shaken by the encounter. William was simply relieved that no blood had to be shed. On the other hand, John seemed oddly indifferent to it all.

"Sorry bout' that yaw. We best be moving on," he said. "Mrs. Catto is a sweet lady but she's fussy about folks coming late to supper. She's not much of a cook but there ain't a kinder woman on God's green earth."

∞∞∞∞∞∞∞∞∞∞

As the Crafts quickly learned, not all of Philadelphia's colored residents were friendly and well-to-do. Their brief visit to the Seventh Ward revealed a level of poverty that caused them to adjust there initial utopian impressions. There were indeed two Philadelphias and colored people lived in both of them. Yet they also realized that both rich and poor Negroes enjoyed a standard of living that far surpassed the dreary and cruel environs of the slave quarters from which they came. There was no doubt about it. Their situation had dramatically improved.

Heading north, back toward center city, William silently reflected on the events of the day. The morning was truly memorable. It was the first time he slept in a bed and the first time in his adult life that he could remember sleeping past sunrise. His entire life had been one of dismal, mind-numbing routine. The train ride was another first; a pleasant experience despite the indignities involved in their stressful passage out of Baltimore. Yet far and away, he would never forget the almost surreal experience of seeing colored people walking the streets as free men and women, walking tall, walking proud.

His eyes moistened as he thought about the simple freedoms that had been denied him all of his life. He developed a lump in his throat as he mentally savored the *new world* that he had just entered. It was a world of unlimited possibilities, a place where a colored man could experience the sweet motion of freedom and strident self-determination. A huge veil had been lifted from his eyes. He felt both joy and sorrow.

He had lived his entire life in retreat as another man's property, a living, cringing corpse. He now realized that he had only seen the world through the pinhole of his miserable existence on the Ferrette plantation – robbed of hope and crippled by despair and self-loathing. But, that was all before Ellen and before he traveled the streets of Philadelphia, where a colored man could pursue his dreams as a man amongst men and live his life in full measure. The psychological and visual reality of it all was so overwhelming; this place they called "the City of Brotherly Love."

6. The Cattos

"There is no use trying to capture a runaway slave in Philadelphia. I believe that the devil himself could not catch them when they once get there."

Anonymous Slave Master

It was Mr. Still's decision to redirect William and Ellen Craft to the Catto home for temporary safekeeping. Reverend Catto and his wife Sarah were two of his closest friends. They were both active in the Underground and various civic organizations. Like the Crafts, they too were from South Carolina; Charleston to be precise. Reverend Catto was the pastor of the First African Presbyterian Church and had come to be one of the city's most respected clergymen. His charming wife, the former Sarah Isabella DeReef, held membership in a few of the mutual aid societies and literary clubs that had sprung up in the colored communities over the past decade. However, most of her time and energy went to the Shelter for Negro Orphans. She also kept very busy caring for her husband and serving as the pianist for the church choir.

According to Mr. Still's revised plan, after two nights of lodging with the Cattos, William and Ellen were to travel to Boston, and ultimately take up residence in New Bedford, Massachusetts, a town known for its strong abolitionist leanings. The unscheduled emergency meeting of the Vigilance Committee had detained Reverend Catto longer than he had planned. Nonetheless, he managed to get home in time to have dinner with his wife, Mr. Still and their two guests.

William consumed a large second helping of fresh baked bread, beef stew and apple cobbler. Afterward and at Mr. Still's request, William recounted the harrowing details of their bold escape from South Carolina.

"...and so I say to the man on the train, I be sorry sa but my massa here is mahty sick."

The dinner party roared with laughter; all except Ellen, who registered a pained expression on her face. Oblivious to her reaction, William continued on.

"You know, I almost feel embarrassed relating our story to you on account of the total deception we were obliged to use."

Suddenly, Ellen erupted.

"Are you crazy? I feel no embarrassment whatsoever. When I think back on the horror of our existence, and poor Ned and Matilda. I just want to..."

Her body began to quake and she started to weep uncontrollably. Sarah handed her a handkerchief and her tears stopped momentarily.

"I do apologize everyone. I think my nerves are just plumb raw from the journey."

"No apology necessary, sweetie. What you need is a good night's sleep and you'll feel like new in the morning," said Sarah, gently patting her on the back.

William instantly regretted his remarks. How could he have been so thoughtless; so insensitive to her mental anguish? Pushing aside a palatable wave of guilt, he pulled his chair closer to hers and put a comforting arm around her shoulder. Sarah stood up and her huge abdomen accidentally knocked over some glassware, spilling lemonade onto the table. She was six months pregnant and still learning to adjust to her new size.

"I'll just clean that up and clear the table. The quicker I finish, the quicker we can let you remarkable thespians get some shut eye."

"Let me help you Sarah," said Ellen, regaining her composure.

The two women departed for the kitchen while the three men remained seated.

"What say we change the subject men?" suggested Reverend Catto.

"Yes by all means. Tell me Mr. Still; John Ansar said there's going to be a big convention here next week."

"Yes indeed William; it's going to be the largest gathering of the American anti-slavery movement. Delegates from over eleven states will be calling for the immediate emancipation of the Negro. We've secured the commitments of an impressive group of religious leaders. Father Kendrick will be speaking on behalf of the Catholic Archdiocese and a group of Jewish rabbis from New York will be coming to join us. How's that for an interfaith coalition? At last count, we're expecting over three hundred men and women, all staunch abolitionists committed to ridding this country of race hatred and the barbarism of slavery. Reverend Reynolds is even going to get the Mayor to bring greetings on behalf of the city. The finishing touches on Pennsylvania Hall will be completed in just a few days. It's a grand structure, dedicated to an even grander purpose. It's a shame you and Ellen won't be here to join us. Your train to Boston leaves in two days. But, believe me, it's going to be a…"

He was suddenly interrupted by the loud sound of glass breaking and Ellen's piercing scream. The men rushed into the kitchen where a large brick had been thrown through a window and had hit Sarah in the head. She was lying unconscious on the kitchen floor and bleeding profusely. Blood gushed from her left temple and ear and small shards of glass were lodged in her face. Reverend Catto and Ellen frantically looked for something to stop her heavy bleeding.

William bolted out of the kitchen door and chased the assailants down a dark alley behind the house. Mr. Still followed close behind with his pistol drawn. He fired four shots in the direction of two men they saw at a distance, scaling a fence whooping it up and laughing in a derisive manner. One of the men appeared to be white, the other Negro; although in the darkness of the alleyway, Mr. Still could not be sure. Nor did he get a good look at their faces. On the other side of the fence, a horse-drawn carriage awaited the assailants who were spirited away by an accomplice. At that point, William and Mr. Still abandoned their chase and returned to the house. Meanwhile, Reverend Catto had placed Sarah on the living room sofa and was still trying to contain her bleeding. But judging by the deep red saturation on the upholstery, he was fighting a losing battle.

"How is she?" William asked as he re-entered the house.

"She's still unconscious. This is as far as I dared to carry her. We had better get a doctor."

Mr. Still immediately left to get Doc Minton who came within minutes. The prognosis for Sarah was not very encouraging.

"Well Doc, is she going to be alright?"

"She's suffered a severe head trauma Reverend. She has a severe concussion and a massive hematoma. We have to get her to a hospital immediately!"

∞∞∞∞∞∞∞∞∞∞

It took twenty-one stitches to close the gash in Sarah's head. She had lost a lot of blood and the heartbeat of her unborn baby was alarmingly faint. Dr. Minton was also concerned about the possibility of permanent brain damage. Sarah Catto had always been a frail woman. Her husband silently wondered if she would ever be the same again.

7. Suspicions

"The mind does not take its complexion from the skin."
Frederick Douglass

The following morning, Mr. Still returned to the Catto home. He and Reverend Catto assumed that last night's assault was intended as a warning to the Underground and to all who were supporting the abolitionist cause. Many perplexing questions arose in the wake of this vicious attack. Why did the assailants attack then and there? Who would they strike next? And, if they had the temerity to assault the home of a Christian minister, was there no limit to their madness and criminality? Finally, was it possible that one of the perpetrators was in fact a Negro?

The lighting in the alleyway behind the Catto house was poor and he wondered if he could really believe what appeared to be. Of course, the presence of rats, both white and colored, was of no surprise to him. However, the Negro rats were usually content to collect blood money for revealing the location of fugitives to the slave-catchers who reaped the largest rewards. They merely sold information (and their tainted souls). But, now it was entirely possible that colored men were now being hired as henchmen and paid thugs. The very thought of it sickened them.

After hours of discussion, they were absolutely convinced that the attack and the presence of the Crafts that particular evening were more than coincidental. And, if that were indeed the case, perhaps someone in their ranks had betrayed them. Only a few people knew when, where and how the Crafts were to arrive in Philadelphia. This worrisome fact had to be faced head on. For over two hours, they retraced William and Ellen's carefully planned movements. Their disguises, coupled with their remarkable acting skills made their identities virtually undetectable. Therefore, they reasoned that someone in their ranks must have known that the Crafts were arriving in Philadelphia and were being taken to the Catto home.

Consequently, they compiled a list of all persons who were privy to this secret information. Each one of them had to be watched carefully in the future. Meanwhile, they thought it best to tighten their circle of trust to include only long-serving operatives and members of the clergy who were responsible for carefully recruiting their parishioners for this sensitive and demanding work. After their shared exercise in "rat detection", Reverend Catto showed Mr. Still to the door. Before leaving, Mr. Still paused and turned to him with a distressed expression. His friend could feel his deep anguish.

"Don't be so downhearted Still. We'll find out who's behind this. God willing, we'll smoke them out."

With tears in his eyes, Mr. Still gulped hard, and then spoke in a low and remorseful tone.

"It's not that Reverend. It's Sarah...poor Sarah. I feel like I brought this trouble to your doorstep. If I hadn't ..."

Reverend Catto refused to let him finish his thought and placed his hand on Mr. Still's shoulder.

"Listen to me. It's not your fault Still. You hear me? It's not your fault. This is the work *we* chose. This is God's work! The victory is already ours. We'll get through this."

And with that expression of magnanimity and unwavering trust, their deep bond of brotherhood endured; and they never spoke of that horrible incident again.

∞∞∞∞∞∞∞∞∞∞∞∞

Time moves on and love abides; even in the silence. Truth, like the rising sun, brings hope for new beginnings. And forgiveness cleanses the soul and replenishes the earth; much like the rains.

8. The Consecration

"No one has greater love than this, to lay down one's life for one's friends."
John 15:13

Little did those assailants know, Reverend Catto was not a man who could be easily intimidated. He bore the attack on his wife and unborn child with a remarkable restraint and determination that was beyond most people's comprehension. With his wife clinging for her life, he was now paying a heavy price for his involvement in the Underground. And more likely than not, he himself was a marked man.

The next day, Sarah's health appeared to have worsened. She occasionally regained consciousness but her speech was very slurred. Apart from a few involuntary spasms, she was motionless and unable to move from a prone position. Seeing Sarah in that condition, Ellen refused to leave her side. After consulting with her husband and Reverend Catto, it was decided that they should delay the next leg of their trip for at least a week. Reverend Catto was grateful for Ellen's willingness to help care for Sarah. Without her unsolicited assistance, it was doubtful if he would have ever left the house. The unplanned presence of both Ellen and William gave him the peace of mind that Sarah was getting proper care and very close attention.

As it turned out, three weeks passed and Sarah still showed no appreciable signs of recovery. Despite Ellen's bedside encouragement and tender care, Sarah could barely muster an occasional smile and the faint whisper of "thank you" as Ellen attended to her every need. While Ellen was providing this vital service, William was growing restless. He was beginning to hear the whispers of the *time bandits*, mocking his ineffectuality. He was not the type of man who could sit idly while others performed useful tasks. Although he was just a visitor, he asked Mr. Still if he could participate in some of the secret work of the Vigilance Committee. He also began to ask questions about the Committee's more secretive operations.

Mr. Still promised to give his request due consideration. He could certainly use more trustworthy and stout-hearted operatives. However, he felt it was much too soon to admit William into the underground's inner circle. He liked William more than most. But, it was far better to err on the side of caution; at least at that point in time. Instead, he offered to take William to some of the Committee's general meetings and build their future relationship in a slow and deliberate manner. The incident at the Catto home had firmly reinforced Mr. Still's excessively cautious nature. He simply did not have the luxury of making misjudgments about people (colored or white) who professed an interest in aiding their cause. Good intentions aside, he had imperiled his best friends and he vowed that it would never happen again.

In fact, trust never came easy for Mr. Still. He had learned years ago to keep others at a safe emotional distance. It was his way of limiting his exposure and making himself less vulnerable to disappointment. That was how he managed his personal life. But, of course, that approach to life and living was ill-suited for his work with the Vigilance Committee and its underground faction. This work at its root was cooperative in nature and well beyond the scope of individual activists operating in isolation. It required skillful planning, organization and a keen ability to coordinate the efforts of countless operatives stretched from Maine to Florida and throughout the expanding westward territories

Mr. Still was an extremely self-reliant man. But, as the recognized leader of the Underground, he would have to learn how to trust. He eventually came to realize that trust was indispensable and indeed, the cornerstone of their operations. Thrust into his leadership position, he gradually learned how to delegate responsibility and depend on others. Eventually, the recurring question in his mind wasn't to trust or not to trust; but rather, *whom* to trust.

∞∞∞∞∞∞∞∞∞∞

As promised, Mr. Still escorted William to his first weekly meeting of the Vigilance Committee. He arrived at the Catto home to pick William up at 6:15 p.m. He wanted to introduce him to a few members before the 7:00 p.m. call to order. During their ride to Mother Bethel Church, William took the liberty to discuss the attack on the Catto home and inquired if any suspects had been identified. Mr. Still bristled at the question. He remained very sensitive about that tragic incident. Unmindful of Mr. Still's discomfort, William continued to pursue his line of questioning.

"John Ansar told us that there are a lot of snitches around here. Do you think it might have been one of the neighbors?"

"It's possible. Anything's possible," he tersely replied.

"Tell me something Mr. Still. How long have you known John Ansar?"

"About a year or so."

"I thought you knew him a whole lot longer than that. No disrespect, but that's not a long time to get to know a man. Ya know what I mean?"

It was an innocent comment but one that evoked a stern response. Mr. Still immediately pulled the hand brake on his wagon and brought his team of horses to a complete stop.

"Now you listen to me. John Ansar is the last man on earth that I would suspect of such a thing. Yeah he's got some rough edges, but he also has a heart of gold. Salt of the earth that man is. They don't come any better. You remember that!"

"I'm sorry. I didn't mean him or you any offense."

Mr. Still paused for a moment, then responded.

"No William, I'm sorry for over-reacting. Believe me; I'd trust that man with my life. But, since you asked about him, let me tell you about how we first met."

He then proceeded to tell William the story of John's arrival in Philadelphia. It was one of the first stories Mr. Still had recorded and placed in his growing collection of fugitive escape testimonies. William listened intensely as Mr. Still recounted the tale.

∞∞∞∞∞∞∞∞∞∞

John came to Philadelphia from Ohio as a fugitive slave running away from an insanely violent master. On that particular evening, there was a blinding winter blizzard with snowdrifts up to the knees. After a three-mile trudge through the snow, he spotted the home of a white minister whom he had previously met. He hesitated for a while before approaching. His body was numbed with pain and his frozen hands could barely grasp the door knocker.

"Who is it?"

"It's me Reverin Lovejoy. John…John Ansar from the Hatcher Plantation."

Opening the door, he said,

"John, what in blazes are you doing out on a night like this?"

"I'm on the fly sa. I decided to take ma chances."

Their conversation awakened Mrs. Lovejoy who entered the living room.

"Good gracious, you're frozen to the bone. Come sit here by the fireplace," she said in a pleasant tone.

"Now see here John, why would you pick a night like this to run away? It's not safe out there for man or beast."

"I know Reverin, that's why I done chose this here night. Mr. Hatcher and his hounds ain't likely to give chase with this blizzard kicking up the way it is."

"But you haven't given us a chance to make arrangements for your passage. And you can't stay here. They're bound to notice you missing in the morning and come here looking for you."

"I know sa, but if I could just thaw out here for awhile, I'll be moving on before daybreak."

"Sure you can. I'll fetch you some warm blankets and a coat to wear. You're bound to catch pneumonia in those clothes."

"I'll heat you up some tea."

"Thank ya kindly ma'am."

Reverend Lovejoy re-entered the room with a tattered coat and two woolen blankets.

"The way I see it, you can go one of two ways. North to Cleveland and then catch a ferry to Canada. Or, you could go due east through Morgantown and on into Pennsylvania. Try to make your way to Philadelphia. You'll be safe there. Ask someone to direct you to a Mr. William Still. Tell him I sent you. He'll take care of you. Believe me; you can trust him. Look here, I only have five dollars but you're sure welcomed to it."

"Thank ya Reverin, I reckon I'll go east and find that Still fella."

"Good, I'll write to Mr. Still and let him know you're coming."

John left early that morning on foot and made it safely into West Virginia. On the fourth day, trouble struck just as he had it made across the Monongahela River. It was his practice to sleep in caves or trees at night to avoid detection. Fatigue had overtaken him and he overslept in a cave, only to be awakened by a band of Negro slaves accompanied by a white overseer. They were chopping down a grove of trees and getting very close to the entrance of the cave where he was hiding. Unfortunately, the cave had only one entrance, so John decided to stay hidden until sunset. He assumed they would eventually pack up to leave by nightfall or perhaps sooner. As anticipated, all of them left at dusk, except one old colored man who was sitting on a stump, staring down at the ground.

"The Lawd is my shepherd. I shall not want…"

John stepped out and approached him.

"Excuse me sir…"

"Good Gawd boy, ya pert near scared the be-Jesus outta me. Where'd ya come from anyway?"

"I've been hiding in that cave over yonder."

"You a runaway or sumptin?"

"Yeah."

"So waz yo name bruder?"

"John."

"Well dey call me Rufus. But my real name is Baraka. Yep…Baraka's ma name. So how long you been in dat dere cave?"

"All last night and today."

"Well you must be plenty hungry".

"Yeah, I ain't had a meal in a long time. And I'll tell ya sumptin. I'd be mighty obliged if ya was to take this five dollars into town and buy me something to eat."

"Yeah, I can do that fer ya. But, you sure you want to give that much money to me?"

"Well, I ain't exactly giving it to ya now am I? Besides, I ain't got much choice."

∞∞∞∞∞∞∞∞

Less than an hour latter, the old man returned and John started to walk out of the cave, only to be stopped in his tracks by the sight of six armed white men following closely behind the old man. John instantly assumed that the old man had betrayed him. Unfortunately, when the old man went to the store with that five-dollar bill, it aroused some suspicions. Slaves didn't have that kind of money so the storekeeper surmised that Rufus must have stolen it.

In turn, he notified the slave foreman who decided to whip the old man for his apparent thievery. The old man took them to the location where John had given him the money. Yet for some inexplicable reason, the old man refused to lead them to where John was hiding. As a result, they stripped him of his shirt and tied his hands around a tree trunk while the foreman took a few practice lashes with a blood-stained whip. John remained hidden in the cave, silent and gripped by fear. He peered helplessly at this gruesome scene, with his heart pounding and his mind simmering with deep regret.

"I done told yaw I didn't steal no money! A colored fella gave it to me."

"Oh yeah? Then where is he?"

"I don't know."

"Who do you think you're fooling?" yelled the foreman.

A lash landed across the old man's frail body, and John cringed helplessly in anguish as he witnessed the heart-breaking spectacle. The foreman drew back to deliver a second blow.

"I'll teach you not to steal, you lying heathen!"

"It ain't my fault iffen the man who done give it to me ain't here now."

The old man quickly glanced toward the cave as he continued to take his unearned punishment. John continued to look on powerlessly as tears streamed down his face.

Ten minutes into this horrific ordeal, one of the overseers became bored with the exercise.

"I do declare George if you keep going, your likely to kill that old bastard. Hell, you done already whipped five dollars worth out of him anyway. Let's go, our supper is probably cold by now."

The others nodded in agreement. So they cut him down and left him lying on the ground. As they cleared out, John ran out of the cave and tried to comfort him. He sat on the ground crying and holding the dying old man's head in his lap.

"Lay still; you hurt preddy bad. I'll get sumptin to stop ya bleeding."

"Neva you mind John. I ain't gonna make it... (gasp)... But, I want ya ta do sumptin fo me."

"Sure...anything."

"Well... when ya git to dat freedom land, and you sittin under ya own fig tree somewhere nice and peaceful, I want you to say a prayer for ol Baraka. Will ya do dat fo me? "

Before John could respond, a contented smile came across the old man's face as his body went limp. He gripped John's hand and his tearful eyes fluttered for the very last time.

∞∞∞∞∞∞∞∞∞∞

They must have given that poor soul thirty lashes. But he refused to give John up. John would never know for sure why the old man sacrificed himself like that. Yet he soon came to believe that the good Lord spared him so that he could be a blessing to others, just as Baraka had been to him. That gut-wrenching experience transformed John's life forever and marked the beginning of his lifelong dedication to the Underground Railroad. From that day forward, he vowed to spend the rest of his life trying to fulfill what he considered to be his sacred obligation to that kindly old man and all of those who were experiencing the misery of human bondage.

Since his arrival in Philadelphia, John had taken up residence in the cellar of Sol Abrams' store where he worked as a deliveryman and one of Mr. Still's most dedicated operatives. Despite his rather meager existence, John was a sublimely contented man. He took great pleasure in volunteering his time to the Underground. So did Sol, who often provided food and supplies free of charge to the fugitives who were temporarily entrusted to his care. John's duties typically involved transporting fugitives to various relay stations and delivering food, water and firewood to the safe houses scattered throughout the city. Occasionally, and whenever the need arose, he would even rendezvous with fugitive slave parties in Maryland and the contiguous slave states and guide them into Pennsylvania. For him, there were no sacrifices or burdens too great to bear.

∞∞∞∞∞∞∞∞∞∞

After hearing the story, William regretted his thoughtless comment and was somewhat embarrassed by his misplaced suspicion. Yet he was glad Mr. Still had taken the time to share this poignant tale, which he assumed was common knowledge among the Underground's inner circle. In this regard, he felt a modicum of acceptance and an even greater respect for John Ansar, Sol Abrams and the man they respectfully called "the General".

They continued their ride to the church in complete silence. Mr. Still pondered his short list of suspected rats who could have infiltrated their ranks and imperiled the Cattos. William's thoughts were elsewhere. The story of John's harrowing experience reminded him of his dismal life on the Ferrette plantation. It also reminded him of Ned and the puzzling circumstances surrounding his death. Ellen had yet to tell him what she knew about the brutal murder of his closest friend.

9. The Vigilance Committee

"...But this is certain that in Philadelphia, the free colored people are a respectable class, and in my opinion quite as intelligent as the more humble of the free whites."

Frederick Marryat

Mr. Still and William arrived at Mother Bethel Church a few minutes before the scheduled meeting. William had never been in a church before, let alone one that was owned by colored people. His religious rituals consisted of weekly sermons and occasional camp revivals. These events were usually held in tattered tents and organized by self-appointed Negro parsons who typically preached without the benefit of basic literacy and a written text.

He stood outside and reverently scanned the sacred edifice. Its stately steeple and stained glass windows were an imposing sight that filled him with awe and utter solemnity. Once inside, he beheld the simple elegance of its long mahogany pews, its upper galleries and its well-crafted nave. There were many larger and more ornate churches scattered throughout the city. Philadelphia's diverse congregations tended to spare no expense in constructing their houses of worship. Yet Mr. Still intimated that Mother Bethel had the tallest and widest doors of any church in the city. He explained to William that these disproportionately larger doors were more than an architectural anomaly. The church elders wanted to convey the simple point that the doors of Mother Bethel would be opened wide to all people, to *all who seek the Lord.*

Mr. Still took his customary seat in the first pew and discreetly looked over his shoulder to observe the behavior of the eighty or so men and women in attendance. He scanned their faces in search of some inexplicable clue that might somehow help him identify the suspected traitors who might be present. This brief exercise in mind reading proved to be fruitless. Yet he remained certain that one day, and one day soon, they would be uncovered. Perhaps some unguarded comment, some self-revelatory action would lead him to his prey.

Upon hearing the loud whack of a gavel, he and William faced forward. True to form, the meeting was called to order at precisely seven o'clock by the committee's venerable Chairman, Reverend C. Thomas Reynolds. Reverend Reynolds was at least ten years older than

Mr. Still and Reverend Catto who both served as the Committee's Vice-Chairman. Reverend Reynolds was a man of broad learning who had a voracious appetite for knowledge, old and new. In fact, he was the only known colored clergyman in Philadelphia who could read the scriptures in both Hebrew and Greek. He was also a man of unsurpassed erudition and was by far, the organization's most eloquent and persuasive elocutionist. He insisted that spoken words had a definite vibratory force and had the power to uplift or destroy. That is why he was so cautious and deliberate in his use of them.

Although he was short in stature, Reverend Reynolds had a commanding presence. Always neat and impeccably dressed, one would instantly recognize him as a man of unmistakable refinement. With his graying temples and receding hairline, he impressed William as the type of distinguished gentleman he would like to be in the twilight of his years. But he was not alone in that assessment. Both the younger and more senior members of the church held Reverend Reynolds in the highest regard because of his well-known family lineage and the force of his character. For these and many other reasons, he was chosen over Mr. Still as the principal spokesperson for the Committee and its liaison with city officials and other civic organizations.

The meetings of the Vigilance Committee had always included lively exchanges of ideas and opinions. As a newcomer and invited guest, William sat in silence and listened attentively as the Committee engaged in a lengthy discussion of the Fogg case and its far-reaching implications. Two weeks earlier, one of its members, Mr. Fogg, was denied the right to vote in a nearby county where he and his family had resided for well over forty years. The Foggs were free men and women of color, who like the other members of the Committee, were gainfully employed, tax-paying citizens. In fact, some of committee members were affluent businessmen and skilled artisans who could trace their family lineage back some seventy years before the American Revolutionary War.

The denial of voting rights was an especially bitter pill to swallow for some of the older members of Mother Bethel Church. Reverend Reynolds in particular, remembered well the civic virtue of his father and Reverends Richard Allen and Absalom Jones. In 1793, they were asked by Mayor Matthew Clarkson, to help combat the yellow fever epidemic that eventually claimed over 5,000 lives; an estimated one-tenth of Philadelphia's citizens. At that time, it was believed that the colored population had a special immunity to the disease.

Consequently, they were tasked with caring for the sick and burying the dead.

In addition, some church members were old enough to remember when Reverends Allen and Jones organized the Black Legion to defend Philadelphia in the War of 1812. They were particularly incensed by the selective amnesia demonstrated by city officials who conveniently forgot that colored residents had been contributors to the common good long before America was a nation and after the subsequent framing of the United States Constitution that was adopted in Independence Hall just a few blocks away from the hallowed sanctuary of Mother Bethel A.M.E. Church.

Experienced in the ways of Philadelphia politics, Reverend Reynolds saw the Fogg case as a harbinger of things to come. He also saw it as part of a well-orchestrated effort to relegate the colored population to a permanently inferior status in the state. He linked the Fogg case to his reason for calling last week's emergency meeting.

Reverend Reynolds had been totally outraged by the appearance of some derogatory cartoon drawings that appeared in Philadelphia's leading newspapers. These drawings depicted Negroes as ignorant, pretentious and unfit residents who were merely cheap imitators of "white civilization". Many, if not most of the committee members believed that on the scale of things, the publication of these drawings, as offensive as they were, hardly constituted "an emergency". But, in respectful deference to Reverend Reynolds, the emergency meeting drew an unusually high attendance. Reverend Catto for one, thought there were far more pressing matters to attend to, such as meeting the needs of a the increased flow of fugitives coming into Philadelphia from the states around the Ohio river region. But he too, dared not challenge the sovereign judgment of the esteemed Reverend Reynolds who made his position on the matter quite clear.

However, he and many others agreed with Reverend Reynolds' position regarding the pivotal importance of Negro voting rights. As usual, Reverend Reynolds set the tone for the weekly meeting.

"Brothers and sisters, we have to take a stand, but we've got to be level-headed about it. For nearly fifty years, the free Negro has voted all over the State of Pennsylvania. And we'd be blasted fools to let them take away the vote from us now. The law is the law! Read it to them Reverend Catto."

In compliance, Reverend Catto opened a book and cited Article III, section I of the Pennsylvania Convention of 1790. In verbatim, it read:

"In elections by the citizens every freeman of the age of twenty-one years, having residing in the State two years before the election, and within that time paid a State or County tax which shall have been assessed at least six months before the election, shall enjoy the rights of an elector*".*

"And that gentlemen and ladies is as plain as plain can be!" Reverend Reynolds added. At that moment, he was interrupted by Pastor Cleophas Hightower, an obese man whose body weight was only exceeded by his verbosity. Slowly rising from his seat in the first pew, he replied,

"Yes, but that was then and this is now. Over the past few years, this city has been swamped with no-account, shiftless sinners who give the Negro a bad name. Many of them don't know the first thing about their duties and responsibilities as law-abiding citizens!"

His remarks were followed by several nods of approval and intermittent affirmations.

"Ain't that the truth."

"Amen Brother!"

Reverend Reynolds agreed with that particular point and felt compelled to chime in.

"Well, brother minister, I must confess, you are right about that. We can't let those less educated brothers and sisters hold us back. They seem to be turning public opinion against us. First, those infernal cartoons; now they want to deny us the vote. There's an ill wind blowing and we have to take drastic action."

On the other side of the aisle, Frances Harper reacted in total disgust. She had a prim and proper demeanor and very rarely raised her voice above a whisper. As usual, she was well-groomed and wore a brightly colored dress that accentuated her slender form. Before rising to her feet, she cleared her throat and discreetly adjusted the knot of hair she had neatly gathered in the form of a taut bun.

"Pastor Hightower, you can't expect uneducated and severely oppressed men and women who have been treated like animals to assume, let alone understand, their place in a civilized society. It is our duty to teach them, to show them a better way. It's as simple as that!"

Ms. Harper was one of the committee's most learned members who understood all too well, the importance of public schooling as a proven remedy to public ignorance. Robert Purvis, a handsome young businessman and one of the city's most eligible bachelors, immediately rose to her defense. He too took great exception to Pastor Hightower's comments.

"With all due respect Pastor Hightower, I've always believed that a man gives *himself* a bad name. It is not thrust upon him by the deeds or misdeeds of others."

Out of the corner of his eye, Mr. Still could see Reverend Reynolds nodding in approval. His subtle authoritative nod was usually a sought after gesture, signifying that a valid point had been made. They were all conditioned to look for it. In contrast, the younger Pastor Hightower was far less articulate. Worse yet, he was not a man who could tolerate his opinions being publicly challenged and contradicted. Raising his voice above the others, he stammered as perspiration seeped from every pore in his body.

"Now yaw can er…er sit up here denying the truth if you want to. But, yaw know that the criminal element in the Seventh Ward is growing out of control."

Again, his loyalists nodded in agreement and endorsed his position with a chorus of further affirmations.

"Tell it like it is Reverend!"

"I know that's right!"

"Speak the truth and shame the devil!"

Mr. Purvis was quick in his rebuttal.

"But surely, you're not suggesting that their existence justifies stripping hard-working, law-abiding free men of color of their right to vote?"

"No it doesn't, Mr. Purvis. I'm merely saying that you can't expect white folks to feel safe around us. Besides, things haven't been the same in this city since Nat Turner butchered those white folks down in Virginia a few years ago. They tell me he even killed a couple of innocent women and children down there."

His calculated reference to Nat Turner's rebellion in 1831 did not have the desired effect he intended to have on the audience. Although it had occurred eight years earlier in far away, Southampton County, Virginia, no one could forget that horrific uprising and the chilling effects it had on race relations in America. At least fifty-one whites were murdered on the evening of August 21st. Nat Turner was a religious man who believed that he was prompted by mystical voices urging him to fulfill a dream of liberating his people from bondage.

Following the massacre, the white community hunted down the Negro assailants and killed an undetermined number of "suspects". In the aftermath, the Court ordered sixteen men executed. Many more were jailed and transported to other localities. Nat Turner was sentenced to the gallows and died totally unrepentant of his deeds. He had declared,

"I have too much sense to be raised, and if I was, I would never be of any service to anyone as a slave."

Nat Turner's insurrection sent shock waves throughout the slave-holding states of the South. Several state legislatures enacted stringent laws called, "black codes", designed to restrict the movement of slaves and forbid them the right to read. In his much-publicized confessions, Nat Turner had insisted that his course of action was inspired by the teachings of the Bible. Hence, the teaching of slaves to read or write was expressly prohibited by most Southern laws. Violators were subject to heavy fines and the threat of imprisonment.

Many Southerners believed that Turner's revolt was encouraged by "outside agitators". Some even argued that the revolt was directly related to the strong anti-slavery writings of one man, William Lloyd Garrison. Two years after the insurrection, the American Anti-Slavery Society was organized in Philadelphia under Garrison's leadership. A New Englander by birth, Garrison moved to Philadelphia shortly after he was dragged through the streets of Boston by pro-slavery advocates opposing his particular brand of militant abolitionism. The allegations linking Garrison's activities to Turner's insurrection were specious at best and were never substantiated. Nonetheless, in the wake of the massacre, the abolitionist movement in the North lost considerable momentum. In the South, fear and endless cycles of indiscriminate violence against Negroes were the order of the day.

Pastor Hightower's attempt to relate the Turner uprising to the Fogg case in Pennsylvania drew additional fire from some of the more learned elders of the Committee. With considerably less decorum than the courtly Robert Purvis, Mr. Fogg leapt to his feet.

"Now what in tarnation does what Nat Turner did in Virginia have to do with the free man's right to vote in the land of his birth? Our fathers voted. Besides, there are no *innocents* (as you say) in war!"

"War!" scoffed Pastor Hightower. "Since when have we been at war?"

Almost on cue, some of Hightower's loyalists snickered in support. Unable to hold his silence any longer, James Forten, one of the most respected businessmen in the city, stood to deliver a sharp and well-measured diatribe. He was well known throughout the city for his wealth and his very direct manner of speaking. The entire group was riveted to its seats as he fixed his piercing gaze on Pastor Hightower.

"My God, look around you man! In the South, 95% of our people are in a human hell, brutalized and terrorized; families torn apart and sold like animals on the auction block. Heartbroken mothers driven to murdering their own children to spare them the absolute horror of slavery! Hard-working and underfed people deprived of the fruits of their own labor. Are you blind? Are you insane? In the North, the colored man can't even earn a decent wage; white folks try to keep him out of the trade guilds and skilled professions. And, you've got some of them who think the low-wage factory jobs are too good for us. The only place he is safe and welcomed is right here in the Seventh Ward. Oh yes sir, we are most definitely at war. I'm just surprised that you haven't taken notice!"

Before he could finish, Robert Purvis chimed in with another verbal assault.

"And I'll tell you something else Reverend. That war started long before ol' Nat Turner decided he wouldn't take it anymore. And, how dare you, a man of the cloth, equate the heroism of Nat Turner with the common thieves and pickpockets in the Seventh Ward! Nat Turner was a martyr...a Christian martyr who struck a blow for freedom rather than endure his veritable hell on earth."

"A Christian martyr you say", chuckled Pastor Hightower. "You sir, must be reading a *special* Bible; a different Bible than the rest of us."

Annoyed by his snide sarcasm, Purvis fired back,

"And you sir, must be a *special* kind of fool; an educated man with the mentality of a slave!"

Deeply offended, Pastor Hightower tried to counter Purvis' surprisingly harsh recrimination.

"I'll have you know that my father purchased my freedom for me over thirty-years ago!" he shouted.

With impeccable timing, one of the Committee's more rambunctious members, Uncle Blue, stood up and hollered back.

"Well, you need to give him his money back for all the good it did ya!"

Uncle Blue was a testy and somewhat irascible man who had developed quite a reputation for his outspokenness. However, on this day he seemed particularly annoyed with Pastor Hightower and was extremely intolerant of his sheepish followers. By this time, Pastor Hightower was beyond himself with anger. It was William Craft's first meeting, so he kept quiet and listened intently as the debate escalated and took on an uncomfortably combative tone.

"Why, I've never heard such imprudence!" said Pastor Hightower.

He rose from his pew and headed for the exit, along with several others who were members of his congregation. Reverend Reynolds politely waited until all of the dissidents had exited the church. As the door closed behind them, he struck his gavel in an effort to refocus the discussion.

"Order, order! Let me remind you that we have a motion before us to support a legal action, in the Supreme Court of Pennsylvania against the judges and inspectors of election in Luzerne County who deliberately and unlawfully deprived Mr. Martin Hobbs, a free man of color, of his right to vote. Are you ready for the vote?"

"Just a point of order," said Reverend Catto.

"Do we have a sufficient quorum to justify a binding decision by this body? It seems like Pastor Hightower has left with what looks like a half of our members. I don't see how we can vote unless we can persuade him to come back."

From the pew in front of him, William heard Uncle Blue whisper to Frances Harper.

"I know how ta git him back; just throw a big ol' pork chop in da pulpit and he'll come a runnin' with those other boot lickers right behind him."

"Uncle Blue, behave yourself."

"Well, it's the truth and you know it girl!"

Acknowledging the question, Reverend Reynolds began to count those who remained.

"Let's see, 1-2-3... Well, we've got forty-two, just enough. Are you ready for the vote? Hearing no further comments, all in favor say "aye" and signify by raising your right hand...The ayes have it and the motion is carried. Let the record show we have unanimous consent.

At this point, I'd like to ask Reverend Catto and Mr. Purvis to prepare a preliminary brief for the Court of Appeals in two weeks. Is there any new business before we adjourn?"

"Just one announcement," said Mr. Still. "I want to remind everyone that the joint plenary convention of the Philadelphia and Boston Anti-Slavery Committees will be held next week in the newly constructed Pennsylvania Hall. It is an extraordinary facility. We look forward to receiving abolitionists from all over the country in support of our cause. I hope to see all of you there for what promises to be a history-making event."

"Are there any other announcements? Hearing none, this meeting is adjourned," said Reverend Reynolds.

Most of the audience filed out of the church. A few lingered behind to socialize a bit. Frances Harper approached her friend, Harriet Forten, the twenty-five year old daughter of James Forten.

"You know Harriet, I like good oratory as much as the next person but I declare, sometimes it seems like we do more *speechifying* than doing."

"What do you mean?"

"I mean, while we're having grand conventions, whatever happened to my suggestion to start a high school for the children in the Seventh Ward? Most of them can't read and those that can, aren't permitted to go beyond the sixth grade."

"Then why don't you bring it up at the next meeting?"

"Don't think that I won't!"

"Well, are you coming to the big convention Frances?"

"I wouldn't miss it for the world. And, I know for sure *you'll* be there Harriet."

"Why do you say that?"

"I see the way you look at Mr. Purvis."

"Why Frances Harper what ever do you mean?"

"You don't fool me Harriet Forten. I see the way your eyes light up when Mr. Purvis enters the room."

"You're delirious."

"Am I? You forget; I know you. You can't…"

Before she could finish her comment, Uncle Blue tapped her on the shoulder.

"Come on Ms. Harper if you want to ride with me. I got work to do, places to go, people to see."

"I have to run. We'll talk tomorrow, okay?"

Frances hugged Harriet and walked toward the exit. Before she could leave, Harriet called back to her.

"Frances?"

"Yes?"

"Is it *that* obvious?"

"As the nose on your face. I gotta go girl before Uncle Blue leaves me. See ya."

Harriet was smiling wistfully when her blissful reverie was interrupted by Reverend Reynolds.

"May I offer you a ride Ms. Forten? I've got a new buggy and team of horses I'd like to show you."

"No, thank you Reverend. It's such a beautiful night, I think I'll walk."

"Okay, but don't linger. You shouldn't be walking along South Street unescorted. There's a lot of riff-raff out there young lady."

∞∞∞∞∞∞∞∞∞∞

Reverend Reynolds' admonition was quite appropriate, considering the sharp increase in street crimes throughout the city. However, Mr. Still had a different and more expansive view of Philadelphia's criminal element. There were other and equally vile criminal forces at work in "the City of Brotherly Love". The Seventh Ward in particular was being stalked by bounty hunters in search of fugitive slaves and capture rewards. These men were being paid by other "respectable" criminals who dwelled in high places where greed and profiteering dominated all other human values.

These types of criminals were the business elite of the city who greatly profited from the perpetuation of slavery. Slavery was essentially and undeniably good for business. It was the common capital of a sinful enterprise that served both the southern and northern states. Thus, commercial interests and the quest to acquire added wealth effectively drowned out the moral impulse to abandon slavery and see it as the inhumane and exploitative social evil that it truly was.

Mr. Still understood all too well that Philadelphia had become a haven for both abolitionists and the ruthless *time bandits* who were determined to keep Negro men, women and children in perpetual bondage. The practice of slavery and slave catching was escalating in Philadelphia and throughout the nation. Thus, the stage was being set for a social and political battle of epic proportions.

10. Assault on God's Citadel

"In defending the great cause of human rights,
I wish to derive the assistance of all religions and all parties."
William Lloyd Garrison

The long-awaited anti-slavery convention opened in Pennsylvania Hall located at 6th and Race Street, in the heart of the city. The great Hall was to be the headquarters of the Pennsylvania Anti-Slavery Society and a printing and distribution center for its various publications. Its majestic Greco-Roman pillars and enormous size presented an imposing sight for the hundreds of pedestrians and onlookers gathered outside. The streets surrounding the grand edifice were crowded and abuzz with excitement and curiosity. There was infectious electricity in the air as countless pro-slavery and anti-slavery advocates surrounded the building in tense anticipation.

Reverend Catto had agreed to be the master of ceremonies for the occasion. Still heart-broken and worried about Sarah's condition, he showed no outward signs of stress or discomfort. This important event had been planned for over two years. For three full days, colored and whites would defy custom and brazenly celebrate their common humanity and call for an immediate end to slavery in the United States. In addition, women were stridently breaking with longstanding tradition and daring to give public speeches and participate in important social discourse. The Hall had a seating capacity of 3,000 and was completely filled. Outside, an anxious overflow crowd clamored to be let in on a standing room only basis.

Reverend Catto walked gracefully to the podium and called the convention to order. He was a tall man with an intense demeanor, befitting the seriousness and importance of the occasion. His first task was to introduce the mayor.

"Ladies and gentlemen, if I can have your attention; I am Reverend William T. Catto, your master of ceremonies and moderator for this morning's session. And, on behalf of the Philadelphia Vigilance Committee, the Pennsylvania Anti-Slavery Society, the Society of Friends and last but not least, the Philadelphia Female Anti-Slavery Society, it is my distinct pleasure to welcome you to this historic convention. We are honored this morning to have with us the Mayor of the City of Philadelphia, the Honorable Mayor Wilford B. Swift. Please join me in welcoming him to the stage."

After a robust applause, the Mayor shook the hands of several dignitaries and eventually made his way to the podium. He was a large man, noted for his winning smile and an unusually thick handlebar mustache that accentuated his rather large nose and bloated face. Clearing his throat, he struck an authoritative pose and leaned on the podium that seemed to quiver under the weight of his wide body.

"Thank you Reverend Catto. To Reverend Reynolds, Rabbi Jacobi, Father Kendrick, Mr. Cope and the several distinguished gentlemen and ladies of the dais, I welcome you all to Philadelphia, the birthplace of American freedom and our nation's cradle of liberty. On behalf of the City Council and all of our citizens, I welcome you and salute you for the noble purposes and humanitarian causes you represent here today. And, I want to tell you…"

ꝏꝏꝏꝏꝏꝏꝏꝏ

His perfunctory greetings were followed by the public recognition of over twenty-four city officials and local dignitaries who each received their own separate rounds of applause. Reverend Catto considered this part of the program to be superfluous and a bit vain. However, he was over-ruled by Reverend Reynolds who was known to be a stickler for proper protocol and decorum.

As these lengthy introductions were taking place, Mr. Still was wading through throngs of people gathered outside. He had been momentarily delayed due to an interview with a local newspaper that had gone beyond its scheduled time. Ordinarily, Reverend Reynolds would give such an interview, but he was still smarting about those disparaging political cartoons depicting Negro "backwardness". As a result, he refused to have anything to do with reporters or anyone associated with the press. His sense of outrage ran that deep. Mr. Still agreed to give the interview in his stead. He thought it was unwise to snub the press. Moreover, be wanted to use the newspapers as a means to raise public awareness about the purpose and critical importance of the anti-slavery convention. Mr. Still, by nature, always shunned the limelight and avoided public speaking. But at the time, his handling of the interview seemed like a reasonable division of labor.

As he approached the entryway of the building, he noticed one of Philadelphia's leading politicians, Judge Huntsfield Andrews. Judge

Andrews was conversing with a small group of the city's wealthy elders. You could always identify them by their decidedly homogeneous attire – well-tailored suits, velvet broadcloth vests and silver-tipped walking canes to accentuate their air of superiority. Mr. Baldwin, a leading banker, appeared to be the center of attention.

"I never thought I'd see the day when gentlemen of property and standing would tolerate such an event in this city. Have you looked inside Judge Andrews?"

"No Mr. Baldwin, I have not."

"Well let me tell you. They have Negroes and whites and females in there sitting together like peas in a pod. It's scandalous, simply scandalous"

"You don't say. Excuse me Mr. Baldwin but there is someone over there that I simply must speak to."

The judge quickly made his way over to the entryway and intercepted Mr. Still who was hoping to avoid him.

"Ah, Mr. Still. Fancy finding you here. Will you be participating in the festivities inside by any chance?"

"Good morning your Honor. As a matter of fact I will."

"So tell me Mr. Still, how is the transportation business these days?"

"Excuse me?"

"Come, come Mr. Still. My sources in Maryland tell me you do a brisk business transferring certain *property* across the Mason-Dixon Line."

"Well I wouldn't know anything about that. I am sure your Honor knows that I am just a simple clerk working only two floors beneath your chambers. I would like to chat further, but I am already running behind schedule. Good day to you sir."

As Mr. Still walked away, the Judge resumed his conversation with the others.

"There's a man who definitely bears watching," he said with a sinister smile. "He's a sly one. First, he's managed to get his people fraternizing with whites. Now, I'm told they even want to give voting rights to women and niggers. Imagine that! I tell you it's absolutely ridiculous and totally immoral!"

∞∞∞∞∞∞∞∞∞

. Mr. Still found one of the last remaining seats in the back, just in time to hear Reverend Catto make his next introduction.

"And now my Brothers and Sisters, it is my distinct pleasure to introduce to you our keynote speaker, a true son of liberty and champion for justice, from the great state of Massachusetts, Mr. William Lloyd Garrison."

Garrison had a broad reputation for being a persuasive writer and a stalwart champion of the abolitionist movement. Earlier that year, he published the first edition of his anti-slavery newspaper, *The Liberator*. On its front page, he featured a drawing of the "great bell' that so proudly hung in Philadelphia's Independence Hall. The great bell was also printed on all of the anti-slavery pamphlets and broadsides announcing the long-awaited convention. Garrison got the idea from an abolitionist poem entitled, *The Liberty Bell*, which represented the first documented use of the name "liberty bell". Thus, the Liberty Bell, the preeminent icon of American democracy would soon become the adopted symbol of the entire anti-slavery movement. Ironically, the revered bell, with its wide crack came to be a bitter metaphor for the freedom that was being denied to the nation's Negro population.

The bespectacled Mr. Garrison was greeted with a tremendous round of applause. He was a studious-looking man whose appearance suggested a certain frailty or perhaps sickliness. However, that initial impression was immediately dispelled as he briskly walked to the podium and began to speak at a high volume and emotional tone that totally belied his diminutive body. The audience was momentarily stunned as this deceptively passive man transformed himself into a forceful polemist who attacked the practice of slavery in the strongest of terms.

"The history of mankind is crowded with evidence proving that physical coercion is not adapted to moral regeneration; that the sinful dispositions of men can be subdued only by love; that evil can be exterminated from the earth only by goodness. But, I say to you in the matter of slavery, I will be as harsh as truth itself and uncompromising as justice. On this subject, I do not wish to think, or speak or write with moderation. No! No! Tell a man whose house is on fire to give a moderate

alarm; tell him to moderately rescue his wife from the hands of a ravisher; tell the mother to gradually extricate her child from the fire into which it has fallen – but urge me not to use moderation in a cause like the present. I am in earnest – I will not equivocate – I will not excuse – I will not retreat a single inch – and I will be heard!" And, I say to you, that..." [1]

William Lloyd Garrison

Outside Pennsylvania Hall, the crowd was growing larger and increasingly restless. It appeared as though the pro-slavery advocates were in the majority. On the west side of the building, a sinister conspiracy was being hatched. A gang of Irish teenagers gathered around their leader, Jack O'Toole, a man of notorious reputation.

"What's all the damn excitement about Jack?" asked Sean, one of his underlings.

"Big meeting. Looks like a bunch of nigs and some blue bloods from New England."

"Geez, it's like a blasted beehive out here."

"Hell, they even have Father Kendrick in there. God only knows what an Irish Catholic priest is doing with the likes of them!"

"Are you sure Jack?"

"Sure as I'm looking at ya."

"Listen, there's three dollars in it for each of us. Easy money I tell ya. Are you in Mike?"

---

[1]**Editorial Note**: While *The Rains* is a work of historical fiction, this quotation and all other subsequent quotations are designated in bold type to indicate the actual (verbatim) spoken or written words of an historical personage or organization.

"Hell, I'd do it for free."

"Fine, then I'll be having Mikey's cut," Sean added.

"Seems a pity though. That there is a handsome building," said Mike.

"Yeah, well pity we can't say the same about you! But, you know you're right; it puts me in mind of the cathedral in County Cork."

"Now Jack, tell us what would you'd be knowing about a cathedral, ya hooligan!"

"I never said I went *inside*, now did I? Ya big ox!"

∞∞∞∞∞∞∞∞∞∞

Back inside, Robert Purvis was speaking to a very attentive audience.

"...And I say to you that we can ill afford to ignore the inextricable linkage between slavery and the ubiquitous hatred of the Negro. It has been said there are a thousand people hacking at the branches of evil, compared to one who is striking at the root. Racial hatred, borne of an attitude of superiority is the root cause of a million branches of social and institutional cruelties and injustices. Racial hatred is both the parent and the child of slavery. It is racial hatred the prevents this country from extending full rights to our people."

At this point, Mr. Purvis was suddenly interrupted by a man seated in the first row.

"This is the white man's country!" he yelled. "We don't need all of this friction between the races. Why don't you people just go back to Africa where you belong and where you can have all the rights you want. I say again, this is *the white man's country!*"

Mr. Purvis was swift and sure in his rebuttal.

"Not so sir. This is the red man's country by natural right and the black man's by virtue of his suffering and toil. Your fathers by violence drove the red man out and forced the black man in. The children of the black man have enriched the soil by their tears, sweat and blood. Sir, we were born here and here we shall remain.

I elect to stay on the same soil on which I was born, and on the plot of ground which I have fairly bought and honestly paid for. Don't advise me to leave and add insult to injury by telling me it's for my own good; or that I am to be the judge. It is vain that you talk to me about *the two races* and their mutual antagonisms. In the matter of rights there is but one race and that is the *human race*."

Harriet Forten applauded vigorously as her eyes twinkled in admiration. Frances Harper applauded his passionate speech, but found herself laughing at her friend who was clearly smitten with Mr. Purvis. Uncle Blue discreetly nudged Harriet and gave her a rascally wink.

"Calm yourself girl, you look at that man like you could sop him up with a biscuit."
She did not seem to mind his teasing. Nor did she refute the comment.

As the crowd outside became more agitated, a group of city policemen were dispatched to the area. Police Sergeant McKilroy was the first to arrive with some of his officers.

"We've got to keep this crowd moving men. Don't let them block the exits. I'll wager you they'll be coming out soon for a break."

"How do you know that sergeant?"

"There's a limit to human tolerance laddy. You can only stand all of that blasphemous hot air but for so long – including that of our beloved Mayor. Saints preserve him; he can shovel it with the best of them!"

The sergeant noticed a group of elderly white ladies hovering around the entranceway, trying to get a closer look inside. He yelled to his patrolmen without the slightest subtlety.

"You men, keep those rubbernecks moving!"

"I'm sorry ladies, but you've got to move on. Nothing to see here."

"I beg your pardon. Nothing to see? You obviously haven't looked inside officer!"

"Instead of harassing law-abiding citizens like us, you need to break up that foolishness inside. I've never seen such goings-on!"

"Listen lady, I'm just doing my job. Don't get your bonnet in a twist."

"Well, you won't be having your job for long if you don't do something about the crimes being committed in there, right under your big red nose! Just what is your name anyway sonnie?"

"You tell 'em, Abigail, give 'em hell!"

"Listen lady, I'm just following orders. I'm an officer of the law."

"Oh yeah? Well, you can put a pig in a powdered wig and robe, but that doesn't make him a judge!"

The vociferous group of senior citizens eventually moved on, but not without letting their feelings be known.

∞∞∞∞∞∞∞∞∞∞

Late in the afternoon, the convention adjourned for the day. Outside Pennsylvania Hall, hundreds of pro-slavery advocates lingered to taunt the conventioneers with a combination of jeers, insults and icy scowls. By most accounts, the convention was a huge success. Several strong resolutions were passed and promptly forwarded to President Andrew Jackson, the Massachusetts legislature and most of the Atlantic States.

Regrettably, word quickly got around that whites and coloreds were openly fraternizing inside and unescorted ladies were daring to appear in public to express openly their abolitionist opinions in Pennsylvania Hall's marketplace of ideas. The tension outside was so thick you could cut it with a knife

Reverend Catto immediately left the premises through the rear of the building and rushed home to his ailing wife. Ellen reported that Sarah's left ear had been bleeding off and on all day. Observing his wife's contorted face and wan complexion, he immediately sent for Dr. Minton again. Unfortunately, Dr. Minton's diagnosis was bleak and worried him further. Apparently, the brick had caused major damage to her inner ear. This injury carried with it the ever-present risk of infection, uncontrollable dizziness and the possibility of a permanent loss of hearing. Sarah was gravely ill and appeared to be slowly slipping away from him. He knelt beside her bed while Ellen showed Dr. Minton to the door. She took the opportunity to ask him the obvious question that was on everyone's mind.

"Be truthful with me Doctor. I can handle it. Is she going to make it?"

"It's really hard to say. I've done all I can do for her. It's a waiting game at this point. One thing is for sure, she needs plenty of rest."

"Believe me. I'll make sure she gets a lot of sleep."

"By the way, you look like you could use some sleep yourself young lady."

"I'm fine, just fine. One more thing Doctor…is the baby going to be all right. I've been praying for him all day and night."

"The baby seems to be okay. But why do you say *him*? It could be a girl you know."

"Oh it's a boy alright. It's definitely a boy."

∞∞∞∞∞∞∞∞∞∞

Night fell on the city and the residents of the Catto household finally got to sleep. However, William arose around midnight to say his prayers and meditate in the quiet and stillness of the evening. Never in his wildest dreams had he imagined the prospect of living as a free man. That simple but profound thought sent a shudder down his spine. It was all so overwhelming. He took for granted that at the estimated age thirty-five, he was well beyond the mid-point of his life. That assumption made him think deeply about time; irreversible, irreplaceable time. Time lost and time left. Slavery and the *time bandits* had robbed him of precious time. The tragedy and injustice of it all momentarily saddened him.

But, when he recalled all the miraculous things he had witnessed on the streets of Philadelphia, his outlook changed. He began to think to himself that life, if viewed correctly, is ever expanding and always pregnant with possibilities. He told himself that his earthly journey may or may not be half over. But, perhaps his best years were ahead of him. He would no longer submit to the wiles and whims of *the time bandits*. Maybe he would eventually claim the final victory over them.

This brief epiphany left him with an indescribable feeling of elation and spiritual reconciliation. He felt free from the past. Not free from the memory of slavery, but free from its haunting and debilitating effects. He was in a word, healed. And, now he could see his life and the entire world with new and hopeful eyes. Slavery had been for him and millions of others, a long and devastatingly brutal experience. However, he now realized that slavery's greatest evil lied not in its physical cruelty and shameless economic injustice. Its greatest harm was inflicted on the Negro's *spirit*. It instilled in him negative and self-defeating habits of mind. It forced it victims to "stand in fear" of their masters and grovel for mere survival. It robbed them of their forward vision and an appreciation of the fullness of life.

But William's mind was awakened now and brimming with unprecedented ideas and aspirations. Stretched in this manner, his mind took new shape and dimension and could never return to its previous state. A great veil had been lifted. It was as if he were born anew. He got up from his knees and went back to bed. Staring out his window, he savored the peacefulness of the evening. He gazed intently at the soft streaks of light that cleaved the darkness and gave the star-filled sky a purple hue that announced the coming dawn. The serenity of this celestial dance took him to the edge of tranquility. Minutes later, his reverent repose was suddenly and rudely disrupted by the harsh clang of fire bells piercing the quiet of the night. He stood and peered out the window.

All of a sudden, the households along South Street were awakening and candles were being lit in rapid succession. Off at a distance, he could hear the repetitive shouts of "**Fire! Fire! Fire!**"

Women gathered their children outside of their homes as the men hastily dressed and ran in the direction of the all too familiar sound. Most of the residents of South Street and the Seventh Ward lived in adjoining row homes and had learned to respond quickly to the threat of flash fires. These infernos had wiped out entire neighborhoods in the past. Smoke billowed in the sky and large plumes arose, leading the startled neighbors to the location of the huge conflagration that was at least eight blocks away.

Pennsylvania Hall was on fire. More fire bells were rung and the shrill of crude police sirens filled the night air. The Negro residents of South Street raced to the great hall. Some immediately formed bucket brigades to help fight the blaze while others frantically tried to beat back the mounting flames with wet blankets. However, most of the white residents came to merely gawk at the fiery spectacle.

The Chestnut Street Fire Station was the only group of trained fire fighters to arrive.

"Chief, where do you want us to position our bucket brigades?"

"No need!"

"Yeah, but chief, I think we can contain this one. The fire is mainly on the west side, we can control the damage."

"When I want your opinion Shaughnessy, I'll be askin' for it."

Meanwhile, a group of about sixty colored and Quaker men formed a long bucket brigade to help extinguish the fire. Women and children assisted by hastily returning empty buckets to the back of the line for refilling.

"Step lively men and keep it coming," yelled John Emlen, a well-known Quaker elder.

He doused the fire with water and reached for another bucket. For the next thirty minutes, he and the bucket brigade bravely fought the fire, but apparently to no avail. The fire grew out of control and soon engulfed the building. Meanwhile, the streets were filling with idle spectators and local residents mocking the futile efforts of the civilian fire fighters. John Emlen was undaunted and reached for another bucket that was half filled.

"Where is the rest of the water?"

"I think that's all there is," Mr. Still replied.

Infuriated, Emlen walked over to the fire chief who was smoking a cigar and was clearly disinterested in the fire that was rapidly gaining in strength.

"See here chief, if thou willst not assist us, let us at least use thine water."

"And exactly who will be replacing that water if we have another fire later tonight? Tell me that Mr. Emlen?"

"We can't lose this building!"

"I beg to differ with ya kind sir. You *can* lose it," he said, blowing smoke in Emlen's face. "And you shall!"

"Thou art insane man!"

Emlen instantly grabbed the chief by the lapels. In turn, the Chief's entire fire company immediately assaulted Emlen and attacked the others who were trying their best to fight the uncontained fire. A frantic free-for-all broke out as several white spectators joined the attack on the Quakers and Negroes who were outnumbered and unarmed. Shots were fired, followed by screaming, pleading and total pandemonium. A massive street brawl ensued against the backdrop of the great Hall, which was at that point, collapsing and fully engulfed in flames.

∞∞∞∞∞∞∞∞∞

The Burning of Pennsylvania Hall

That night, the abolitionists lost Pennsylvania Hall, along with a huge portion of their faith in humanity. In the aftermath of the fire, Pastor Hightower widely disseminated the unsubstantiated rumor that the fire was started by colored arsonists who were known for this type of destructive behavior. He had the unfortunate habit of passing along highly questionable information without the benefit of reasonable verification. In stark contrast, Reverend Catto and Mr. Still advised everyone to suspend judgment until further facts could be ascertained. The abolitionists suspected foul play and were outraged by this senseless violence and destruction. The situation clearly called for Reverend Reynolds' type of steadying influence. In times of crises, he was always the voice of reason and restraint.

The following morning, Reverend Reynolds led a small delegation that would ask Major Swift to conduct a formal investigation to determine the cause of the fire and identify those who might be responsible for it. He was accompanied by Mr. Still and two Quaker elders, Alfred Cope and John Emlen who represented the politically powerful Society of Friends that had provided most of the funding for the building. Emlen's arm was in a sling. His face was also badly bruised during last night's brawl. Mr. Cope, the oldest of the group represented the Quakers and Reverend Reynolds spoke for the Vigilance Committee, playing his customary diplomatic role. The delegation was greeted with unfriendly scowls from the Mayor's receptionist and four police officers guarding the outer lobby of his office.

"May I help you?"

"Yes, we are here to see Mayor Swift."

"Do you have an appointment?"

"No, but if thou wouldst kindly let him know that Mr. Cope of Spring Garden Street is here, I am most confident he will see us."

"Just a minute."

After a brief visit to the Mayor's inner office, she returned with a wry smile.

"The Mayor will see you. This way."

In the inner office stood the Mayor, Joe Flanagan, the belligerent fire chief and Patrick Duffy, the city's head constable.

"Ah, Mr. Cope, what an unexpected pleasure. Do come in and have a seat. Let me introduce you to Joe Flanagan, our fire chief and you know, Constable Duffy, I presume."

"Reverend Reynolds thou knowst of course, and this is Mr. Still and John Emlen, one of our brethren who was injured in last night's fire," said Mr. Cope

"Yes, I believe Mr. Flanagan and I have met, but with respectful deference to Mr. Cope, it was not the fire that injured me," said Emlen in a contemptuous tone.

Leaping to his feet, Flannagan blurted,

"You bet your ass we've met! Now see here Mayor, why do I have to be here with the likes of him and these nig..."

Before he could finish his tirade, Mayor Swift interrupted.

"That'll be enough Flanagan."

Calmly lighting a cigar, the Mayor continued,

"Mr. Cope I'm not much of a psychic, but I presume you are here to discuss that unfortunate fire last night. A pity; what a terrible waste of labor and material. I shutter to think how much that building must have cost you Quakers. They tell me it went quickly."

"On the contrary, I am told by our brethren that it lingered for at least an hour while thine firemen stood idly by," responded Mr. Cope.

Again, Flanagan reacted in a rage.

"I don't have to sit here and listen to this malarkey. You're a damned liar, so is he and your nigger friends!" shouted Flanagan as he stormed out of the room. The Mayor nonchalantly continued on.

"I do apologize for the rudeness of the Chief. He has been under quite a strain. It's not easy for a man of his ability to see a brand new building like that go up in flames. It's an affront to his professionalism and to the efficiency of the men under his command."

Mr. Cope remained calm and focused on the business at hand.

"I shall not mince words with thee Mr. Mayor. We have several eyewitnesses who can attest to the fact that thine own fire brigades were as much to blame for the loss of Pennsylvania Hall as the scoundrels who set it on fire."

"But Mr. Cope, I was led to believe that the fire was an accident; an unextinguished candle or something of the like."

With that remark, John Emlen could no longer control his anger.

"Mr. Mayor, if thou please. The fire was clearly ignited from the *outside* of the building. A child of five could clearly see that! And, when it occurred, thine men did nothing; absolutely nothing to put it out!"

"Oh well, then we are talking about arson and dereliction of duty then aren't we? In that case, if you all have witnesses, I would be pleased to have Constable Duffy and his men take their names. In fact, I will do better than that. I will appoint a special committee to investigate the matter. Yes sir, they will be sure to ferret out the truth and bring the guilty parties to justice."

"Yes, it would indeed please us if thou would indeed recognize the truth and fulfill the requirements of justice," said Mr. Cope.

"Then that settles it. You'll be hearing from my office in a few days and we will take all the necessary legal depositions."

John Emlen was flabbergasted by the Mayor's pretentious civility.

"But, but…

"Come along, Brother Emlen", said Mr. Cope. "We have taken enough of the Mayor's time. I thank thee sir and believe that thoust willst be a man of thine word and will be earnest in thine pursuit of the truth."

Slapping Reverend Reynolds on the back, the Mayor concluded,

"You betcha. And you all have a pleasant day now."

Uncle Blue, William Craft, John Ansar and several members of the Vigilance Committee had been anxiously waiting outside City Hall.

"Well? How did it go?" asked William.

"The Mayor promises to conduct an investigation into the matter," Mr. Cope answered.

"An investigation? Surely thou dost not judge the Mayor to be an honorable man?"

"The Lord seeth and knowth the secrets of all hearts Brother Emlen."

Mr. Still too could not believe Mr. Cope's apparent gullibility.

"You're kidding of course? Flanagan is totally unrepentant. Why he as much as confessed to his guilt and complicity!"

"The wheels of justice grind, slowly my friend," Mr. Cope muttered in a somber tone.

"Yeah and so does my grandma's teeth!" blurted Uncle Blue, "Except she has the good sense not to go biting into a brick thinking it's a cream pie."

"Thou mayst be correct. However we must wait upon the Lord."

Mr. Cope walked away leaving the others stunned and confused. Emlen followed him.

"Alfred, please wait up."

"Yes, what is it?"

"Please tell me. Why didn't thou challenge or at least question the bold face lies Flanagan was telling us?"

"Chief Flanagan is the very least of our concerns my dear brother. He has exteriorized his evil intent, revealing all that he is and is predisposed to do. And, unlike the good Mayor, he at least doesn't smear his misdeeds over with a hypocritical show of virtue."

∞∞∞∞∞∞∞∞∞∞

Meanwhile, in the Mayor's inner chamber, Chief Flanagan returned to continue their discussion. The Mayor was not pleased in the least with his unbridled display of emotion.

"You idiot! I told you to shut up and let me handle the situation!"

"Handle it how? By pandering to some mealy-mouthed Quakers? They act like they own this city. Them with their high-falootin' talk. Hell, you can't even understand what they're saying half the time, with all their stupid "Thees and Thous". Sounds to me like they all swallowed a Bible or something!"

"Let me tell you what I do understand! They're a powerful force in the business community and they have tons of influence with the Governor, who is one of them; or did you forget that?"

"Yeah, well maybe you're forgetting something too Mr. Mayor."

"What's that?"

"*Thou* are the bastard who gave the order to burn it down in the first place!"

11. The Resurrection of the Just

*"And thou shall be blessed; for they cannot recompense thee;
for thou shall be recompensed at the resurrection of the just."*
                                                    Luke 14:14

Later that morning, Mr. Still sat alone in his house, thinking about the destruction of Pennsylvania Hall and the escalating wave of violence against the abolitionist movement. He also began to wonder about his friend, Alfred Cope, a man of supreme patience and forbearance. He wondered if Cope was a saint or a fool. This much he did know. Forgiveness is one thing; gullibility is another. He viewed gullibility as an unmanly trait and a costly and dangerous luxury. Anyone who could forgive Chief Flanagan so easily was a saint. But, anyone who thought the Chief did all he could to save Pennsylvania Hall was simply gullible beyond repair.

As promised, the Mayor's office conducted a thorough investigation into the cause and aftermath of the fire. Reverend Reynolds dutifully collected thirty depositions and the police interviewed no less than seventy-five witnesses. In the end, the investigation concluded that the fire was of "unknown origin" and that Chief Flanagan and his men had "acted appropriately."

But three weeks later, all questions and doubts about the true causes and motivations behind the destruction of Pennsylvania Hall were put to rest. A riotous white mob burned down Reverend Catto's First African Presbyterian Church on Lombard Street. This flagrant act of arson absolutely stunned the city's entire colored population. Never had they witnessed such a vile assault aimed at a house of worship. The message was clear and unmistakable. Negroes were viewed with utter contempt and not even their sacred precincts were respected and exempt from hateful destruction and mob violence.

True enough, many of the city's white residents were beginning to show less and less fondness for their colored residents. However, many believed that this horrific act transgressed all requisites for civilized behavior. If places of worship could be blatantly defiled, were there no limits to human degradation and man's inhumanity towards man? It remained to be seen if they would raise their voices in protest and bring the guilty parties to justice. If not, Philadelphia, in all probability would disintegrate into a lawless society where vicious race crimes were tolerated and blithefully passed over.

∞∞∞∞∞∞∞∞∞∞

Reverend Catto was undoubtedly a major target of these assaults but the entire Seventh Ward was in a state of siege. Mayor Swift ordered a six p.m. curfew in the city and twenty-four hour police protection for Reverend Reynolds. Armed Negro parishioners guarded Mother Bethel Church around the clock. Two weeks passed without incident so the Mayor eventually lifted the citywide curfew. There seemed to be a cessation of the racially motivated violence, but the anti-Negro forces were now moving on other fronts.

The anti-slavery convention was a successful rallying point for the abolitionists. But apparently, it had also produced a huge political backlash. It galvanized the pro-slavery forces and enflamed the racial bigotry and pro-slavery sentiments of many of the city's white citizens. Many of them were Irish and Italian immigrants who were competing with the colored population for scarce jobs and resources. One city councilman even called for the enactment of laws to bar "ignorant, indolent and depraved persons of color" from entering the state. The city's well-established white "Nativists" and the newly formed communities of European immigrants now seemed to be solidly unified in their common contempt for the city's colored population.

In response to this worsening state of affairs, a special meeting of the Vigilance Committee was held to formulate appropriate counter-measures and to better prepare the Seventh Ward for vigorous self-defense. Reverend Catto decided to forego the meeting and attend to Sarah whose condition had not stabilized. Mr. Still arrived late to the meeting, just as they were discussing a lesser but no less disturbing development; the final disposition of the ongoing Fogg case against the County Board of Electors.

Reverend Reynolds asked Robert Purvis to provide an update. He stood and turned around to face a packed audience.

"Well it's really quite simple; we lose," he said. "The Negro has been legally stripped of his right to vote in this state."

The members all gasped in utter disbelief. James Forten was the first to question him.

"How can that be? Didn't Judge Andrews recognize the decision of 1795 that was read to us? It clearly stated that every free man, twenty-one or over has the right to vote!"

"You're right Mr. Forten. His decision was an obvious straining of the law and common sense. But the opposition somehow persuaded the judge that the word "white" was intended to be in the 1795 statute and was taken out to prevent insult to dark colored, white men."

"Is that true?"

"Of course not! There is no written record of it and no persons who attended the Constitutional Convention were brought forward as witnesses. Nonetheless, Judge Andrews ruled that a Negro, though free, could never be a free man. The state legislature has followed his lead and has even voted 77 to 45 to insert the phrase "*qualified white voters*" in the new statute to prevent us from making further legal appeals."

The entire Committee fell into stunned silence. Uncle Blue was the first to speak up. As a former resident of the South, Uncle Blue had suffered more than his fair share of insult and social humiliation. And, as one of the Cattos' closest friends, he was well beyond his capacity for tolerance and reconciliation. The attack on the Catto home and the burning of the First African Presbyterian Church were the most outrageous acts he had ever experienced. His facial muscles twitched as he strained to vocalize his anger.

"Well, are we gonna let 'em get away with it?"

"I don't see where we have any choice Blue. Any further appeals would be useless."

"Well, if that there don't take the tin off the can! I never thought I'd see the day when you would quit like that Purvis!"

"Believe me, I'm as disappointed and frustrated as you Blue, but now we've got to choose which battles we're going to fight and determine those we think we can win."

"I'll tell yez what I think. I think yaw are losing the will to fight. That's what I think! And, that judge…well he ain't got no more legal smarts than my Aunt Suzie! And, if we wasn't in the house of the Lord, I'd tell ya what I *really* think!"

The aging lion was out of his cage, indomitable, and on that day, totally inconsolable. He rose from his seat and prepared to leave. Before slamming the door behind him, he yelled back.

"If anybody's interested, I'm going to go check on Sarah Catto. Yaw remember Sarah don't cha?"

∞∞∞∞∞∞∞∞

Uncle Blue was very close to William and Sarah Catto. He met them in Charleston, South Carolina ten years earlier when he worked as a carpenter for Sarah's father, Mr. Morris DeReef. The DeReefs were one of Charleston's wealthiest mulatto families and had five children, four sons and one daughter. The sons worked in the family's thriving lumber business and Sarah aspired to become a renowned concert pianist. It was a childhood ambition that her parents encouraged at every turn.

His real name was Silas Kincaid, but everyone in Philadelphia came to know him as plain ol' "Uncle Blue". He was born an only child and was raised as an orphan by one of the "Geechy" families that settled in the Gullah Islands near the coastlines of South Carolina and Georgia. Thus, he was in truth, no one's uncle. The DeReefs gave him that honorific title to reflect his closeness to the family and Sarah in particular. The men in the lumberyard used to say that his skin was so black that is was blue. That is how the appellation, "Uncle Blue" came into being. And that was fine with him. He was a man who took great pride in his deep, dark complexion and insisted that it reflected the "purity" of his African lineage. In fact, he often bragged to them, "Ain't no cream in this coffee". Of course, he had the cracked and calloused hands of a carpenter. Yet he was quick to remind everyone that the rest of his skin was "as smooth as a baby's behind."

His special relationship with Sarah began when Mr. DeReef commissioned him to help build an exquisitely crafted piano on the occasion of her sixteenth birthday. It proved to be a magnificent instrument and one that Sarah would rarely play without thinking of him. Uncle Blue loved her piano playing and she especially enjoyed playing classical standards for him in addition to her own original compositions. Sarah played like an angel and he was gratified by the thought that some of his craftsmanship had helped her acquire her musical wings.

Reverend Catto married Sarah five years later; much to the displeasure of her parents. They had many misgivings about their daughter marrying a "penniless preacher". To make matters worse, the young couple would soon leave Charleston when he was invited to be the minister of the First African Presbyterian Church in Philadelphia. This move did not sit well with the DeReef parents who were not at all happy about being separated from their one and only daughter. That fact was compounded by the observation that Reverend Catto had no visible means to "care for her in the manner to which she is accustomed". Uncle Blue kept silent on the matter. But, he secretly liked Reverend Catto a lot and thought that it was a good thing for Sarah to assert herself as a mature woman and leave her pampered existence in the DeReef family nest.

Protestations aside, Sarah joyously married the tall and quite handsome clergyman and off they went to Philadelphia. Uncle Blue followed them six months later when he was asked to deliver Sarah's piano to her. Like Reverend Catto, he had grown weary of South Carolina's oppressive racial policies and humiliating civil codes that restricted the rights of its colored residents. At that time, the city of Charleston was beginning to require all colored people (slave and free) to wear tags identifying their occupations. Things were getting to be more than both men could bear. When Uncle Blue arrived in Philadelphia, he took an instant liking to the relative freedoms enjoyed by the city's colored residents. And as things turned out, he vowed never to return to the Gullah Islands or the Palmetto State ever again.

∞∞∞∞∞∞∞∞

The meeting at Mother Bethel Church resumed with a lengthy discussion of ways to fortify the Seventh Ward against further attacks. A tentative plan involving around the clock neighborhood watches was roundly endorsed with the details to be put forth by a special sub-committee within twenty-four hours. That endorsement was followed by a discussion of ways to confront the latest wave of political maneuvers designed to deprive the colored population of its basic citizenship rights. Some suggestions included the formation of more mutual aid organizations, the exclusive patronization of Negro businesses and the launching of a campaign to seek federal interventions.

The conversation took a different turn when Pastor Hightower stood to offer his views. He began with his familiar contention that the anti-Negro sentiments held by whites were the direct result of the misbehaviors of those "shiftless, Negro ne'er-do-wells" who were continuing to give the colored population a bad name. He specifically referred to those who where concentrated along South Street where "crime, alcoholism and Sabbath-breaking have run amok."

He then reiterated his argument that unless and until moral reform was achieved, whites would never look favorably on Negroes nor would they be willing to grant them full citizenship rights. As usual, most of the committee members considered his position to be a gross oversimplification of a complex and multi-faceted social problem. Some of the older members were growing weary of his sweeping generalization that somehow, the entire Negro race was in need of reformation. They considered themselves to be the victims of white racism and *not the cause* of the growing social cancer.

Pastor Hightower then proceeded to outline his curious plan for moral uplift and social improvement. It began with his suggestion to have an inter-faith picnic to help foster Negro unity. That idea was warmly embraced. Secondly, he called for the creation of a new "Negro Moral Reform Society". This idea was vague and received a lukewarm response. Finally, he proposed the establishment of a fund to buy hundreds of Bibles and distribute them to the residents of the Seventh Ward. This suggestion was the least popular idea among the group who immediately responded with a combination of stone silence and suppressed snickers. Undaunted and oblivious to the offense taken by many of the members, Pastor Hightower asked Reverend Reynolds for permission to take up a collection immediately in support of this endeavor. Before Reverend Reynolds could respond, John Ansar rose from a pew in the rear of the sanctuary and asked for permission to address the group.

"Excuse me Reverend Reynolds, but I got something to say."

"Why of course John, go ahead."

"What I want to say is…well, er…Yaw know I'm kinda new to da city. And, I just started coming to dees here meetings…And Lawd knows, I ain't had much book learnin', but I'd be the last man on earth to say that books and Bibles ain't good for ya. And Pastor Hightower, I figger you to a mahty fine, God-ferring man, so please don't get me wrong. It's just that I'd hate to see dis committee spend what liddle bit of money it do have on some Bibles, when we got so many other needs, namely the men, women and children in the safe houses. Some of yaw know what I'm talking and the rest of ya gonna have to take my word for it. We's really struggling just to keep 'em fed. And, when the winter sets in, I don't see how we gonna have enough coal and firewood to keep 'em warm. I say we gotta do for those that are the *worst off*. The way I figger, them runaways are our first duty, they have been placed in our care, and we gotta do for them; least ways until we can find a way to get them further north and out of danger. Well...dat's all I got to say."

Everyone was taken by surprise. It seemed like John spoke more words in that minute than he did the entire year they had known him. He was right though. Things were extremely difficult in the safe houses. The runaways were in constant fear of being recaptured. They were literally trapped in Philadelphia and subject to the treachery of paid rats and slave catchers. Until they could be moved further north, they were in effect, prisoners – unable to seek employment and fearful of showing themselves in the light of day. To make matters worse, some of the children became infected with smallpox and needed medicine. They had to be separated from the others and were in no condition to travel.

But there was something else bothering John; something the others didn't know. Mr. Still received news earlier that day that one of his helpers, Reverend Elijah Lovejoy, the man who helped John escape to Philadelphia, had been murdered by a drunken pro-slavery mob. John was devastated. It was the first time Mr. Still ever saw him cry, but it wouldn't be the last.

∞∞∞∞∞∞∞∞∞

The meeting went on for four more hours and adjourned after midnight. Mr. Still returned home and sat at this desk to write a letter of condolence to Reverend Lovejoy's family before going to bed. It was a painful and difficult task to be sure. He had only met Reverend Lovejoy on one occasion but had corresponded with him on a regular basis. In addition, he had compiled over twenty stories given to him by fugitives like John Ansar who spoke of the Reverend's great courage and extraordinary kindness.

Words continued to fail him. He paused for a moment and stared out his window at the rain falling on nearby rooftops. It was then that he suddenly realized yet another use for his stories. These stories could do more than unite fractured families. They could also help people to remember. In a real and meaningful way, Reverend Lovejoy's work and sacrifices were permanently memorialized in the written testimonies Mr. Still had already amassed. He drew great satisfaction from that simple fact.

Reverend Elijah Lovejoy

By all accounts, Reverend Lovejoy was a high-minded man. He was conscious of the risks involved in the Underground, yet he was even more conscious of his duty to God and his fellow man. Though he was white, he made the ultimate sacrifice for an enslaved people who bore him little physical resemblance. He was truly a faithful helper and a living witness to the oneness of humanity. As Mr. Still began to concentrate on these simple virtues, the words somehow became easier. He finally finished the letter and enclosed some money for Reverend Lovejoy's widow.

It had been an exhausting day, but it was his nightly habit to read a portion of the Good Book before going to sleep. Thumbing through its pages, he happened upon Luke 14:14. It read, *"...and thou shall be blessed for they can not recompense thee; for thou shall be recompensed at the resurrection of the just."* He read the text three times, savoring its profound meaning. Then he extinguished the candle on the night table beside his bed and listened to the gentle sounds of the rains outside his window. As sleep approached, his soul resonated to the thought that he might indeed meet Reverend Lovejoy again; perhaps in another existence; at the resurrection of the just, the gathering of the good and the great festival of the forgiven.

12. Earthly Pursuits

"Work is the grand cure for all the maladies and miseries that ever beset mankind - honest work, which you intend getting done."

Thomas Carlyle

For the next two months, the Crafts remained as guests in the Catto home where their presence was greatly appreciated. William and Ellen expressed no interest in continuing their travel to Boston any time soon. Sarah was very near childbirth. It had been a difficult and worrisome pregnancy. Her recovery had been slow, but she was at least able to stand and walk short distances. Reverend Catto was pleased that Ellen and his wife were becoming good friends. He knew that Sarah could hardly care for herself, let alone a new baby. When the baby arrived, it was his intention to ask the Crafts to stay with them indefinitely. He assumed that Ellen would agree. She was a woman who liked to be needed and gladly took on all household duties in exchange for room and board.

William also believed it was a mutually beneficial arrangement. However, he was still a bit uneasy with it all. Reverend Catto had been exceedingly gracious towards him. No one had ever showed him such friendship; that is no one except Ned. As usual, William was constantly reminded of Ned's old axiom,

"A true friend wants for his brother what he wants for himself."

Was it possible that the same spirit animated Reverend Catto?

"Of course not," he silently mused. "There never was, nor would there ever be a truer friend then Ned. Not in this world."

The truth be told, William had difficulty accepting anything resembling charity. He wanted and needed to find employment. Eventually, he found day work unloading crates at one of the wharfs on Delaware Avenue. The job was strenuous, but he had no complaints. He was accustomed to hard labor. Shortly thereafter, he found work closer to home at a nearby carriage factory. Fortunately, the job paid a decent wage and allowed him to walk home for lunch. He was to begin this job in a few days. It was to be his first full time employment as a free man. It was indeed, his first victory over the *time bandits* who had shamelessly laid claim to his body, his mind and the fruits of his labor.

∞∞∞∞∞∞∞∞∞∞

One Monday morning, an apparent breakthrough occurred. Sarah awoke with a keen appetite and asked to have breakfast in the dining room with the rest of her new "blended" family. Step by step, her husband guided her downstairs and sat her at the dining room table; a place she had not visited in more than two months. Ellen prepared a scrumptious breakfast and the four of them enjoyed fine food and fellowship. Sarah's speech was still slurred and slow, but Reverend Catto thought he saw glimmers of her old self.

William was not the kind of man who was accustomed to lingering over a meal. With a subdued belch and a sigh of contentment, he was the first to rise from the table.

"Well if you'll excuse me, I'm off to work. Don't want to be late on my first day."

"I'm on my way out as well. Can I give you a ride?" asked Reverend Catto.

"Sure, if it's no trouble Reverend."

"No trouble at all. Sarah can I bring you something back this evening?"

Sarah was totally unresponsive to his question. Apparently, her head wound had not completely healed. Her bandage was stained by a thick pinkish residue that indicated continued hemorrhaging beneath the surface of her scalp.

"Sarah, Sarah I said…"

"You all run along Reverend Catto", said Ellen. "She's probably a little tired. I'll take care of things here."

"No, I think I'd better stay."

"Nonsense, you all run along now. Don't you worry about a thing Reverend, she's in good hands," insisted Ellen.

Reverend Catto kissed his wife on the cheek while William and Ellen embraced at the front door.

"Be careful out there honey, I love you."

As the men departed, Ellen walked back to the dining room where she saw Sarah staring at an empty wall in a trance-like state.

"Sarah, can I get you some more tea?"

"Huh…"

"More tea dear?"

"Where is my husband?" said Sarah in a whisper. "He knows he's got to get those roosters out of our bed. There's twelve of them hiding under the quilt."

Ellen looked at her sadly,

"He's gone to a meeting dear."

"Oh, that's nice," she answered with a vacant look on her face.

"You know Sarah, I've been thinking of getting a job too, and you'll have a new job soon taking care of that baby. And I'll tell you something else. It looks like you're going to have it any day now."

"That's…that's…nice."

Ellen forced a smile and tried her best to cheerfully carry on the conversation, fully aware of Sarah's obvious mental impairment.

"Yeah, and you know the first thing I'm going to do when I get my wages? Well, I'm going to get you one of those pretty shawls that all the fashionable ladies are wearing nowadays. Would you like that?"

Sarah was still unresponsive, but Ellen continued with her optimistic monologue.

"Yeah, you'd like that. And, you'll be turning heads by the dozen. Come on sweetie; let's get you back in bed."

∞∞∞∞∞∞∞∞∞

Reverend Catto dropped William off at the carriage factory, and then continued on to a meeting at Mr. Still's house. William was greeted at the loading dock by Charley O'Rouke, a white foreman who called out to Amos Jones, one of his Negro wheelwrights.

"Amos, this is William Craft. He'll be working with us starting today."

"Pleased to meet cha. You can leave your coat over there. No need soiling it on these greasy axles."

"Thanks Amos."

A few minutes later an unusually large carriage with gilded gold trim rolled up. A red-faced white man with bushy eyebrows and blotchy skin stepped down and immediately began to scan the area His extended belly put a noticeable strain on the buttons of his gaudy plaid vest and brown trousers that perfectly matched his tobacco-stained teeth.

"How's it going Charley?" he asked in an unusually jovial manner.

"Just fine Mr. Conley. We'll have eight coming off the line this morning and ready for shipment by this afternoon."

"Where are they going?"

"Looks like Richmond, Virginia."

"Richmond. You don't say. I've got a fine filly down there in Richmond. Those southern girls are pretty as a picture, but not very bright. Two qualities I do so admire in a woman."

"I wouldn't know much about that kind of thing. My wife's about to have a baby. No sir, I'm a happily married man."

"Why so am I lad. So am I," said Conley with a chuckle.

He paused for a moment as he spotted William working on the far side of the factory.

"Who's the new fella over there?"

"His name is Craft, William Craft."

"Is he any good?"

"Can't say, he just started today. We need a good man to help us forge and lift those center wheels so I thought I'd give him a chance, even though I know some of the boys are bound to give him a rough go of it. He seemed fit to me, and that's all I care about."

"Ah, O'Rouke, always the clear thinker. Them nigs have strong backs, but weak minds. Perfect match for our crew huh?"

O'Rourke inwardly bristled at his caustic remark but didn't bother to respond. The other workers went about their work, ever mindful of Conley's dark presence. William curiously whispered to Amos.

"Who's that?"

"That's Boss Conley. He owns this place and half the beer joints in Kensington. He runs prostitution rings and is involved in every kind of thievery that you can imagine. He gets the single men falling-down drunk in his saloons and brothels then sends his crew out to burglarize their apartments. Burglary and hijacking—that's how he makes his big money. The boys on the docks say his word is law down there too and he gets a cut out of everything that comes into the docks."

"You don't say?"

"Yep, and he's not a man to be trifled with either. They say step out of line and his goons will show you no mercy. But he don't scare me none. Look at him, barking orders and looking like a stuffed pig!"

After inspecting the shipping manifests and collecting his cash box, Boss Conley strolled back toward his chauffeur-driven carriage. O'Rourke watched him walk away and murmured under his breath.

"What a pompous jackass!"

Two white workers obsequiously tipped their hats to him as he crossed their path. It seemed like the entire work crew breathed easier as they watched his deluxe carriage ramble down the street.

∞∞∞∞∞∞∞∞

Reverend Catto arrived a few minutes later to a secret meeting at Mr. Still's house. They were joined by John Ansar and Sol Abrams. Mr. Still wanted to meet privately with his most trusted friends to discuss two recent incidents of recapture. One occurred near Cincinnati to the west and the other, to the south, just outside of Baltimore. Mr. Still and his helpers had carefully planned the escape routes for both fugitive parties that were making their way to Pennsylvania from different points of origin. In both cases, the fugitives were recaptured by heavily armed slave catchers and sheriffs who were apparently waiting in ambush. The helpers involved in both escapes were charged with receiving "stolen property", jailed and held without bail. Mr. Still reasoned that the captors in both instances must have had prior knowledge of the planned escape routes and rendezvous points.

Recaptured fugitive slave

The implications were clear. The Underground was being betrayed by someone who had access to very sensitive and privileged information. After the attack on the Catto home, Mr. Still decided to have secret meetings with his inner circle of operatives in what be considered a secure location in the basement of Mother Bethel Church. Therefore, he concluded that whoever leaked the escape plans must be a member of the Vigilance Committee or someone associated with the church. No other conclusion could be drawn. They were not being betrayed by rats. Instead, *moles* were clearly at work. They too worked underground and hid in the shadows.

"We've been infiltrated by moles," said Mr. Still, pounding his fists on the table.

"Moles?"

"Yes, colored moles. And they're very close to us!"

"Do you have any suspects?" asked Sol.

"You bet I do! It's got to be someone who…"

Before he could finish, they heard frantic knocking at the front of the house. John reached for his pistol and accompanied Mr. Still to the front door. Sol and Reverend Catto remained seated in nervous anticipation. Much to their relief, the man at the door was Uncle Blue. He was totally flustered and gasping for air.

"Where's Reverend Catto? I been looking all over for him. Sarah is fixing to have that baby!"

Reverend Catto instinctively climbed aboard Uncle Blue's wagon and away they went. Under normal circumstances, he would have declined Uncle Blue's transportation. In addition to this carpentry work, Uncle Blue provided a fine delivery service for the shut-ins and the older ladies of the neighborhood. However, his old wagon had seen better days and his eyesight seemed to have gotten worse in recent years. He was not the type of man you wanted to be transporting you at high speeds through the narrow streets of the Seventh Ward. However, to his credit, he managed to get Reverend Catto home in one piece.

Reverend Catto sprinted up the stairs and into his bedroom where Ellen and Doc Minton were attending to Sarah.

"How is she Doc?"

"She's running an awful fever and her pulse is weak. You remember Reverend. I warned you this would probably be a high-risk delivery. But so far, she's hanging in there."

"And the baby?"

"Strong heart beat. He's giving her a good run of it. Now why don't you wait downstairs? I'll send for you as soon as we know something, okay?"

∞∞∞∞∞∞∞∞

It was to be a long and prayerful morning for the Catto household. It was also a particularly busy morning for Mayor Swift and his business partners. They had to review architectural plans for the new indoor market that was to be built on the site where Pennsylvania Hall had been burned to the ground. The land had been leased to the Quakers but it was owned by the City. With Pennsylvania Hall lying in ruins, this land could now be utilized for commercial purposes. It was an ideal location that promised to generate windfall profits for the Mayor and his silent partners who were major investors in the project.

That meeting was followed by a more private session with Boss Conley and a few of his political cronies who were also venture capitalists with a keen appetite for high-yield investment opportunities. They discussed ways to confiscate the land where Reverend Catto's church once stood. It too enjoyed a strategic location – in the heart of the Seventh Ward. The Presbyterian Church owned the land outright. However, Reverend Catto and his Board of Deacons were men of limited means and did not have the wherewithal to rebuild the Church any time soon. There was considerable doubt that the financially strapped Negro Presbyterians of Philadelphia would voluntarily surrender the land, even at a reasonable price. And, it would be virtually impossible to get them to sell it if they ever got wind of the plan that was afoot.

Boss Conley was determined to strengthen his raptorial grip on the city and extend his financial empire into the predominantly colored Seventh Ward. He proposed that they pay a respected Negro leader to persuade Reverend Catto to relocate his church elsewhere. Once the sale was consummated, he wanted to build a large saloon and dance hall on the property and place it under "Negro management". According to his plan, it would be popularly perceived and operated as a thriving Negro business, but legally incorporated under the name of "Conley Enterprises Inc". All revenues would be proportionately distributed to key white investors. Moreover, Conley as lead investor, would have a lucrative opportunity to tighten his entrepreneurial tentacles around the Seventh Ward.

If Conley and the time bandits had their way, they would have expanded leverage to sink their fangs into the already limited economic lifeblood of the Seventh Ward. There appeared to be no limit to their greed, no end to their efforts to reduce the Negro to the lowest level of human consciousness and the highest level of frivolous distraction. Such were the ways and the wiles of the time bandits.

13. The Miracle Baby

"If we love a child and the child senses that we love him, he will get a concept of love that all subsequent hatreds in the world will never be able to destroy."

Howard Thurman

Sarah survived an excruciating childbirth that was complicated by the extensive physical injury she had incurred. It was a boy; and a remarkably healthy boy, considering everything that had happened. Ellen called him *her* miracle baby. And there was no one to tell her otherwise – particularly since Reverend Catto had asked her to be his godmother. They named the boy, *Octavius Valentine Catto*. Reverend Catto proudly asserted that it was an unusual name for a most unusual child. Uncle Blue had a different opinion on the matter. He thought it was "unusually cruel" to give the boy a name like that, especially "a precious little fella who ain't done nothing to nobody". Nevertheless, they all got used to the appellation; even Uncle Blue who deemed it a high honor to be named his godfather.

In the following months, Sarah slowly regained her strength. Her overall health showed a marked improvement with the exception of dizzy spells and episodic hearing losses. Fortunately, she received plenty of help from Ellen and several friends and neighbors who took an immediate liking to the miracle baby; but none more than Uncle Blue. On any given day, he could be seen proudly pushing the newborn around the Seventh Ward in a lopsided and semi-functional baby buggy that he had built with his own hands. Uncle Blue's skills as a carpenter and a wheelwright had diminished quite a bit since he was diagnosed with acute arthritis. The odd-looking buggy soon became a familiar, if not comical sight in the neighborhood. It tilted to the left, much like Uncle Blue's rickety wagon and Uncle Blue himself.

The following year, 1840, brought major changes to the Seventh Ward. The year witnessed a resurgence of racial antagonisms and physical violence aimed at the city's colored population. Reverend Catto had every reason to worry about the bitterly contentious state of the world that his son would inhabit. Philadelphia was facing unprecedented challenges as its population grew in size and diversity. The city was also being rapidly transformed by industrialization. Manual jobs were being lost to mechanizations that were more cost-efficient. New waves of European immigrants and steady streams of colored fugitives and migrants from the south were being compressed into already crowded neighborhoods. For colored citizens and the Catto household in particular, it was a year of mixed blessings.

Shortly after the birth of his son, Reverend Catto was offered the position of Assistant Pastor at Mother Bethel Church, working under Reverend Reynolds. This appointment was a godsend. He had been unemployed for weeks and was beginning to worry about how he was going to support his family. Fortunately, Reverend Reynolds had developed a high regard for Reverend Catto's elocutionary skills and his tireless devotion to community service. It was a timely appointment given the loss of his church. It also enabled Reverend Catto to continue his work with the Underground. This time he would be working on the inside of Mother Bethel and would be in a much better position to help snuff out the rats and moles that had apparently been undermining their work. Meanwhile, William was still enjoying the benefits of full-time employment at the carriage factory. Thus to no one's surprise, the Crafts completely abandoned their plans to settle in Boston. This was due in no small measure to the birth of Octavius and the deep bonds they had formed with the Catto family.

On occasion, Reverend Catto would be called upon to deliver Sunday sermons at Mother Bethel when Reverend Reynolds was away on travel. Apart from his supervision of the children's Sunday school, his duties were pastoral in nature. He was grateful for the opportunity to work again in that capacity. Reverend Reynolds was very active in political affairs and in high demand for various speaking engagements and ceremonial occasions. Unfortunately, he was becoming increasing unavailable to his flock. But Reverend Catto was always glad to fill in when necessary. The congregation of Mother Bethel was seven times larger than Reverend Catto's Church. Therefore, he was always in great demand. It felt good to be useful again.

One of his assignments was to promote the work of the newly formed Negro Moral Reform Society that was the brainchild of Pastor Hightower. At the time, it was a fledgling organization that Reverend Reynolds had strongly endorsed. Yet Reverend Catto had little enthusiasm for this nebulous undertaking. To be honest about it, he was never quite clear about the new organization's social mission. The name itself was problematic for him. After all, were *all* Negroes in need of reform? Was the Negro in general, so innately flawed that he required a *special* redemptive cure? And, through what process of spiritual alchemy would Pastor Hightower and his learned colleagues achieve their stated goals? He believed his fellow clergymen and the other self-appointed members of the Society were well-intentioned. Thus, and in respectful deference to Reverend Reynolds, he began to attend their meetings that were held in the annex adjoining the church.

The first meeting Reverend Catto attended had one and only one item on the agenda. Once again, Reverend Reynolds was very agitated about the reappearance of more vicious anti-Negro political cartoons in the local newspapers. Somehow, these cartoons offended him in ways that brought out an uncharacteristically angry side of his nature. Most of these latest cartoons offered crude representations of ignorant, intemperate Negroes who were unfit for *civilized* city living.

Some of these cartoons played on the racial prejudices of whites by depicting middle-class colored men and women strutting about the city and riding in coaches driven by white footmen. Others poked fun at what were referred to as the pathetic pretensions of "Cullud Sassiety". In a very rare fit of rage, Reverend Reynolds held up a cartoon entitled, "Miss Cloe" as drawn by cartoonist, Edward Clay. Clay had recently published a number of derogatory cartoons in his *Life in Philadelphia* series, which was offered for the amusement of white readers. This particular cartoon depicted a Negro man and woman in clownish attire and denigrated the assumed ignorance of Philadelphia's Negro citizens.

Life in Philadelphia (Edward Clay)
The dialogue under this cartoon reads:
" How you find youself dis hot weader Miss Cloe"
" Pretty well I tank you Mr. Ceaser only I aspire too much."

Reverend Reynolds was livid and went on to say how the mockery of colored citizens was part of a pervasive pattern of "Negrophobia" designed to drive them out of the city. He wanted to retaliate by calling for an immediate boycott of all newspapers and magazines that published these cartoons. His words were calm but his jittery body language suggested that he was very upset.

"...and I'll tell you this. Intelligent white people of strong Christian influence respect the Negro. They know that we have been here for decades as decent law-abiding citizens. It's our uncultured brothers and sisters from the South that are undermining all the progress we and our ancestors have achieved in this city. Now the whites want to lump us all together as a bunch of depraved and ridiculous buffoons. These offenses will not stand!"

The Society's members unanimously endorsed the proposed boycott effective immediately. However, some were surprised by Reverend Reynolds' harsh stereotyping of lower class Negroes. Such sweeping generalizations were far more typical of Pastor Hightower and his all too familiar rants. But, as usual, no one was willing to challenge Reverend Reynolds' opinion or oppose his recommendation.

Reverend Catto made a deeper and more analytical assessment of the situation. In his view, the cartoons were more than mean-spirited caricatures. He believed they had a subtler, twofold intent. On one hand, they were meant to ridicule the city's entire Negro population as being hopelessly ignorant. That much was obvious. However, they were also designed to besmirch middle-class Negroes in particular. In this way, the cartoons effectively discredited educated Negroes who were pressing for social reforms. The strategy was fiendishly diabolical. First, it reinforced a widespread negative stereotype of Negroes as being uneducated and uncultured. But, it also insidiously belittled those who clearly did not fit that negative stereotype.

These cartoons carried a message that played well in the halls of city government. Their message also resonated in the communities of new European immigrants fighting to establish a foothold in an increasingly competitive economic and political environment. None of these groups wanted to extend full citizenship rights to the colored population. "Negrophobia" was in full effect and uniting the city's white population in common cause.

As the meeting adjourned, Reverend Catto still remained
ambivalent about the Negro Moral Reform Society's social agenda.
There was indeed much need for moral reform in Philadelphia. But,
that need was not restricted to the Seventh Ward and the denizens of
Soapfat Alley. Reform was needed in the city's seats of power where
anti-Negro legislation and social policy were being shaped. He left the
church still churning these thoughts and wondering if these
observations would ever find their way into the political strategies of
the learned society of Negro moral reformers.

∞∞∞∞∞∞∞∞

Returning home, he was surprised to find Sarah in the parlor,
seated at her piano. He could not remember the last time he heard her
play it. It had always been one of her deepest pleasures. Sarah's close
friend, Frances Harper was visiting and Sarah had decided to entertain
her with a rendition of Beethoven's *Pathetique*, which she announced as
one of her favorite pieces. He took a seat next to Frances and looked
on with joyful anticipation as Sarah struck her first notes. Her finger
movements were as graceful as ever. A smile of contentment appeared
on her face as she beamed with the rapturous joy of making music
again.

She went on playing for a while before Reverend Catto decided to
interrupt her. He and Frances lifted Sarah from the piano stool and
gently placed her on a nearby sofa. It was an eerie performance that
bore no resemblance whatsoever to Beethoven's tender sonata. For
three uncomfortable minutes, her husband and best friend sat in silence
as she erratically pressed keys that produced nothing more than random
noise. It was a sad performance that flooded the room with discordant
sound and filled their eyes with disquieting tears.

14. A Hostile Stream

"There is not perhaps anywhere to be found a city in which color is more rampant than in Philadelphia. Hence, all the incidents of caste are to be seen there in perfection."

Frederick Douglass

Sarah's medical condition caused Ellen to abandon her search for full-time employment. Instead, she searched for a part time job outside of the Seventh Ward. After a week of canvassing center city, she found employment working afternoons in Ezra Sloan's dress shop and millinery. Her attractive appearance and refined manners made her a popular saleslady, particularly among Mr. Sloan's wealthy clientele.

"Ellen, I just want to say, you're doing a splendid job. Your sales are outstanding and the customers seem to like you a lot."

"Why thank you Mr. Sloan. I had no idea I would enjoy this work so much. And, I am pleased that you are pleased."

"Yes indeed, and I wouldn't be surprised if you didn't receive a tidy little raise at the end of the month."

"You are too kind. Thank you sir."

Ellen appreciated the compliment but she was uncomfortable with his remarks. She wasn't entirely sure, but he seemed a bit flirtatious. Then again, it could have been her imagination.

Later in the week, Sarah Catto had an unusually good morning. This time, her speech was lively and coherent and she was even able to walk without any assistance. To celebrate this rare occasion, Sarah suggested that she and Frances Harper pay a surprise visit to see Ellen at the dress shop. Frances Harper was very uneasy with the suggestion, but ultimately yielded to Sarah's insistence. She arranged for a babysitter and asked Uncle Blue to ride them to center city. He too thought the outing was a good idea… at the time.

They arrived at the dress shop at about two o'clock that afternoon. Ellen was hanging clothes and had her back to the front door. Frances Harper tiptoed up behind her while Uncle Blue shielded Sarah from Ellen's immediate view.

"Ellen, look who I brought you," said Frances.

"Oh my Lord, Sarah. How did you get here?"

"Praise God, she just sat up this morning and said she wanted to go for a ride and here we are!" Frances explained.

"That's a fact, and she walked in here on her own two feet. Yes she did," added Uncle Blue.

"Yes Ellen and in honor of the occasion, I thought I'd treat myself to something special," said Sarah.

"Well, Sarah, you've come to the right place and the right saleslady. Come over here. We just received some exquisite broadcloth straight from Paris, France. I just know you're going to love it. And Uncle Blue, you might want to buy a scarf for your lady friend. You know the big interfaith picnic is coming up."

"Ain't no need for me to do no looking around in here. I'm so poor right now, I can't even pay attention. I'll wait for you ladies outside. Y'all take your time."

Two white sales ladies were standing nearby and eavesdropping on their conversation. They were apparently very suspicious of Ellen.

"Did you hear that?" said one of them. "She called that horrid man *Uncle.*"

∞∞∞∞∞∞∞∞∞

That Sunday, they all gathered in Fairmount Park for the interfaith picnic. It was a day of merriment and fine fellowship. The festivities were livened by local musicians, singers, and a drum and bugle corps from the Seventh Ward. As usual, children were jumping rope and participating in various athletic contests. At 12:30 that afternoon, they stopped for lunch in the picnic grove at Belmont Plateau where countless culinary delights were the fare of the day. Mr. Still was a guest at the Forten family's picnic table but he was not in a festive or talkative mood. He surveyed the crowd and discreetly scanned the faces of two people he suspected of being the moles in their ranks. Out of the corner of his eye, he saw Robert Purvis approaching the Forten table.

"Ah, excuse me Harriet but I've been asked to deliver these napkins to you."

"Napkins? We have plenty of napkins Mr. Purvis. But I thank you nonetheless."

"But I don't understand. Ms. Harper specifically asked me to bring them to you."

Harriet suspiciously glanced over at Frances Harper who was seated three tables away. Frances smiled, then sheepishly stared down at the table to avoid direct eye contact with Harriet. She instantly realized that it was yet another one of Frances' playful connivances.

"*Oooh, I seeee*...Well of course, you can never have enough napkins now can you?"

"I suppose not."

"Father, Mother – you all know Robert Purvis don't you?"

"Why of course I know him. Good day to you Mr. Purvis. Harriet talks so much about you. There is scarcely anything I don't know about you. No sir, not a thing I don't know", said Mr. Forten.

"Father please!"

Mrs. Forten discreetly elbowed her husband in the ribs.

"What? What did I say?" he responded, blissfully unaware of his blunder.

Mr. Purvis went back to his table and Harriet excused herself from her family's table to have a private conversation with Frances.

"Frances will you please tell me why you pulled that napkin stunt?"

"Because I'm worried about you, that's why! I think you're blowing it. Have you figured out how you're going to snag Mr. Purvis yet?"

"Frances please, you're embarrassing me," she said in a low voice.

"Now you listen to me Harriet Forten, you're no spring chicken. Wasn't it Shakespeare who said, if it be done, then twere well it be done quickly?"

"Something like that."

"Well, you get my meaning."

"I do indeed Frances. But may I remind you that it was Aesop who taught that the race does not always go to the swift. I will approach Mr. Purvis in due course."

"You better do more than *approach* girl or he's libel to get away from you. What you need is a plan."

"I'm not so sure."

"Well, why on earth do you say that?"

"Well...I can't swear to it, but I think I felt a spark between us. And just the other day, I caught him eyeing me."

"And?"

"And what?

"That's it? What about *a plan* dearest?"

"Well, if you must know Frances, I do have something of a plan. Step one, get him to notice me. Step two, get him talking and step three, get him listening."

"And next?"

Fluttering her eyes, Harriet responded,

"Why back to step one, of course, silly!"

Despite Harriet's confident words, Frances knew she was painfully shy and a shrinking violet at heart. She had serious doubts about the effectiveness of Harriet's so-called plan, but nonetheless saw it as forward progress.

To the left of them was a large picnic table where the Cattos, the Crafts and Uncle Blue were seated. Pastor Hightower stepped out of a shiny carriage and strolled toward them with his faithful entourage of minions following closely behind. He was in a very jovial mood.

"Good afternoon Reverend Catto and everyone. And, Mrs. Catto, so nice to see you up and about. It looks like our inter-faith picnic is a smashing success, wouldn't you say Reverend Catto?"

"It looks that way Brother Reverend. Won't you join us?"

"Would that I could Reverend. But, I'm afraid that if I don't get over to sample Ms. Shepard's fried chicken, she'll never forgive me. Perhaps later. You all have a blessed day."

As he walked away, Uncle Blue whispered to Sarah,

"Well somebody betta git over there and warn Ms. Shepard!"

"Warn her about what?" whispered Sarah.

"I done seen that man eat. After he takes that last piece of chicken, he's libel to gnaw off a few of her fingers."

Suddenly, Ellen happened to catch a glimpse of a carriage off at a distance. It was slowly moving up a path towards the picnic grove. One of the white sales ladies from Mr. Sloan's dress shop clearly noticed her amongst her friends. She nudged her husband and pointed directly at Ellen.

"I knew it. I just knew it! Wait till Mr. Sloan hears about this!"

"What are you caterwauling about now? Just a bunch of Negroes minding their own business; as you should. She's not the only white lady that's ever kept company with coloreds."

"Shows what you know! She's not white and I seriously doubt if she's much of a lady!"

∞∞∞∞∞∞∞∞∞∞

The laughter and gaiety of the picnic was diminished when John Ansar arrived and summoned Mr. Still and Reverend Catto. He brought dire news of the recapture of a fugitive slave family in Anne Arundel County, Maryland. As in the previous incidents, the County sheriff was obviously informed of their precise location. He arrived with armed slave catchers who came prepared with leg irons and a cattle cart to whisk the fugitives away to the slave pens of north Baltimore, just below the Mason Dixon line. These fugitives had managed to make it all the way from Georgia. Mr. Still had carefully planned their strenuous northward passage, which required the support of a dozen families who offered their homes as safe havens. The weary fugitives had come a very long way only to be arrested and turned back just a few miles from the Mason-Dixon Line. It had been an arduous journey and an absolutely heart-breaking experience for all who supported their brave attempt.

Mr. Still and Reverend Catto left the picnic at once. They wanted to privately retrace the source of this particular information leak. A few suspects were discussed but there was room for some doubt. Meanwhile, all rescue missions would have to be suspended until the moles in their ranks could be identified and publicly exposed. They spent the rest of the afternoon at Mr. Still's home, agonizing about what could have gone wrong. Had they overlooked some obvious suspects? Were there glitches in their own logistical planning?

Meanwhile back at the picnic, Reverend Reynolds thanked everyone for attending and especially thanked Pastor Hightower for his patented sermon on "the wages of sin".

∞∞∞∞∞∞∞∞∞∞∞

The following Monday morning, Ellen was summoned to Mr. Sloan's office.

"Ellen, may I speak to you for a moment?"

"Of course, Mr. Sloan, what is it?"

"Well, I don't know how to put this delicately; so I'll just come out with it. I've been told by a reliable source, that you are a mulatto…a …a colored woman. Is that true?"

"It is."

"Well then, that puts me in an awkward position, now doesn't it? You should have told me."

"You didn't ask; and furthermore, I didn't know that being white was a requirement of this job; a job you said I was doing quite well."

"Now see here, I don't have anything against your people. But, it's not fair to my sales ladies or to our valued customers. They simply wouldn't understand."

"Some of your customers are colored, are they not? I'm extremely disappointed in you Mr. Sloan."

"Now listen to me. There's no need mincing words. I've got to let you go...Now here's your wages for the rest of the week. I'm sorry."

"Keep it!" she shouted furiously.

Ellen turned and stomped out of the shop while glaring at the white sales lady who was silently gloating.

∞○○○○○○○○○○○

She then wandered aimlessly over to Market Street in deep contemplation. She barely noticed Mr. Abrams sweeping the sidewalk in front of his store.

"Well hello there Ellen. Fancy seeing you here; and looking quite prosperous I must say."

"Hi Mr. Abrams", she muttered.

"Yeah, I was just saying to John that I haven't seen much of you these days. Wasn't that long ago that you first visited me, shall we say, in somewhat different attire."

He chuckled as Ellen responded with a forced smile.

"What's wrong dear? You look like you've got the weight of the world on your shoulders."

Mr. Abrams was indignant but hardly surprised about the story she told him. He had heard of and experienced many variations of its familiar theme. It seemed not long ago when his father first encountered the brunt of Philadelphia's racial and religious intolerance. He was only a child then, but he had indelible memories of the day when the city's white Nativists tried to have his father run out of business and arrested for his strange, "anti-Christian" beliefs and practices.

Mr. Abrams, and his father before him, had seen that type of bigotry plenty of times. His family was a part of the Jewish immigration from Germany and Central Europe that began around 1810. He remembered all too well, Philadelphia's earlier municipal codes that made it illegal to offer food or lodging to Jewish immigrants. The city's

Protestant Nativists made it clear that the Jews were to be socially ostracized without exception. All Jews were lumped together with the Catholics and other "heretical" groups that had found their way to Philadelphia.

Since taking over the family business, Sol was one of only a handful of Jewish merchants who operated stores on Market Street. Most notably, he was one of the few merchants who was willing to extend lines of credit to the struggling Negro families in the Seventh Ward. For as long as he could remember, Philadelphia had always been a harsh environment for those not fortunate enough to be born within its precincts. Despite the city's benevolent reputation, it had a stubborn habit of discriminating against ethnic and religious outsiders who simply "didn't belong there".

Ellen really needed an empathetic ear. She had come into the store downhearted but left relieved that someone else understood her pain. She also left with an unexpected gift. Mr. Abrams gave her a bag of freshly baked breads and bright red wine sap apples that he claimed to have had difficulty in selling.

∞∞∞∞∞∞∞∞

Ellen turned right onto Sixth Street, past Independence Hall and continued her southward walk home. Suddenly, her somber meditations were halted by a most unusual sight. A parade was about to begin. Apparently, some men from a Negro lodge had organized this parade to celebrate "Jamaican Emancipation Day", as their lead banner so proudly proclaimed. It was a small but festive gathering staged primarily for the residents of the Seventh Ward.

However, it was not the type of celebration that the Vigilance Committee and other abolitionist groups were inclined to participate in. Mr. Still, for one, believed that parades were just a colossal waste of shoe leather. On the other hand, men like Reverend Catto viewed the emancipation of Jamaica as a partial victory at best. True enough, British Parliamentary legislation had recently abolished slavery in Jamaica. However, that same legislation offered no reparations to the slaves or the families of slaves who had been massacred in several bloody uprisings. In fact, an Act of Parliament made thirty million dollars available to white slave owners as compensation for the nearly 300,000 liberated slaves who had previously lived and died under British oppression. This recent legislative enactment caused Ralph

Waldo Emerson to sarcastically describe Jamaican sugar cane as being so good that "nobody could taste the blood in it."

The parade moved on as curious colored men, women and children gleefully followed the musical Jamaicans down Bainbridge Street. When the parade crossed Fifteenth Street, a group of white spectators began throwing stones, bricks and rotten vegetables at the marchers. Some were bludgeoned with ax handles and clubs as the agitated whites attacked the unarmed paraders and colored spectators who fled in total fear and panic. They were caught off-guard and found themselves significantly outnumbered.

In their exuberance, the celebrants had made a fatal error. They crossed over Broad Street, the invisible dividing line separating a poor Irish community from the Negroes who made up most of the Seventh Ward. Several innocent bystanders were injured before the police could restore order in about an hour. But peace didn't last long. Later that afternoon, a gunshot from a colored man's house wounded a white teenager. Shortly thereafter, a crowd of more than two hundred whites went pillaging the Negro community. This time they burned down the Negro Temperance Hall and Pastor Hightower's church. Some knew it was safe to run into Sol Abrams' store. Others sought shelter in the Moyamensing Street police precinct while others ran into some of the abandoned warehouses along the Delaware River.

∞∞∞∞∞∞∞∞∞∞∞

The next morning, Mr. Still accompanied Reverend Catto and John Ansar to survey the ruins of yesterday's arson and carnage. They stopped to inspect the remains of Pastor Hightower's church that was still smoldering. No one outside of the Seventh Ward seemed willing to discuss what exactly sparked the horrible riot. Later on, some Irish residents would claim that it was the Jamaican banner that offended them. They thought the parade banner's picture of a black man breaking his chains against the backdrop of the sun, advocated the fiery death of the entire white race. Whether they believed that or not, no one could say for sure. But when you're spoiling for a fight, any excuse will do.

The sight of Pastor Hightower's incinerated church and several severely damaged homes distressed Reverend Catto. He stooped down to pick up a well-dressed doll that was in his path and imagined that it must have been dropped by some terrified little girl fleeing for her safety. Overtaken with sadness, he dreaded the type of cruel and violent environment that awaited young Octavius and the other colored children of the city.

"Is there no limit to our degradation? How could they destroy that beautiful church? Well…at least Mother Bethel still stands. But we better post men there day and night. By the way, has anyone seen Pastor Hightower?" Reverend Catto asked.

"Not since yesterday. They say he high-tailed it over to Camden," said Mr. Still.

"Pardon me for asking Still, but you seem almost glad that Pastor Hightower's church was torched."

"Of course not; it's just that…well; let me put it this way. John and I have had our eyes on him for some time now. We think he could be one of the moles."

Reverend Catto paused for a brief moment, then responded.

"I know he has some strange ideas, but I don't think he's capable of such a thing. Lord forgive him if he is. God save us from this insanity."

"We had better save ourselves Reverend. Looks like it's going to be a long, hot summer," grunted John.

Two weeks later, Reverend Catto secretly violated the newspaper boycott proposed by Reverend Reynolds. He secured a copy of the Philadelphia Gazette. News of the *"Negro Riot"* and its aftermath still claimed the front page. The Gazette reported that seven people were dead, all Negro. Thirty arrests were made and all were Negroes. In the end, the local magistrate ruled that the riot was caused by the Jamaican *zealots* whose parade was described as "untimely and ill-advised".

∞∞∞∞∞∞∞∞∞∞

Later in the evening, the rains came to cleanse the blood soaked streets of the Seventh Ward. Fragrant garden plots came to life and clusters of honeysuckle vines along Bainbridge Street stretched to receive the welcomed refreshment. To the west, the sassafras trees and multi-colored shrubs along the Schuylkill River rose up in aromatic revolt to challenge the stench of racial hatred that was once again polluting the atmosphere of the city.

15. Beauty for Ashes

"...to appoint unto them that mourn in Zion, beauty for ashes..."
                                                        Isaiah 61:3

The Jamaican Emancipation Day riot was the beginning of an extended period of unrestrained racial violence. In addition, economic hardships gripped the residents on the Seventh Ward who were losing their jobs at an alarming rate. The Negro shops along South Street were beginning to close. White customers no longer felt safe visiting these shops and Negro customers no longer had the means to patronize these businesses that were once the cornerstone of the neighborhood economy.

However, in the midst of these downturns, a few positive trends were developing. Interest and participation in the work of local charities grew. Public interest in formal schooling dramatically increased and a plethora of Negro literary societies and reading clubs flourished throughout the Seventh Ward. Interest in public education was at an all-time high. The Vigilance Committee opened two small private schools in the vacated storefront properties along South Street. Even the city government announced plans to build three new elementary schools to serve the expanding Negro community.

Meanwhile, the Underground's work slowed to a crawl as its resources became stretched to the limit. The safe houses were in dire need of food and supplies. Ironically, these shortages created living conditions that mirrored the bleak existence that some of the fugitive families had fled. All rescue missions remained suspended at Mr. Still's direction until the Underground's "mole problem" could be resolved.

Reverend Catto began to put in long hours at the church. However, he was paid a modest salary that did not begin to meet Sarah's escalating medical expenses. Consequently, he was compelled to take on a weekend job as a waiter at Bookbinder's seafood restaurant in the old colonial section of the city. He thought this second job was a better option than selling the land under his demolished church. After an exhausting day, he walked home to enjoy the comforts of hearth and home. As he turned the corner of Sixth and South Street, he was jolted by the sight of Dr. Minton's carriage parked in front of his house. He sprinted into the house, ran up the stairs and into the bedroom where Ellen stood holding the baby as Dr. Minton examined Sarah.

"Reverend Catto, thank God you're here. I just sent William and Uncle Blue to get you", she said.

"Doc, what's wrong with her?"

"This doesn't look good," he murmured, probing Sarah's abdomen.

"Can't you do anything for her?" asked her panicked husband.

"She has suffered a massive stroke. Her vital signs aren't good and I suspect she has severe internal bleeding. I've given her some medicine but I'm afraid there isn't much more we can do at this point but keep her comfortable."

He knelt beside the bed and began to wipe the perspiration from his wife's brow and dab her lips with a wet cloth. Blood trickled out of Sarah's left ear as she laid unconscious and unresponsive to his tender touch.

∞∞∞∞∞∞∞∞∞

They buried Sarah eight days later. The DeReefs had been informed via telegraph. They immediately left their home in South Carolina and arrived in Philadelphia by train; just in time for her funeral. Reverend Catto insisted that the funeral would not go forward without their attendance. They appreciated his courtesy but proved not to be very gracious guests in the Catto home.

Reverend Catto was not at home when the DeReefs had a frank discussion with Uncle Blue the following day. Mrs. DeReef expressed her desire to take Octavius back to South Carolina with them. Mr. DeReef supported the idea and reasoned that his grandson would be better cared for in a large and loving family that had more than ample means to provide for him. Uncle Blue vehemently disagreed and advised them not to broach the subject with Reverend Catto. He assured them that he and the Crafts would assist Reverend Catto in providing for Octavius' every need. Ellen silently agreed as she eavesdropped on their conversation from an adjoining hallway. In the end, it appeared as though Uncle Blue's counsel had prevailed and the DeReefs left for Charleston two days later.

In was good that Reverend Catto never participated in that surprising conversation. He knew that the DeReefs did not approve of his marriage to Sarah. And, he would have surely seen through their thinly veiled disapproval of the humble lifestyle that he had afforded their cherished daughter. And of course, Ellen and Uncle Blue knew exactly how he would have reacted to such a suggestion. It was good that the DeReefs left Philadelphia so soon and even better that he never learned of their audacious proposal. Some ideas are well intentioned but ill advised. Some words are heartfelt, but better left unspoken.

∞∞∞∞∞∞∞∞∞

It seemed like the entire Seventh Ward went into mourning. For two full weeks, scores of friends and neighbors streamed in and out of the Catto home to offer condolences. More often than not, they were received by Ellen in Reverend Catto's constant absence. Reverend Catto was grief-stricken but refused to take any time off from work. He immediately quit his job at the restaurant and threw himself into the work of the church and the Underground with renewed vigor. It was as if Sarah's death had energized him in some way. He worked long hours offering pastoral care to the parishioners of Mother Bethel and even longer hours tending to the inhabitants of the safe houses. He would return home in the wee hours of the morning but was unwilling to sleep in the bed he once shared with his wife. Ellen worried about his lack of sleep and loss of appetite. She tried to help by leaving fresh linen on the parlor sofa along with light snacks, which he rarely ate. This routine went on for nearly three weeks as he struggled to fight back his grief and find peace in a world that had tragically ended Sarah's life and decimated his.

A month later, Reverend Reynolds was called out of town and it fell to Reverend Catto to deliver the Sunday sermon to the congregation of Mother Bethel. True to his diligent nature, Reverend Catto declined offers to have Pastor Hightower or some other clergyman substitute in his place. On that Sunday, he delivered a powerful message of healing and deliverance. Those who knew him best, understood that it was as much a message of encouragement and fortification for his own battered soul.

"...and in The Book of Isaiah, Chapter 61 we read:
'The Spirit of the Lord God is upon me; because the Lord hath anointed me to preach good tidings unto the meek; He

hath sent me to bind up the broken-hearted, to proclaim liberty to the captives, and the opening of the prison to them that are bound…'

And, listen to this, it says further, '…to appoint unto them that mourn in Zion, beauty for ashes'. Let me say that again. He will offer them this exchange – *beauty for ashes*, the oil of joy for mourning, the garment of praise, for the spirit of heaviness. Not a bad deal huh!?"

The congregation listened with rapt attention and deep empathy. Mr. Still became worried and wondered if his good friend was going to have the strength to finish. Reverend Catto's speech suddenly became labored and his body began to sway. Sitting in the first pew, Mr. Still readied himself to catch him if he should fall. Then Reverend Catto's back surprisingly stiffened and his strained voice rang out with even greater volume and intensity.

"Now I know there are many of you here today who labor in the shadow of fear and doubt. There are many lonely lives, hearts, and minds that have said good-bye to happiness; your souls are filled to the brim with anxiety, despair and unspeakable loss. But, I'm here this morning to tell you that there is but one cure for your afflictions and for mine. I don't know nothing else to tell you this morning! When trials and tribulations come your way, when the dark clouds of worry blanket the sky and when the storms of oppression beat upon your house, know that our God is a present and mighty Helper. And know that He will protect and He will prevail. And, do you know why? I said; do you know why? Because **He is able… He is able…He is able!!!"**

∞∞∞∞∞∞∞∞∞∞

After this powerful crescendo, the congregation was absolutely spellbound. Outside, the swirling winds rattled the stained glass windows of the church and the unrelenting rains could be heard pounding on the roof of the sacred edifice. Inside, spirits soared as hope firmly reasserted itself and openly defied the fury of the mounting storm. Hearts were lightened, faith was rejuvenated and the specter of the time bandits was in full retreat.

16. The Chastening

"Know how sublime a thing it is to suffer and be strong."
Henry Wadsworth Longfellow

In a very profound sense, the loss of Sarah transformed Reverend Catto in ways that he himself did not fully understand. It was as if the void created by Sarah's death had been filled with a vortex of new energy. Something inexplicable had happened to him. His soul was on fire. His bereavement seemed to have been replaced by an unleashing of a fountainhead, abundantly supplied by wellsprings of unknown origin.

Ellen and William were the first to notice the beginnings of this transformation. The work of the Underground had emerged as his utmost concern. He began spending less time on his church duties and even less time with his newborn son whom he adored. Instead, he became preoccupied with assisting the fugitive families who were precariously living in the safe houses. It began with his decision to open his home to some of them for brief periods, usually two or three days. Later on, he invited a family of four to occupy his bedroom for a month, while he slept in the parlor. William and Ellen managed the home, while Reverend Catto's time and resources were spent helping those he considered to be in the greatest need.

Even though the resources of the Underground were stretched thin and the moles were still at large, he wanted to resume rescue missions into the South. He even propositioned Mr. Still to allow him to lead a rescue party into the Tidewater, Virginia area. His request was respectfully denied. However, it became increasingly clear that his energies were intensified and his commitment to their holy cause was indeed boundless.

In the privacy of his thoughts, Mr. Still worried about the mental health of his good friend. Sarah's murder had shaken him to the core. He wondered if Reverend Catto's feverish activities on behalf of the Underground, as commendable as they were, might be masking a deep pain that eventually threatened to overtake him. William and Ellen had a different view. Maybe his all-consuming concern with the fugitives was his way of paying homage to Sarah. In this way, each life saved and each life enriched was a living tribute to her precious memory. Uncle

Blue and John Ansar weighed in with a theory of their own. They read fearless defiance into Reverend Catto's obsessive behavior.

"Those cowards who killed sweet Sarah are gonna learn soon enough, ain't no way Catto is gonna be beat down. That's for sure," said Uncle Blue.

"You sho right about that!" John concurred. "And if they think he ain't gonna keep coming, they're as wrong as they can be. And guess what? We gonna be right there with him!"

Theories, like most other human inventions, are imperfect but often contain some elements of truth. There was no way of knowing how and why Reverend Catto had become so radically transformed. Some called it by its simple name—*grace*. Years later, many years later, Reverend Catto would refer to it as "the chastening".

∞∞∞∞∞∞∞∞∞

In February 1846, Philadelphians would hear the ring of the Liberty Bell for the last time. The great bell was tolled to commemorate the birthday anniversary of George Washington and was rendered unringable thereafter. For some, the bell's defect was an ominous sign that the fight for liberty was dead, or had at least fallen into a deep slumber. The cruel irony of this event did not escape the attention of the Vigilance Committee when they held an emergency meeting at Mother Bethel the next day. The sanctuary was filled to capacity with anxious residents. Everyone was concerned about a new wave of violence and escalating tensions between Negroes and the Irish living in the Seventh Ward.

On that day, Robert Purvis was the most outspoken.

"It's gotten so bad; we aren't free to walk the streets! And just the other day, poor Mr. Dunbar was attacked with bricks by a gang of Irish boys, right in front of this church. And do you think the police did anything about it? Of course, not! So what do you think we should do Reverend Reynolds?"

"Now I'm not condoning violence, but I think we had better do something to protect ourselves."

As usual, Uncle Blue was never at a loss for words. He offered the group some of his homespun wisdom.

"You're right about that Reverend, like I always say, *those that bite shall be bitten, and those that don't bite, shall get et up!*"

Reverend Catto clearly understood his simple witticism. Uncle Blue had repeated it many, many times before. However, an uncomfortable silence ensued. Apparently, Uncle Blue's meaning was not fully grasped by the other men. Or perhaps they thought his words were shallow and not particularly useful. Seconds later, he impatiently blurted,

"Don't yaw act like you don't know what I'm saying 'cause ya do! Reverend Catto, you catch my drift don't cha?"

"Of course I do Blue. And, I strongly suggest that the men gather right after this meeting to discuss plans to protect the neighborhood, by force of arms if need be. Let's adjourn this meeting and have the men gather in the basement in fifteen minutes. I don't think we should have our meeting in the sanctuary. Besides, we'll have more privacy downstairs."

∞∞∞∞∞∞∞∞∞

Pastor Hightower did not attend the meeting in the basement. The men assumed he was uncomfortable with the idea of meeting the violence against Negroes with armed resistance. Reverend Reynolds did not attend either. In retrospect, Reverend Catto wondered if he should have asked for his permission to have such a meeting in the church.

The meeting was well attended and after two hours of discussion, a decision was made to establish a comprehensive neighborhood watch. In addition, the group agreed to develop an inventory of available firearms and makeshift weaponry. Reverend Catto ended the meeting with a closing resolution.

"So it's agreed, we'll meet at Belmont Plateau and make our way over to Wissahickon Creek for target practice. Bring your pistols and your rifles for inspection. Before we adjourn, does anyone else have something to add? Yes Uncle Blue, did you have something to say?"

"Yeah, I'm gonna bring the musket that my cousin passed on to me. They say it was used by Crispus Attucks himself, that Negro patriot who died for the American Revolution at Bunker Hill. Yep, that's what they say!"

Regrettably, a small group of younger men started laughing at Uncle Blue, so Reverend Catto felt compelled to intervene.

"Do you fellas have something to say? Hosea what's so funny?"

"Nothing really Reverend; it's just that Blue can sure tell some whoppers that's all."

It was obvious that Uncle Blue was getting agitated. However, before anyone could defuse the situation, he lashed out.

"Whatchu mean boy?"

"Well no disrespect intended, but, well...first of all, Crispus Attucks was unarmed when he got shot and secondly; he was killed at the Boston Massacre, not at Bunker Hill."

"You callin' me a liar boy?"

Hosea's more belligerent friend, Stephen Gloucester quickly inserted himself into the conversation.

"Well, if he ain't, *I am!* You sure can tell some tall tales old man."

At this point Uncle Blue was beyond reconciliation and briskly walked over to his young critic.

"Now you listen to me young buck. You oughta show me more respect. I could have been your daddy, but the dog beat me up the steps!"

Reverend Catto and the other men would long remember it as the day Stephen Gloucester spoke out of turn and received a little "chastening" of his own.

17. A Decade of Disillusionment

"The American people have this to learn; that where justice is denied where poverty is enforced, where ignorance prevails and where any one class is made to feel that society is an organized conspiracy to oppress, rob and degrade them, neither person nor property will be safe."

Frederick Douglass

For the next few years, the issue of slavery continued to be hotly debated in the halls of Congress and in several seats of state and regional government. Tenacious and unyielding, the Southern slaveholders continued to defend their "God-given right" to hold men and women as chattel. In the north, the moral abomination of slavery was decried by outspoken critics like William Lloyd Garrison, Lucretia Mott, Levi Coffin, Samuel Ringgold Ward, Frederick Douglass and thousands of abolitionists who sought to turn the nation away from "the peculiar institution".

On the local front, Philadelphia continued to experience unabated animosities between Negroes and whites in the Seventh Ward. True enough, the Nativists had their quarrels and resentments toward the waves of Irish immigrants that were swelling the ranks of the city's unemployed. And, the Italians of South Philadelphia certainly had little tolerance for the eastern European clans who were trying to establish a foothold in the city's commercial districts and shipping industries. But, despite their cultural differences, those of European descent were unified on one essential point. The Negro, be he slave or freeborn, was worthy of distain and well beneath their respective social stations. His darker hue was proof positive that he belonged to an inferior breed of humanity. It was to be sure, an unfair and self-serving political conviction.

The Negro's very existence in the city had become problematic and barely tolerable. By custom and by law, the Negro was reminded that while he resided in the newly formed America, he was most certainly *not an American*. He would have to work out his own salvation in the new Republic through hard work, thrift and moral temperance.

A majority of whites were beginning to subscribe to a rigid racial ideology. Yes, let the Negro work out his own salvation, — *but with his own kind!* And, let him not presume to lay claim to the rights of full citizenship and the comfort and dignity of social acceptance. Such was the reality of Reverend Catto's existence as he steadfastly prepared to raise his son in the City of Brotherly Love. Philadelphia was nowhere near a utopian ideal. But, it was home for him. And it offered a far better life than the one he and the Crafts left behind in South Carolina.

During this period, the Crafts essentially raised young Octavius. Given his father's frequent absences, they now took the place of both parents. And, there was Uncle Blue, Frances Harper and a few others who surrounded the boy with the love of a dedicated extended family. Octavius was undoubtedly the center of their attention. He evolved into a comely, but somewhat precocious young boy. William called him spoiled. Ellen preferred the term, "well cared for".

One thing was for sure. He could get out of all sorts of trouble with his effervescent smile and his charming and well-practiced (appearance of) innocence that was so disarming. By all indications, he was exceptionally intelligent. He could read and write by age four and was the acknowledged head of his class at the local Vaux Primary School established for the colored children of the Seventh Ward. However, his fifth grade teacher, Ms. Mapps noted in his latest report card that the child was "bright but regrettably overactive". Naturally, Ellen vehemently disagreed. She thought of him as being bored and "under-challenged".

∞∞∞∞∞∞∞∞∞∞∞

The weather was warming and it was time for the Catto household to celebrate Octavius' tenth birthday. Ellen gave him a silver dollar to save or spend on anything he wanted, other than candy. Frances Harper baked him one of her highly coveted apple pies. That beautiful spring afternoon, Octavius and Ellen were playing arithmetic games on the stoop in front of the Catto home. William has whittling a piece of wood and listening to Octavius who was reciting the multiplication tables without flaw or hesitation. Ellen beamed with pride and blissful vindication as William finished his whittling of an exquisitely detailed wooden lion.

"There you go sport. Happy birthday. What do you think?"

"Wow! I love it Uncle Will. Aunt Ellen can I go over to Uncle Blue's house and show it to him? Oh, never mind, here he comes now."

Uncle Blue came riding toward them in his rickety wagon whose creaking axles and badly hinged sideboards annoyingly announced his arrival. Before he could dismount, Ellen walked over to him for a private conversation.

"Octavius wait over there; I want to talk to Uncle Blue for a minute."

"Well howdy Ms. Ellen, how ya doing this fine afternoon?"

"I'm fine. Listen, I want you to do something for me. While you two are out gallivanting around the city, I wish you'd talk to Octavius about his fighting. Maybe he'll listen to you. He's already been suspended from school three times this month."

"Sure thing Ellen."

"Thanks Uncle Blue. I knew I could count on you. Take care."
As she returned to the stoop, Uncle Blue yelled out,

"Ready to go boy?"

"Sure thing!"

As they rode off, Uncle Blue carefully initiated his assignment.

"Hey birthday boy, wanna stop by Mr. Abrams' store and get us some candy?"

"No thanks, Auntie Ellen says it's bad for my teeth."

"Yeah, well so is fighting! Tell me something boy, your Auntie Ellen says you've been getting into trouble at school. Sez you been fighting a lot."

"Well, I don't mean to get into trouble."

"That's what I figured. Sometimes you don't go looking for trouble. Sometimes trouble comes looking for you."

"That's right"

"I know that's right! You just remember what I taught you boy. *Those that bite?*"

"*Shall be bitten*", Octavius cheerfully answered.

"*And those that don't bite?*"

"*Shall get et up!*" answered Octavius.

"That's my boy!" said Uncle Blue; quite pleased with his godson's well-learned responses.

Their conversation was briefly halted by a crackle of thunder as dark clouds began to roll in.

"Looks like it's gonna rain Uncle Blue. You think we should head back home?"

"No way boy! We gotta make some deliveries to the safe houses. Besides, that rain ain't nothing but some liquid sunshine. That's all…liquid sunshine."

∞∞∞∞∞∞∞∞∞∞

After Octavius left, William and Ellen continued their conversation on the stoop.

"You know Ellen, in a few months we'll be able to buy our own home. Would you like that?"

"I don't know. I'm worried about Octavius. He's growing like a weed. Reverend Catto hardly has any time for him. I know that boy is mischievous but God, I've grown so attached to him."

"I know; we all know. But, maybe it is time for us to have a child of our own. What do you say?"

"In this city? With all these hateful people? I don't think so."

"All right, then we'll buy us a farm and raise a family in the country. Amos Jones says there's some good pasture land over in Christiana."

"Just as many hateful folks in the country as in the city. Doesn't seem like they want us anywhere."

"You can't start thinking like that."

"Look who's spoiling him now. What are you going to carve with that other block of wood? He doesn't need two lions."

"This one isn't for Octavius. It's for Jake, his baseball buddy."

"You mean, Jacob White?"

"Yeah, he's the one. And, like I always say; want for your brother what you want for yourself."

"Oh I see, teachings from the Book of Ned," she murmured under her breath.

"And, if you give me the go-ahead Ellie, I'll start in on a third lion, for our little man."

"I wouldn't bet on it if I were you William my love. I'm probably more like that lion then you realize."

"How's that?"

"Neither of us can breed in captivity!"

∞∞∞∞∞∞∞∞∞∞

Ellen's views were shared by most of the city's colored residents. Despite its reputation as "the Athens of the New World", Philadelphia was losing its standing as a place of high culture and social tolerance. Anti-Negro riots were simultaneously breaking out in several cities like Cincinnati, New York City and Providence, Rhode Island. However, Philadelphia appeared to exhibit a level of anti-Negro violence that was unparalleled. The city was fast becoming a cauldron of racial hatred, the kind of hatred that has a powerfully disintegrative effect. Like a social cancer, it infiltrated the population and moved from human heart to human heart, strengthening and spreading its demonic dominance. The city seemed no longer able to resist its corrosive power. Philadelphia was becoming like the roots of a tree that indiscriminately absorb and transport poisons that could very well destroy it.

More and more European immigrants were coming to America to escape oppression and seek economic opportunity. Unlike the Negro, most of them were welcomed. Some were peaceable people, but some brought with them old animosities and deep social divisions that challenged the public peace. The Irish joined the coloreds in the Seventh Ward and the Kensington section, while the Italians laid claim to most of South Philadelphia. To the north, the Germans and Swedish were seeking their fortunes, while the English-speaking Quakers and the Protestants and the Nativists controlled center city, municipal government and the outlying areas to the immediate west.

Despite the death and destruction caused by the rioting, it did accomplish one useful purpose. Faced with the possibility of total anarchy and mob rule, the city's leading citizens were concerned about law and order and the security of their homes and businesses. The city elders and religious leaders wondered how they could effectively address this chaos and avoid the possibility of a ghastly war of all against all. And, what about the children? How were they to be educated in the ways of racial tolerance and civic responsibility? With new waves of European immigrants and runaway slaves flooding the city and its economic markets, they were desperate to learn how to make peace and how to preserve it.

If nothing else, the riots forced civic leaders to confront the fact that, if left unchecked, this widespread violence was going to choke the very life out of the city. Violence settled nothing. It was far better to bring these animosities to the surface and treat them in the daylight of reason and public discourse. Most importantly, the rule of law had to be re-established. Anarchy was never a tenable option. Even Mayor

Swift and *his* decidedly pro-Irish police force understood that something had to change.

As public schools proliferated, the city's rigid educational policies became a major political concern. By 1849, Negroes were taught in segregated schools that only went up to the sixth grade. The need for a Negro high school was quite apparent. But, there seemed to be no political will to bring it into existence.

The Irish on the other hand, had a different set of concerns. The city admitted them to high schools but they wanted their children to be taught in schools that respected their strong Catholic beliefs and practices. However, the city's largely Protestant Board of Controllers saw no need to accommodate their preferences. This controversial issue would soon come to a boil when Charley O'Rourke, William's immediate boss at the carriage factory, shared a distressing story with his priest, Father Kendrick.

∞∞∞∞∞∞∞∞∞∞

O'Rourke had recently sat down with his wife and son for an early supper.

"I fixed your favorite, lots of cabbage but I'm afraid it's a wee bit skimpy on the corned beef side," said his wife.

"Well, I'm glad to have it and grateful to have a fine lassie like you preparing it for me. Isn't that right Joey?"

"Yeah, I guess so."

"So how was school today son?"

"Okay."

"So what kind of things are you learning there?"

"All kinda stuff. Hey Dad, what's a Papist?"

"A what?"

"A Papist. Our principal says that Catholics are Papists and they all worship the Pope instead of God."

"That does it! I'm taking you out of that school tomorrow. Those blasted Protestants! If they think they can ram their beliefs down our throats, they've got another thing coming!"

"Now Charley, don't be getting yourself in a rage. It's not good for ya digestion," said his wife.

"Sorry Dad."

"No need for you to be apologizing for the likes of them. It's not your fault son."

"Dad, may I be excused from the table?"

"What's your hurry? Trying to get another game of stick ball in before the sun goes down?"

"No, I gotta collect a bunch of rocks; as many as I can. Shamus and some of the older fellas are going to hunt the nigs later tonight. And they said I can help them get ready for the fight."

"What did you say?"

"We're going to hunt the nigs! Shamus says we got to keep them in their place and teach them some lessons they'll never forget."

"Now you listen to me boy! Shamus O'Toole and his brother are nothing but a bunch of idlers and their dad, saints alive is one of the biggest drunks that ever set foot out of Dublin. Hear me son and hear me well! When a man has honest work and a family to raise, he doesn't have time to go around picking fights. And when you're right within your soul, there's no need to hate other people for the sheer hell of it. Now you march yourself up to your room and think about what I said!"

When Joey departed, his parents resumed their conversation.

"You were a bit harsh with him don't you think? He's just a little boy."

"Yes, but little boys grow up to be big jackasses, like the O'Tooles. My God Maggie, I've seen better families in a snake pit. I'll not have my son following in their ways, that's for sure!"

"Well he's only repeating what he hears out in the streets."

"Of course dear. That's why it's our job to teach him better. Live and let live, I say. Why hate the coloreds? Why stop there? Hell, it was just a year ago that the Italians got chased out of the Third Ward by the Nativists. What kinda malarkey was that? How can they be so-called *natives* when their fathers and grandfathers came here from England? They're selfish hypocrites, the whole lot of 'em. Once they climbed the ladder to the top, they wanted to snatch it away from the rest of us. And believe me, they didn't exactly roll out the welcome wagon for the Irish either.

First, they managed to get a foothold here in the States. Then they wanted to slam the door shut on the Irish and wanted to extend the period of naturalization to twenty-one years. Imagine that! They wanted to fix the law to say that *only they*, the so-called native-born could vote in public elections. The guys at the factory tell me that it wasn't more than twelve years ago that the Irish were the hunted ones. I guess they don't even remember the anti-Catholic riots of 1844! I suppose O'Toole has amnesia; no doubt brought on by all the whiskey he's been drinking."

"Please finish eating Charley. You've hardly touched your food."

"Aw forget it, I've lost my appetite!"

∞∞∞∞∞∞∞∞∞∞

This account greatly angered Father Kendrick who was one of the leading political advocates for Philadelphia's rapidly growing Irish community.   Father Kendrick was born in Ireland but emigrated to America with his uncle and aunt in 1801. He was only seven years old at the time, but could vividly recall the turbulent events that tore him away from his mother country. Both of his parents had been killed during Ireland's Rebellion of 1798. They were part of a courageous movement of Catholic peasants who fought for sorely needed social and political reforms. In the 1790s, the Protestant ruling class comprised only 10% of Ireland's population. Yet they owned most of the land and were the only citizens allowed to vote or sit in Parliament.

His parents and the other Irish rebels were inspired and emboldened by the French and American revolutions. They were determined to bring about sweeping land reforms and create a new Irish government based on democratic principles and freedom of expression. Their political activism had cost them their lives and orphaned Father Kendrick at a very tender age. Yet the martyrdom of his parents had created in him a certain "fire in his belly" (as he called it) and a raw and fearless passion for issues concerning Catholic rights and social justice in general.

After hearing Charley O'Rourke's story, he immediately scheduled a meeting with Mayor Swift to press his concerns. The Mayor had invited James Cahill, the President of the powerful Board of Controllers to help mediate the discussion.

"...Yes, but Father Kendrick, the Board of Controllers has already ordered that the King James version of the Holy Scripture is to be used as the basic devotional text in all Philadelphia public schools. What more can I say? What more can I do?"

"I'll tell you what Mr. Mayor, it's really quite simple. The Catholic children should be allowed to read our authorized Catholic version of the Scripture and Catholic teachers should not be forced to read the

King James Version during reading exercises. Our catechisms will do just fine. Justice man, simple justice that's all we're asking for."

"It'll never work," said Mr. Cahill. "With all due respect Father, we've tried that already in the Kensington schools. We had hundreds of Catholic students waiting nosily outside in the halls, while we tried to do our bible reading. It was totally disruptive."

"Then what do you propose Mr. Cahill?"

"I don't know for sure. But, might I suggest that we suspend *all* Bible reading until such time that the Board of Controllers devises a better method for excusing Catholic children from the exercise. At least then we could get on with the business of teaching."

"That may do for the moment. But don't think this will be the end of it!"

"Well Father, we'll certainly take your recommendation under advisement. Now if you'll kindly excuse me, I've got an eleven o'clock visitor that I dare not keep waiting."

"Well, then good day ta ya Mr. Mayor. We'll certainly see you in the voting booth next year!"

Father Kendrick and Mr. Cahill left the Mayor's office and saw Boss Conley waiting in the reception area. The Mayor warmly ushered him into his office.

"Conley, come on in. How the hell are ya?"

"Fit as a fiddle and ready for love. But you look a little piqued Mr. Mayor."

"I tell you Connie I see trouble brewing. No offense, but if I give the Irish Catholics what they want, the Protestants will want to run me out of office. It would be political suicide. I can read the headlines now; *Mayor Swift Kicks the Bible Out of the City Schools.*"

"Yes, but I know my people", said Conley. "You can't push them around. And that Father Kendrick, he's a feisty cuss. He's in O'Grady's pub every other day, yet he wants to limit the drinking and gambling in my wards. He's a hand-full and a vindictive man too. I tell ya, he really scrapes my ass. You really gotta watch that one."

"So what are you going to do Conley?"

"Absolutely nothing! With the potato famine in Ireland, they're going to keep coming to the States in droves. Pretty soon, there won't be enough jobs for the men to support themselves and their families. Between them and the out of work niggers, it's like fishing in a barrel.

Like I always say, nothing takes the edge off the blues like a good stiff belt of booze. And that's where I come in; offering comfort and joy to the masses. Why I wouldn't be surprised if they nominated me for sainthood in a few years."

"You're a piece of work Conley," said the Mayor with a smile.

"And did I tell ya? We're opening up a new line of business."

"Stop, let me guess; you're going to sell reading glasses to the blind."

"No, better than that Mr. Mayor. We've got tons of nigger runaways coming through here trying to make their way further North. A lot of 'em squat here in Philadelphia for a while until they can plot their next move. Sneaky devils they are."

"So?"

"So? Do you know how much money we can make in capture rewards? Twenty, fifty, seventy-five dollars a piece. I tell ya, we're sitting on a gold mine. Sure, I'll be making a tidy profit. But the way I see it, I'm also creating employment opportunities for the boys. Free enterprise Mr. Mayor, free enterprise…God I love this country!"

"Well, I hate to break it to you; but O'Toole and his gang have been doing that kind of work for years."

"Well thank you Captain Obvious! That's why I've come to see *you*. You and your constables can give me the competitive edge I need. They know every damn thing – who comes in and out of the wards, who's on the take, who's on the bottle. I want to sort of deputize them to be my eyes and ears…for a modest fee of course."

"It's not that simple you know. Pennsylvania is legally a free state. Those runaways aren't breaking any state or local laws. We have no legal justification to arrest them or those who hide them; at least that's what Judge Andrews keeps telling me."

"Don't mention that petticoat chasing wino to me. I've been paying him for years and that greedy bastard still wants more. Besides, I'm not talking about arresting them. I'm talking about snatching them, collecting the capture rewards and paying your men, and you of course, for good surveillance at a reasonable price."

"I see your point Conley…free enterprise."

"Precisely!... Free enterprise indeed."

18. The Visitor

"In the nightmare of the dark, all the dogs of Europe bark,
and the living nations wait, each sequestered in its hate."
W.H. Auden

Mr. Still's personal diary and ongoing record keeping marked May 13, 1849 as the very first day he received a very unusual visitor to Philadelphia. She had made a few very brief visits since. But this time, Reverend Catto had agreed to accommodate her in his home for a week. Ellen took an instant liking to their newest temporary resident. She made her feel at home and asked Frances Harper to introduce her to some of the other ladies of the Seventh Ward. It was suggested that the weekly meeting of the Vigilance Committee would be a good place to start in getting her more familiar with the city. At the end of the meeting, Frances began to introduce her to some of the ladies in attendance.

"Harriet, Harriet… over here. I want you to meet someone."

"By all means, hello I'm Harriet Forten"

"Pleased ta meet cha, I'm Harriet Stoker."

"Well, fancy that; two Harriets. How will we ever tell you apart? " asked Frances.

The two Harriets stared at each other from head to toe and simultaneously looked at Frances in utter amazement. The two Harriets looked nothing alike and were nowhere near the same age. More tellingly, Harriet Forten was stylishly dressed, much taller and very light-skinned. Harriet Stoker was a shorter woman, dark-complexioned and shabbily dressed. Her well-worn shoes curled at the toes and the stitching in her soles were clearly beginning to unravel. They shared a laugh together at Frances' expense even though it was clear that Frances was referring to the name they shared, not their appearance.

"Okay, okay, that may not have been the smartest thing that ever came out of my mouth. But moving right along, I was just about to invite Harriet to join our Female Literary Association. Wouldn't that be nice?"

"Yes, you'd love it. We talk about all kinds of subjects; the Bible, Shakespeare and Alexander Dumas – he's part colored you know. My how our ladies love Dumas!"

"Well, thank you kindly, but I reckon not. Never had much use for book learnin'. Besides, I don't spec I'll be here fer long anyways."

"I understand perfectly. Between the mean-spirited white folks and the common thieves and pickpockets in the Seventh Ward, it isn't safe to walk the street anymore. But it wasn't always like this. We're determined to live here in peace, surrounded by family and people who love, respect and care for one another."

"So where are you from Ms. Stoker?"

"Well I was born in Maryland, on da Eastern Sho."

"I see, so I assume that you will be moving north from here?"

"No, I spec I'll be goin' south in a few days."

Frances and Harriet Forten were dumbfounded by her curious answer. Standing nearby, Mr. Still wisely thought it was a good time to interrupt before the other women started to pry any further.

"Ahem, excuse me ladies but Ms. Stoker is plumb tuckered out from her travels. If you will excuse us, I'd like to let her get some rest."

"Of course, Mr. Still, we'll have plenty of time to get acquainted. By all means, do get some rest honey; we'll catch up with you later."

He took Harriet Stoker back to the Catto home while Frances Harper and Harriet Forten stayed behind to socialize a bit.

"Did you hear that? She's going south. Now why would a colored woman want to leave Philadelphia and go *south*?"

"Well Harriet, maybe that's where her family is. Maybe she has a husband down there. Say, speaking of husbands, how is Mr. Purvis doing?"

"Just fine. He's been visiting with me off and on for a few weeks now."

"Step two, huh? Time to reel him in girl!"

"Not quite Frances. My grandfather was a fisherman and he always taught me not to yank up your line until you're sure you have a good, strong bite."

"You're so right. A man and a fish are a lot alike. Both of them are slippery as all get out. And even when they do take the bait, it's hard getting them into the boat."

∞∞∞∞∞∞∞∞∞∞∞

That same evening, Mr. Still had dinner at the Catto home with the Crafts, Uncle Blue and Harriet Stoker. Uncle Blue sat next to Harriet and seemed to take a personal interest in her. She was a seasoned woman who appeared to be about his same age and temperament. That aside, the dinner conversation focused on the mood of the city and the strong racial tensions that were coursing through its veins.

"I can feel it in my bones. It's like there's this huge volcano out there and it's going to erupt any day now," said Reverend Catto.

"We've been through tough times before, but I never had you figured for a pessimist," replied Mr. Still.

"Pessimism is a sin Still. I'm simply a realist."

Uncle Blue joined the conversation.

"I feel it too. Those white folks over on Carpenter Street are spoiling for a fight. They even have children throwing rocks at us and calling our women all kinds of names. What do *you* think Ms. Stoker?"

"Well, I'm new to da city, but I tell yaw what. Once the white man git it in his head that you's afred of 'em, he'll try to crush you in da dirt! You may as well stand up and fight for yo'self. You might get kilt. But, if you're lucky, you just might take two or three of 'em wit ya."

"You're right as rain about that Harriett...er, er, I mean, Ms. Stoker. And I'm sure your husband would agree with that too," said Uncle Blue.

"Excuse me, but I ain't got no husband Mr. Blue."

"*Oh I see.* That's mighty hard to believe," he said with a noticeable twinkle in his eyes.

"Well anyway Ms. Stoker, I believe that all God's children have a right to defend themselves. Like I always say, *those that bite shall be bitten; and those that don't bite, shall get et up!*"

"Now ain't that the truth! I declare, you sure do have a way with words Mr. Blue," she responded, with an amorous glance of her own.

19. Twilight in the City of Brotherly Love

"Despair, black as the pall of death hangs over us.
The bloody will of this cruel city is to destroy us."
                                        Letter from Robert Purvis

She may have been new to Philadelphia, but Harriet's predictions and the Underground's worst fears soon came to pass. On the evening of June 4, 1849, that volcano erupted and touched off a new round of anti-Negro race riots. Irish street thugs terrorized the Seventh Ward, throwing rocks, bricks and whiskey bottles into Negro homes. Innocent men and women were openly attacked as street thugs roamed from street to street, setting fires to homes and businesses. Reverend Catto's heart was sickened by this latest episode of unbridled racial hatred.

On the next day, the colored residents of the Seventh Ward prepared themselves for another all-out war. The city police showed no interest in restraining or pursuing the attackers; so the Seventh Ward prepared for the worst. Some of the men who could afford it, sent their families away. James Forten for one, sent his wife and daughter Harriet up to Boston on the morning train.

A week passed and the Negro residents still considered themselves to be in a state of siege. Nightly patrolling continued, as each end of a twelve block area was fortified with a makeshift barricade made of wooden crates and chicken wire. The guards hardly had enough candlelight to detect movements and very little ammunition to repel a full frontal attack. The truth be told, their flimsy barricades provided scant fortification and were more of a psychological benefit than a physical deterrence. Nonetheless, there was the widespread belief that readiness and "the hand of God" would prevent further death and destruction. At the corner of Seventh and Bainbridge Streets, Mr. Still stood watch with Uncle Blue who was staring at Robert Purvis seated on the ground and writing by candlelight.

"Whatcha writing there boy?" asked Uncle Blue.

"Just a letter; writing relaxes me."

"Listen here, no need to be fretting. Them fellas know we ready for 'em this time. You go on with your writing. Ain't much going get pass these eyes."

If only that were so. Everyone knew that Uncle Blue could not see more than ten feet in front of him. But who dared to confront him with that unfortunate truth?

"Blue?"

"Yeah ?"

"I just wanted to say, well er...Thank you for being you."

"Now *who else* would I be? I declare; for an educated man, you sure can say some dumb things."

Robert Purvis went back to writing his letter and Uncle Blue left to inspect the barricade at the opposite end of the street. Purvis' letter to Harriet Forten read in part:

"...I know not where I should begin, nor how, I can describe the wantonness, brutality and murderous spirit of those who are aligned against us, nor of the apathy and inhumanity of the whole community in the matter. The press, church, magistrate, clergymen and devils are against us. The measure of our suffering is full. I am convinced of our utter nothingness in the public's estimation. Here and there, the image and bright countenance of your smiling face strengthens me. Save that, there is for me nothing redeeming."

Robert Purvis

Inside the Catto home and just outside of Octavius' bedroom, William was tiptoeing downstairs to avoid waking him. However, a creak in the floorboard caused Octavius to stir.

"Who's out there?"

"It's just me; you go on back to sleep now."

"Uncle Will?"

"What is it?"

"Where's Auntie Ellen? I thought she was going to tell me a bedtime story."

"She turned in early son. I'd help out but I've got to go. It's time for me to stand watch. You get some sleep now okay?"

William walked down the steps and headed for the front door. This time he woke Harriet Stoker who was asleep on the sofa in the parlor.

"I'm sorry Ms. Stoker; I didn't mean to wake you."

"Dat's all right, I wasn't sleep. How's Octavius?"

"Restless, like most of us. He wanted me to read him a bedtime story. Ellen is fast asleep and I have the next shift. You don't suppose you could…"

"Sorry, I ain't exactly proud of it, but I can't read a stitch. But, I'd be glad to go up and check on him."

"Thanks, I'll be back in a few hours."

"Take yo time."

Harriet put on a robe and walked upstairs to Octavius' room. She knocked twice before pushing the door slightly ajar.

"You up in there?"

"Yes, ma'am."

"Mind if I sit a spell wid ya?"

"Sure, are you gonna read me a story?"

"No chile, Ms. Harriet ain't much on reading, but I do have plenty of stories to tell ya. Now scoot on over and let me tell you about the first time I tried to come to Philadelphia."

"You mean you've been here before?"

"Yeah chile, a couple of times."

"Well, did you ever meet my momma?"

"No baby, I never had the pleasure. But, they say she was a mighty fine lady."

"So what did you do in Philadelphia?"

"Well ya see, me and Mr. Still been doing a lot of business. He knows all about me. He even keeps records of my doings. That man sure does write a lot. So any way…where was I?"

"You were about to tell me about your first trip to Philadelphia."

"Oh yeah, let's see. Well, not too long ago, a bunch of us decided to escape from ol' Massa Joe's plantation on the Eastern Sho of

Maryland. He was a mean ol cuss. I declare, he treated his horses better than most of us, 'cept da lucky ones that got to live in da big house. Tell ya da truth, taint none of us knew where we was going, but we knew we had to leave dat place. For some reason, they chose me as dere leader. Funny thing, bout being a leader, folks have a way of 'specting you to know where ya going, even when you is a liddle bit lost yo'self. All I knew for sure was that we was headed north, up to Salisbury, through Seaford, Delaware and Lawd willin', into Pennsylvania. Course we ain't had no maps. Couldn't read one even if we did. The sky was our map. And, we knew we could always look for the North Star to keep us moving in the right direction."

Ms. Stoker had a razor sharp mind and could remember everything that happened that evening. Octavius drew closer to her as she recounted every step along her journey and every word spoken on that moonlit night. She lied down on her side and continued with the story.

∞∞∞∞∞∞∞∞∞∞

"...yaw keep a movin', we gots to make as much time as possible fo sunrise. Esther, now I done told ya, ya gotta keep dat baby quiet, ya hear me?"

"I know, then we had best stop now so I can feed 'em, Harriet. He ain't et in a while."

"All right then, we'll stop here for a spell. Jarvis you keep watch, while I scout on up ahead."

Harriet walked north and spotted a farmhouse. Off at a distance, she saw a freight train pointed south. The engine was running while some Negro men were loading crates onto it. She walked back to where the group was waiting and was shocked and angered by Jarvis who was lighting up his corncob pipe. She instantly grabbed him by the collar and threw him to the ground. Unfortunately, the two of them started wrestling on the ground and began cursing at each other.

"Ya damn fool. Didn't I tell ya we cain't be lighting nuthin' up 'round here. Are ya crazy?"

"Wad the hell is wrong wid you woman! Cain't nobody see a little fire in all dees trees. Get offa me!"

Their scuffling caused a commotion. As the others tried to break them apart, the baby started crying. Its shrill voice could be heard loudly against the silence of the night. In addition, their loud noises awakened residents in the darkened farmhouse. Candles were lit inside and four men with guns and rifles emerged. They also released four rabid dogs that came running ahead of them in hot pursuit.

"Come on yaw, let's git!" Harriet commanded.

Harriet led the startled group sprinting in the direction of the southbound train. They hurriedly crossed the tracks and hid behind the train that was idling and ready to pull off. At a distance, they could see the farmers headed in their direction. All of a sudden, Harriet caught the eye of a Negro man who was shoveling coal from the coal car into the train's furnace. He too saw the men giving chase. The coal stoker quickly reacted.

"What chaw goin' ta do?" he asked.

"Looks like we gonna spill some blood," Harriett said as she pulled out her pistol.

"Listen here; there's some room left in the next freight car. Yaw better jump on. Deys gaining' on ya," yelled the coal stoker.

"Come on yaw let's go!" shouted Harriet.

"Are you crazy woman? Dis train is going south where we done come from!" shouted Jarvis.

"Now ya listen ta me. It don't rightly matter what *you* think. Ya lucky I don't just kill ya where ya stand! Yo dumb ass can stay here for all I care. Come on yaw!"

They all jumped aboard the freight train just as it pulled off and gradually picked up speed. The chase party fired their weapons in frustration as the southbound train accelerated and disappeared out of sight.

∞∞∞∞∞∞∞∞∞∞

By this time, Octavius was hanging on her every word. However, the story left him a bit confused.

"I don't understand. You mean to tell me you hopped a train going south. In the wrong direction?"

"Sure did. And it landed us just about three miles from where we started."

"Wow! That sure was strange."

"I know chile. Life can be strange like dat. Some times ya gotta move backwards fo ya can move ahead. But, I'm glad we all finally made it up here and I'm alive here tonight ta tell ya da story. Yep ol

Harriet Tubman ain't lost a passenger on da Underground Railroad yet. Tank da lawd!"

"Tubman? I thought your last name was Stoker?"

"Well ya see chile, when ya on the fly it wouldn't be too smart ta use the last name of yo massa. Especially these days, when dem slave-catching hyenas is on da lookout fer ya. So I chose the name Stoker."

"But why *Stoker*?"

"Ain't you been listening chile? Stoker was dat fella dat was stoking the engine of dat train when we run up on 'em. Wazzint fer him, we would have been a goner! Now ya git some sleep Octavius."

"Ms. Harriet, can I tell you something?"

"What is it baby?"

"Well…I'm a little bit scared. What if they come for us tonight?"

"Now you listen to me. Anybody think dey gonna harm a hair on yo head, got another thing comin'! Ain't no harm gonna come ta ya while Ms. Harriet's around, dat's for sho."

"But aren't you just a little bit afraid…I mean…for yourself?"

"Is you kiddin' me? The Lawd done brought me dis far and he ain't bout ta leave me now. I's been plenty scared in my life. But ya know what?"

"What?"

"Da Bible says, if God be fer us; who can be agin us?"

"I don't get it."

"Well…ya know how snug and cozy ya feel under dat blanket?"

"Yeah"

"Well da Lawd's promise is just like dat. It's my blanket. And, as long as I stay under it, ain't nothing and nobody going to do me no harm. Do ya understand?"

"Yes ma'am."

"Good! Now close those angel eyes of yours."

"Ms. Harriet?"

"What is it now boy!"

"I like you."

"And I like you too. But, I'd like ya more if ya'd let me get some shut eye."

∞∞∞∞∞∞∞∞

Four years would pass before Octavius saw Ms. Harriet again. She left the next day to conduct *some business* she had been secretly planning with Mr. Still. Her visit to Philadelphia was brief and her departure necessary and quite advisable. However, before leaving, she shared some valuable advice with Reverend Catto and Mr. Still regarding the *mole problem* that they were trying to fix. She also left just in time to avoid the catastrophe that was about to befall all of those who dared to support the work of the Underground and its intrepid freedom fighters.

Harriet Tubman

20. The Fugitive Slave Act

"This Fugitive Slave Act is an affront to every freedom loving American. It mocks our Constitution and violates its very spirit and purpose. It reeks of sin and inhumanity. It is at last, a covenant with death and an agreement with Hell."

William Lloyd Garrison

William Still was the first to receive the disastrous news. Years later, he would record this event as the day their lives dissolved into chaos. The news first came in the form of a one-page bulletin that had apparently been slipped under his door in the middle of the night. Unknown couriers had also made the same delivery to various churches, schools and business establishments throughout the city. Local politicians and law enforcement agents hailed the news as a major victory in their *war against crime*. Most of the morning newspapers in Philadelphia heralded it as a triumph of free enterprise and the protection of property rights in the United States. Nevertheless, many Americans vehemently opposed it. From his home in Concord, Massachusetts, Ralph Waldo Emerson, the widely perceived moral voice of the nation, condemned it as **"the most detestable law ever enacted by a civilized society."**

As the bulletins proclaimed, on September 18, 1850, the United States Congress, with the support of President Millard Fillmore passed a comprehensive Fugitive Slave Act. This sweeping legislation stipulated that all fugitive slaves would no longer have a safe haven in the northern states. All Negro fugitives and those suspected of being fugitives were subject to arbitrary detention, arrest and re-enslavement. Furthermore, this new federal law empowered U.S. marshals to arrest anyone caught aiding and abetting fugitives. Such persons faced costly fines, imprisonment and the possible loss of their homes and farms. The enactment of this ominous legislation was a pivotal triumph for the pro-slavery south and the lawyers, businessmen and bounty hunters who represented their interests. For Mr. Still and his legions of helpers, it spelled utter doom. Philadelphia would no longer be a refuge for fugitives. Moreover, those who gave them asylum would now be punished to the fullest extent of the law.

The next day, an emergency meeting of the Vigilance Committee was called to discuss the meaning and probable impact of it all. All of the Underground's helpers could lose their homes and their farms if they continued to lend their assistance. Before the passage of the Act, their involvement was a personal matter of conscience. Now it was a matter of courage. If they continued to support the Underground Railroad, they stood to be imprisoned and vigorously prosecuted. These helpers could now be fugitives themselves; living in fear and constantly worrying about *their own* freedom. It remained to be seen how many helpers would continue to support the cause. In light of this new legislation, Mr. Still wondered if it was even right to ask them to incur such risks.

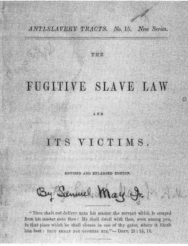

The Fugitive Slave Act would have precisely the kind of effect it was intended to produce. The social and political landscape had definitely changed. The fear and intimidation tactics inherent in the Act surely tested the moral resolve of the Underground. Fear claimed many victims and many were those who yielded to the pressure of it all.

With the full weight of federal law bearing down heavily upon them, many Underground helpers began to withhold their support. The United States Congress had sided with the pro-slavery forces and had effectively issued its gravest challenge ever to the Underground's scattered army. Justice and morality had been sacrificed at the altar of racism and unbridled greed. Again, Emerson's scathing criticism captured best the sentiment of the nation's abolitionist movement and all freedom-loving Americans. He angrily wrote, **"This has ceased to be a responsible government when the statute itself fosters penalties of treason on acts of common humanity."**

Ralph Waldo Emerson

As the meeting went on, Reverend Catto sat alone with his thoughts; contemplating less immediate and perhaps more philosophical ramifications. The Fugitive Slave Act had even deeper meaning for him. For the first time in his life, he began to think about the merits of colonization to Africa. For well over twenty years, he bitterly resented those who argued that Negroes should all resettle in Africa. On this disappointing day, even that impractical idea seemed appealing.

His silent ruminations were suddenly halted by the pounding of a gavel and the call for a vote. Reverend Reynolds read a draft of the Committee's response to the United States Congress' cruel and well-calculated legislation. In times of crises, Reverend Reynolds was always the calm amidst the storm. They could always count on him to ably convey the sentiments of the Committee. On his recommendation, they would issue and widely disseminate an intensely defiant public proclamation of their own. It was *their* "Declaration of Independence". By unanimous consent, it read in part:

> **"...And be it resolved that we deem the laws of God paramount to any human laws: and that in obedience to the command to hide the outcast and betray not him that wandereth. But, seeing clearly and knowing fully, the unjust prejudice existing against us, and using only those moral means of truth, sufficient as we deem them by a**

certain process, to the "pulling down the stronghold" of the injustice and wrong that now affect us; yet in view of the unheard of atrociousness of the provisions of this infernal Fugitive Slave Bill, we solemnly declare before the most high God, and the world, to resist to the death any attempt to enforce it upon our persons!"

The meeting adjourned and a dejected Reverend Catto walked home, uncertain of the future. The Fugitive Slave Act would undoubtedly have enormous consequences for the fugitives and the defenders of freedom everywhere. However, little did he know, it would soon have a profound impact on his immediate household.

21. The Parting

"When the storm of life is raging/Stand by me."
Anonymous slave

In the following weeks, the Underground was effectively pushed back on its heels. A citywide campaign was waged to apprise citizens of the new law and warn the general public about the penalties to be incurred by those who dared to violate it. Large three-foot bulletins were tacked on street posts and mounted in all public buildings. Schools and churches were asked to assist by distributing handbills urging citizens to give law enforcement agents their full cooperation.

Slave catchers residing in Philadelphia and the surrounding areas were especially emboldened by the arrest powers provided to them by the Fugitive Slave Act. They began to offer larger rewards for those providing information leading to the capture of any suspected fugitives or their abettors. These rewards gave added incentive to the moles that had already been menacing Mr. Still's operations. This increased bounty also provided inducements for recently unemployed citizens who previously had no interest in such immoral profit-making ventures.

This pervasive campaign also included the proliferation of "wanted" posters describing escaped fugitives in detail. These ubiquitous wanted posters would re-appear just as quickly as the Vigilance Committee could tear them down. The message was clear. Philadelphia was no longer a safe refuge; it was to be a danger zone. And, all fugitives (real or imagined), would be aggressively hunted both north and south of the Mason Dixon Line.

As expected, incidents of arbitrary arrest and flagrant kidnapping became widespread. Most of them occurred in border cities near the Line. To the west, cities scattered along the Ohio River were overwhelmed with cases of kidnapping whereby bounty hunters did not make the slightest attempt to distinguish free men of color from escaped slaves. All Negroes were fair game. Mr. Still grimaced as he read a letter from one of the conductors operating near the Ohio-Kentucky border. It read in part:

"Dear Mr. Still:

Our friends in Cincinnati have failed finding anyone to assist me in my return. Searching the country opposite Paducah jail, I find that the whole county fifty miles round is inhabited by Christian wolves. It is customary, when a strange Negro is seen, for any white man to seize and convey such Negro through and out of the State of Illinois to Paducah, KY, and lodge such a stranger in a Paducah jail, and there claim such reward as may be offered by the master."

$150 REWARD.

RANAWAY from the subscriber, on the night of Monday the 11th July, a negro man named

TOM,

about 30 years of age, 5 feet 6 or 7 inches high; of dark color; heavy in the chest; several of his jaw teeth out; and upon his body are several old marks of the whip, one of them straight down the back. He took with him a quantity of clothing, and several hats.

A reward of $150 will be paid for his apprehension and security, if taken out of the State of Kentucky; $100 if taken in any county bordering on the Ohio river; $50 if taken in any of the interior counties except Fayette; or $20 if taken in the latter county.

july 12-84-tf   B. L. BOSTON.

William Craft was also worried about these new developments. He returned from work one evening and found Ellen seated at the dining room table with Reverend Catto, Mr. Still, John Ansar and Uncle Blue. Judging from the sad expressions on their faces, he sensed that something was horribly wrong.

"William we need to talk," said Ellen as she stood and rushed to his side.

"Well good evening to you too. Hey, what's wrong with you all?"

"William, we've been tossing this thing around and we think…"

Before she could finish, Uncle Blue rose from the table.

"Come on John. We best be moving on."

"Yeah we have deliveries to make," added Mr. Still.

After seeing the three of them to the door, Reverend Catto returned to the dining room where he saw Ellen crying with her head on William's shoulder.

"I think you two need some privacy. Call me if you need me."

And with that said, he walked into his den and Ellen began to tell William what had happened.

∞∞∞∞∞∞∞∞

"Mr. Still said he can arrange passage for us to Boston tomorrow. We could stay with Harriet Forten and her family. He said there's work for us to do with the abolitionist groups up there."

"Slow down Ellen. What are you talking about? We haven't discussed Boston in years. Why would we go there now? I'm just a few months away from buying that homestead in Christiana, or did you forget that?"

"Honey, we don't have any choice in the matter."

"Oh believe me, we have a choice. I'm not going to let some stupid fugitive slave law cheat us out of our dream and chase us away from our friends. And, what about you? Are you telling me you're willing to leave Octavius? I'll believe that when I see it!"

"You know good and well I would never want to leave that boy. But there's no other way!"

"Listen to me Ellen because you obviously don't know me very well. I won't be scared into running. You go on up to Boston. Me and Octavius will be just fine right here in Philadelphia. Drop us a line every once and a while, will ya."

Ellen became totally exasperated and pulled away from him. She ran up the stairs and slammed the bedroom door behind her. William followed her to their bedroom and found her lying on the bed and writhing in anguish.

"Ellen please talk to me. I need to know what's going on here."

She composed herself long enough to walk over to a dresser, pull out a folded bulletin and place it in his hand. The bulletin was blazoned with the headline that screamed, **$800 Reward** in large, boldface type. It provided the following subscript:

TWO NEGRO FUGITIVES!!!

"Mr. Clyde Ferrette of Chatham County, South Carolina is offering a sizable reward to any persons providing information leading to the arrest and safe return of two runaway slaves; a tall, dark-complexioned negro man answering to the name of William and his alleged mulatto wife, a Negress of small stature who answers to the name of Ellen. These fugitives may be residing in Philadelphia or its general vicinity. They are known to be dangerous and not at all reluctant to use all forms of violence, theft and chicanery to avoid capture and prosecution. Any and all citizens possessing knowledge of their whereabouts are kindly encouraged to contact a local magistrate and/or a duly appointed officer of the law. All information received will be handled with utmost discretion by Mr. Ferrette and his agents who will provide prompt and considerable remuneration to all persons instrumental to the process of helping him reclaim his rightful property."

The bulletin also provided a drawing of the couple that bore a striking resemblance to them. Ellen went on to say that Uncle Blue had seen it posted in some of the store windows along Market and Chestnut Streets. William was thunderstruck. He slowly placed the bulletin back in the dresser and turned to Ellen in silence. Holding her close, he struggled for words.

"How could this happen? How could Ferrette track us here after all these years?

"I don't know William. I was so careful. You know what John Ansar told us years ago; trust no one."

"Wait a minute. I did tell someone about our past. Let me think...yes, Amos Jones from the carriage factory. I told him about our escape. We got to be close. I've spoken to you about him. He's the one who told me about the cheap farmland in Christiana. Do you think he could have...?"

"Oh William, you didn't!"

"Yeah, I did. But I really don't think he would have..."

"Oh my God, I told someone as well."

"Who Ellen?"

"Frances. You know...Frances Harper. But she's as good as gold. She would never...

"Sure she was Sarah's friend, but how well do you *really* know her Ellen? Every time you see her, she's got her nose buried in some book. I swear, you women can't keep a…"

"Please, I beg you William, do not; I repeat, do not finish that sentence!"

William paused for a moment and then decided to spin the conversation in another direction.

"Well answer me this. Ferrette is one of the richest men in Chatham County. Hell, he owns half the land, a shipping company and probably over three hundred of us sweating and slaving under his whip. Why would he take all this time and trouble to track us down?"

"He's an animal. No, that man is the devil incarnate!" Ellen shouted.

"Yeah, *but why pick on us?* Why is he so determined to get *us* back there?"

"Who cares? Let's just go William. Let's just go to Boston," she screamed.

Her voice traveled downstairs and caused Reverend Catto to come running out of his den.

"Yaw alright up there?"

"We're okay," responded William. "Everything's fine."

Ellen's outburst re-ignited a suspicion that William had harbored for a very long time. She obviously knew more than she was saying about Mr. Ferrette and what went on in his mansion years ago. His thoughts immediately traveled back to the murder of Ned and Ellen's sudden insistence that they leave the Ferrette plantation at once.

"You're holding back on me Ellen. It's time for you to tell me; I think I have a right to know."

Tears welled up in her eyes and her lips began to quiver uncontrollably. He sat on the bed pulling her forward, and gently placed her head on his shoulder. Stroking her hair, he continued his line of questioning in a far more relaxed manner.

"Ellen, I'm your husband. I love you. I will always love you. But I need to know what happened."

The pause was painful for both of them. Finally, Ellen summoned the courage to reveal the secret she had kept from him for so long.

∞∞∞∞∞∞∞∞∞∞∞∞

She haltingly informed William that on the night before Ned's murder, Mr. Ferrette returned home drunk and stumbled into the pantry where she was preparing a snack for Mrs. Ferrette. He forced himself on her and swore to kill her if she told anyone, especially Mrs. Ferrette. Ellen took the threat to heart, but decided that she had better warn Ned's wife, Matilda. A man who could do that to her would have no reservation in doing it again to others. The next morning, she told Matilda about his beastly attack but swore her to secrecy. But, for some unknown reason, Matilda broke her promise and told Ned. And that is when the problem escalated.

"I can understand why you would want to warn Matilda. But, why didn't you tell me Ellen?" asked William. "I would have killed him! I would have snapped his neck with my bare hands!"

"Yes, I knew that. And so did Ned!" she whimpered. "He knew exactly what you'd do, so he went to do it himself! To spare you…to spare us!"

The rest of the story was increasingly painful. When Matilda told Ned, he became furious and there was nothing she could do to restrain her hot-tempered husband. He grabbed an ax handle and immediately went looking for Mr. Ferrette. A few minutes later, he found him in the dairy. Ferrette saw Ned racing toward him and reached for his pistol. But, before he could raise it, Ned lunged forward and managed to strike him a blow before tripping over a milk bucket. Four of the other slaves immediately ran to restrain Ned before he could inflict any further harm on their master. That explained the large contusion on Ferrette's head the night he whipped Ned to death. It also explained why Mr. Ferrette did not assign Ned's punishment to one of his foremen.

Ned had inflicted both a physical and psychological wound on Mr. Ferrette. He had injured his manhood and sense of complete invincibility. But more importantly, Mr. Ferrette knew that he had to hide his lustful deed from his wife and her powerful father who never approved of their marriage in the first place. He knew he risked tremendous social and financial loss if his sexual indiscretion was ever revealed. First, he ran the risk of a divorce that would surely nullify any claim he had to his wife's vast inheritance. Secondly, he knew he would incur the wrath of his powerful father-in-law. In all likelihood, Colonel Knight's public rebuke would diminish Mr. Ferrette's standing in the local business community and tarnish his reputation as an upstanding deacon in Chatham County's polite religious community. Faced with these possibilities, he concluded that Ned had to die. Therefore, he contrived the rumor about Ned stealing from the smokehouse. It was a deliberate and well-calculated lie designed to hide his unspeakable crime.

William now understood with certainty what he had suspected for so many years. He knew all along that Ned had not stolen that pork shank. If he did, he would have surely shared it with him. It was as simple as that. Ned never wavered from their brotherly code; their solemn pledge of fidelity. *"A true friend wants for his brother what he wants for himself."* Mr. Ferrette had committed a grave offense against Ellen. That offense extended to William and in a deeply personal way, extended directly to Ned himself. Ned knew how William would react to this violation of Ellen and apparently decided that *he* would personally deliver the lethal retribution to Ferrette.

William was stunned by Ellen's account of the devastating incident. It was now easy for him to see why she kept such a horrific secret from him. But his blood still boiled at the very thought of Ferrette's indecency. He gulped hard and began pacing back and forth, as he considered what must have gone through Ned's mind at the time. William knew that Ned was impulsive and quick to react. Therefore, it was not difficult to comprehend why Ned did what he did.

Yet on second thought, he was struck by a staggering alternative explanation. Maybe Ned's actions were premeditated. Maybe Ned knew *exactly* what he was doing. Maybe this time, he had the presence of mind to make a deliberate and thoughtful decision. By killing Ferrette, he would in effect, save William's life and spare Matilda a similar fate. Perhaps Ned had consciously decided to sacrifice himself and willingly bear whatever consequences might befall him. Such a sacrificial act was well within the scope and depth of Ned's character. William clenched his teeth and wiped away a tear as he recalled Ned's unwavering dictum, *"a true friend wants for his brother what he wants for himself."* It was a code they lived by, and one that Ned was apparently willing to die for. Perhaps it was as simple and painful as that.

∞∞∞∞∞∞∞∞∞∞∞

All things considered, it would just be a matter of time before Mr. Ferrette's legal reach would extend to Philadelphia where the godless moles roamed the streets and the Fugitive Slave Act held sway. Now Ellen and William both knew the dark secret that their former master so desperately wanted to conceal. He was a maniacal man who was quite capable of killing to assuage his wounded pride. He proved that with Ned and he would certainly prove it again through his relentless pursuit of the Crafts whose very existence posed a major problem for him. To be sure, they represented far more than "lost property".

In truth, Ferrette had learned of William and Ellen's whereabouts through an abolitionist newspaper that was brought to his attention. The newspaper featured a well-intentioned but extremely ill-advised article describing the Crafts' clever escape from South Carolina to Philadelphia. The article infuriated Mr. Still who learned of its publication after it had already been released. He could not believe that his abolitionist partners could be so careless in protecting the Crafts' identities. It also enraged Ferrette who was shocked and embarrassed to no end. He immediately began to fear that Ellen might divulge other damaging details; sordid details that might also surface in the South Carolina press.

The Crafts carried with them a dangerous and damaging secret that he had hoped to bury by murdering Ned years ago. And for that reason alone, they had to be destroyed. With the legal impetus of the Fugitive Slave Act, he could now pursue and re-capture them with great efficiency and unprecedented legal support. However, Ferrette did not really want them to be returned to South Carolina. On the contrary, he paid his northern agents a hefty fee and gave them explicit instructions to kill both William and Ellen in any manner they saw fit. That way, the ghastly secret they bore would finally die, once and for all.

After hours of agonizing debate, William and Ellen reluctantly decided to accept Mr. Still's offer to help them relocate to Boston, a safer abolitionist stronghold that was a much further distance away from the slave catchers and kidnappers who were clustered near the Mason-Dixon Line. They agreed that it would be safer to travel separately. Ellen would leave by train in the same disguise she donned years ago. William would travel by coach and rendezvous with her three weeks later in the home of George and Millicent Hilliard, two of Mr. Still's most trusted helpers in the New England area.

"Well, I guess I'd better go find some scissors," said William.

"Excuse me?"

"Well you don't think you can get all that pretty hair under a top hat do you?

Ellen gasped as she suddenly realized the price she would have to pay (yet again) to earn her freedom. William went about his barbering task in complete silence. Ellen sat perfectly still as her long, wavy tresses fell to the floor. She was thinking about an even more disagreeable task; one that she and only she should perform. Someone had to tell Octavius. It was to be a difficult and agonizing parting. It could not have been otherwise.

∞∞∞∞∞∞∞∞

The next day, William, Ellen and Octavius arrived at Pennsylvania Station, just in time for Ellen to catch the afternoon train to Boston. Ellen and Octavius walked into the train terminal and sat in the waiting area while William searched for a place to hitch his wagon.

"Now Octavius, I am counting on you to be strong. I want you to listen to your Auntie Frances while I'm gone. She's going to keep a close eye on you. And you listen to your Uncle Blue...well, to *most* things he tells you. And no more fists fights. You've got to learn how to get along with people, all people you hear me?"

"Yes ma'am."

"Come here and give your Auntie a hug...Don't cry...you'll get me to bawling. You know I don't want to leave you, don't you?"

"Yes ma'am"

"Listen, I'll be back as soon as I can. Until then, you have to be strong honey. And take care of your father too. He's got a lot of things on his mind."

"Yeah, I know. I hardly see him anymore. He doesn't care about me."

"Honey, you're as wrong as you can be about that. You listen to me young man. Your father loves you more that anything in this world. Everybody knows that. God Himself knows that! It's just that he's a little distracted; that's all."

"*Distracted?* What's that mean?"

"Well, it means he's got a lot on his plate; important things to get done. A lot of folks are counting on him. And like the rest of us, he only has twenty-four hours in a day to get it all done."

It was the first time that Octavius ever mentioned his inward anxiety and his apparent alienation from his father. It was difficult for a young boy to understand how a father, who professed to love him so much, could be so blind to *his* emotional needs. To his young eyes, it seemed as though Reverend Catto wanted to save the whole world and did not care one bit about his own son's well-being.

But Ellen knew better. She believed that Reverend Catto still wrestled with feelings of guilt stemming back to the evening of Sarah's life-threatening injury. His was a psychological wound that never really healed. And, the fact that Octavius looked so much like his mother did not help matters at all. He saw Sarah in Octavius' body movements, in his eyes and in his gentle smile. At times, he could not bear even to look at his son. Wherever Octavius was, there was too the haunting and heartrending memory of his beloved wife.

Before they could continue their conversation any further, William entered the terminal and walked toward them in a hurried pace.

"Ellen please, you're going to miss that train if you don't get a move on."

"One minute William…You listen to me Octavius Valentine Catto and listen well. I *never* lied to you and I don't intend to start now. Your father loves you in the deepest possible way. And trust me; one day we'll all be together again. You can bet on that. So straighten those shoulders and give your Auntie a hug. God I love you (sigh)…I truly do."

22. Buried Treasures

"Nothing of tragedy can be written, can be spoken, can be conceived, that equals the frightful reality of scenes daily and hourly acted on our shores, beneath the shadow of American law, and the shadow of the cross of Christ. And now, men and women of America, is this [slavery] a thing to be trifled with, apologized for, and passed over in silence?"

Harriet Beecher Stowe

The morning after the Crafts left Philadelphia, Mr. Still sat alone in his den contemplating a much different dilemma imposed by the Fugitive Slave Act. By 1850, he had already conducted well over five hundred interviews of escaped slaves. His notes from those interviews were written in painstaking detail and contained the names of the underground passengers as well as their points of origin and destination. His extensive notes were supplemented with secret correspondences that delineated travel routes, means of conveyance and even the names and locations of the countless helpers who had assisted these slaves in their escapes. Federal law now deemed these helpers to be law-breakers who were subject to harsh penalties. There was no way Mr. Still was going to expose them to such prosecution. For him, that was an *unthinkable* possibility.

He knew that a few of his stalwart supporters would continue to harbor and transport the fugitives in total defiance of the new law. But clearly, he could no longer commit any more interviews to writing. Any further record keeping would provide incontrovertible proof that he and his helpers were willfully violating Federal law. He simply could not place his faithful friends and their families in such jeopardy.

The decision to abandon further record keeping came easy. However, he was now confronted with an agonizing dilemma. What was he to do with the irreplaceable records he had already amassed? They contained vital information that could be of invaluable assistance to fugitive families who were desperately seeking their displaced loved ones. Without the benefit of his richly detailed information, they stood little chance of ever being reunited with relatives who, like his brother Peter, had been scattered to the winds. For nearly fourteen years, he was propelled by a deep desire to help those families experience the joy of similar reunions. He was now betwixt and between in the worst possible way. Time was of the essence. It probably would not be long before the police came to his door with warrants in search of fugitives and prosecutorial evidence.

After hours of soul searching, Mr. Still decided that it was best to destroy his priceless collection of interviews and correspondences. He concluded that their immense value was outweighed by the enormous danger they posed to his devoted army. In the end, this was the wisest and safest course of action – or so he told himself. Rising from his desk, he paused to peer out of his window at the heavy rain outside. The grayish, mid-day sky added to his already dismal mood. He gathered all of his cherished manuscripts and piled them beside the fireplace in his parlor. Adjusting the flue in his chimney, he shuddered at the thought that he would soon release into the atmosphere, a grainy smoke fed by the destruction of his irreplaceable documents.

Most of his firewood and kindling were stored on the porch in the rear of the house. Opening his back door, he suddenly realized that he had another problem. High winds had channeled the rain onto the porch and had saturated most of the wood, rendering it unusable. Mr. Still gasped as he frantically picked through the bottom of the woodpile to find dry, combustible pieces. Some of the bottom logs were dry enough to use so he quickly gathered them in his arms and made his way inside. Time was running out.

Unfortunately, the height of the wood stack obstructed his vision and before he knew it, he had tripped over a shovel that was leaning against a wall in the hallway leading to his den. Lifting himself off the floor, he began to curse with a fury. He cursed at the shovel that had sent toppling. He cursed all slaveholders. He cursed the United States Congress for passing the Fugitive Slave Act and he cursed the city constables and U.S. marshals who might be knocking on his door at any moment. A huge primal scream was stirring in the center of his chest and making its way up to his esophagus. Then, in a split second, an inspired idea flashed into his mind. That shovel had provided a serendipitous clue; an alternative to destroying his precious documents.

He would not feed his documents to the fire after all. Instead, he would *bury* them. The idea was simplicity itself. He would bury them in a secret place, a place no one would look. His first and best thought was of Mount Lebanon Cemetery, the place where he had buried his first love. Mount Lebanon was the designated colored cemetery for the residents of the Seventh Ward. It was owned and operated by the Deacon Board of Mother Bethel Church. Mr. Still had been its unpaid treasurer for several years. And with Reverend Catto serving as the church's assistant pastor, securing a plot would be no trouble at all. In fact, he knew of two prepared plots that were available for immediate occupancy. The cemetery had the added advantage of being located only twelve blocks from his home and only a few blocks from the city's market district.

His plan would be easy enough to implement. Its main virtue was that it did not require anyone else's direct assistance. He would gladly assume all the risks in transporting the cherished contraband to the cemetery. Accordingly, he gathered his documents in small bundles and tied them each with yarn. He would boldly go to the cemetery in broad daylight, using two large suitcases as a means of conveyance and a perfect decoy. To travel at night would only serve to arouse suspicions. He waited until the afternoon when he could inconspicuously walk through the market district amidst the swarm of shoppers and pedestrians usually found in that congested area.

∞∞∞∞∞∞∞∞∞∞∞

The clock in his den struck one o'clock and he began his walk to the cemetery carrying two overstuffed suitcases that strained every muscle in his body. As anticipated, the noisy streets were bristling with energy and the usual fast-paced activity found in the market district. From there, he would take a side alley to the cemetery and bury his materials in one of the available plots. He safely made his way to the corner of Market and Ninth Street. It was there that his plan began to unravel.

Straight ahead of him, he saw Judge Andrews and Constable Duffy supervising a group of policemen who were handing out and posting bulletins announcing the recently enacted Fugitive Slave Act. The Judge spotted a beautiful young woman and stopped her for a brief flirtation. Mr. Still assumed they would be sufficiently distracted and continued to walk in their direction.

"Well, Ms. Trueheart, I hope you will have time this week to visit me in my chambers so we can finish our most stimulating conversation. Now if you'll excuse me, I see someone I must speak to."

The judge then walked toward Mr. Still and literally blocked his path.

"Ah, Mr. Still, so nice to see you. Are you perchance going on a trip today?

"Yes, your Honor is most perceptive. Now if you'll excuse me, I have to …"

"Just a minute Mr. Still. I've been meaning to ask you something. What exactly are your thoughts about Congress' new and improved Fugitive Slave Act?

"Well sir, my opinions are of no importance. But I suppose we all must learn to live within the law."

"You're damned right about that Mr. Still."

"Now your Honor, if you don't mind, these suitcases are quite heavy."

"Well sit them down; no need straining yourself. Besides, you look like you could use a rest…Hey wait a second. I do believe that I have just made a little pun. You get it don't ya? I said you could use *'arrest'*…as in handcuffed and hauled off to jail. Tell me Constable Duffy; don't you think Mr. Still deserves arrest?"

"I do indeed your Honor; but all in good time; all in good time."

"I suppose you're right about that Constable. We must wait for the proper occasion. What say you Mr. Still?"

"Well sir, I think your Honor is as wise as he is humorous. Now gentlemen if you please, I must be moving along."

Mr. Still stooped to pick up the suitcases and walked another fifty paces before he encountered yet another delay. Pastor Hightower arrived at the next intersection in his carriage; an ornate conveyance that never failed to attract attention.

"Good afternoon Mr. Still. Are you going on a trip?"

"Yes I am Reverend. I'm on my way to the train station; but I'm running a little late."

"Well hop on in then. I can take you."

"No thanks Reverend, I don't want to impose."

"Nonsense, I'm going that way anyhow."

He climbed down from the carriage and reached for one of the suitcases. Instinctively, Mr. Still clutched the handles tighter to resist the Reverend's meaty grip. Their tense but friendly tug-of-war made one of the latches become undone. One of the suitcases popped open, causing the bundled manuscripts to strike the ground and spew all over the sidewalk. Off at a distance, two more attractive women had diverted the Judge's gaze. He and Constable Duffy engaged them in conversation and did not see the spillage directly in front of them. With cat-like agility, Mr. Still hastily stuffed the contents back into the opened suitcase. Pastor Hightower helped by stepping on some of the documents to keep them from being blown away by a brisk wind. With his assistance, Mr. Still recovered the contents and quickly lifted the suitcases into his carriage. Pastor Hightower had now become suspicious. He saw no clothes in the luggage and had apparently scanned some of the documents. However, he did not utter a word. Their ride to the train station was brief, but palpably uncomfortable for both men.

"Thanks for the lift Reverend," he said, trying to make direct eye contact with him.

Pastor Hightower looked downward and responded.

"My pleasure Mr. Still. You be *real* careful now."

Mr. Still was flooded with misgivings as he watched Pastor Hightower continue down the street. How much had he seen? Did he understand what the contents of the suitcase were? Did he fully grasp what had just transpired? Most importantly, could Pastor Hightower keep a secret? Would he betray him? Worst yet, was he *truly* one of those despicable moles whom John Ansar and others had suspected of being in collusion with the slave catchers?

Mr. Still completed his mission as planned, but spent that night pondering these and other nagging questions.

23. The Amazing Story of Henry (Box) Brown

"Go and carry the news. One more soul got safe."
Harriet Tubman

Reverend Catto was a man of integrity and one who tried very hard to keep his hypocrisies to a minimum. He found it increasingly difficult to ask the families of his operatives and helpers to accept dangerous assignments when he was unwilling to put his own family at risk. Thus, he agreed to allow Octavius to serve as a lookout during the Underground's nightly transfers of fugitive slaves. Octavius had just turned eleven years old. Prior to that time, he was only allowed to make deliveries to the neighborhood safe houses. Now he was being asked to serve in a more mature capacity. Octavius gladly accepted this new responsibility and proved himself to be a reliable and conscientious worker who was always glad to lend a hand.

However, there was one particular day when he failed to meet his responsibilities. He had promised to help Uncle Blue make deliveries to some of the safe houses that were in need of food and medical supplies for the children. Octavius had forgotten this assignment and was instead on Bainbridge Street, playing with Jacob White, Jessie Glasgow and his familiar group of friends. He apparently had been lured into a baseball game. When Uncle Blue found him otherwise engaged, he reluctantly decided to handle the deliveries himself. That evening, he caught up with his godson.

"You listen to me Octavius, or I'll knock you down where you stand! You oughta to be goddam ashamed of yourself. Those families were counting on you and you let them down. Anybody that is that damned selfish ain't fit to live. A man that only cares about himself is not worth a bucket of spit! I ought to hit you upside your head with one of those baseball bats of yours!"

His unanticipated reprimand was stern and cut Octavius to the core. He had never seen that side of Uncle Blue's personality. It was a bitter and shocking introduction to adult reality and a poignant reminder of the underground's unwritten code of conduct. Sure, baseball had its place. But selfishness was sin; and dependability was an indispensable virtue. From that day on, Octavius never missed a delivery and Uncle Blue never again raised his voice to *his special boy*; the one he had grown to love more than life itself.

∞∞∞∞∞∞∞∞∞∞

It was to be a difficult and erratic passage into adolescence for Octavius. In the absence of Auntie Ellen's steadying influence, his already tenuous commitment to school began to wane. His interests turned to sports; baseball in particular. That shift of attention was accompanied by his discovery of members of the opposite sex. One girl in particular seemed to have caught his eye, the attractive and quite popular, Rachel Porter.

One bright spring afternoon, Octavius completed his deliveries and gathered Jacob, Jessie and a few of the neighborhood boys to play baseball at their familiar haunt, a vacant lot on the corner of Eighth and Bainbridge Street. Octavius had emerged as the group's best batter. Jacob considered himself their best pitcher. It was a classic showdown between two friends who competed in just about everything. Octavius confidently walked to home plate wishing Rachel were on hand to witness what he intended to do with Jacob's tricky curve ball.

"I tell ya what I'm going to do. I'm gonna smack your curve ball right over that roof," he boasted.

"Well, we'll see about that," said Jacob.

"Strike him out Jake. He swings like a rusty gate!" yelled Jessie.

Uncle Blue was watching the game from a distance. He cheered as Octavius swung the bat and sent the ball sailing high above the rooftops and over to the next street.

"That's my boy", he hollered as he rode off in his rickety wagon.

"A lucky hit," shouted Jacob. "That's all…Pure luck! And don't think I'm going to go after it."

"Aw, come on. We'll go get it together," insisted Octavius.

All of the boys left to find their one and only baseball. When Octavius and his friends walked over to the next street, they were confronted by a group of Irish boys. One in particular, named Shamus O'Toole, held the ball tightly in his hand. He had delightfully claimed it as if it were dropped like manna from heaven. Octavius was the first to react.

"Hey that's my ball!"

"Well, I don't see your name on it."

"No, but it's *my* ball."

"Well, seeing that you watermelon-eating apes don't have no right to be over here, I reckon, we'll just hold on to it. Besides, I don't think you're as tough as everybody says you are!"

"Naw, he don't look that tough to me," chimed in Joey O'Rourke.

Jacob instantly charged forward and punched Shamus square in the nose. Octavius immediately joined the fray. A veritable free-for-all broke out between the Negro and Irish boys. Father Kendrick saw this out his parish window and ran out to break up the melee. He grabbed Octavius with one hand and Shamus with the other.

"All right all ready. That's enough of that! Have you boys taken leave of your senses?"

"He started it Father!" Shamus shouted.

"Yeah Father, them nigs came over here where they don't belong," added a badly bludgeoned Joey O'Rourke.

"I don't care who started it. You boys had better learn how to get along. Now go on about ya business! And Octavius, I know your father wouldn't approve of this kind of nonsense."

"Sorry Father."

As the boys started to walk away, a policeman came running to the scene and instantly grabbed Octavius by the collar.

"What's going on Father? Ms. O'Malley says we had a bit of an altercation. No doubt, this one is behind it all."

"Not really officer. Just a friendly discussion between these fine young lads."

"A discussion ya say? About what Father?"

"Well, as far as I can tell, there were some differences of opinion concerning potatoes and their nutritional superiority over the watermelon."

"Well, Father if you say that *discussion* is over, I'll let this trouble maker be."

"Capital idea officer."

"All of ya best get moving or I'll run the lot of ya in. Go on now!" shouted the policeman.

As the boys departed, Father Kendrick walked back toward his rectory and heard the voice of the policeman calling out to him.

"Excuse me Father, but do you have a minute?"

"Yes I suppose so. What is it?'

"Well, I've been meaning to ask you something. Why is it that you always seem to take the side of those burr heads?"

"Burr heads? I don't particularly care for that kind of language officer."

"Sorry Father, no disrespect intended, but you sure don't make our job any easier."

"Oh really? How so?"

"Well, we're the ones that have to keep those coloreds in line. And, it seems to a lot of us that you care more about *those* people than your own kind. That's all I'm saying."

"Well I can assure you, that's not the case at all; but I thank you for your observation. And might I also offer *you* a bit of worldly advice?"

"Sure."

"My dearly departed uncle was a great admirer of the English poet and clergyman, John Donne. Didn't care much for Donne's church politics but he sure did like his poetry. Ever hear of him?"

"Can't say that I have."

"Well then, I certainly commend him to you. I believe it was Donne who once wrote:

"No man is an island, entire of itself...any man's death diminishes me, because I am involved in mankind; and therefore never send to know for whom the bell tolls; it tolls for thee."

"Yeah, but what's that got to do with us keeping those burr...I mean... er... coloreds in their place?"

"*Everything my son; everything.* Have a good day."

"You too Father. See ya in church."

∞∞∞∞∞∞∞∞∞∞∞

Given their failure to retrieve the ball, the boys walked back to Bainbridge Street totally dejected. The game was canceled and the boys disbanded. Octavius and Jacob walked east in the direction of Mr. Abrams' general store.

"I hate those Irish. I could kill them all."

"But you're the one who started it Jake. One little scuffle and you want to kill all of 'em? That's crazy! Anyway, forget that. What about that Rachel? Did you ever notice how she looks at me?"

"Forget Rachel! You trying to tell me that you don't hate them boys? You don't fool me...I saw it in your eyes. You liked kicking their tails, I saw hate."

"Naw, I was just angry with 'em. Colored folks have been living in this neighborhood long before their scrawny butts jumped off the boat from Ireland. And some of them are slave-catchers. They're the worst of the bunch. My Uncle Blue calls them the scum of the earth; trading on colored folks' misery."

"That's what I'm saying! They think they can come in here and push us around just cause they have us outnumbered."

"Yeah, but all I'm saying is it ain't right to hate white folks. Actually, it's not right to hate anybody. Besides, they're not *all* bad."

"I swear to God boy, I think that Rachel girl has caused you to lose your mind."

"Naw that ain't it. It's just that I know for sure, a lot of 'em are good people. As a matter of fact, we had one of them over for supper last week."

"Yeah right!"

"No, I'm dead serious. Before last week, I had never seen one of them on our street, except for Father Kendrick and a few bill collectors. I couldn't believe it. But, there he was, with his boots under our dining room table and my Dad and Aunt Harriet sitting up there treating him like a king. I found out later that the man's name was Samuel Smith, if I remember right. He must have talked for hours. And there they were, hanging on his every word. Come to find out, he had helped a lot of runaway slaves; one in particular by the name of Henry Box Brown."

∞∞∞∞∞∞∞∞∞∞

The miraculous story of Henry Brown's escape to Philadelphia was well known by the inner circle of the underground. It was one of the many stories that Mr. Still had recorded; stories that now resided in the depths of Mount Lebanon Cemetery. Henry Brown was a slave on the Culpepper plantation, just outside of Richmond, Virginia. One evening, he staggered into the livery stable of Samuel Smith, the local blacksmith. He was bludgeoned and bruised by a severe beating he had just received at the hands of three drunken overseers. They found amusement in hog-tying him and taking turns at whacking him with an iron spiked wooden paddle. He was further exhausted by a three-mile walk, but somehow managed to find his way to Mr. Smith's stable, where he collapsed in the entranceway. His face and legs were badly swollen and his shirt was soaked in blood.

"Henry, is that you? Oh my God, what have they done to you now?

"I... I didn't do anything. I ...I...was just there... I didn't do ..."

"Never mind Henry. You save your strength."

He helped Henry limp over to a pile of hay and gave him a ladle of water. Smith was horrified by the sight of his deep and gaping wounds.

"I ain't never goin' back there. I'd rather die right here than let dem beat me like that agin."

"Lord knows I understand Henry. But how are you going to escape? Do you have any money? They probably have the hounds and half their men out looking for you already."

"Naw, they done had their supper and they's in fer the night. Been sipping that corn licker all day and night. I don't spec they'll know I'm gone til tommorra."

"Listen up. It's about time for me to quit for the day and have my supper. You can stay here for the night, but you best be moving out by early morning. There're sure to come this way looking for you."

"Thank ya Mista Smith."

Then came a familiar voice, summoning him to the house.

"Samuel, Samuel, its awfully late. Come on and eat!"

"Listen Henry, that's Alice calling me in for supper. You lay still and I'll bring you something to eat later on. I'll be back as soon as I can."

∞∞∞∞∞∞∞∞∞∞

Samuel sat opposite his wife nervously tapping his fingers on the table, lost in thought.

"Peas?"

"No thank you."

"What's the matter dear? You look so forlorn and you barely touched your food. I thought you enjoyed my cooking."

Samuel became perturbed and pounded his fists on the table.

"You know I do Alice! So why would you say a foolish thing like that!"

He stormed out of the kitchen and went into the bedroom where he lied down. Alice followed and sat down beside him.

"Samuel, what is it? What on earth is bothering you?"

"I gotta help him."

"Help *who* Samuel?"

"Henry, from the Culpepper place. Alice...I've never seen a man beaten like that. And just for the sport of it; those drunken fools. It ain't right I tell ya, it just ain't right!"

"Where did you see him?"

"He came staggering into the livery a few minutes ago."

"Oh Samuel no, don't tell me you took him in?"

"Alice, what else could I do?"

"But you know the Culpeppers have plenty of men and bloodhounds. They're sure to track him down and they'll track him right here to us Samuel, to us!"

"You think I don't know that?" he retorted.

"Then why Samuel? Why would you put us in danger? You know the law here. Anyone caught helping a runaway faces fines and imprisonment. And have you forgotten? Charles Torrey got six years in jail for trying to help those runaways. The poor man was snatched from his family and died in prison from tuberculosis? Is that what you want?"

"No; but I can't just stand by and let them do this again and again. I have a moral duty."

"Yes and your first duty is to your family. (She paused for a moment.) "I swear, if anything happens to you, I'll kill those Culpeppers myself – every last one of them."

"Now don't get yourself all upset. I'll figure something out. I'll find a way...or make one."

"Samuel Smith, you are an incurable jackass!"

She stood up and stared out the bedroom window, transfixed by ominous looking rain clouds, stretched across the eastern sky. Minutes later, she walked briskly into the kitchen.

"Where are you going now? Home to your mother?" he asked as he followed her.

"No Samuel. If you must know, I'm going to fix him some food. That is, if it's all right with you. The poor man must be starving."

"But I thought you said...."

She placed her hand over his mouth and then wrapped her arms around his waist.

"And I'd thank you kindly to bring back my good plate when you're finished."

"I want you to know, I love...."

Before he could finish, she placed her hand over his mouth again, then slapped him on the butt.

"I know, I know. Now go eat your supper. I'll have his ready in a minute."

Samuel finished his supper and walked back to the livery with food and a jug of water in hand. Henry was sound asleep. He woke him and placed the plate on a nearby crate. After pacing around for a few minutes, it came to him; the solution to his problem – the crate. He would ship Henry in a crate to Philadelphia on the morning train out of Richmond. He merely had to telegraph Mr. Still to arrange a parcel pick-up in Philadelphia. The only remaining problem was the crate itself. Unfortunately, it measured only two feet, eight inches deep, three feet wide and four feet long. Henry would have to curl himself in a fetal position to fit inside.

The next morning, Mr. Still wired back to the Richmond telegraph office to acknowledge receipt of Smith's message. With that assurance, Smith would send Henry Brown by train on a dangerous and harrowing twenty-six hour journey. Smith collected some clothes and found some cotton baize to line the crate. Once Henry was inside, he cut some hickory hoops to strap around it for added cushioning.

"Henry, these clothes may be a little big on you, but they're all I have. Now you eat up; eat all you can. You'll only have a flask of water and some soda crackers. We don't what to attract the hounds with unnecessary food scents. And here's a gimlet. You can use if you need to drill more holes for air."

The long trip to Philadelphia was made no easier by the fact that Henry would spend about half of that time literally standing on his head. Somewhere around Harve de Grace, Maryland, the train made a sharp turn, causing the crate to fall from a stack and land upside-down; wrong side up.

∞∞∞∞∞∞∞∞∞∞

Some people found this story to be too incredible to believe. But, those who knew Mr. Still knew beyond a shadow of a doubt, that he did not traffic in fictions or fantasies. Mr. Still remembered that remarkable episode very well. Sol Abrams had agreed to keep his store open a few hours past sunset on the Jewish Sabbath just so he could receive the special delivery from Richmond. Uncle Blue and John Ansar then transported the crate to Mr. Still's house. As they laid the crate on the living room floor, Uncle Blue said aloud what the others were already thinking, but dared not say.

"I don't know, yaw. I can't see how somebody could survive a trip like that in such a little crate."

"Never you mind Blue, just hand me that crow bar," replied John.

"Why would a man do a fool thing like dat? Lord, I sure hope he's alive in there," said Uncle Blue as he feverishly worked with a hammer claw.

"He's alive all right," murmured Reverend Catto.

"How do you know?" Mr. Still asked.

"I just know."

John and Uncle Blue simply looked at each other. They were confused by Reverend Catto's sublime confidence.

"Well, he just better be!"

"Why do you say that Blue?"

"You mussa not ever smelt a dead body before, have ya? I tell you, it's worse than spoiled milk; worse than pig feet that's been out in the sun for two weeks; worse than a baby that done poo…"

"Blue, Blue I think we get your point," interrupted Reverend Catto.

As they removed the lid, they saw Henry's body covered in sweat and dried blood.

"Good Lawd, he feels like he done swam up the Delaware River", said Uncle Blue.

He was completely still. In his right hand was the small gimlet that Samuel Smith had given him. The handle was broken off, so apparently he had died from asphyxiation. They lifted his lifeless body out of the crate and placed him on the sofa. Reverend Catto kneeled and touched his forehead and then his wrist, feeling for a pulse, but none was detectable. Uncle Blue gently placed a blanket over the still body and whispered.

"Rest in peace young buck. You did what you could do and that's what counts, ya hear me?"

Tears welled up in his eyes and he reached for his handkerchief that had dropped on the floor. As he bent down to pick it up, he saw a slight twitch in Henry's fingers.

"Don't you be blaming yourself Reverend. We got him here as fast as we could. I think he would have made it if that drill hadn't come apart on him."

"But John, I was so sure that he…"

Just then, they heard Uncle Blue shout.

"Look yaw, look!"

Henry's eyes began to flicker. His limbs began to move ever so slightly. John Ansar immediately began to rub Henry's arms and legs. Reverend Catto looked on in total amazement and utter joy. He dropped to his knees and knelt beside Henry offering a prayer of gratitude.

"Praise the Lord, the one and only God; the giver of life and death. In His hands is all good. He hath power over all things."

It was yet another amazing story that Mr. Still never grew tired of telling.

∞∞∞∞∞∞∞∞∞∞

"Wow, Octavius, that's some story all right! But, what does that have to do with white folks being good. The way I see it, Mr. Smith didn't do anything but put some nails in a crate and send Mr. Brown on his way. That doesn't make him a good person to me."

"Well, there's more to the story. You see, a little while later, Mr. Smith was arrested and convicted for boxing up two other runaways. The police were dead set on punishing him for what he had done."

"And you know what? They sentenced him to prison. For five months, he was chained in a cell, four by eight feet long. They even bribed one of the prisoners to kill him. He took five stabs aimed at his heart, but he still made it through."

"So what happened to him?"

"Well he was pardoned after a few years in prison. He knew he couldn't stay in Virginia because they would have killed him for sure. So he and his wife moved to Boston I think."

"I see what you're saying. He was a good man. But, ol' Mr. Brown almost lost his life traveling all that time, pent up in that little crate. That took a lot of guts. He's a real hero."

"My father doesn't exactly see it that way. He says Mr. Brown, being a slave and all, had everything to gain and nothing to lose. So he took his chances. On the other hand, Mr. Smith had *everything* to lose and *nothing* to gain by helping him. *So he's the real hero.*"

"You know something?" asked Jake, stopping in his tracks.

"What's that?"

"Your father is a pretty smart guy."
"Yeah, I know," said Octavius with a somber nod.

24. A Beacon of Hope

"Prejudices, it is well known, are more difficult to eradicate from the heart whose soil has never been loosened or fertilized by education. They grow there, firm as weeds and stones."

Charlotte Bronte

The rains cleanse the air and saturate the earth with new possibilities. On some occasions, they come as unexpected harbingers of better days to come. It is always darkest before the dawn. Hope can be fragile and often difficult to maintain amidst despair and the apparent victory of evil over good. Yet it has been proven time and time again that Divine precipitation blesses those who work and wait.

∞∞∞∞∞∞∞∞∞∞

There was no denying the fact that the Vigilance Committee was disheartened by the shameful enactment and swift enforcement of the Fugitive Slave Act. Re-captures, interceptions and blatant kidnappings were occurring on a regular basis. It was high season for the parasitic rats and moles trafficking in blood and betrayal. A month after the Act was passed; another special meeting of the Vigilance Committee was called. Mr. Still knew something unusual had happened. Frances Harper was ordinarily so poised and unflappable. However, on this evening, she was fidgety and could hardly keep her seat. After his customary invocation, Reverend Reynolds called the meeting to order.

"I want to thank you brothers and sisters for coming out in such inclement weather for this special meeting. For those of you just coming in, let me point out that we have some more room in the umbrella racks to my left. Now without delay, I will turn the floor over to Ms. Harper who will introduce our invited guest."

"Thank you Reverend Reynolds. I am delighted to introduce to some of you and re-introduce to others, a distinguished citizen of our city, Mr. Alfred Cope. I tell you I'm so excited, I feel like my heart is about to jump out of my chest. Go ahead, Mr. Cope you tell them!"

"I thank thee, Ms. Harper. I come to thine meeting today as a representative of the Society of Friends. We have as thee well know, our central office on Arch Street and many meetinghouses throughout this state. We are a people vehemently opposed to ignorance, intemperance, violence of all manner, war and alas, slavery. Tis our duty and our sacred trust to oppose these human weaknesses in every sphere of our existence. And, I..."

Before he could finish, Ms. Harper had lost her patience.

"Go on, go on and tell them the news Mr. Cope!"

"Ahem...Yes, by all means. I shall get to the point. Tis my duty to inform thee that one of our recently deceased Quaker brothers, Richard Humphreys has bequeathed a fund of ten thousand dollars for the establishment of a high school for colored children."

The members all applauded with excitement. Then Mr. Cope continued.

"I have been charged with the execution of his will which stipulates that said school will be devoted to the instruction of students of African descent, in the higher branches of learning and in agriculture and the various trades. This school is to be chartered by the Legislature of Pennsylvania and to be named the *Institute for Colored Youth.* Furthermore, I am also pleased to inform thee that the initial endowment has been increased by several donations from our brethren across the state, such that the initial corpus stands at $16,312. Finally, we have purchased a lot in the Seventh Ward, at the corner of Sixth and Lombard Streets, which shall be the site of its permanent establishment."

"Well Mr. Cope, on behalf of the Vigilance Committee, I simply can't thank you enough. Are there any questions or comments from our members?" asked Reverend Reynolds.

William Whipper, one of the staunch supporters of the Vigilance Committee had a particular concern.

"I want to extend to you my heartfelt gratitude Mr. Cope. But I do have a question. I'm in the lumber business and I can't see how you're going to build a decent school with only sixteen thousand dollars."

"Thine estimates are quite right and they remind me of a few details I have neglected. Another Friend, who wishes to remain anonymous, has increased that fund to...let me see...yes, here it is...an additional $8,000."

The committee members applauded again as he began to flip through a thick document.

"Yes, we have concluded that this is enough to begin construction immediately, while we raise the projected total of $28,000 needed to complete this undertaking. The balance of which is to be raised by future subscriptions by our Society of Friends."

Not to be argumentative or unappreciative, Reverend Catto asked another probing question.

"Mr. Cope, if you please, what about teachers? There can't be more than a handful of white folks in this whole city who would be willing to teach in a colored high school."

"Thou art correct sir. But, it was always our assumption that the school would be operated by colored instructors, while our role would be that of a Board of Managers."

Always the pragmatist, Sarah Mapps joined the discussion.

"I would deem it an honor sir to teach in such a school, but we have lost so many of our educated people in the last five years. The riots have prompted them to leave the city for greater security. And now, with that infernal Fugitive Slave Law in effect, they're leaving for Canada in droves. It's unlikely we can find many who would be willing to risk their safety by moving back here."

Once again, Mr. Cope had a ready answer.

"I have been charged with the responsibility of recruiting the best scholastic talent among thy race, and to offer them suitably attractive wages to induce them to come to Philadelphia and join us in this most worthy endeavor. In fact, I have here a written commitment from a Mr. Charles L. Reason, a colored gentleman of some note, who has agreed to be the school's first principal as soon as the building is complete and he disposes of his duties in New York City."

"Well, what are we waiting for? Let' get on with it!" shouted Ms. Harper.

Uncle Blue chimed in.

"She's right. No more jawboning yaw. We gotta get the word out and about. Nothing comes to a sleeper but a dream. We gotta help him find us some colored teachers!"

"Well, I suppose that's as good a note as any to end on," declared Reverend Reynolds. "Do I hear a motion to adjourn?"

"Ya sho nuff do!" replied Uncle Blue.

"Very well then; we stand adjourned until next Tuesday."

At the striking of his gavel, the Committee members swarmed to the front of the church to energetically thank Mr. Cope for bringing such a priceless gift; a bountiful gift that suddenly appeared like divine precipitation, revitalizing a socially barren landscape, on a cloudless evening.

A week later, Reverend Catto welcomed Harriet Tubman back to Philadelphia and hosted a late supper and strategy session at his home. Despite the efforts of Boss Conley and the time bandits of his ilk, the work of the Underground resumed; albeit on a much smaller scale. After the planning session, Harriet Tubman went upstairs to say goodnight to Octavius. Reverend Catto was glad to have her back again. In many ways, her presence helped made up for the loss of Ellen Craft who used to shower Octavius with so much attention. In time, Octavius grew to anticipate his nightly chats with his newly adopted "Auntie". Before retiring for the evening, she knocked on Octavius' door.

"Come in."

"Hi baby, I was hoping ya wazzin't sleep yet."

"What took you so long Aunt Harriet?"

"Well, I had to go over some things wit yo' daddy."

"What kind of things?"

"Well fo' one thing, ya Aunt Harriet is leaving soon. Me and ya' Uncle John is going ta make a trip to da low country. First thing tommorra, I'm going to get me a new pair of boots. Some fella named Tom Garrett's going to pay for them. I can't wait. They sho goin' to spare me a world of pain. All God's children need good shoes to protect their feet. Like I always say, if yo' feet ain't right, ain't nuthin' right. So chile, I want you to always take good care of yo' feet, ya hear me"

"Okay. Will you be away for long?"

"Now I caint say fo sure, a lot of things could happen down there."

"Aunt Harriet, do you think I might be able to go with you on one of your trips?"

"I don't know bout dat chile. Yo daddy would miss you somethin' awful."

"I guess your right."

"I know I'm right. And besides, you gots ta go ta that new school they's building just fo da colored children. Dat's what *you* need ta do."

"I don't want to go to high school. I could work with the Underground Railroad, just like you. Ask anybody, I'm not afraid of those slave catchers."

"I know that. But listen ta me chile. We's all called ta do different things. Everybody knows you's a top-notch student and you's bound ta be a leader and maybe even a teacher. You's called ta study dem books; dat's yo calling, ya hear me?"

"Well if studying is so important, how come I've never seen you reading a book?"

"Well maybe its cause yo Auntie don't know how. Ya see, where I come from, dem white folks didn't let us near no books and twern't nobody going ta break da law and try to teach us. But, I'll tell ya dis much. I always figered dere was somethin' powerful and good in dem books; or dem slaveholders wouldn't be so dead set on keeping dem out of our hands. Dat's what I figered! So ya go on ta dat school and make yo Auntie proud. And while you're at it, make your momma proud too."

"You know something? I wish I could talk to her."

"Well what's stopping ya? She's always near. When I wanna talk to somebody's that's passed over to the other side, I just dream about em."

"Dream?"

"Yeah chile, dream."

"Okay, I'll try that…Aunt Harriet?"

"Yeah baby, what is it?"

"Did I tell you about my new girlfriend?"

"Ya mean dat preddy little girl, Rachel?"

"Yeah, that's the one!"

"What about her?"

"Well…do you think she'll be going to the new high school?"

"Well now, I cain't say fo sho, but I figer yaw are bout da same age, so I wouldn't be surprised if she went ta dat school wid cha. And I'll tell ya something else…"

"What's that?"

"Dey say she's a preddy fine reader herself. Yes dey do."

"Now how would you know that?"

"I done told ya; yo Aunt Harriet knows everything. Now stop ya gabbin' and git ta sleep."

∞∞∞∞∞∞∞∞∞∞∞

Needless to say, not everyone welcomed the advent of the new colored high school. Most of the white residents of the Seventh Ward opposed its establishment. Boss Conley and his goons saw it as yet another sanctuary for "uppity niggers". He expressed his extreme displeasure at one of his frequent meetings with the Mayor.

"What's this I hear about niggers building a school in the Seventh Ward Mr. Mayor? I thought we had an agreement to chase as many of them out of there as possible. A new school is bound to give them a stronger foothold."

"Now there really wasn't much I could do about that, could I? Those crazy Quakers are behind this. Hell, they've got a legal charter, signed and sealed by the Governor, and all of the construction financing already in place."

"Who's doing the construction?"

"They say McCloskey and Company got the bid and he'd gonna be working with a bunch of darky sub-contractors."

"I'll be damned. That McClosky will do anything for a dollar. Imagine that! A white contractor for a nigger school. That man has no scruples whatsoever!"

"Let's face it; there aren't many of us honorable businessmen left nowadays."

"You can say that again Mr. Mayor. But, you know what? A building like that will probably take them twelve to fifteen months to complete."

"Yeah, that sounds about right."

"Well, the way I see it, with the right amount of kerosene, it'll probably take about twelve to fifteen minutes to burn it to the ground."

"And who would you get to do such a thing Conley?"

"Are you kidding me? Some of my men would do it for a song. Hell, I know some niggers in the Seventh Ward who would do it themselves for a case of Jamaican rum!"

"Ah, Connie always plotting, always thinking ahead."

"Why thank you Mr. Mayor, I consider that a high compliment coming from the likes of you."

"Indubitably me lad, indubitably!

25. Kidnapped!

"I would fight for my liberty as long as my strength lasted, and if the time came for me to go, the Lord would let them take me."

Harriet Tubman

From her stoop on Bainbridge Street, Rachel Porter could see the tall scaffolding for the new high school towering over the adjacent row homes. Unlike Octavius, she looked forward to it its completion with great excitement. Her friend, Marva Walker was indifferent about the matter; scarcely listening as Rachel braided her hair.

"Are you excited about going to the new high school Marva?"

"Not really."

"Why do you say that?"

"Who needs that reading, writing and studying all the time? Girl, I have better things to do with my time."

"Like what?"

"Well, making money for one thing. I want to open my own dress shop one day. Maybe even sell hats and shoes and the like."

"Yeah, I bet you'd be good at it too. You always dressed your dolls the best. But, if you're going to start a business shouldn't you know something about arithmetic and money handling?"

"Aw girl, my husband can handle all that stuff."

"I don't know about that. Seems to me you ought to know something about how to make money and how to spend it. You know, just in case."

"Just in case what?"

"Well, they say money makes people do strange things. You can't be too careful when it comes to money."

"Listen girl, I'm an *artiste*. I don't have time to be doing no ciphering and all."

"If you say so."

"Well, what do you wanna do when you grow up?"

"I'm going to be a schoolteacher, like Ms. Mapps. I'm going to miss her when I graduate and go to the new high school."

"Are you done yet?"

"Almost, sit still!"

Lifting her head up, Marva saw a homely looking little girl sitting alone across the street.

"I tell you what you need to do next. You need to go over there and comb that girl's nappy head. Now you know she ain't got no business coming out the house looking like that! And look at those raggedy clothes. That's a sin and a shame!"

"Who is she?"

"Can't say. She's new and doesn't talk much."

"I think I'll go introduce myself."

"Suit yourself girl, I got chores to do."

"See you in church Sunday?"

"Do I have a choice?"

Marva left and Rachel walked over to the tattered little girl.

"Hi my name is Rachel, do you live here?"

"Kinda"

"What's your name?"

"Dey call me Missy."

"Well Missy, how do you like it here?"

"It's a sight better din where we come from."

"Where's that?"

"Papa said I ain't supposed to say. So I reckon I won't. He says you can't trust a lot of folks around here."

"Yeah, I know what you mean. My father says the same thing. Rachel don't say this, don't do that; don't go here, and don't go there."

She mockingly imitated her father's deep baritone voice, which made Missy laugh.

"See that, I knew you had a pretty smile hidden under there."

"And that's a pretty ribbon you got on Rachel."

"Do you really like it?"

"Uh-huh"

"Well, you can have it. Turn around Missy."

"Tanks, ain't nobody ever gave me nuthin, specially, nuthin as preddy as dis. But what you gonna do fer a ribbon?"

"Girl are you kidding me? I have more like that at home. Besides, my mother is taking me over to Oxford County to a store where they sell them in all kinds of colors. I'll get us some more. Maybe your mother will let you go with us one day."

"I don't think so. Momma said we had better lay low on account of dem slave catchers."

"Well, we'll see...Hope springs eternal!"

"Huh?"

"Well…it's just a way of saying that you shouldn't let people or things stop you from believing in yourself and seeking your own happiness. Ya know what I mean?"

"Uh-huh."

"Listen, I gotta go, but I'll look for you when we get back okay?"

"Okay Rachel, I'll be seeing ya."

∞∞∞∞∞∞∞∞

Three months after its enactment, the Fugitive Slave Law had not precipitated the windfall profits that Boss Conley had expected. He called his nefarious gang to a meeting at his office in the back of O'Grady's pub. His obsequious underlings knew beforehand that he was extremely displeased with their performance. Without any preamble, he began one of his infamous tirades.

"You men listen to me and listen damn well. I've got twenty-five duly signed warrants that came to me just this week! Hell, the city is crawling with runaway niggers. Do you all mean to tell me you can't find any of them? Look here, you got descriptions, you got warrants and you got the power of the law behind you. I didn't buy you those deputy badges for decoration!"

$600 REWARD!

Left the service of the subscriber, near Port Republic, Calvert Co., Md.,

About the 19th of APRIL,

3 NEGRO SLAVES

He threw a stack of fugitive slave advertisements in the air and continued his vitriolic rant.

"Now somebody needs to tell me what the problem is. Cause if I can't get any better results than this, I just might have to get me some new men who are a damn sight more motivated than you slackers."

His men stared at the floor and occasionally at each other. Finally, one spoke up.

"Well Boss, ya see it's like this…some of us are a might skittish about taking on some of them bucks. It ain't like they're willing to go peacefully, if you know what I mean. Geez, I had one of them cut my rope and come after me with a knife. Jasper had to shoot 'em in the leg, just to get 'em to settle down."

"Yeah and there was this other one that fit the description of a runaway to a tee! So we grabbed him," added Jasper.

"And?"

"Well, the nigger said he had a er…er some a…what did he call it Tom?"

"He said it was a manumission paper or somethin like that, which done proved that he was a free man and couldn't be taken."

"And what did you do Tom?"

"Well Boss, being that I don't read much, I couldn't rightly say if he was telling the truth or not. So we let him go."

"Ya see, that's what I'm talking about! You nitwits had him and let him go? All you had to do was snatch that piece of paper from him and burn it. Now what's he going to do? Nothing! It's his word against yours. Now who's gonna take the word of some no account nigger over a white man? Your job is to arrest them and bring them to us so that we can rush them down to Baltimore as soon as possible."

"But Boss, what if he really was paid for, free and clear? What if he was telling the truth?"

"Now ya see Tom, there comes a time in every man's life when he has to use his head for something other than a hat rack. Who gives a rat's ass if he's telling the truth? The truth you moron, is that you had better find a way to get some jingle in your pockets and keep the wolf away from your own door! Do you understand me? Do any of ya? Now you all bring me in some niggers or I'll find some others who know how to get the job done. Now git outta here, all of ya!"

As the men headed for the door, Jasper tried to offer an additional explanation.

"Boss, I was only trying to say that…"

On Boss Conley's command, one of his henchmen pulled out a blackjack and Jasper wisely decided to move on.

∞∞∞∞∞∞∞∞∞∞∞∞

As planned, Rachel Porter accompanied her mother to a popular store in Oxford County, due west of the city. It was a sunny Saturday morning and a perfect day for the bi-weekly mother-daughter outing that both of them always looked forward to with great anticipation. They traveled their usual route from Philadelphia that merged with Old Baltimore Pike, a scenic and well-traveled country road. Rachel beamed with excitement as she carefully observed the diverse flora and fauna of the area. Mrs. Porter encouraged her daughter's interest in naturalistic studies and was pleased to make several stops along the way to enable Rachel to collect leaves and multi-colored flowers. This aspect of their trip was almost as satisfying as the purchases they would make later in the day.

The store was crowded as unusual, but the twosome managed to get most of the items on their shopping list, including an assortment of brightly colored ribbons.

"We best be going Rachel. I want to get back to the city before sunset."

"Okay momma."

"Oh my goodness. I stood up there and left the corn meal on the counter. You wait here with the groceries Rachel. I'll be right back".

Just as she re-entered the store Jasper and Tom McMullen appeared carrying a fugitive slave advertisement. It offered seventy-five dollars for the return of a runaway Negro girl. Seeing Rachel unattended, they quickly grabbed her and stuffed a dirty rag in her mouth to prevent her from screaming. Just as quickly, her legs and arms were bound with leather straps and she was violently thrown into a crude wagon used for transporting pigs and animal hides. Their immediate objective was to rush her to the Perryville depot, south of the Mason-Dixon Line. She was to be swiftly taken from there, relayed by train to Baltimore and sold into slavery.

When they arrived at the depot, Rachel's hands and legs were unbound, but Tom McMullen had a concealed pistol aimed at her back. There were several travelers on the platform including a middle-aged couple, Mr. and Mrs. Tappan. Mrs. Tappan was the first to become suspicious.

"Do you see anything peculiar about that situation?"

"Not particularly."

"That girl. There's fear in her eyes. She's afraid, awfully afraid."

"You'd be afraid too if you were a runaway. Of course, you know I don't approve, but it's all so perfectly legal these days. I'm sure that deputy has his orders."

"She's no runaway. Look at her pretty dress. It's all soiled with grease and what looks to me like blood. Who would dress a girl like that, then let roll her around in the muck and mire? And look at her posture and bearing. Mark my words, she's no slave."

"What are you saying?"

"I'm saying we have to do something! That girl is probably being kidnapped against her will and right here in front of us. We have to do something!"

"What do you propose we do dear? The train will be here in ten minutes."

She paused for a moment before responding.

"I'll tell you what. You get on the train and trail them when they get off. I want you to telegraph the Sheriff's office as soon as you know where they have taken her. Meanwhile, I'll go see Sheriff Barker myself."

"Have you taken leave of your senses woman? We don't need to get involved in this!"

"Just do it dear! I have a very bad feeling something awful is going to happen to her."

A reluctant Mr. Tappan boarded the train and successfully trailed the two to Baltimore. They took Rachel to a slave auctioneer who maintained a hog pen and warehouse just a few blocks from the Baltimore train station. Rachel was chained to a large granite slab situated in the center of the pen. She scanned the area around her and saw endless trails of moldy garbage and two very active male swine that were free to roam the disgusting habitat. By this time, both of her ankles were severely swollen from the tight leg irons that restricted her movement. And her thirst had become unbearable. Nearby was a trough of dingy water that was just beyond her reach. The cold, damp ground beneath her offered little in the way of comfort as she finally shivered herself to sleep.

∞∞∞∞∞∞∞∞∞∞

Meanwhile, in Oxford County, Mrs. Tappan barged into the sheriff's office and interrupted a conversation he was having with his deputy and Joseph Miller, a local resident. The sheriff patiently listened to her story. However, his reaction bordered on indifference; or so it seemed at first.

"No disrespect ma'am, but that was not a smart thing for your husband to do. He could get himself killed."

Miller however, took an immediate interest and exhibited a far greater sense of urgency.

"Excuse me ma'am, but can you describe the girl?"

"Of course, she was about ten or eleven years old; quite attractive with a beautiful lilac dress with frilled collar and a deep purple ribbon in her hair."

"That's the one!" shouted the Deputy. "About an hour ago, I saw a hysterical colored woman over at Rankin's General Store. She said her daughter just up and disappeared. I didn't do anything though. I assumed they must have had a spat and she ran away or something. You know how kids are. So what do you want to do sheriff?"

"Well, there's really nothing I can do at this point. That is, unless we can prove that she's not a fugitive. If she really is a kidnapping victim, I suppose we could get an order from the court to detain her in Baltimore and make those who have taken her show cause why she should not be released to the care of her mother. Deputy, you run and fetch Judge Murphy so we can get started on that court order."

"Pardon me Sheriff, but what if they decide to move that girl before we can get to the proper legal authorities in Maryland?"

"Well, Mr. Miller, I suppose we'll just have to pray that they don't."

"I believe in the power of prayer as much as the next man," said Miller. "But I refuse to treat it as a substitute for action. If we are serious about saving that child, we had better act and act now! For all we know, she could be headed further south even as we speak."

"So what do you suggest?"

"I'm prepared to board the next train to Baltimore. It leaves in three hours. I know some fine attorneys down there. When Mr. Tappan wires to tell us where they've taken her, I'm confident that we can get a Baltimore magistrate to serve her captors a cease and desist order with the utmost dispatch."

Upon receiving Mr. Tappan's telegraph, Joseph Miller left for Baltimore with five armed men. The next day, the Baltimore sheriff's office delivered a warrant halting any movement of the young girl until it could be proven that she was a freeborn minor, and not the slave

McMullen claimed her to be. Unfortunately, on their way back North from Baltimore, Miller and his men were confronted by an angry, pro-slavery mob. The entire rescue party boarded the train, but Miller was forced onto the back platform and became separated from his men. He never made it back to Pennsylvania.

The next day, Miller's body was discovered hanging from a tree at Stemmer's Run Station, just a few miles outside of Baltimore. In response to the ghastly murder of Joseph Miller, his uncle, John Miller Dickey, a well-respected citizen of Oxford County, threw himself into the legal battle over Rachel Porter. The protracted case soon became a controversial and much publicized affair.

The Commonwealth of Pennsylvania was persuaded to enter the case and scores of attorneys joined the fray. While Rachel remained in protective custody, Dickey mobilized the whole community to come to her defense. The kidnapping of freeborn Negroes grew into a burning social issue that deepened the hostilities between abolitionists and the pro-slavery forces that inhabited the area.

In the end, Rachel was returned to Pennsylvania. However, her family thought it best to relocate further north, as far away as possible from the relentless time bandits. She never had the opportunity to attend the new high school in Philadelphia, nor did she ever see Octavius again.

∞∞∞∞∞∞∞∞∞∞

On September 13, 1852, the city's first colored high school was opened at Sixth and Lombard Streets, in the heart of the Seventh Ward. Despite threats of violence and arson, the colored community attended the dedication ceremony with great delight. It was a grand occasion, full of hope and high expectations. Reverend Reynolds gave a most stirring speech:

"…This is a day that we have worked and prayed for. At last, we have a school where our children can pursue a higher education, an education driven by their hope and our expectation that they might go forward and contribute to the progress of humankind; that they might play some significant part in this drama of life; that they might consecrate themselves to the pursuit of knowledge and truth for the benefit of others, for the preservation of this republic and,

above all, for the Glory of God. Therefore, it is with great
pride and utter solemnity that we dedicate this fine facility. Let
it henceforth be known as the *Institute for Colored Youth.*"

At the conclusion of his speech, Uncle Blue passed scissors to the
platform speakers, including Mr. Cope, Father Kendrick, Reverend
Reynolds and Mr. Charles L. Reason, the Institute's first principal.
Everyone beamed with joy as they cut the ceremonial ribbon and were
saluted with a thunderous round of applause by a crowd of over three
hundred well-wishers.

It was a major leap forward for the Seventh Ward and a bitter
setback for the sinister time bandits who doggedly preyed on the fertile
minds of Philadelphia's youths.

The Institute for Colored Youth

26. The Christiana Uprising

"Rebellion to tyrants is obedience to God."

Thomas Jefferson

As it turned out, Reverend Reynolds' message of hope was soon overshadowed by an explosive new development. Another emergency meeting of the Vigilance Committee was called the next day. This time, there was trouble brewing in Christiana, forty miles southwest of the city. Slave-catchers, led by a white man, Thomas Gorsuch, surrounded the farmhouse of a Negro farmer named William Parker. Parker and his family occupied the house with William Craft's friend, Amos Jones and his wife. Acting under the authority of the dreaded Fugitive Slave Law, Gorsuch attempted to raid the farm and capture some Negroes whom he believed to be his rightful property. A fierce gun battle ensued as armed Negro farmers defended themselves and routed the white intruders.

In the end, Gorsuch was shot dead. His son was also wounded along with several Negroes who swore that they would not be taken alive as slaves. An intense manhunt was ruthlessly conducted by the United States Marshal, a company of marines, and a large civilian posse who scoured the countryside, indiscriminately attacking, or as they put it, "interrogating" Negro homesteaders. Not one of them bothered to question the guilt or innocence of their Negro victims.

Back in Philadelphia, the incident made the front page of several newspapers, drawing the attention of the Vigilance Committee and unsavory slave catchers like Boss Conley. At the Committee's emergency meeting, Robert Purvis read aloud an article that appeared in the Philadelphia Daily Ledger the next day.

"There can be no difference of opinion concerning the shocking affair which occurred at Christiana, on Thursday, the resisting of a law by a band of armed Negroes, whereby the majesty of the Government was defied and life taken in one and the same act."

Across town, Boss Conley read to his men a somewhat different account of the incident as it appeared in the Philadelphia Examiner:

"According to reliable sources, several well known
abolitionists are implicated in the Christiana murder. All
the ascertained facts go to show that they were the real, if
not chief instigators. White men are known to harbor
fugitives in the neighborhood of Christiana and these
white men are known to be abolitionists and vehemently
opposed to the Fugitive Slave Law. No less than three
white men are in the Lancaster prison, and were arrested
as the accomplices in the dreadful affair on the morning
of the eleventh. Twenty-seven colored rioters are also in
custody in the Moyamensing prison awaiting trial for
insurrection and treason."

The Christiana Uprising

Their alleged "leaders", William Parker and Amos Jones were both
at large and were traveling along two different escape routes. Parker
managed to find his way to Lewes, Delaware and eventually escaped by
sea. Jones could only make it as far as Philadelphia where he was taken
into the protection of the Vigilance Committee.

While Mr. Still and his colleagues discussed how to assist Jones
move further North, Boss Conley called a meeting to discuss how he

might be captured. He had been informed that Jones was hiding out somewhere in the Seventh Ward and quickly summoned all of his men to a secret meeting in O'Grady's pub.

"Now I ask ya boys, where could a nigger like that hide out?" asked Conley.

"Most likely in a coal bin," answered McMullen jokingly.

"No boys, unless I miss my guess, he's probably headed this way. He knows the law is after him and he's gotta move fast and head for Canada, if he's got any sense. But, he's gonna need food, money and a lot of help... Yeah, he's gotta come through the city all right. You boys stakeout the train station. You all scour the neighborhood and keep your eyes open. McCreary, Kelly, and you other men come with me!"

"Where are we going Boss?" asked McCreary.

"We're going to church."

"Church? Why are we going there?"

"Let's just say a little black bird told me to," responded Conley with a sinister smile.

∞∞∞∞∞∞∞∞∞

Just as the emergency meeting at Mother Bethel church was ending, Father Kendrick and Mr. Still entered.

"Where is this Jones fella?"

"He's in the basement."

"Do we have a plan?"

"Well Father, yes and no. We can get him to a schooner headed for Boston and we can transfer him over to New Bedford from there. But, they have the church surrounded. Safe to say, they know he's in here."

"But how? How could they trail him here? John, I thought you said no one followed you."

"I'm sure of it. I reckon someone must have ratted us out. That's what I figger."

"Let me get this right. Then the only thing we have to do is get him out of here undetected and over to the wharf?"

"That's about the size of it Father."

∞∞∞∞∞∞∞∞∞

Outside the church, Conley and his men were keeping a careful watch.

"What do ya think they're doing in there Boss?"

"Plotting and a scheming. But they won't get away this time. That Jones nigger is mine! I'm gonna show you lads how it's done. I'll have him and my capture reward before sundown."

"Now tell us Boss, how in the hell did you know he was holding up in there?"

"Well, I'll tell ya, McCreary. My dear father used to say that the key to fishing is to find the right bait. It turns out that one of them darky preachers has a special fondness for fine coaches. And you know me; I aim to please. Got it for him at cost. I think of it as an investment. Yep, there's no substitute for good inside information."

Conley pointed to a fine coach that stood out among a long line of older and less attractive carriages and buggies parked outside of the church. An hour later, the front doors of the church slowly opened and eight men emerged carrying a coffin with Father Conley and Uncle Blue in the lead.

Before the colored pallbearers could load it onto Uncle Blue's wagon, they saw Conley and his men, standing about forty feet in front of them.

"Heads up boys, here they come," whispered Conley."

"Looks like they're a fixing to bury somebody Boss."

"Bury my ass! Do you notice anything peculiar about this funeral party?"

"Can't say that I do."

"Flowers. You ever see a funeral without flowers? And what's Father Kendrick doing with them? Now I ask ya, what self-respecting white, Catholic priest is going to preside over a nigger funeral? The newspaper said they were being helped by some abolitionists, but I never figured Father Kendrick would sink so low. Let's go. You other men stay back and be ready to move on my command."

As the funeral party walked closer toward them, Father Kendrick whispered to Uncle Blue.

"Here comes Conley. I declare; I've seen better heads on cabbage."

"What do we do now Father?"

"Let me handle it," he responded.

"Good day to ya Father."

"Good day to you, Conley. And a glorious day it is."

"Tell me Father, you haven't seen any suspicious goings-on in there have you?"

"Why Conley, whatever do you mean?"

"I think you know *exactly* what I mean Father. We are duly sworn deputies of the law and we aim to catch that nigger murderer. And that's that!"

"Well, I'll tell ya Conley. That's an interesting vocation you have chosen for yourself. And I'd really like to chat with you some more about it; but as you can see, I've got some business to attend to."

"Of course Father; so I don't suppose you'd mind if me and my men join you."

"Well, to tell you the truth, I don't see how our business is of any concern to you, but you're welcome to come along."

"Yeah, we'll do just that. You can bet on it."

Uncle Blue drove his open wagon with the coffin in it and headed toward center city. He was followed by an entourage of four carriages, forming the appearance of a funeral procession. They slowly moved down the street with Conley and his men following closely behind. All of a sudden, Father Kendrick gave a nod to Uncle Blue, who immediately whipped his horse into a full gallop. The funeral entourage's horses galloped, as did Conley's horses. A wild chase ensued, as they cut sharp corners, upset fruit carts and barely missed several startled pedestrians. Nevertheless, Conley's men could not be eluded. They tenaciously followed the funeral party until Uncle Blue's wagon hit a bump in the road. All of a sudden, the coffin slid off the wagon and hit the ground with a loud thud. The frenzied chase was over.

Uncle Blue and Father Kendrick immediately stepped down from the wagon. Conley and his men also dismounted and cautiously surrounded the coffin. A large crowd of curious spectators moved in for a closer look.

"Careful Boss, they say he's armed and dangerous."

"You're right, no need taking any chances. All right boys, we'll fire on my count."

As Conley and his men drew their guns and rifles, the funeral entourage and onlookers inched back in silence. Conley was the first to fire at the coffin. His men followed and completely discharged their weapons. The coffin was totally mangled by their loud and devastating barrage of bullets and shot gun pellets. As the gun smoke slowly cleared, Conley smugly turned to Father Kendrick.

"Well Father, what do you have to say for yourself?"

"Why I'm speechless Conley; absolutely speechless."

"Now why in tarnation would you do something like that?" Uncle Blue asked Conley.

"As if you didn't know. You're not fooling anybody you old coon!" Conley's verbal attack on Uncle Blue was abruptly halted by a group of policemen who quickly waded through the crowd.

"Alright, what's going on here?" Sergeant McKilroy asked.

"Well, Sergeant I appreciate your backup. But we've got everything under control here. Seems we done caught us a runaway-- a thieving, murdering runaway," boasted Conley.

"What are you talking about?" asked Sergeant McKilroy

"See for yourself Sergeant. We've captured that nigger Amos Jones; the one that led the massacre over in Christiana. And I'll be stopping by the precinct latter to collect my bounty. See for yourself."

"You men check it out!" commanded the sergeant.

The group of policemen pried the lid off the mangled coffin. But much to their surprise, Jones was not in it.

"It's empty sergeant," reported one of them.

Conley walked over to the coffin in shock.

"It can't be!"

"Care to explain yourself Conley?"

"Well Sergeant, I… I…er…"

"Well, it really is quite simple officer," interrupted Father Kendrick. "These men from Mother Bethel Church were kind enough to escort me to the lumberyard on Chestnut Street. We had to add some side rails and other finishing touches to this coffin. And the next thing I know, Mr. Conley and his wonderful associates are chasing us like bats out of hell."

Pointing to Conley, Uncle Blue added,

"Yeah, and then he starts shooting at a poor defenseless coffin. Didn't make much sense to me. That coffin ain't never did him no harm. And I oughta know. I've been with it all day."

"Yes, he's right officer. It was quite an unusual sight," said Father Kendrick. "And I can tell you, in all my born days, I've never seen a man display such a strong dislike for cedar."

∞∞∞∞∞∞∞∞∞

Back at Mother Bethel Church, Mr. Still said goodbye to those who had remained inside. He walked out the door towards his carriage with a heavy heart. He had strong suspicions, but is was not until the Christiana incident that he and the others knew for sure who had been conspiring with their enemies. Reverend Reynolds and Pastor Hightower also exited the church together. Pastor Hightower climbed aboard his carriage and rode away. As Reverend Reynolds prepared to leave, John Ansar called out,

"Excuse me Reverend Reynolds, could you give me a lift to Broad Street?"

"Well…I suppose I could; come on."

"Hold on, let me just grab something I left in the sanctuary."

Reverend Reynolds waited impatiently in his luxurious carriage. He faced forward and began to casually polish the brass trimmings of his carriage with the sleeve of his soft cotton shirt. A few seconds later, John Ansar came out of the church with Amos Jones walking behind him. John walked up to the carriage on the left side, quickly pulled out a gun and pressed it against Reverend Reynolds' rib cage.

"Don't move and don't say a word Reverend. Now smile and say hello to Mr. Jones."

Amos Jones appeared on Reverend Reynolds' right side. He mounted the carriage and the three of them rode down the street as the horse assumed an easygoing trot. Reverend Reynolds was visibly shaken as he sat between them.

"What are you going to do to me?"

"Never you mind, Reverend. Just keep moving."

"This man is a fugitive from the law. And you helping him makes you just as guilty. You are an accessory to a major crime. Did you know that John? You could go to jail for this."

"Well now Reverend, I appreciate your concern. But if I were you, I'd be more worried about my own backside right about now."

"You wouldn't dare harm a man of the cloth."

"Whatcha say, Amos? Ya think we should harm this *man of the cloth*?"

"I don't know John. I mean to say, I sho nuff see the cloth but ain't no *man* in it. Not that I can tell."

John pressed the gun in Reverend Reynolds' side for the entire ride. Fifteen minutes later, they stopped at a dilapidated section of a deserted wharf along the Delaware River.

"Git out Reverend!"

Reverend Reynolds slowly dismounted and struck an authoritative pose.

"You can't take my carriage. It was a gift to me."

"Yeah, we know."

"Now what John? Do you really think you're going to kill a man of my stature and get away with it. You've got to be crazy!"

"Well, now I wasn't planning on killing ya; but I am going to give ya five seconds to jump into that river."

"You'll never get away with this. Besides, what makes you think I won't tell the police?"

"Oh I doubt if you'll have much to say. That is unless you want Reverend Catto and the others to tell your congregation that they've got themselves a Judas for a minister. Do we understand each other?"

"Yes, I suppose so."

"Good! Now git! Times a wasting. We got things to do and you, well…looks like you gotta lot of swimming to do to make it over to Camden."

Standing on the ledge of the embankment, Reverend Reynolds issued one final plea.

"But what do I do?"

Cocking the trigger on his pistol, John yelled,

"Try the backstroke!"

27. Anatomy of a Traitor

"The heart is deceitful above all things and desperately wicked; who can know it?"
Jeremiah 17:9

It was not until the Christiana incident that the inner circle of the Underground knew for sure who had been betraying them. Their suspicions were first aroused after one of the anti-Negro attacks on the Seventh Ward. One of Mr. Abrams' white customers had nonchalantly told him that the attacks were part of a conspiratorial plan to limit Negro migration into the city and to force Negro residents out of the Seventh Ward through fear, intimidation and even murder if necessary. Whites and *"respectable coloreds"* who lived in and around the ward, were told to keep a candle burning in their windows between the hours of ten and eleven o'clock p.m. if they wanted their homes to be spared by the nightly arson and violence of the mobs.

Armed with this knowledge, Mr. Still and John Ansar made an early morning inspection of the window ledges to determine who among them were co-conspirators in this secret plot. They were shocked to find several waxy residues on the windowsill of Reverend Reynolds' home. Even then, Mr. Still was not entirely convinced of his guilt. He did not want to pass judgment until further evidence could be obtained.

It was Mr. Abrams who first learned of the sinister plot against the Negro residents of the Seventh Ward. But, it was Harriet Tubman who recommended the trap that would finally put Reverend Reynolds' guilt or innocence to the test. Reverend Reynolds was invited to a secret meeting in Mother Bethel Church to help plan an escape route for Amos Jones. As anticipated, he left that meeting to attend a secret meeting of his own. They trailed Reverend Reynolds back to O'Grady's pub where he apparently divulged their escape plan to a grateful Boss Conley. Little did he know, the committee members only told him a small part of their elaborate plan; the part they assumed he would dutifully leak to Boss Conley.

There were some among them who wanted to kill him then and there. But cooler minds prevailed and they decided to let him live with the shame of what he had done. Reverend Catto reasoned that to expose him for his miserable crimes would severely disillusion the countless people who viewed him as the embodiment of all that was decent and virtuous. Mr. Still took a different view. He suggested that they could use Reverend Reynolds in a plan to pay back and discredit

Conley and his men. He was tired of their legal maneuvering and their ceaseless aggressions. It was time for the Underground to take the offensive for a change. It was time to give the slave catchers a dose of their own medicine.

Ever since he was exposed, the inner circle of the Vigilance Committee tried to understand what went wrong with their esteemed leader. The sting of his betrayal was especially felt by those like Mr. Still and Reverend Catto who so completely trusted and revered this complex man. How could he have done such a thing? And how could they have been so naïve? The elusive mole was right there under their very noses. Somehow, the entire world didn't make sense anymore. They didn't think they would ever fully understand the mask Reverend Reynolds wore and why he chose to wear it.

However, in retrospect, the signs were there all along. For instance, in the aftermath of the Pennsylvania Hall burning, Reverend Reynolds seemed to be the only Negro in the entire Seventh Ward who held Mayor Swift blameless for what really happened that fateful night. He even solicited depositions for the Mayor's "special investigation".

Furthermore, John Ansar recalled that during the first racial riot, Reverend Reynolds' church was not destroyed by the arsonists. Reverend Catto and the others had naively attributed this to "divine providence". But in fact, Mother Bethel Church was spared the torch because of a deal he had already worked out with the Mayor and Boss Conley.

Mr. Still's memory was also getting sharper. As they further discussed these events, he recalled Reverend Reynolds' total passivity when the Fugitive Slave Act was enacted. Even though he was the organization's official spokesman, he made no *public* denouncements whatsoever of the Fugitive Slave Act. Yet and still, he wanted to boycott the press and wage a full-scale public relations campaign to protest those innocuous cartoons that were so vexing to him.

Mr. Still had always been such a keen observer of human nature. He blamed himself for not seeing this obvious inconsistency much sooner. Perhaps he was, like so many others, too caught up in dealing with the immediate consequences of the Fugitive Slave Act to pay close attention to Reverend Reynolds. Admittedly, he was preoccupied with safeguarding his manuscripts and dealing with other emergencies at the time.

Reverend Catto also began to see things clearer. He would be the first to admit that Reverend Reynolds was a learned man and an extraordinary public speaker. However, he should have also been the first to comprehend that there is no necessary correlation between education and virtue, and absolutely no correlation between fine oratory and ethical integrity. He knew these things in principle, but he too was deluded by Reverend Reynolds' towering prestige and social influence and thus failed to notice this incongruity.

Reverend Catto spent long hours agonizing over Reverend Reynolds's enigmatic personality and limitless treachery. After all, they worked closely together, dined in one another's homes and worshipped side by side, professing their love of God and affirming their ties of Christian brotherhood. How could he have so totally misjudged the man? Were there *two* Reverend Reynolds; *two* halves of a divided and diabolical mind?

As he reconstructed the events of the past few years, a frightening pattern began to emerge. It surprisingly led him to conclude that Reverend Reynolds had indeed been at the very center of the Underground's recent woes. In addition, he was struck by yet another realization that chilled him to the bone. Reverend Reynolds might be directly responsible for the attack on his home and the death of his beloved wife. He was more than a hypocrite and a walking mass of contradictions. He was apparently something far worse. He was by all indications, a fiendish traitor who had Sarah's blood on his hands.

In retrospect, the attack on his home occurred on the day that William and Ellen Craft arrived in Philadelphia. Reverend Reynolds had called an emergency meeting to discuss the Committee's response to the published anti-Negro cartoons while Mr. Still was called away to Delaware. The meeting went longer than anticipated and Reverend Catto had to excuse himself so he and Sarah could receive William and Ellen who were scheduled to come in on the afternoon train from Baltimore. He distinctly remembered whispering into Reverend Reynolds' ear.

"Listen Reverend, I've got to leave now. John Ansar is delivering two *packages* from South Carolina. I mustn't be rude to my guests."

As he recalled, Reverend Reynolds bristled at his comment. More tellingly, no one other than Mr. Evans (from South Carolina), Mr. Still, Mr. Abrams and John Ansar knew of the Crafts' escape plan, and all four men were well above suspicion. Thus, by a process of elimination, Reverend Reynolds must have been the mole in their midst. He must have informed Boss Conley that same day. In turn, Conley then directed his thugs to attack the Catto home as a high visibility target that could help launch their well-planned terroristic campaign. Apparently, that marked the beginning of Reverend Reynolds's long list of betrayals and his close collusion with the enemies of the Underground.

The subsequent series of recaptures could also be traced back to his duplicity. Reverend Reynolds had either participated in or eavesdropped on several meetings in the basement of Mother Bethel Church, where the Underground secretly discussed escape plans and travel routes for the fugitives. It all made sense now. Reverend Reynolds had committed himself to ridding the city of "undesirable Negroes" and had made an unholy pact with the white political establishment and the slave catchers to do just that. On the surface, he endorsed several high-sounding initiatives such as the Negro Society for Moral Reform. However, in his heart, he loathed those whom he considered to be beneath him and innately unworthy of permanent residence in the city.

The Vigilance Committee might never know for sure how or when Reverend Reynolds began his descent into darkness. But Reverend Catto could now at least trace it back to the first appearance of those demeaning anti-Negro cartoons in the local newspapers. If that was not the beginning of it all, perhaps it was the breaking point. Those depictions deeply offended Reverend Reynolds's immense pride in his distinguished family lineage and the established reputations of Philadelphia's free men and women of color. Rather then blaming the creators and distributors of these derogatory images, he blamed the Negro fugitives from the South. In his view, it was *they* who were responsible for spoiling the good reputation and social standing of the city's *respectable* Negroes.

He despised their broken English, their "uncultured" ways and their obvious lack of a rudimentary education. He saw the growing influx and settlement of fugitive slaves as a direct threat to the Seventh Ward's quality of life and the social and political well-being of all free persons of color. In essence, he believed that these unrefined, uneducated and unmotivated Southern Negroes were "ruining it for everyone". They and they alone were responsible for the city's growing animosities toward the Negro. Thus, he saw it as his moral duty to stem the tide of Negro "undesirables" entering the city.

Strangely enough, he perceived them as being responsible for their own previous enslavement. However, in truth, these fugitives were victims of the social order that imposed upon them every type of disadvantage and discouragement enforced by American law and custom. As he saw it, the Negro fugitives had no one to blame but themselves for their social condition. In his twisted logic, *they* were responsible for the unfettered racism that systematically and relentlessly limited their employment options, deliberately deprived them of schooling and pushed them down to the lowest level of human existence. Thus, he concluded that their criminal activities in the city were the *real reason* why people of color were being denied the right to vote. In his ideological framework, the citizenship rights of the more established Negroes were going to be permanently compromised by the uncivil behaviors of the few who were fast becoming a majority.

In this regard, his political opinions were more like Pastor Hightower's irrational viewpoints than anyone had previously imagined. Pastor Hightower was a simple-minded man and openly subscribed to the "blaming the victim" brand of social commentary. He was not a particularly educated or articulate man, but to his credit, he at least let his opinions be known. In contrast, Reverend Reynolds hid his opinions behind a veil of pious rhetoric and cloaked himself in a lifetime of political posturing and gamesmanship.

Finally, Reverend Catto was led to yet another bizarre conclusion. Reverend Reynolds had a precise reason for offering him the position of Associate Pastor at Mother Bethel Church. And, it had nothing to do with the fact that the church needed to expand its pastoral care and charitable service activities. As recaptures increased, the Underground was beginning to close ranks and share its escape plans with a select few. At all cost, Reverend Reynolds wanted the inner circle of the Vigilance Committee to keep having their secret meetings in Mother Bethel. That way, he could either eavesdrop or extract information from Reverend Catto and other parishioners who would never in their wildest dreams, suspect him of being the mole who was sabotaging their operations.

There was apparently no limit to Reverend Reynolds's degeneracy. His agile and chameleon-like mind had the capacity to deceive and had been placed in the service of diabolical and evil men whose acceptance he desperately craved. The bitter truth was that race pride can easily conceal race-hatred; or more accurately, self-hatred. Reverend Reynolds certainly did not commit his treacherous crimes for the capture rewards or the fine carriage that Boss Conley provided. By any comparison, he was a wealthy man and could easily afford to purchase the finer things in life. Money was by no means the lure that seduced him. His moral perversion and grand delusions ran deeper, much deeper.

What he craved most was *acceptance*. Social acceptance was his personal reward; his thirty pieces of tainted silver. And for it, he would betray his own people and abandon the teachings of the Living Christ. He hungered for white folks' acceptance. The more they withheld it, the more he coveted it. Despite his formal education and extensive knowledge, he never grew to an appreciable level of *self-acceptance*. Thus, he was forever doomed to look for his own reflection in other men's eyes.

Through this strange obsession, he developed an unexplainable identification with those in power. He thought his acts of betrayal would be viewed as evidence of his unquestioned respectability and his transcendence of the negative racial characterizations and stereotypes heaped upon the Negro. He assumed that his loyalty to men of wealth and power justified their acceptance of him as one of the city's foremost "distinguished" and "acceptable" Negroes; one certifiably worthy of great esteem. However, long after he had achieved high social standing and acquired all the material trappings of wealth, he still found himself obsessed with this strange need to repeatedly *earn* their respect and continuously *prove* his worth.

Ironically, Reverend Reynolds' aberrant views on race relations blatantly contradicted the fundamental teachings of the African Methodist Episcopal Church. In 1787, the A.M.E. Church's founder, Reverend Richard Allen, broke with the Methodist church over the issue of white racism. Reverend Allen was a devout Methodist, but he refused to accept the church's practice of having segregated pews and separate burial plots for its Negro parishioners.

His defiant protests against these practices were a direct denunciation of white supremacy and its various social manifestations. Reverend Allen insisted that Negro take his place as a man amongst men. He forcefully argued that Negroes and whites were equal in the sight of God. Thus, Negroes were not required or expected to submit to white supremacist viewpoints and practices. There was no need to "measure up" to white social standards. On the contrary, Reverend Allen had always urged his congregation to uphold the highest *moral standards*. In practical terms, that meant serving as exemplary models of Christian faith and good citizenship, not begging for social acceptance from whites or pandering to their hardened bigotry and racial prejudices.

As Reverend Reynolds so often proclaimed, he grew up in the venerable A.M.E. church and was well versed in its teachings. His family ancestors were staunch abolitionists and leading clergymen in the A.M.E. movement that flourished in Philadelphia during the early nineteenth century. In time, he ascended to the leadership of Mother Bethel Church and became its most widely recognized representative. In light of these facts, members of the church and the closely aligned Vigilance Committee reluctantly decided not to publicize his treachery and betrayal. They concluded that he had done enough harm and that the public airing of his misdeeds would only lead to widespread disillusionment and alienation from the church.

Looking back on it all, Reverend Catto believed that they were wrong for not exposing Reverend Reynolds. Surely, the congregation of Mother Bethel Church would have been shocked but they would not be shattered. The spiritual roots of the venerable church ran deep and its parishioners were nurtured by an unshakable faith that no power on earth could destroy. Moreover, Mother Bethel meant so much to so many people. It was more than a place of worship. It had become the spiritual and political hub of the black community. The distinguished reputation of the church could never be soiled by the misdeeds of one man; never in a million years. Reverend Reynolds' replacement proved to be a man of towering integrity. And sure enough, he was followed by a long line of successors who were outstanding civic leaders and were steadfast and true to the church's moral teachings.

But for the moment, the lesson was lost. People in Philadelphia's faith community needed to learn that their leaders often have a shadow side. There are deep maladies that are often bred in the inner recesses of the soul. Holy rhetoric and silvery platitudes can easily mask the workings of a deceitful heart and can prevent people from acknowledging their leaders' blatant inconsistencies. In retrospect, Reverend Catto believed that they should not have shielded the congregation from those uncomfortable truths.

They were wrong on yet another account. Two weeks after the incident, they found Reverend Reynolds in his home with a bullet through his head. Rumors swirled throughout the city as to the cause of his shocking demise. Most residents of the Seventh Ward believed he was the victim of a senseless hate crime. Others, like Mr. Still and John Ansar, assumed that Conley's men had killed him. Reverend Catto thought otherwise. He believed Reverend Reynolds was a tortured soul who ended his own life. Reverend Catto's suicide theory seemed quite plausible. He believed that the human mind has great difficulty in reconciling itself to oceanic moral inconsistencies over time. Eventually, one's moral conscience rebels against the strain of it all. This process of moral corruption and psychological implosion had been known to happen before. It often occurs one moral compromise at a time until the line separating good from evil all but vanishes.

As Reverend Catto explained the matter, it was as if Reverend Reynolds' moral center broke away from its spiritual moorings. Apparently, a series of moral squints had turned into moral blindness. And, in the end, he became duped by the greatest deception of them all. He forgot that the spirit precedes the word. Sadly, he lost sight of the spiritual principle that deeds are appropriately judged by their intentions and there are no actions that can escape the judgment of God. In his zeal to safeguard his family's distinguished legacy, he forgot one simple, but important thing. If there was true *greatness* in his ancestors, it was because there was *goodness* in them. Virtue always was and always will be its own reward.

"God be his judge," said Reverend Catto. As he so often reminded them, "Vengeance is mine saith the Lord."

Reverend Catto liked to teach from the Bible. However, he was equally fond of quoting the Bard who once wrote:

"The quality of mercy is not strained; it droppeth as the gentle rain from heaven. It is twice blessed; it blesseth him that gives and him that takes. Tis mightiest in the mightiest; it becomes the throned monarch better than his crown."

∞∞∞∞∞∞∞∞∞

The Underground's inner circle would be bewildered by this mystery for years to come. Yet, the world has always had its fair share of hypocrites and profiteers masquerading as holy men. Nor has there ever been a shortage of unscrupulous leaders who care nothing about worthwhile causes but simply use them to advance their own selfish objectives. Treachery and religious demagoguery did not begin with Reverend Reynolds; nor were they likely to end with him. He was not the first unreformed reformer to enter their lives, nor was he likely to be the last.

"Beware of wolves in sheep's clothing," says the Good Book. And Mr. Still would add to that counsel his own wisdom: "Guard ye against the seductive whisperers; the twin sirens of power and privilege. They promise you a brand of self-importance that is illusionary at best. They promise you a peace they can never deliver."

Despite all his intelligence and erudition, Reverend Reynolds was unable to resist the hypnotic lure of the time bandits. They are the great deceivers, the demonic forces that have dwelled among us since the world began. They pollute the spirit and cloud the mind. They beckon us to a weightless existence where form precedes substance, and truth yields to mere appearances.

They control us through manifold sophistries and seductions. They wear a million disguises and tempt us to enter arid places; places that the rains do not visit; places where shadow vanquishes light. They are the time bandits; puppets and purveyors of the living dead. They serve the one-eyed King who reigns supreme in the Land of the Blind.

28. Vital Lessons

"He who neglects learning in his youth, loses the past and is dead for the future."
Euripides

Mr. Still and Reverend Catto did not go to Reverend Reynolds' funeral that weekend. They simply could not bear to be among the hundreds of tearful mourners who attended the massive outpouring of grief for that "great man." Pastor Hightower delivered an emotional eulogy, followed by a lengthy memorial citation read by the Mayor himself.

Instead, Mr. Still and Reverend Catto turned their thoughts to the opening of the Institute for Colored Youth. That weekend was spent collecting several boxes of books that had been donated by the Negro literary societies and some of the city's leading Negro bibliophiles.

Octavius reported to Sarah Douglass' classroom for his first day of instruction at the Institute. From the very beginning, he was recalcitrant and easily distracted.

"Michael Abele?"

"Present."

"Constance Bustill?"

"Present."

"Octavius Catto? (silence) Octavius Catto?"

"I'm here."

"Mr. Catto, the correct response is *present*. That is present in mind and body, if you get my meaning. Jessie Glasgow?"

"Present, and most pleased to be here ma'am."

Octavius, Jacob and some of the other boys rolled their eyes at Jessie who was an obvious apple-polisher, determined to win Ms. Douglass' affection.

"Bertha Hampton?"

"Present."

"Caroline LeCount?"

"Present."

"Rebecca Paschal?"

"Present."

"Rachel Porter? Rachel Porter?"

"She won't be with us ma'am. Her family has moved up North," answered Jessie.

"Oh I see, well then we shall miss her. Jacob White?"

"Present."

∞∞∞∞∞∞∞∞∞

Unbeknownst to Ms. Douglass, Octavius was despondent and totally inconsolable. Rachel's sudden departure had left a huge void in his life. It was a disappointment that wounded him deeply and one that had clearly dampened his enthusiasm for attending the Institute. As the day wore on, Octavius became increasingly downhearted. By nightfall, he thought it best to confront his father who was up late studying in his den.

"Come in."

"I just came in to say, to say...well..."

"What is it son? You obviously have something on your mind."

"Well dad, I don't know how to tell you this but I decided that I don't want to go to that high school."

"*You* decided?"

"Yes, sir."

"I see...and what if *I* decide otherwise?"

"Well sir, the law does not say that colored children have to go beyond the third grade. So in a way, me being in high school now, well...I guess you could say I'm *over-educated*, at least better educated than most colored boys my age."

"Oh, I see. And, you have thoroughly researched this matter? You've thought it through I presume?"

"Yes sir, most definitely!"

"Well son, let me put it to you this way. A horse that can count to ten is a remarkable horse, but not a remarkable mathematician. Do you understand me?"

"Not exactly."

"What I'm trying to say son, is you can't accept low standards of achievement. You can't go through life comparing yourself to what the majority of people do. Your job is to develop your mind and your body to the highest possible level; to realize your unique potential."

"Yes, but the truth of the matter is that most colored boys don't have any need for the science, history, math and that other stuff they're going to teach us at the Institute."

"The *truth* of the matter son is that you're looking for excuses not to go to school. Truth! Since when is truth decided by a majority vote? Do you hear yourself? It's like saying eat manure; a billion flies can't be wrong!"

"Maybe you're right."

"I think I am son. Come here; let me show you something. Read this."

He reached into a lower drawer of his desk and handed Octavius an old document. It read:

"Be it enacted by the Honorable State and House of Representatives of the State of South Carolina and by the authority of the same. If any person shall hereafter teach any slave to read or write, such person if a free white person upon conviction thereof shall for each and every offense against this act be fined $100 and imprisoned not more than six months; or if a free person of color, shall be whipped not exceeding fifty lashes and fined not exceeding fifty dollars, at the discretion of the Court of Magistrates and freeholders."

"Well, I think I understand your point, but…"

"No, don't stop son; read on."

"…and if any free person of color or slave shall keep any school or other place of instruction for teaching any slave or free person of color to read or write, such free person of color or slave shall be liable to the same fine and corporal punishment as by this act imposed."

"Understand something son; we left the South for precisely that reason. And I thank God every day of my life, that you are not being raised in an environment where someone has the audacity and the power to limit how fast and how far you can develop your mind and cultivate your talents. That school you're attending is a mighty blessing to you and all the teenagers of the Seventh Ward. We cannot afford to waste this opportunity. It would be an insult to God himself and an utter travesty if you don't continue on your path."

"My path?"

"Yes son. Your path. I happen to believe that you're going to contribute something significant to this world."

"Well I don't feel that way. I just don't."

"I'm not surprised. But be patient and prayerful. In time, you will come to know. Good night son."

"Good night."

"Octavius?"

"Yes sir?"

"I'm sorry, truly sorry about your friend Rachel. But you know, her leaving was probably for the best. At least she's safer now."

"Maybe. But it seems like every time I get to liking someone, they have to leave. First Auntie Ellen, then Auntie Harriet and now Rachel."

"I understand your feelings son. But you know, loss is a part of life. In time you will understand that too."

"If you say so. But, right now, I'm still angry and a bit confused. Nothing makes sense. Do you ever get like that?"

"All the time. All the time son. Good night."

"Good night dad."

∞∞∞∞∞∞∞∞

Later that night, Octavius lied awake in bed, unable to sleep. He wondered what his Mother would think about his idea to discontinue his schooling. Auntie Harriet had insisted that she was reachable through his dreams. It was a spiritual medium he had never explored. His experience that night seemed so real. He heard his mother's voice and looked into her loving eyes.

"Come in."

"I came to say good night."

"You're so sweet. Come sit and talk with your mother for a while."

"Sure thing!"

"Auntie Ellen tells me you have a little girl friend."

"Well, she really isn't my girlfriend...yet. But, she sure is pretty, just like you momma."

"What's her name?"

"Her name is Rachel; Rachel Porter and she lives over on Bainbridge Street. Well any way, she used to live there."

"Well, I'm sure she's as attractive as you say. But remember what I told you. *Pretty is as pretty does.*"

"I know, you done told me a thousand times."

"*You done?* What kind of language is that Octavius?"

"I mean you *have* told me."

"Much better. You know, that's why I want you to go on to that high school. It's important for you to learn how to properly express yourself. I think people are going to want to listen to what you have to say young man."

She suddenly grimaced in pain as blood oozed out of her left ear.

"Octavius, be an angel and get momma a wash cloth over there on the dresser."

"Yes, ma'am."

He gently dabbed her ear to stop the bleeding.

"I hate those white folks for what they did to you! I hate them!"

"I've told you before, you can't allow yourself to hate. Life is too short to hate."

"That's what Auntie Ellen says too."

"And she's right you know. If your heart is full of hate, you won't have enough room to love."

"I'm too young to love, any way."

Tickling his belly, she responded,

"That's what you think. That's what you think."

They playfully wrestled for a few seconds. Then her body suddenly went limp. She lied on her back, completely still. Octavius sadly pulled the blanket up to her neck and kissed her cheek. Tears ran down his face as he closed the bedroom door behind him.

It all seemed so real; so strikingly real.

∞∞∞∞∞∞∞∞∞

Reverend Catto was right about the future efficacy of the Institute. With financial support from the Quaker Mangers, Principal Charles Reason was able to recruit the best colored teachers in the country to participate in what he called a "grand experiment." He immediately began to establish the Institute as a strong academic center. Classes in the Institute were systematized and trigonometry, Latin, Greek and philosophy were added to the curriculum. The Institute and its students quickly became the pride of the neighborhood and the talk of the city.

However, Octavius showed no signs of recovering from his emotional malaise. Ms. Douglass clearly knew that he was not performing up to his potential.

"And so if x equals 5, by simple deduction y must be…Mr. Catto?"

Once again, she was annoyed when she called on Octavius for the answer. He was oblivious to her question and was instead whispering something in the ear of a classmate, Caroline LeCount, who was giggling. They had inadvertently disrupted the class. Caught off guard, Octavius answered

"Yes, ma'am?"

"Would you like to give us the correct answer Mr. Catto?"

"Yes, I'd like to, but… ah…"

"But you can't! And, do you know why you can't Mr. Catto? Because, while the rest of the class is trying to learn, you feel compelled to make a nuisance of yourself. I suggest that you pay more attention to your lessons and hold whatever you have to say to Ms. LeCount until class is dismissed. Do I make myself clear Mr. Catto?"

"Yes ma'am."

"Now, if there are no further interruptions, who can solve this equation?"

Jessie Glasgow raised his hand.

"Yes, Jessie please come forward and show us how we derive the answer."

Jessie smugly strolled up to the blackboard. Octavius and some of the other students smirked at Jessie's arrogance and his zeal to impress Ms. Douglass. Jessie began to write on the black board and a few seconds later announced the correct answer.

"Then "y" must be 25."

"That is correct. Thank you Jessie, you may be seated. So you see class, by holding all other variables constant, we can deduce that…"

Before she could finish her thought, Octavius stuck his foot into the aisle and tripped Jessie who went sprawling to the floor. The class erupted in laughter and the large veins in Ms. Douglass' forehead began to noticeably throb.

"I saw that! Now you gather your belongings Mr. Catto and march yourself over to Principal Reason's office. I'll join you there shortly."

∞∞∞∞∞∞∞∞∞∞∞

In the waiting room, just outside the principal's office, Octavius stared at a drawing of Benjamin Banneker reverently hanging on the wall. Shortly thereafter, Ms. Douglass walked past him and directly into the Principal's office. Minutes later, she came out and again walked past Octavius without uttering a word. Her veins were still bulging and she had apparently developed a curious facial twitch that Octavius had never seen before. He stared at the floor in order to suppress his urge to laugh out loud. Fortunately, his self-discipline won out and he avoided making an already bad situation worse.

When she exited the room, Octavius continued to scan the pictures on the wall. To his left was a portrait of Reverend Richard Allen, founder of the A.M.E. Church. To his right was a drawing of Phyllis Wheatley, the famous Negro poetess. It was his first visit to the Principal's office. Looking at that gallery of Negro notables, he began to regret being there for such an unworthy purpose. As punishment for his impulsive prank, Principal Reason suspended him for two days. Walking home from school, Octavius contemplated what, if anything, he was going to tell his father.

29. Trouble in the Cradle of Liberty

"I would much rather starve in England a free woman, than to be a slave for the best man that ever breathed upon the American continent."

Ellen Craft

Octavius reluctantly told his father about the incident and regretfully accepted an additional punishment – no baseball for two weeks and more household chores. The following morning, Reverend Catto had a strategy meeting in his home with John Ansar and Mr. Still. He had just received some distressing news from Boston.

"When are you gonna tell Octavius about Ellen and William?" asked Mr. Still.

Octavius came downstairs just as his name was being mentioned. He then walked into the dining room to greet their guests. Reverend Catto responded nervously. He had a large blue envelope in his hand and quickly shoved it under his Bible. Octavius seemed to notice his father's uneasiness and apparently had heard a portion of their conversation.

"Tell me what dad?"

"Oh it's nothing son, nothing at all. You run along now. Aren't you supposed to be making deliveries with Uncle Blue?"

"Yes, I suppose I should go. Well, I'll see you all later."

They waited until the front door closed behind him before resuming their conversation.

"Reverend, you know I've never been one to meddle, but you gotta tell him sooner or later," said John.

"You're right John, but not now. He has to concentrate more on his schoolwork. I don't want to upset him with any more bad news."

Mr. Still thought Reverend Catto's concerns about his son's state of mind were perfectly understandable. He knew what the Crafts meant to Octavius. He had been in correspondence with them and their hosts in Boston, George and Mary Hillard.

Three weeks earlier, the Hillards were visited by one of their closest friends, Dr. David Bowditch. His frantic knock at the door foretold the regrettable news he would deliver.

"Why Dr. Bowditch, what an unexpected pleasure. Do come in."

"Good evening George. I'm sorry to call on you unannounced, but I'm afraid I come with terrible news."

"What is it?"

"I've been informed that a warrant has been issued for your friends, William and Ellen. It seems they are wanted as fugitive slaves in the State of South Carolina."

"Surely you jest. They have been living here as decent, law-abiding citizens. They have even remarried here in Massachusetts according to the laws of a free state. How in blazes can they be arrested as lawbreakers because of some barbaric code of Southern justice?"

"It's that infernal Fugitive Slave Law! Since the U.S. Congress passed it, I'm afraid no colored fugitive will ever be safe under the stars and stripes, not even in Boston. A certain Mr. Ferrette has secured a federal warrant and claims they are his rightful property. He demands that they be released to the court for extradition to Chatham County, South Carolina. Apparently, he read about the Crafts' clever escape in one of our abolitionist newspapers that found its way down there. That newspaper article has probably made him the laughing stock of the whole state."

"I must warn them immediately. We cannot let this happen. Mary, come quickly!"

"What is it George?"

"Dr. Bowditch has brought us some distressing news. It looks like some southern bounty hunters want to snatch the Crafts from under our noses and take them back to South Carolina as slaves. Can you believe it?…as slaves!"

"Is that true Dr. Bowditch? Can they really do that?"

"I'm afraid so ma'am. It's a federal law. And might I add, one that stipulates that any one that assists these fugitive slaves is subject to a minimum sentence of six months in prison and a $1,000 fine."

"I'd like to see them try it," answered Mr. Hillard. "This is an effrontery. I will not stand for such nonsense! This is free soil in a free state and I'll be damned if I'll let some witless bounty-hunters determine my fate or the destiny of my friends."

"Do you know where they are George?"

"Ellen is upstairs and William should be coming in from work any minute now."

"Mrs. Hillard, might I suggest that you tell her immediately. The U.S. marshals can't be far behind me."

"I'll go get her."

"I don't believe it. This can't be happening."

"I'm sorry about this, but I thought you should be warned as soon as possible."

Their conversation was interrupted by a knock at the door. It was William Craft and one of Mr. Hillard's cousins, Theodore Parker.

"William, Theodore get in here. Dr. Bowditch has informed us that we can expect a visit from some marshals who are coming to arrest you and Ellen as fugitive slaves. But William, I want you to know we have no intention of cooperating with them."

"But you must", said William, with an unexplainable calmness.

"Are you insane? Do you really think I would surrender the two of you?"

"No, not for a moment. But you must be practical. You are a United States Commissioner. If we were found in your home, you would probably have to resign your office and incur the full penalty of the law. I will not subject a friend to such a punishment for the sake of our security. I won't do it!"

"Now see here...we have a saying here in Boston, *Give me liberty or give me death.*"

"And we have a saying where I come from; *A true friend wants for his brother what he wants for himself.* I will not have you jeopardize your reputation or your liberty on our account. And that's final!"

"Theodore, talk some sense into him will you?"

"I've got only one thing to say William. I strongly suggest that you take this pistol and this knife and use them in the manly defense of your wife and yourself. It is your decision alone. And that dear cousin, is all I have to say on the matter. You have only to say the word William and we can get dozens of men, strong and true, who will defend to the death your right to stay here."

Theodore's expression of support was greatly appreciated. Nonetheless, the Crafts decided to leave-- in a hurry. They hastily packed and were transported to Boston Harbor within two hours. And with Mr. Hillard's support, they were ticketed for a schooner to England. Mr. Still was subsequently apprised of these developments and afterwards agreed with the decision to relocate the Crafts to London. There they could start a new life as paid lecturers for the abolitionist cause. It all happened so quickly. There was no time for sensitive goodbyes. The bloodthirsty time bandits were in full pursuit.

∞∞∞∞∞∞∞∞∞∞

Despite all the secrecy surrounding the Crafts' situation, Reverend Catto would soon discover that his precautions were for naught. On that evening, Octavius arose from his bed and crept into his father's den. On the side of his father's desk, he saw the Bible with the mysterious blue envelope lying beneath it. His curiosity had gotten the best of him. He placed his candleholder on the desk and began to read the letter his father had tried to conceal from him. It was from Ellen Craft and read:

Dear Reverend Catto:

By the time you get this letter, we should be in route to England. Today we leave with little hope or expectation of ever returning to the land of our birth or of seeing the two of you any time soon. Once again, we are on the run. It appears that the widespread publications describing our escape and our abolitionist activities in Boston may well have contributed to our undoing.

Given what happened last week to that poor man, Anthony Burns, we have concluded that we may never live in this country in peace. Mr. Burns was a friend of ours and a fine upstanding man who was suddenly robbed of his freedom and arrested as a fugitive slave. Hundreds of citizens, white and colored rallied to his defense. A group of freedom loving abolitionists including Wendell Phillips and Theodore Parker held a protest meeting in Fanuel Hall. On May 26, the abolitionists stormed the courthouse where Mr. Burns was being held.

In the ensuing riot, a deputy marshal was shot and killed. After that unfortunate occurrence, things went completely out of control. Over 50,000 people flooded the streets, some of them supported Mr. Burns and others were angry over the senseless death of the deputy marshal. The mayor ordered two artillery companies to help keep the peace. President Pierce decided to send in the U.S. Marines as a show of force to demonstrate to all that the Fugitive Slave Law would be strictly enforced, even if it meant bloodshed. Mr. Burns was recaptured by force and ultimately sent back to slavery in Virginia.

After consulting with our friends, we concluded that we should find a country where we would not be in constant fear of slave-catchers who are backed by the government of the United States. So off we go to England in search of peace, carrying with us our crusade to rid the earth of slavery and its many abominations. We will be sure to write to you once we have established residence in London.

Kiss my little man for me and tell him how often we think of him and how warmly remembered he is by his Auntie Ellen and Uncle William. Please share with him the enclosed pamphlet written by a colored Bostonian, David Walker. It is entitled, An Appeal to the Colored Citizens of the World. In so many ways, it captures our deepest hopes and aspirations as oppressed people in this land of freedom. But alas, it does not appear that we will be around to see our aspirations realized. Nonetheless, it is our fervent prayer that Octavius will one day live in a society that can accept the fullness of our humanity and grant to us, the very rights and freedoms they demand for themselves.

With warm regards,
Ellen

Poster protesting the kidnapping of Anthony Burns

After reading the letter, Octavius reached inside the blue envelop and began reading David Walker's Appeal, cover to cover. Afterwards, he walked slowly back to his bedroom where he lied awake for hours; thinking about what he had discovered and contemplating the powerful message of David Walker's stirring treatise. It was one of the most controversial publications ever written by a colored man. In it, Walker explained the history of colored people with great passion and delineated their current state of affairs and their sacred duty to break the chains of slavery – at any cost. This short but powerful book, like no other, fired Octavius' imagination. It placed in sharp focus the signs of the time and the social and political obligations of all colored people in America.

Ellen had proven herself to be a woman of great courage and resilience. But the warrant for their arrest, coupled with the Anthony Burns affair in Boston devastated her. She and William had gone through enough. They simply refused to live their lives under the constant threat of re-enslavement.

In a broader sense, the arrest of Anthony Burns in Boston marked a dark day for freedom and justice. Interestingly enough, the police captain who took Burns into custody immediately resigned. Some of Boston's most influential citizens reacted in total outrage. The renowned humanist, Henry David Thoreau wrote in bitter reaction, **"My thoughts involuntarily go to plotting against the State."**

Later, on the Fourth of July, William Lloyd Garrison protested by burning the Fugitive Slave Act and the United States Constitution on the steps of the Boston Court House.

Henry David Thoreau

30. Remembering David Walker

"It is a notorious fact, that the major part of the white Americans, have, ever since we have been among them, tried to keep us ignorant, and make us believe that God made us and our children to be slaves to them and theirs."

David Walker

After the secret readings in his father's den, Octavius returned to school the next day with a new attitude toward learning and a solid commitment to finish his course of study at the Institute. Ms. Douglass was very pleased with this apparent turnaround, which also seemed to have affected some of his friends – Jacob White in particular. The next day she decided to jokingly coax Jacob along in his Latin recitations.

"Now, Jacob I want you to say it slowly and correctly. And, I declare, if you mispronounce it this time, I do believe I will just throw myself out this window. You may begin."

"Veni, vidi…"

"Just a minute Jacob."

A knock was heard at her classroom door. It was Principal Reason.

"Good afternoon Mr. Reason. What a pleasant surprise. How may I help you?"

Principal Reason had a broad smile on his face..

"I'm sorry to interrupt your lesson Ms. Douglass, but I just received the greatest news and I wanted to share it with you and your class before you dismiss them for the day."

"By all means, what is it?"

"For some time now, I have been talking to the Board of Managers about establishing a guest lecture series. The idea is that we would invite outstanding educators and leaders to the Institute and have them lecture to us on various subjects and discuss the affairs of the day. Well, it looks like we've scheduled our first speaker. And do you know who he is?"

"Oh, please tell us!"

"None other than Frederick Douglass himself!"

"You mean to say, *the* Frederick Douglass?

"I do indeed; and he'll be here this Friday."

"Why I must say, that is great news!"

"Yes and I wanted your class to be the first to know."

"Thank you Mr. Reason. We can hardly wait."

"Well class, I think we should end the day with that wonderful announcement. We will resume tomorrow morning with you Jacob. Class dismissed."

As the students stood and gathered their belongings, Jacob whispered to Octavius.

"You ever hear of this Frederick Douglass fella?"

"Nope, never heard of him."

"Well, I'll tell you one thing."

"What's that Jake?"

"If he's half as boring as our Latin recitations, I think I'll throw *myself* out the window! We still going to play baseball later on?"

"Yeah, I just gotta change my clothes and do a few chores first. I'll come by and get you when I'm done."

"Alright, I'll see you later Octavius."

Octavius left the building and walked down the street. At the corner, he saw Frances Harper walking toward her apartment carrying two large grocery bags.

"Hi Aunt Frances."

"Why hello there stranger, I haven't seen you in awhile."

"I've been doing a lot of studying these days. Can I help you with those bags?"

"Aren't you sweet. Alas, chivalry is not dead."

"So how is school?"

"Alright, I guess."

"Just alright?"

"It's okay. I like my teachers…but sometimes we don't see eye to eye."

"I see, well here we are."

"I can carry these in for you if you want."

"Okay."

He walked inside and climbed three flights of stairs to get to the tiny apartment that she rented in the rear of an old tenement building. He placed them on her kitchen table and headed for the door.

"Well I best be going now."

"Octavius, would you like to have a piece of my fresh baked apple pie and maybe some milk to go with it?"

"Yes ma'am, but I can't stay long. I have chores to do."

"Okay you just have a seat and I'll get that pie. I remember when you were a little boy. You always took a special liking to my apple pie."

"Still do!"

"So how was school today...And don't just tell me *alright*. What did you study today?"

"The usual stuff...math, grammar, Latin...philosophy, history, geography, and science."

"Well those sound like useful things to learn. What else?"

"Well...the principal told us today, that we were going to have some sort of lecture series. Starting on Friday, we're supposed to have visitors come in and talk to us."

"Who's coming this Friday?"

"A man named Fred Douglass"

"You mean, *Frederick Douglass*?"

"Yeah, I think so. Do you know him?"

"Do I know him? Why he's only one of the most respected colored men in the country! He's a well-known abolitionist and they say, quite an eloquent speaker. He's also the founder and editor of a colored newspaper, *The North Star*. I'm sure I have a copy of it in my den. Frederick Douglass, here in Philadelphia. Praise the Lord!"

"So you do know him?"

"Well, not really. I should say I know *of* him. But, I sure would like to make his acquaintance. He is truly one of our most gifted leaders."

"Wow, I guess I'll have to listen to what he has to say."

"I should say so young man."

"Aunt Frances?"

"Yes?"

"Have you ever heard of a man named David Walker, from Boston?"

"Yes, indeed. Who could forget him?"

"Yeah, I just read his book, *An Appeal to the Colored Citizens of the World*".

"You read David Walker's *Appeal*?"

"Yeah."

"Well, I'll be! Where did you get a copy of it?"

"From my father."

"You mean to tell me, your father, Reverend William T. Catto, gave you a copy of *the Appeal*? Well I must say, that's mighty mature reading for a young man your age."

WALKER'S
APPEAL,
IN FOUR ARTICLES;
TOGETHER WITH
A PREAMBLE,
TO THE
COLOURED CITIZENS OF THE WORLD,
BUT IN PARTICULAR, AND VERY EXPRESSLY, TO THOSE OF
THE UNITED STATES OF AMERICA.
WRITTEN IN BOSTON, STATE OF MASSACHUSETTS,
SEPTEMBER 28, 1829.

"Well anyway, I was thinking that we might invite him to be one of our guest speakers."

"Honey, David Walker is dead."

"Dead? He can't be."

"I'm afraid so. He died back in 1830. You know his book caused quite a stir. Some of the southern Congressmen wanted to stop him from distributing it. They even asked the Mayor of Boston to arrest him for inciting slaves to revolt against their masters."

"Really? So how did he die?"

"Well, we really don't know for sure. He was a relatively young man, I do know that much. He died shortly after the book was published. Some folks suspect foul play. They say he was poisoned. But, I'm surprised your father didn't tell you all that."

"That's too bad. I really wanted to meet him."

"But honey, you have met him! You shared his innermost thoughts. That is what books are for, to acquaint you with wonderful people and their ideas; to travel, no to soar!; to wander through the corridors of time and understand the wisdom of the ages! And, oh my goodness...to sail to the shores of eternity! I believe it was Milton who wrote:

"A good book is the precious life blood of a master spirit, embalmed and treasured up on purpose, to be a life beyond life."

Yes indeed, that is what good books are for – *to be a life beyond life!* Come with me."

She grabbed his hand and led him into her den that contained several shelves of books and magazines. Her desk was cluttered with more books, newspapers and political tracts. Octavius was impressed by the sheer volume of reading materials crammed into the room.

"Now let me see, Douglass...Douglass. Aha! Here it is! Frederick Douglass, *My Bondage and My Freedom*. Now ordinarily, I don't lend out my books. They are my most treasured possessions. However, being as you are one of my most favorite people in the whole wide world, I'm going to let you borrow it. That is, if you promise to read it."

"Oh I'll read it all right. Thanks Aunt Frances."

"Oh I almost forgot. Come over here. Let's see; it's in here somewhere."

She took him over to her desk that was buried under a mountain of newspapers.

"Aha, here it is, *The North Star*, that's his newspaper. Hmmm, and I must say, not a bad looking man either...Now you read this too. I want you to be prepared when Mr. Douglass comes to the Institute."

"Thanks."

"You are oh so welcome dear."

"Well...I should be going now."

"Of course, give my best to your father, okay?"

She walked Octavius to the door and headed back to her chaotic den, muttering to herself.

"Now that man ought to know better than to give a young boy David Walker's Appeal...too much...too soon...too dangerous!"

Octavius and his Aunt Frances had completely forgotten the apple pie that was abandoned on the kitchen table. Their elevated conversation had stirred his thoughts and stimulated his appetite for a different kind of nourishment; new and provocative food for thought.

∞∞∞∞∞∞∞∞∞∞∞∞

Frances sat behind her desk and decided to jot down a few notes before they were forgotten. But first, she had to clear a space to write.

That task alone took a few minutes. Fortunately, she had grown accustomed to keeping blank paper, an ink well and a quill in a lower drawer, all to themselves. That way, she was always prepared to write whenever an inspiration came to her. Unfortunately, she had not quite mastered the habit of keeping the surface of her desk free from clutter. Many were the times when she would "straighten up" her desk with a sweeping wave of her right arm. Of course, she would eventually have to pick all those reading materials off the floor. But better that, than waste the sudden urge to write and lose the fruits of the creative streams of creative consciousness that flowed through her mind at all hours of the day and night.

Her greatest love had always been poetry and she became quite good at it. In 1854, she published a popular book of poetry with the unassuming title, *Poems on Miscellaneous Subjects*. Most of her poems spoke of racial pride, the quest for human rights and the ongoing evils of slavery. Some literary critics referred to her evocative verses as "protest poetry" of a powerfully moving nature. However, there was much more that could be said regarding the range and depth of her writings. This book (and several reprintings) brought her national acclaim and a steady income apart from her intermittent earnings as a domestic servant. And, the subsequent success of other equally fine essays and novels earned her the title of Philadelphia's preeminent *scholar-in-residence*. She rather liked the title, but shunned the public attention that came with it.

Above all things, she cherished her privacy and carefully guarded it. As far as anyone could tell, she rarely dated or received gentleman callers in her apartment. It was her sanctuary and very few entered it without invitation or a very compelling reason. Many of the neighborhood women wondered why someone as smart and pretty as Frances never married. Some speculated that she was just "too picky" for her own good. But truth be told, she rather enjoyed socializing with men. However, she simply enjoyed *her own* company the most. What people couldn't understand was that she could actually be alone for days and not feel lonely whatsoever. She liked men for sure, but not just any men. She was not picky, just *selective*. And as a rule, she always preferred solitude over bad company.

In the ensuing years, her writings brought her something more valuable than fame. With the royalties from her books, she was able to move out of her tiny apartment and buy a house of her own. It was a modest row home on Bainbridge Street with weatherworn shutters and a sagging front porch. No one would describe it as spacious or attractive. Her furnishings were sparse and her six windows had no curtains or drapes. Hers was a very Spartan-like existence but it was one of utter contentment. She had the glorious freedom to read and write whenever the spirit moved her to do so. She had control over her time and a space to create. Her psychological liberation was at hand.

Moreover, she now had the financial wherewithal to devote her time freely to being a speaker and a publicist for the ever-widening abolitionist movement. At last, she had the freedom to follow the dictates of her heart and engage the world on her own terms. It was Archimedes who purportedly said, "Give me a fulcrum, and I will move the Universe". Frances' humble dwelling on Bainbridge gave her such leverage. From that unadorned place, she would shape the thoughts and fire the imagination of a whole generation of readers. It was sublimely purposeful work that was most satisfying.

A few years later, she did in fact marry a man who loved and respected her as the vibrant and intelligent woman that she was. True love, that most elusive of elixirs, had finally come to quench her thirst for intimate companionship. The porch on Bainbridge Street was fixed within three months of their nuptials. The curtains and drapes came shortly thereafter.

Frances E. W. Harper

31. Frederick Douglass Speaks Out

"We cannot censure others for doing what we would be likely to do under the same circumstances…The white man's happiness cannot be purchased by the black man's misery."

Frederick Douglass

It was a grand day. Principal Reason decided to open the Institute's first public lecture to the entire city. Some of Philadelphia's most prominent Negro citizens were in attendance. And of course, there were the Quaker Board of Managers and the ladies from the Minerva Club and the Negro Women's Literary Society. The auditorium was filled to capacity and there were several people standing on the sides and in the rear. Mr. Still arrived just in time to hear Mr. Douglass' concluding remarks.

"…so you see, education is our most vital weapon. That is why I say to you young students that you have an awesome responsibility and a sacred duty to perform. While most of our people are tormented and weighed down by the yoke of slavery, you have been given the singular blessing of pursuing a higher education; one that I trust you will utilize for the uplift of our race and for the good of humanity. Remember always, *education is the great equalizer.* Each one, teach one. Educate to elevate! The day is not far when we will reassert our humanity, demand dignity and respect and secure for ourselves the sacred liberties of full citizenship and equality before the law."

Frederick Douglass

Most of the audience leapt to their feet and gave him a standing ovation. It was apparently one of the most stirring speeches he had ever given. As their applause subsided, Principal Reason announced that Mr. Douglass had a few minutes to entertain questions from the audience. No one was surprised that Jessie Glasgow was the first to step forward.

"Ah...ah...Mr. Douglass...I have a question. Are you by any chance related to *our* teacher, Ms. Sarah Douglass? I mean to say, I wouldn't be the least bit surprised if you were. I mean, you all having such great minds and all."

Octavius and some of the other students snickered at Jesse's blatant attempt to curry favor through his thinly veiled flattery. Principal Reason registered a look that clearly indicated that he was disappointed by the shallowness of Jesse's question. Frederick Douglass was also taken aback and somewhat amused by the question. Nonetheless, he answered politely.

"Well son, I would say we're probably not directly related. You see, I was born Frederick August Washington Bailey. My mother was a slave on the Eastern Shore of Maryland and my father was her slave master, Captain Aaron Anthony. When I escaped to freedom, you can understand why I didn't keep my master's last name. So you see, it is unlikely that Ms. Douglass and I are *directly* related. But of course, all colored folks are related in one way or another."

Frances Harper posed the next question.

"Mr. Douglass, what is your assessment of the recent arrest and extradition of Mr. Anthony Burns in Boston. Is there not any relief or remedy to the Fugitive Slave Act?"

"Oh there's a remedy alright! A good revolver, a steady hand and a determination to shoot down any man who attempts to kidnap you. I think every colored man should make up his mind to live by this, and if need be, die by this! That will put an end to kidnapping and slaveholding too for that matter. We blush to our very soul when we are told that a Negro is so lowly and cowardly that he prefers to live under the slave driver's whip than freedom and death. We should have a little more of the manly indifference to death which characterized the heroes of the American Revolution of 1776!"

In the center of the audience, Caroline LeCount, one of the Institute's ablest students, stood to be recognized. Octavius took particular note of her pleasant appearance and her quiet confidence.

"Mr. Douglass I want to thank you for an excellent presentation. I just have one question though. Are you really advocating physical violence and murder as means to achieve our emancipation?"

"No, I am certainly not proposing violence or murder. However, please understand this. Slavery is murder in the highest degree. Every slaveholder is a murderer. And, those who apologize for them and turn a blind eye to the issue of slavery are worst than murderers. Those who passively condone slavery commit the severest form of violence. Slavery is true violence; it violates our self-respect and nullifies our very humanity. That is why I say that even those who are apathetic and indifferent to the evils of slavery are indeed murderers."

Without being recognized, Pastor Hightower responded angrily.

"Well if that's your position, I must say, you are most definitely advocating violence and bloodshed. And, that is in total opposition to the teachings of the Bible! Young lady he is most certainly condoning violence! And, let me remind you young people, the Good Book teaches that *he who lives by the sword, dies by the sword.*"

Douglass was swift and calm in his response.

"Does not the Bible also teach us, 'an eye for an eye'? Let me put it to you this way. Suppose one of those foul kidnappers barged into the home of a white man with the intention of binding him hand and foot and delivering him to slavery. And, let us suppose that this same white man shot that intruder. Would we not all consider that an act of righteous retribution?"

"Well er…er…yes, I suppose so."

"Now take the case of a colored man like Mr. Burns who is living quietly in Boston, a peaceful law-abiding citizen living one mile from the Bunker Hill Monument. He is free, God created him free! And, he attempts to break

loose from slavery's iron grasp, but a U.S. Marshall is killed in the process. That appointed Marshall, consented to be invested with the power to rob Mr. Burns of his God-given rights and that Marshall...that miserable hireling is shot to death. Now I ask you, is the man who shot him through his stony heart a murderer? He would not be considered so if the parties involved were white! If Burns and his defenders are murderers, George Washington was one, and all those brave men who wielded swords and bayonets under him in defense of liberty were all cold blooded murderers."

Again, the audience applauded; that is except Pastor Hightower, a few of his loyal followers and the Quaker managers. Finally, Octavius rose to ask the next question.

"Mr. Douglass, have you ever met David Walker or read his *Appeal to the Colored Citizens of the World*? If so, what do you think of it?"

"No son, I've never met Mr. Walker, but I'm certainly familiar with the Appeal and the central premise of his book. That is to say, I believe in peaceably rescuing fugitive slaves if possible. However, I believe in rescuing them forcibly if need be. We should by all means and by all rights kill the man who would dare lay his hand on us or our brother or sister in an attempt to enslave them. And, we should feel no pain of conscience in doing so! So I strongly agree with Mr. Walker's position. We simply cannot and should not censure others for doing what we would likely do if we were under the same circumstances."

Reverend Catto sat erect in total silence. He was proud of the way his son had handled himself, but surprised to know that Octavius had apparently read the book that he had decided to keep from him. And, with that final answer, Principal Reason called an end to the program.

"I'm afraid that's all the time we have for questions. Please join me in thanking Mr. Douglass for a most stimulating lecture."

The audience responded by giving Douglass another standing ovation. Afterwards, several people walked on stage and shook his hand. Others stayed behind to chat and some headed for the exits. All of the Institute students stood and began to leave through the exit at the rear of the auditorium. Octavius and Jacob left together. Jacob saw Jesse walking out and ran over to tease him.

"Hey Jessie! That was a *real deep* question you raised; very profound indeed."

"Yes, I thought the question and answer session was quite illuminating. What did you think of Mr. Douglass' speech Octavius?"

"Well, I agreed with most of what he said and I really liked his answer to Caroline's question.

"You mean you really liked *Caroline*," said Jacob.

"No really. I liked what he said; but he's as wrong as wrong can be on one point."

"What's that Octavius?"

"Education *is not* the great equalizer."

"Oh yeah, then what is?"

"Baseball!"

Institute for Colored Youth Baseball Team

32. All Hail the Mighty Pythians!

"A faithful friend is the medicine of life."
Ecclesiasticus

That Saturday, the boys talked Father Kendrick into being the umpire for their weekly baseball game in Fairmount Park. He had stopped playing the game years ago, but it was a pleasure to watch the boys play. They were all so gifted; so competitive. By this time, some of the local girls frequently came to watch and cheer them on. Caroline LeCount in particular had become a regular fan and supporter. She made no secret of the crush she had on Octavius. And not surprisingly, he did not attempt to hide his growing affection for her.

"Come on Octavius you can do it!" she yelled at the top of her lungs.

As the game's umpire, Father Kendrick tried his best to maintain an attitude of neutrality. However at times, his special fondness for Octavius would get the best of him. The boys from the Institute were behind in the game, trailing three runs to five, in the bottom of the ninth inning. Jessie had just struck out, missing badly. They had two outs and the bases were loaded, with Octavius next to bat. Jacob walked over to him and whispered,

"Come on Octavius. You're our last chance. We can't let these knuckleheads beat us. We can't!"

As Octavius approached home plate, Father Kendrick discreetly whispered in his ear.

"Remember to widen your stance son. And for God's sake, don't swing at the first pitch."

His teammates all joined in the cheering. Octavius was immensely popular. More to the point, he was in fact their best batter.

The first pitch was low and inside so Octavius let it go by. Pleased with his disciplined restraint, Father Kendrick nodded with approval and added a subtle wink for good measure. The second pitch was clearly outside of the strike zone but Octavius lunged forward and took a big swing at it. The ball soared far and high in the air. The crowd roared and jumped for joy as the opposing outfielders sprinted backwards to pursue the well-hit ball. Octavius took off and was nearing first base before the ball began its descent. Seconds later, the centerfielder fully extended his glove and just barely caught the ball in full stride. The game was over. Octavius and his team had lost.

The opposing team rushed to the pitching mound to congratulate their pitcher and celebrate the victory. A few of them walked over to Octavius and his friends to gloat.

"Hey, Octavius. I thought you boys from the Institute could play some baseball."

"Yeah, well yaw can't even *spell* baseball," shouted Jacob.

"No need to argue. After all, it's only a game," said Jessie in a conciliatory tone.

"Only a game? Are you crazy? At least I hit the ball," yelled Octavius.

Jacob put his hand on Jessie's shoulder and said,

"Yeah, look who's talking; the great interrogator, *Mr. Are you kin to Ms. Douglass'* himself."

"Don't worry, you'll beat them next time," said Caroline.

"Yeah Caroline, but I really can't stand that Kevin and the rest of those Pythons."

"Pythons?"

"Yeah, that's the name of their lousy team."

"Well, what's the name of your team Octavius?"

"We don't have one."

"Hey, I've got it! *The Pythians.*"

"Say what?"

"Why the Pythians Caroline?"

"Surely you've read about Pythias, in Greek mythology. He supposedly killed the python; you know, the fabled serpent that guarded the sacred shrine on Mount Parnassus."

"That's right," said Jessie. "The Ancient Greeks started a festival and athletic competition called the Pythian Games. And, there was this group of mathematicians and philosophers known as the Pythagoreans who were famous for their faithful friendship to each other. And, then…"

Jacob interrupted him,

"Octavius, where did we ever find these two?"

"No, I kinda like it. *The Pythians.* Yeah, sort of like our gang; friends to the end!"

"You see, I am good for something," said Caroline.

"Yes and you're very easy on the eyes too."

Caroline smiled and asked,

"Is that all?"

"Of course not?"

There was a brief silence, deliberately meant to tease her.

"Well? What else?"

"Don't rush me, I'm thinking, I'm thinking…"

Caroline playfully elbowed him. As the boys laughed, the girls walked away in a mild huff.

Before then, Octavius and his friends would frequently refer to themselves as "the band of brothers". But now a new group identity had emerged. That fateful day in May marked the birth of *the Mighty Pythians;* a merry band of intrepid competitors who would claim victory on other days and in other fields of endeavor.

33. Growing Pains

"Men may combine to prevent cruelty to animals, for they are dumb and cannot speak for themselves; but we are men and must speak for ourselves, or we shall not be spoken for at all."

Frederick Douglass

In only three short years, Principal Reason had established the Institute as an outstanding preparatory school, particularly for students who aspired to become teachers. Public exhibitions and examinations generated interest among prominent Philadelphians and several visitors. The time had arrived when the Institute was ready to apply for full accreditation from the Pennsylvania Department of Instruction. Once again, Principal Reason chose Ms. Douglass' exceptional class to hear the news first.

"And now class, Principal Reason has a very special announcement to make. Please give him your full attention."

"Thank you Ms. Douglass. I have the most delightful news. On June 20th, one month from today, a State Accreditation team will visit us. These distinguished educators will be here to determine if the Institute for Colored Youth will be allowed to confer diplomas and teacher certificates authorized by the Commonwealth of Pennsylvania. Starting tomorrow, you will all begin drilling for your final examinations and your performance will form a significant part of our overall accreditation review."

"Well, then by all means, we shall be ready Mr. Reason. We shall be ready," said Ms. Douglass

Jacob whispered to Octavius,

"What did he say?"

"He said, it looks like we're going to be taking more time studying for tests and having less time for baseball."

"Why?"

"I guess if we don't, folks won't respect the kind of work we're doing here."

Their sidebar conversation drew the attention of Principal Reason.

"Mr. Catto, do you have something to say to the entire class?"

Instinctively, the veins in Ms. Douglass' head began to throb again. Octavius' classroom behavior was still erratic and his questions were always so unpredictable.

"No sir...I mean yes sir. I was wondering who our next guest lecturer will be this Friday."

"Well unfortunately, we don't have anyone secured yet, but I will keep trying and will keep your teachers apprised of my progress. Did you have any particular speakers in mind Mr. Catto?"

"What about Reverend Henry Highland Garnet, the famous abolitionist?"

"Well he's an excellent speaker, but I'm pretty sure he resides in upstate New York. Today is Tuesday and we don't have enough time to write to him and get a favorable response by Friday. Maybe we could get him at another time."

"Well it just so happens that he will be in Philadelphia tomorrow speaking to my Aunt Frances' Negro Women's Literary Society. Maybe she can talk him into coming to speak to us."

"Why of course. If she can do that, we'd be pleased to have him."

"Thank you sir."

"No, thank *you* Mr. Catto, and thank all of you young men and women. I know you will make us extremely proud next month."

As he left the classroom, Ms. Douglass continued with her lesson plan.

"Now class, where were we?"

"Yes, Ms. LeCount?"

"We were discussing the trial of Socrates. And you were saying that he was prosecuted for what he said and not for anything he did."

"Yes indeed so. But, what precisely were the charges brought against him? Jessie?"

"Well ma'am, in Plato's Apology it states that Socrates was an enemy of the state because he corrupted the youth and did not believe in the gods the state believed in, but in other spiritual beings. Now a similar account of those charges is offered by Xenophon in his Memorabilia and by Diogenes Laertius in his book, *Life of Socrates...*"

Octavius dropped his head on his desk in mockery of Jessie's long-winded answer to Ms. Douglass' simple question. Other students giggled too but Jessie rambled on, oblivious to their teasing.

"...The latter claims that Favorinus the historian, found the original preserved in the archives of Athens during the reign of Emperor Hadrian in the second century A.D. Then there are others who say..."

Jessie may not have been the most popular boy at the Institute. However, he was certainly Ms. Douglass' favorite, and for reasons that were entirely understandable.

∞∞∞∞∞∞∞∞∞∞

After delivering the news to all of the other classes, Principal Reason returned to his work. He greeted the secretary who was seated in his reception area and straightened the drawing of Benjamin Banneker that was hanging over the doorway to his private office.

"Good afternoon Miss Kearny. Any messages?"

"No messages sir. But Mr. Cope is waiting in your office."

"Thank you."

"Ah Mr. Cope it's a pleasure to see you."

"The pleasure is all mine dear friend. Now if thou wouldst give me a few minutes of thy time, I shall be brief in my interruption."

"By all means, what is it?"

"Mr. Reason…Ah…Charles, we are concerned about the upcoming accreditation review."

"Say no more. Our students and teachers will be ready. Our curriculum is sound and is in fact stronger than any other school in the city; and thanks to you, our library is superb, second to none."

"If thou wouldst indulge me. My concerns lay elsewhere – in the kind of outside speakers thou hast invited to speak before the students."

"I don't understand. Are you referring to last week's speaker, Mr. Douglass?"

"Indeed so."

"I don't get your meaning. Please tell me exactly what the problem is."

"We are very displeased with the militant tone of his discourse and his avocation of violence, even murder to achieve certain ends. Some of the members of our Arch Street Meeting were alarmed and I must say that I too questioned the wisdom of thine decision to invite him."

"I'm sorry; I don't recall Mr. Douglass advocating violence as a preferred means to any end. He is not a pacifist like you and the Society of Friends, and he is certainly not a moderate on the subject of slavery. He presented what I considered a lucid and compelling argument against slavery and its many atrocities. What's wrong with that?"

"Yes, but we do not think his references to the torture of slaves and the sexual defilement of slave women were appropriate subject matter for a speech; any speech."

"But tell me something Mr. Cope. What bothers you most? The fact that those atrocities have occurred and continue day after day or the fact that someone has the humanity and courage to speak out about them?"

"But his comments were hostile and obscene."

"No, I'll tell you what's obscene. The fact that this nation continues to ignore the suffering and total debasement of over three million Negroes who endure violent cruelty, justified and legitimized by established custom and the very law itself. That's what is obscene! And you all know that."

"Clearly, Charles thy thinking differs from ours. Thy way is not ours. But, consider this. The Institute is only provisionally accredited. Members of the accreditation team have been known to drop in on schools unannounced, well in advance of the team's formal visit. We can ill-afford to offend *their* sensitivities. Thou hast worked tirelessly to bring the Institute up to its current level. And we have been faithful in our efforts to recruit the very best Negro teachers in the entire country. Dost thou really want to jeopardize full accreditation and the future of this institution? We are on the verge of reaping the extraordinary fruits of our labor. We simply must win that accreditation. Will thoust at least think about what I'm saying?"

"I understand. And, I will take what you say under advisement."

"Fine, then I shall leave thee to thy plentiful duties. Good day to thee."

∞∞∞∞∞∞∞∞∞∞∞

That evening, Octavius paid a visit to his father's den before going to bed. Reverend Catto was sitting in his favorite winged back chair reading the Bible, as was his nightly habit.

"I just wanted to say goodnight Dad. I'm turning in early. Big day tomorrow."

"By the way son, I understand Reverend Garnet will be speaking at the Institute. I told your Aunt Frances that he's quite a firecracker. I'm really surprised the Quaker managers approved him as a speaker."

"Do you know him?"

"Not personally; but I have attended a few conventions where he spoke. My Lord, he does have a gift. I deeply respect his unapologetic crusade for immediate emancipation. You would do well to listen to what he has to say."

"Well, then why are you surprised that he's speaking tomorrow? Do you disapprove?"

"Not at all. It's just that I didn't think the Quakers would approve of his brand of honesty. He has a way of bringing the truth home, a way of telling it like it is. I thought that the managers would shy away from anyone as controversial as he is, particularly when you all are preparing for state accreditation."

"Who really cares about accreditation anyway? We have a great school with great teachers. And most of us are doing well in our studies. Who could ask for more?"

"It's not that simple Octavius. Listen to me. Shortly after we left South Carolina, there was a powerful Senator there by the name of John Calhoun. Today he is one of the influential men in Congress. I remember him telling the press, '**Show me a Negro who can conjugate a Greek verb, and I may reconsider my views on his innate intellectual inferiority.**' Can you imagine such ignorance; such arrogance? And I dare say, most of the people in this city aren't far ahead of him in their thinking. So it's important that the school be accredited. It's a form of legitimization; a way of proving to the John Calhouns of the world, that your educational accomplishments are just as valid as theirs. This accreditation review could really work in your favor."

"I see...So you think Reverend Garnet shouldn't speak tomorrow?"

"Well, I don't suppose you could un-invite him at this point son. I just hope that the folks in the audience can keep an open mind to what he's probably going to say. He speaks the plain, unvarnished truth."

"Sort of like David Walker, huh?"

"Yeah just like...(He interrupted himself). Say, that reminds me son; I have been meaning to ask you what you knew about David Walker and his Appeal. When Frederick Douglass spoke last week, you gave the distinct impression that you were familiar with Mr. Walker's book."

"I er...er...read it. You see, I er…"

"I know you read it and Aunt Ellen's letter too didn't you? I was planning to tell you about her tomorrow. Instead, you took it upon yourself to violate my privacy. You know you had no right to take things off my desk."

"Well, actually I didn't take them *off* your desk; I read them right there."

"Don't play word games with me boy! You were wrong and you know it! Don't you?"

"Yes sir."

"I'm your father. And as long as you're living under this roof, you will obey me, is that clear?"

"Yes sir. But can I ask you something?"

"What?"

"Why wouldn't you want me to read his book? Do you disagree with it? Shouldn't we be fighting to put an end to slavery now and forever?"

"Of course, it's just that I... I worry about you. I really worry about you in this sick city. There' so much hatred, so much senseless violence against the colored man; especially one who speaks up against injustice."

"I can handle myself."

"And so can Reverend Garnet. But, I bet you a day doesn't go by that he isn't attacked or threatened with life or limb. You know, he only has one good leg now. Listen to me. I love you son. Your mother loved you too...(tears welled up in his eyes). If somebody was to do something to you, I think I would, I would..."

"I know dad, I know. Listen, everything is going to be all right. We'll show those accreditation folks. We'll be ready. Wait till they see our class; and wait till they meet Jessie."

"Yeah, that Jessie. He's a handful alright," said Reverend Catto.

"Hey dad, I've got an idea. Why don't we cancel Reverend Garnet and invite ole Senator Calhoun instead. He and Jessie could debate. I betcha the fur would really fly that day!"

"Yeah and Calhoun would want to break *both* of Jessie's legs."

Father and son enjoyed a hearty laugh together. At last, Octavius had successfully lightened the mood.

"Good night dad."

"Good night son."

∞∞∞∞∞∞∞∞∞∞

The following morning, the auditorium of the Institute was again filled to capacity. In the back row, Mr. Cope and a few of the Quaker managers were talking amongst themselves when Mr. Cahill entered through a side door. He was the Chairman of the State Accreditation Board. Mr. Cope took notice and went to greet him.

"Why Mr. Cahill, 'tis a surprise to see thee with us today. Thou honor us with thy presence. But thou were not expected for three more weeks. Thou knoweth Mr. Emlen and our other brethren, I trust?"

"Yes. Well I do hope that this is not too much of an intrusion. But you will recall that I did give you ample notification that individual members of the visitation committee would be stopping by from time to time leading up to our formal visit."

"Yes indeed, thou spoke plainly on the matter."

Before they could finish their conversation, Principal Reason called the audience to order and introduced the distinguished speaker of the day, Reverend Henry Highland Garnet. His opening sentences foretold the content of his polemical speech. Already, some folks were becoming a bit uneasy—Mr. Cope in particular.

"George Bourne has said, every man who holds slaves and who pretends to be a Christian or a Republican is either an incurable idiot who cannot distinguish good from evil, or an obdurate sinner who resolutely defies every social, moral and divine requisition."

And with that preamble, he launched into a spellbinding oration without the benefit of any prepared notes.

"...Slavery! How much misery is comprehended in that single word? The diabolical injustice by which our liberties are cloven down, neither God, nor Angels or just men command us to suffer for a single moment."

Principal Reason looked back at the Quaker managers and Mr. Cahill in the rear. Their faces were twisted. Then he glanced over to

Octavius and his classmates. They were hanging on Reverend Garnet's every word.

Charles Sumner

"Just last week, a member of Congress, the Honorable Senator from Massachusetts, Charles Sumner gave a four-hour speech on the Senate floor. He entitled it *The Barbarism of Slavery.* In it, he clearly refutes the absurd claim that slavery is a beneficent institution, productive of a high civilization. In fact, he declared that a slave society was no civilization at all. He further states that, 'slavery is barbarous in origin, barbarous in its law; barbarous in all its pretensions; barbarous in the instruments it employs; barbarous in its consequences; barbarous in spirit; barbarous wherever it shows itself.' In essence, he concluded that slavery must breed barbarians!'

No, we do not excuse those barbarians who would brand the Negro like a mule, yoke him like an ox and constantly beat him like a brute; all this I remind you, in accordance with the law. By the license of legalized slavery, an entire race is delivered over to prostitution and concubinage, without the protection of any civilized law.

And shall I tell you what became of our friend, the great Senator from Massachusetts? Why he was beaten by a common thug, caned about the head in the hallowed halls of Congress! And, his attacker, one Preston Brooks was hailed as a hero of the South. I ask you, how could one expect truly civilized leaders to emerge from such a society? I say to you, the halls of justice have been transformed into a den of thieves!

Oh I beg of you, remember the stripes your father bore. Think of the torture and disgrace of your noble mothers. Think of your wretched sisters, loving virtue and purity, as they are driven into concubinage and are exposed to the unbridled lusts of incarnate devils. Think of the undying glory that hangs around the ancient name of Africa – and forget not that you are native-born American citizens and as such, you are justly entitled to all the rights that are granted to the freest."

At this point, some people in the audience were moved to tears.

"There are at this moment over three million slaves in the United States. Merciful God, what a vast number this is. Besides this number, there are more than half a million free men and women of color in the non-slaveholding states who have been prescribed by law, prosecuted, intimidated and abused by racial prejudice."

Octavius and some of the other boys leaned forward in their seats while Jessie sat erect, taking copious note. Twenty minutes later, Reverend Garnet concluded his discourse with a fiery flourish.

"...so I say to you, however much we may desire it, there is not much hope of emancipation without the shedding of blood. If we must bleed, let it all come at once-rather die freemen, than live as slaves. Let the word go forth, that we will reclaim our sacred liberties! And, if there be no speedy and peaceful emancipation, then let this nation prepare itself for bloody war. Let our motto be Resistance, Resistance, Resistance! No oppressed people have ever secured their liberty without resistance. And, brothers and sisters, resist you must. Trust in the Living God. Labor for the peace of the human race, but tell them and tell them at once, we are determined to be free!"

Rev. Henry Highland Garnet

At the conclusion, the audience erupted with thunderous applause. In the rear of the audience, Mr. Cahill sneered at the Quakers and hurried out of the auditorium. Outside the building, on the opposite side of the street, Boss Conley sat in his deluxe carriage and directed the movements of his henchmen who lied in ambush.

"Is McMullen in place yet?"

"Yeah Boss, but it's gonna be hard getting a shot off from where he is. He may have to wait until that nigger preacher comes outside."

"Wait my ass! He'll probably draw a crowd around him afterwards. Then it will be too late! We'd have to kill a dozen of those coons just to get to him. Not that I'm opposed to it. But who's gonna pay us for extra ammunition?"

The side door of the auditorium was wide open. McMullen waited behind it with his pistol drawn at his side. Reverend Garnet and his entourage were about to walk towards the exit, when behind McMullen stepped John Ansar followed by Uncle Blue. John discreetly pressed a pistol in his back.

"Feel that?"

"Yeah."

"Now lower that pistol and give it to that fine gentleman. Now take your left hand and wave at the good Reverend. No wave, like you really mean it!"

As McMullen waved along with several others, Reverend Garnet stepped into his carriage and rode safely away.

Meanwhile, Uncle Blue knelt down to tie both of McMullen's boot strings together with a triple knot.

"See that John, I done told ya them folks got rhythm. All they need is a little coaxing. Yep, look at him, a little nudge and he's a waving before ya can say Jack Robinson."

"Next time I see ya, I'm gonna slit your throats from ear to ear. I'll get you niggers next time," he snarled.

"What makes you think there's gonna be a next time? Blue, get the wagon," said John.

McMullen began to tremble and perspire. He looked into John's steely eyes and thought to himself that perhaps this time, he may have said too much.

∞∞∞∞∞∞∞∞∞∞

As anticipated, Reverend Garnet's speech was eloquent, straightforward and fueled by a deep passion in condemning the institution of slavery and those who actively or passively condoned it. Unfortunately, his controversial presentation served to deepen the divide between Principal Reason and the Quaker Board of Managers. Exactly three weeks later, Charles A. Reason resigned his post as Principal of the much-heralded Institute for Colored Youth. True to his meticulous nature, he announced that his resignation would be effective two days after the scheduled accreditation review. He was not the kind of man to leave things undone.

34. What Are You About?

"The great and glorious masterpiece of man is to know how to live to purpose."
Michel de Montaigne

"As each one has received a gift, minister it to one another, as good stewards of the manifold grace of God."
I Peter 4:10

Upon hearing a rumor about Principal Reason's impending resignation, the students delegated Octavius to confirm its veracity. On the last day of classes, Octavius went to the Principal's office alone.

"Ah, Octavius, it is good to see you. What can I do for you?"

"Well sir, I just wanted to know if it was true."

"Is what true?"

"They say you're resigning just as soon as we finish our examinations and you meet with the accreditation people. Is it true?"

"Yes, it's true."

"But why now? Just when it seems like everything is going our way. You said it yourself, there's not a high school in this whole city, colored, white or polka dot that can compete with us."

"Yes, and I still stand behind that statement. But, I've got some pressing family matters to attend to in New York."

"If you don't mind me saying so sir, they say you got into a big disagreement with the Board of Managers over Reverend Garnet's speech."

"Yes that too. But reasonable men can disagree. It's simply time for me to go. Can you understand that?"

"What I understand is that we have a right to free speech and the right to invite whomever we please to this school."

"True enough, but he who pays the piper calls the tune."

"Yeah, well it stinks!"

"Listen, there's nothing wrong with you students starting your own lecture series. I've told you many times, there's an ocean of learning that takes place outside of the classroom."

"You know something sir, you're right about that!"

"I get lucky sometimes."

"Yeah, we'll have *our own* lecture series and invite whomever we please. We'll start a debating club too. You know, talk about the things we want to talk about!"

"Splendid idea. And you're just the fella that can make it happen."

"Why do you say that?"

"It's obvious to me that the other boys look up to you – even the girls; that is when you're not busy taunting them. There's no question in my mind; you have great leadership potential. You have many talents that I hope you will cultivate as you grow and mature. I expect great things from you."

"To tell you the truth, I really don't care about greatness or anything like that."

"I know; that's what's going to make you a good leader."

∞∞∞∞∞∞∞∞∞

Despite the fallout regarding Mr. Garnet's speech, and Principal Reason's imminent departure, the students did exceedingly well on their examinations. As expected, Octavius excelled in the Latin readings and in oratory, while Jessie was cited with honors for extraordinary talent in the area of differential and integral calculus. It was a great day. Despite the review board's concerns about the school's "questionable lecture series", the Institute was accorded full accreditation. It was a pivotal victory for the school and the residents of the Seventh Ward.

Their happiness and excitement was doubled that same week when they got the news that a group of Presbyterians from Oxford County, led by John Miller Dickey was opening a school offering college level courses to young men of African decent. They named it the Ashmun Institute and later, Lincoln University, after the man who would become the sixteenth president of the United States. The school would go on to be the nation's first recognized colored university. Thus with the establishment of the Institute for Colored Youth and Lincoln University, Pennsylvania had the distinct honor of having two of the first institutions for higher learning ever established for Negro students.

And so it was, on January 1, 1854 on the anniversary of the kidnapping of Rachel Porter, John Miller Dickey dedicated the first building of the Ashmun Institute. Over the entrance way was placed the inscription "*The Night is far Spent, the Day is at Hand.*" It was also an occasion for them to solemnly remember the murder of his nephew, Joseph Miller, the man who risked his life to rescue little Rachel Porter. It would be long remembered as the time when Joseph Miller "chose sides with the angels."

∞∞∞∞∞∞∞∞∞∞

Meanwhile, back at the Institute, the students and faculty welcomed their new Principal, Mr. Ebenezer Bassett, an accomplished and well-known Negro scholar. He was educated at the Connecticut State Normal School and Yale College and had distinguished himself in a broad range of academic disciplines. Building on the solid academic foundations laid by Principal Reason, he expanded the curriculum, brought in additional teachers and successfully lobbied the Quaker Managers to finance a new and larger building at Ninth and Bainbridge Streets to accommodate more students. Skeptical at first, Octavius decided he would approach the new principal about his proposed extracurricular initiative. Three weeks into the semester, he knocked on the door of Mr. Bassett's office.

"Hello Mr. Catto, do come in. How may I be of service to you?"

"I've come to let you know that a group of us plan to start a lecture series and debating club of our own."

"Is that so? Do tell me more."

"Well sir, we aim to meet regularly to discuss matters of importance to the Negro race; to talk about current events with invited guests and lecturers."

"Well I think that's very commendable. But you know, we have already planned a schedule of speakers who will be visiting us starting in two weeks."

"Yes I know, but we prefer to have *our own* lecture series. Hey… I couldn't help but notice; you changed this room around didn't you?"

"Yes Mr. Catto. I trust you approve?"

"Doesn't matter to me sir. Well, anyway I thought I'd tell you about our debate club; even though we'll be meeting outside of this building."

"Well I certainly appreciate the notification. Maybe you'll invite me to one of your meetings some day."

"I suppose."

"By the way, what will your debating club be named?"

"I think we're fixed on *The Banneker Debating Society*. Incidentally, I mean, if you don't mind me asking sir, what happened to the picture of Benjamin Banneker out in the reception area? I liked it."

"I liked it too. Turn around."

Octavius turned around to see the picture hanging on the wall behind him, directly facing the principal's desk. He smiled broadly. It appeared that they were united in their great respect for Banneker.

"Yes, an act of blatant self-indulgence which I hope you all will not begrudge me. I draw such strength and encouragement from it."

"Not at all sir, not at all. Mr. Bassett, can I ask you something?"

"Of course, what is it?"

"Well...what do you think about baseball?"

"Baseball you say? Well, I've been known to take a swing or two."

"Really?"

"Yes, really."

∞∞∞∞∞∞∞∞∞

Saturday's weekly baseball game drew an unusually large crowd. Once again, Father Kendrick was asked to be the umpire. Several students and faculty showed up just to see if Principal Bassett had any particular athletic prowess. Strangely enough, he came to the park in his usual business attire and with his characteristic air of dignity and decorum. When it was his turn at bat, he removed his jacket and beckoned to Jacob White. Jacob took his jacket and neatly folded it over his forearm under the meticulous eye of his new principal.

Octavius batted before Principal Bassett and was on second base, cheering him on to get a hit. The first throw was low and outside. Octavius yelled at the pitcher,

"What's wrong Kevin? Scared to show the old man the ball?"

"I'll show you just how scared I am!"

The second pitch came right down the middle and over home plate. Principal Bassett swung and hit a towering home run. The crowd went wild as Octavius trotted around the bases and waited at home plate to congratulate Mr. Bassett. The game continued.

Off to the side on the playing field, Octavius and Principal Bassett sat alone under a weeping willow tree.

"I knew there was something I liked about you Mr. Bassett."

"Why thank you Octavius. I'm glad I meet with your approval."

"Yeah, with hitting like that, we just might make you an honorary member of the Pythians."

"I can only hope. (He paused) Octavius, tell me something?"

"Sure thing."

"Well son, just *what are you about?*"

"What do you mean?"

"I mean, what is your main purpose in life?"

"Well, I can't say I've thought about it much."

"But you must. Every man and woman is born *with* and *for* a purpose. You must continuously search for and determine what your purpose in life is – what it is that you were born to be and do on this earth. Without a true purpose, life's meaning is clouded. We see the world through other people's lenses and we never quite reach the fulfillment we seek."

"Well I think I'd like to be a teacher."

"That's good, we could surely need use more teachers. But a career is only one dimension of a life. Life is wide and deep. It is full of mystery and has meanings we must constantly explore. I happen to believe that we are put on this earth to do something more than acquiring things, something more significant than simply growing older. Life is like a coin that you can spend anyway you want. But you can only spend it once. That's why I am inclined to agree with Plato; the unexamined life is truly not worth living."

"I suppose you're right…. So what are *you* about Mr. Bassett?"

"Me? I'm about the elevation of our race. I'm about the business of serving humanity. I particularly want to teach our young people *how* to think, not necessarily *what* to think. I want them to be self-aware. I want to fling open the gateways to their minds! I want to provide them with a higher level of education that will make them free-thinkers, capable of leading, willing to serve, and impossible to enslave, ever again. I want to prepare them to do battle against the forces of ignorance, intolerance and injustice. Listen, I have to go. I'll see you in school Monday."

"Yeah, see ya."

When Principal Bassett left, Octavius remained seated under the tree. His eyes were on the game, but he seemed to be in deep reflection. Principal Bassett's unanticipated question and simple answer had the impact of a revelation. His words fell like tiny, but potent seeds that had fortuitously fallen on fertile ground. His counsel had implanted in Octavius' mind a clarion call to maturity and a subtle invitation to manhood.

Principal Bassett had effectively struck a psychological chord that would resonate in the depths of Octavius' soul for days and weeks following their conversation. Octavius would forever recall their encounter as an unmistakable turning point in his life. It marked the beginning of a lifelong determination to understand his place in the world and a fervent desire to contribute something to it. From that day forward, he knew he wanted his life truly to mean something. That was the first time that he began to wonder if his life might be directed by a wisdom greater than his own.

∞∞∞∞∞∞∞

Charles L. Reason   Ebenezer Bassett

The meandering waters of youthful curiosity and discovery run deep and often go unnoticed. Nevertheless, they are quickened by the flow of powerful ideas that can transform tiny streams and narrow rivulets into mighty torrents. Such is the way of abundant and ever-expanding life; such is the providential purpose of the rains.

35. John Brown's Raid

"Whereas slavery, throughout its entire existence in the United States is none other than a most barbarous, unprovoked and unjustified War of one portion of its citizens upon another portion; the only conditions of which are perpetual imprisonment, and hopeless servitude or absolute extermination; in utter disregard and violation of those eternal and self-evident truths set forth in our Declaration of Independence…"

John Brown

On Friday, another special meeting of the Vigilance Committee was called. The long awaited decision in the Dred Scott case had been rendered by the United States Supreme Court. Dred Scott was a slave who sued for his freedom on the grounds that when his master transported him to a free territory, he was no longer a slave. This was the verdict the whole nation waited for with great anticipation. The Negro populace had hoped that it would be an answer to their prayers. It was not. Reverend Catto read the disheartening news.

"Well, it says here that in separate opinions, a majority of the Supreme Court held that Scott didn't even have the right to file suit in the state or federal court, because he was not a citizen of the United States."

Several committee members shouted with outrage and swooned with expressions of disgust and disappointment.

"That's preposterous!" yelled Robert Purvis. "How can we be denied the right to appeal to the highest court in the land?"

"Well Robert, it says here that Justice Curtis of Massachusetts dissented by pointing out that Negroes had in fact voted in five states, as early as 1776 when this nation was founded. Therefore, we had to have been citizens from the very beginning. But, it didn't seem to matter to the others. So much for justice. Well, that's that."

"No it isn't, read the rest of it Reverend," shouted Uncle Blue.

"Well let's see. Oh yeah here it is. It says that the Chief Justice of the Supreme Court of the United States offered a lengthy opinion on the case. In it, he concluded that, **"the right of property in a slave is distinctly and expressly affirmed by the Constitution."** He further added that Negroes could never be considered citizens of the United States and thus do not have a right to sue in federal court."

"Go on…read the rest of it!" insisted Uncle Blue.

"It says …in the opinion he filed with the Court, Chief Justice Roger B. Taney declared that **'the Negro is so inferior, that they**

have no rights which the white man is bound to respect.' And, that's a quote!"

Dred Scott   **Justice Roger B. Taney**

The year was 1857. It was the first time in over ten years, that they disbanded a meeting with no subsequent discussion. The members were all shocked by the chilling verdict and sickened by the thought of its broad implications. Justice Taney's vicious and stinging pronouncement left them in stunned disbelief and total disillusionment. It removed all doubt concerning the government's official position on slavery and its perception of the Negro's citizenship rights. For the first time in his life, Mr. Still began to wonder if their allegiance to the government was foolhardy. After all, if the Supreme Court did not uphold the basic rights of colored people, the laws of the land surely did not *apply* them. And, if those laws did not apply to them, to whom and to what did they owe their allegiance?

While they were initially disheartened by the verdict, it did however serve one useful purpose. Thereafter, it began to intensify Negro solidarity. Even with the legal sanctions imposed by the Fugitive Slave Act, more and more Negro families began to volunteer their support the Underground. In a very deep way, the Dred Scott decision had a unifying effect. It made them feel like all they had was each other.

In the ensuing two years, the collective will of the Seventh Ward was considerably strengthened as its residents vowed to fight to the end, any and all attempts to displace, dishonor and demoralize them. In a broader sense, it sent a clear and undeniable message to the Negro that even though he was *in* America, he was not *of* it. The political veils had been lifted, revealing the ugly intent of those who were determined to squash any and all claims for full Negro citizenship and equal protection under the law.

Against this darkening national backdrop, the Institute for Colored Youth stood as a lighthouse in a raging sea, a beacon of hope. In a city where most colored children were taught in shamefully deficient segregated public schools, the Institute had emerged as an indisputable flagship school; the pride of the community. The success of the Institute reinforced their opinion that there was no power of earth that could defeat any group of colored people who were committed to one another and fused together by high moral purpose.

By 1859, the Institute had graduated two full classes. In September of that year, Octavius Catto and Caroline LeCount joined the faculty of the Preparatory Department, teaching the lower grades at first. Jessie Glasgow had the exceptionally good fortune to receive a full scholarship to pursue advanced studies in mathematics at the University of Edinboro in Scotland. The Quakers planned to ask him to lead the Institute's mathematics department upon completion of his studies. Jacob White was also cited as a potential faculty recruit for the Institute, but he accepted a post as the youngest colored teacher in the Philadelphia public schools.

The Quaker managers were particularly interested in grooming Octavius for a future leadership role in the Institute. This pleased his father greatly as well as those who had watched him develop into a dynamic educator. Octavius had a pleasant, yet forceful voice and a very persuasive manner. His reputation as a gifted orator became widespread and he soon became a frequent speaker at various civic functions and educational meetings. In recognition of his ability, the Quaker managers asked him to be the keynote speaker for the fall convocation ceremony. It was for him, a significant honor and a welcomed task that he did not take lightly.

As he walked to the podium, his countenance was brimming with confidence and his posture was relaxed but at the same time, authoritative.

"...and so I ask you young men and women, *what are you about?* What shall be your guiding principles, your chief preoccupation in life? After all, is every featherless biped to be counted a man and a brother? No! I say to you it is purpose, noble purpose that makes us men and women and binds us together in the pursuit of the greatest good and the least suffering of humanity. Tell me, show me, through your thought and actions, where is your North Star, *what are you about?"*

In the rear of the auditorium, Principal Bassett and Reverend Catto sat together. Not a word passed between them. They sat in silence, marveling in admiration at the man Octavius had become. After the convocation ceremony, all incoming students were all invited to the teacher's lounge for refreshments and fellowship. The mood was upbeat and celebratory as the freshman class introduced themselves and began being indoctrinated into the ethos and atmosphere of high expectation and achievement that had characterized the Institute since its inception.

Jessie Glasgow was still away studying in Scotland and could not attend the festivities. However, he sent a letter of salutation. In addition, Octavius read a short letter from Ellen Craft. She and William had met Jessie in London and were his "fireplace and blanket" in the cold atmospheric and rigid social climate of England. The letter read:

"Dear Octavius:
I am so pleased that you and your new 'friend' Caroline are fulfilling your commitments to teach. By the way, we recently had Jessie over for supper. He is an amiable and intelligent young man, but I must say, a bit talkative. Your Uncle William has invited him over for Sunday brunch this week. He looked a little thin to me so I suppose we will have to fatten him up. Fond regards,
Aunt Ellen."

When Octavius finished reading the letter, Jacob immediately quipped,

"Yeah, that's the best thing for ole Jessie. Keep his mouth full of food so you don't have to listen to his incessant chatter."

∞∞∞∞∞∞∞∞∞∞

However, the gaiety of that moment did not last for long. The next day, the Institute's students and faculty learned of John Brown's raid in West Virginia. On October 16, Brown, a fiercely devoted white abolitionist, tried to seize a United States arsenal and armory at Harper's Ferry in an effort to free the slaves by armed insurrection.

The mission failed and Brown was arrested and sentenced to death. Ten of his men, including two of his sons were killed in the ill-fated attempt. However, with the assistance of Mr. Still and Harriet Tubman, five of his men managed to escape.

Even though the raid was unsuccessful, it focused the nation's attention on the escalating issue of slavery. In this regard, most abolitionists believed that the raid on Harper's Ferry was not a vain undertaking. On the day of Brown's public execution, Henry David Thoreau wrote, **"This morning, Captain Brown was hung. He is not Old Brown any longer; he is an angel of light"**. In Boston, Ralph Waldo Emerson hailed him as a new saint whose martyrdom **"will make the gallows as glorious as the Cross."**

John Brown

Yet Philadelphians reacted to John Brown's raid in polarizing ways that openly revealed their strong and radically different opinions about the future of slavery in America. Many, if not most white Philadelphians reacted in anger and indignation towards the city's mounting abolitionist movement. They immediately began to hang banners and streamers from ships, hotels and public buildings throughout the city proclaiming:
"Union Forever! Pennsylvania Greets its Sister State Virginia."
These banners announced the city's solid support for the pro-slavery South and its fuming animosity toward abolitionists. Five day's after John Brown's execution, they held a "union meeting" and rally near Independence Hall to proclaim and promulgate their views. A

strong anti-abolitionist song was composed that captured their angry sentiments.

> **"The South shall have her rights- O'er her**
> **Our eagle spreads its wings-**
> **The treason plotters, brown or white,**
> **Shall on the gallows swing."**

This rally called for the killing of all *"abolitionists of the John Brown stamp."* Various speakers like Henry M. Fuller stirred the crowd with a vigorous defense of slavery and its continuance. He stridently explained:

> **"Slavery is a fact. We are not responsible for it; the people of the south are not responsible for it. It was brought here before the Union was born. A mysterious Providence has cast upon this continent two races, distinct in origin, character and color."**

In sharp contrast, the execution of John Brown and his men also prompted a display of interracial solidarity that had not been seen in a long time. In several Northern cities, candlelight vigils and church services brought whites and Negroes together in commemoration of his valiant sacrifice. A few weeks after the "union meeting" in Philadelphia, Octavius led the Institute students in a candlelight vigil at Mother Bethel Church. Mrs. Brown, John Brown's widow, was invited to speak about her husband and the meaning of his sacrifice. Trembling and with tearful eyes, her voice cracked as she struggled to suppress her emotions.

"…Yes, my husband had unflinchingly declared war on slavery. His commitment to immediate emancipation and atonement was an all-consuming passion. It was after all, his destiny. I have in my possession a letter from my husband, delivered to me by a United States marshal. Let me read to you a brief excerpt. In it, he says:

> **"I John Brown am now quite certain that the crimes of**
> **this guilty land will never be purged away but with blood.**
> **I had as I now think vainly flattered myself that without**
> **very much bloodshed it might be done. I believe that to**

have interfered as I have done – as I always freely admitted I have done – on behalf of God's despised poor, was not wrong but right. Now if it is deemed necessary that I should forfeit my life for the furtherance of the ends of justice, and mingle my blood with the blood of millions in this slave country whose rights are discarded by wicked, cruel and unjust enactments – I submit; so let it be done."

She became overtaken by grief and could not continue, so Reverend Catto gently escorted her to her seat. Next, he called upon Mrs. Copeland to speak. She was the mother of John Copeland, a young colored man who went to his death along with John Brown.

"We will now hear from a mother who lost her son during the raid at Harper's Ferry".

Mrs. Copeland was assisted to the podium by her elderly husband. She too was choked with emotion and found it difficult to speak.

"…Well, all I can say is my son is gone now…And there isn't much we can do about that but remember him the way he wanted to be remembered and keep working for a cause he sacrificed for. He wrote us this letter, just an hour before his execution. In it, he says:

"…my fate so far as man can seal it, is sealed. But, let not this fact occasion you any misery…for remember the cause in which I was engaged; remember it was a holy cause, one in which men, in every way better than I am, have suffered and died. Goodbye Mother and Father, tell my brothers and sisters to love one another, make each other happy, love, serve and obey your God and meet me in heaven."

John Copeland

And with those last words, she staggered and fell into her husband's arms.

The evening's event concluded with a speech by Frances Harper. She began her presentation by reading aloud a poem she had written to one of John Brown's men who was awaiting execution for his role in the Harper's Ferry insurrection. It read as follows:

> **"Make me a grave where'er you will,**
> **In a lowly plain or a lofty hill;**
> **Make it among earth's humblest graves,**
> **But not in a land where men are slaves.**
>
> **I could not rest, if around my grave**
> **I heard the steps of a trembling slave;**
> **His shadow above my silent tomb**
> **Would make it a place of fearful gloom.**
>
> **I could not sleep, if I heard the tread**
> **Of a coffle-gang to the shambles led,**
> **And the mother's shriek of wild despair**
> **Rise, like a curse, on the trembling air.**
>
> **I could not rest, if I saw the lash**
> **Drinking her blood at each fearful gash;**
> **And I saw her babies torn from her breast,**

Like trembling doves from the parent nest.

I'd shudder and start, if I heard the bay
Of a bloodhound seizing his human prey,
And I heard the captive plead in vain,
As they bound afresh, his galling chain.

If I saw young girls from their mothers arms
Battered and sold for their youthful charms,
My eye would flash with a mournful flame,
My death-pale cheek grow red with shame.

I would sleep, dear friends, where bloated Might
Can rob no man of his dearest right;
My rest shall be calm in any grave
Where none can call his brother a slave.
I ask no monument, proud and high,
To arrest the gaze of the passers by,
All that my yearning spirit craves
Is—Bury me not in a land of slaves!"

The rest of her speech was equally poignant and electrifying in its impact on the large audience. So ended an evening of reverent remembrance and somber reflection. Philadelphians of all races and creeds joined the nation in contemplating the meaning of John Brown's insurrection. The fate of the entire nation was in question and anxious hearts and minds worried about what the future held in store. Emotions ran deep as America precariously stood on the edge of the unknown.

∞∞∞∞∞∞∞∞∞

The next day, Mr. Still and John Ansar met at the Catto home to discuss logistical assignments for the week. Seven refugees from Petersburg, Virginia were expected on Friday. All of the safe houses were filled to capacity, so makeshift accommodations had to be made for them in the cellar of Mr. Abrams' store. Harriet Tubman was distracted and did not seem quite ready to discuss the business at hand. Apparently, she was still grieving over the loss of life during the Harper's Ferry incident.

"Ya know, we got five of' em out. But, couldn't save dat Copeland boy. Dey got to him fo we could. Dem other boys should be half way to Canada by now."

"I know you did the best you could Aunt Harriet," said Octavius.

"The Copeland boy, where did he come from?" asked Reverend Catto.

"Don't know fer sher. I think Kentucky. Ya know, dat boy was sumptin' special. He was as smart as a whip. Dey say he even went ta some fancy school in Ohio."

"Oberlin?" Mr. Still asked.

"Of course *ober land*, ya didn't 'spect him ta fly did ya?"

After a few seconds of silence, they all roared with laughter at Harriet's innocent comment.

"No Harriet, *Oberlin College*, in Oberlin, Ohio", he explained.

"How on earth was I ta understand ya Still when ya sittin' up thar wid ya mouth full of food."

Uncle Blue playfully interjected. He never seemed to resist the temptation to tease her.

"Aw come on Harriet, no need to get upset. You always been the apple of my eye, but ya really need to learn how to enunciate."

"Oh yeah? Well we'll see how much you can eenun-sate when I knock da lidda bit a teeth you got outta ya mouth. Ya ole toothless tiger! You sho is a peeble in my boot!"

"You tell him Aunt Harriet!" said Octavius, laughing out loud.

Reverend Catto thought it best to change the subject. He clearly sensed Harriet's anguish and shared her pain.

"Speaking of *special boys*, I wonder how Jessie is making out in London. I received this letter from Ellen and William today. But, I haven't had time to read it. That Jessie; he's probably talked them to death and eaten them out of house and home."

They all chuckled as he opened the letter and started reading it silently while they watched. His smile suddenly disappeared and a grim pallor spread across his face.

"What's wrong? What does it say?" asked Mr. Still.

Reverend Catto could hardly speak. He gulped once, twice and finally summoned the strength to read it as best he could.

"Dear Reverend Catto:

I regret to inform you that Jessie Glasgow is dead. He died of pneumonia two days ago. The doctors tried to save him, but to no avail."

He stopped reading and lowered the letter to the table.

"It can't be true!" shouted Octavius.

He grabbed the letter and read aloud the rest of it.

"Fortunately, we were with him in his final hours. He asked us to send all of his books to the Institute. You should receive them via parcel post. But, he expressly asked that his volume on Greek mythology be delivered to Octavius. I can't be sure, but he seemed to mutter something about a victory a final victory for the Pythians. Perhaps Octavius will know what he meant."

Octavius dropped the letter and stormed out of the room. The others remained seated while Harriet left the table and ran after him.

"Let me talk to him."

She followed Octavius up to his bedroom, where he was pounding the walls and throwing his books around in a fit of rage.

"Octavius?"

"Leave me alone Aunt Harriet! I don't want to talk!"

"Now you jest simma down boy, ya hear me?"

"I don't understand. I don't understand anything anymore! Copeland, now Jessie. Why God? Why? "

"Octavius!"

"What? What is it? Why won't you leave me alone?"

"Oh, I'll leave ya alone all right. But, first ansa dis fo me. Is God dead?"

"What did you say?"

"Ya heard what I said. I axed ya, is God dead?"

"What are you talking about?"

"Well, if God ain't dead, den we gotta lot more ta do. And we best buck up. Ya hear me; buck up! Cause dere's gonna be mo death and mo blood spilt fo it's all over. And we ain't got no choice but ta keep on fighting. Matta' of fact, I think we's gonna have a war!"

"But Jessie, why Jessie? He never did anything wrong. He had his whole life in front of him!"

"Honey, nobody knows where or when dey's gonna die. But remember what I always told ya. Ain't none of us getting outta dis life alive. We all gonna be called from our labors at some point. Nobody knows when and nobody knows why. So we best keep on keeping on."

Octavius calmed himself for a moment and sat down on his bed. Harriet took a seat beside him.

"Do you really think there's going to be war Aunt Harriet?"

"Yep, after ole John Brown, I feel it in my bones. Dem Southern boys is arming demselves to da teeth. And, da Norf is standing firm."

"I think you're right. I read where Governor Seward is prepared to run for the Presidency. He thinks we're headed for a Civil War. He called it the *irrepressible conflict*."

"Well, I don't spect I know what dat means. But mark my words, we gonna have us a big scrap. I knows that much. And you gotta be ready ta do yo part. Ya hear me? Dere's gonna be war, and we's gonna git our freedom and git it soon."

"You are a beautiful woman," he said as he hugged her.

"Yeah chile, I was quite a looker back in my day."

∞∞∞∞∞∞∞∞∞

Aunt Harriet was all too right. After John Brown's raid, it became increasingly clear that slavery would not be abolished through moral suasion alone. The nation was being torn asunder by sectional differences that could not be reconciled. Tensions escalated and unretractable moral battle lines were being drawn. The political handwriting was on the wall. The issue of slavery, in all likelihood, would have to be settled by blood—and by iron. The skies were darkening and there was little doubt that a hard and heavy rain was about to fall.

36. War!

"Let the word go forth, that we will reclaim our sacred liberties! And, if there be no speedy and peaceful emancipation, then let this nation prepare itself for bloody war."

Henry Highland Garnet

"We must throw aside unpleasant memories of the past and look to the future. Let us show them our willingness and readiness to defend the Union. Such is the government, my brave bothers, you are called upon to uphold with your arms. Such is the government that you are called upon to cooperate with in burying the Southern rebellion and slavery itself, in one common grave."

Frederick Douglass

A dense fog began to roll in and dark clouds continued to thicken on the horizon. War, true to its nature, did not arrive in an instant. It came as a gradual building up of thunder.

In May 1860, the Republican Convention passed over the more popular William H. Seward, and nominated the lesser-known candidate, Abraham Lincoln as their presidential nominee. Lincoln won the election amidst growing tensions that the Southern states might decide to secede from the Union.

On February 22, 1861, President Lincoln stopped in Philadelphia on his inaugural journey to Washington, D.C. He chose Independence Hall as the most appropriate place to deliver these somber words. They truly foreshadowed the fate of his troubled presidency.

"… I have never had a feeling politically that did not spring from the sentiments embodied in the Declaration of Independence. I have often pondered over the toils that were endured by the officers and soldiers of the army who achieved that Independence. I have often inquired of myself what great principle of idea it was that kept this Confederacy so long together. It was not the mere matter of the separation of the Colonies from the motherland; but that sentiment in the Declaration of Independence which gave us liberty, not alone to the people of this country, but, I hope, to the world, for all future time. It was that which gave promise that in due time the weight would be lifted from the shoulders of all men. This is a sentiment embodied in the Declaration of Independence. Now my friends, can this country be saved upon this basis? If it can, I will consider myself one of the

happiest men in the world, if I can help to save it. If it cannot be saved upon that principle, it will be truly awful. But, if this country cannot be saved without giving up that principle, I was about to say I would rather be assassinated on this spot than surrender it...."

∞∞∞∞∞∞∞∞

A few months later, the country was at war; *with itself.* On April 12, 1861, confederate cannons fired on Fort Sumter, a federally controlled garrison in South Carolina. On July 4, President Lincoln called a special session of Congress to declare war on those confederate states that decided to secede from the Union.

Then came the Battle of Antietam in September 1862. It was to be the bloodiest one-day battle of the war. General Robert E. Lee and his Confederate troops boldly attempted an invasion of the North. However, they were repelled by Union General, George McClellan and his Army of the Potomac. It was a costly confrontation. The Union suffered over 12,000 casualties and deaths. The war was at a fever pitch and its outcome was uncertain to say the very least.

That same year, a group of Philadelphia's prominent businessmen, lawyers and civic leaders established the Union League to demonstrate their solidarity with President Lincoln's administration and reinforce the city's support for the war. But here again, not all Philadelphians were of like mind. In 1862, with the war raging on, Pennsylvania's Democrats held a convention to proclaim their firm belief that America was **"a government of white men, and was established exclusively for the white race."** They further speculated that Lincoln's party would **"turn the slaves of southern states loose to overrun the North and enter into competition with the white laboring masses, thus degrading and insulting their manhood by placing them on an equality with Negroes."**

Shortly thereafter came the Day of Jubilee; a day most colored people referred to as the "Coming of the Lord!" Effective January 1, 1863, President Lincoln issued his Emancipation Proclamation stating that all slaves residing in any rebellious State would be **"then and thence forward and forever free."** This bold decision enraged Philadelphia's Democrats. A week later, a "Central Democratic Club" was formed and drafted a constitution that began with a bold preamble announcing its political and ideological convictions. It read:

" That in the State of Pennsylvania all power is inherent in the WHITE PEOPLE and that our government is founded on THEIR authority...and that the FREE INSTITUTIONS established by our Revolutionary Fathers were committed to the charge of the white race; and that all attempts, directly or indirectly, on the part of the Federal Government to frustrate this intention, or change the relative status of the superior white, and inferior black races... are subversive of the original design."

Nonetheless, Lincoln's controversial proclamation held sway and in the Seventh Ward, there were massive celebrations and dancing in the streets. Slavery may have been abolished, but the fight for political freedoms and social equality before the law was far from over. Informed Negro citizens were alarmed and infuriated by the Democratic Party's grim pronouncements. The Vigilance Committee met to discuss these new developments and somberly discuss the meaning of it all.

Mr. Still was the most skeptical. Robert Purvis was more optimistic; bordering on ecstatic. They had very strong opinions and inadvertently engaged in a one-on-one debate that captured the full range of Negro political opinion on the matter.

"The *Great Emancipator* my foot! Back in '58 when he was Senator Lincoln, he openly stated that, **as wrong as slavery is, we can afford to leave it where it is.** And that's a quote!" said Mr. Still.

"So what, he's a moderate," responded Mr. Purvis. "But look at it this way. He did not have the power to free the slaves except as a necessity of war. It should not matter what his motives were. It was a shrewd move on his part. It was designed to induce the majority of slaves living in the Confederates Sates to defect. It breaks the back of the southern confederacy and deprives those states of their main labor force. I say it was a brilliant military strategy. And, it works to our advantage; you can at least acknowledge that."

"Well then tell me this Mr. Purvis, why does the Proclamation contain the proviso that gives the rebel states a hundred days to rejoin the Union *with their slavery laws intact*? You all can celebrate if you want, but a lot of things can happen in a hundred days. It's so obvious, the proclamation was merely a military decree directed at those states that are at war with the Union. Who does he think he's fooling? He had no jurisdiction over those states. He doesn't give a damn about slavery or us! His only concern is to preserve the Union at all cost."

∞∞∞∞∞∞∞∞∞∞

Whatever President Lincoln's motives may have been, it was clear that most of the colored community supported him and the war effort. In June 1863, General Lee's army moved northward toward a climatic showdown with the Union army near Gettysburg, Pennsylvania. In response, Governor Andrew Curtin and Philadelphia's new Mayor, Alexander Henry moved to reinforce the state's militia. Negro recruitment into the Union Army had been previously denied beginning in 1861. Denied admission to the army in Pennsylvania, about three hundred of Philadelphia's colored citizens enlisted in Massachusetts regiments. In fact, one company of the celebrated Massachusetts Fifty-Fourth Regiment was comprised of colored Philadelphians. This was the regiment that would soon gain national recognition after its courageous attack on Fort Wagner on July 18, under the command of Colonel Robert Shaw.

Faced with the looming threat of a Confederate invasion, Pennsylvania and the nation (as a whole) now seemed willing to accept Negro recruitment into the Union Army. Principal Bassett set up an enlistment office in the Institute for the purpose of recruiting Negro volunteers. Frederick Douglass visited the city to lend his support for the Negro recruitment effort. The local white and colored press spoke directly to this need; but not without mentioning the hostile treatment of colored citizens throughout the city and the nation. A patriotic article in the Philadelphia Ledger noted:

"We, the colored people of Philadelphia, throwing aside the unpleasant memories of the past, looking only to the future, and asking merely the same guarantees, the same open field and fair play that are given our white fellow-countrymen, desire here and now to express our willingness and readiness to come forward in the defense of our imperiled country."

Negro Recruitment Poster

As expected, Pennsylvania was especially prominent in its recruitment of colored enlistees, even though they were to be paid less than white volunteers. Pennsylvania raised eleven colored regiments of about one thousand men. Moreover, eight of these regiments were from Philadelphia. To no one's surprise, Octavius was among the first to volunteer and was chosen to lead the newly formed company of ninety volunteers who were leaving to go off and fight General Lee's Confederate army.

Outside Penn Station in West Philadelphia, a company of colored men prepared to board the train to Harrisburg. A huge crowd gathered to joyfully send them off. Principal Bassett also came to offer some parting words of encouragement to the new Negro recruits.

Mr. Still went with Reverend Catto, Father Kendrick, and Uncle Blue to help send Octavius on his way. Bassett spoke first.

"...My brothers, understand that events more mighty then men, eternal Providence, all-wise and all-controlling, have placed us in new relations to the government and the government to us..."

Octavius listened intently to his mentor's moving speech. After hugging his father and Father Kendrick, he turned to Caroline LeCount who had already started to cry.

"You make sure you come back in one piece," she whimpered, with her head pressed to his chest.

"Don't cry. I'll write to you everyday, okay?"

"You better," she sobbed.

Uncle Blue stepped forward.

"Well boy, you best be getting on that train. But, I want ya to remember what I taught ya. *Those that bite?*"

"*Shall be bitten!*" came Octavius' response

"*And those that don't bite?*"

"*Shall get et up!*" Octavius answered.

"I love you boy."

Then Harriet Tubman approached and nudged Uncle Blue out of her way.

"Step aside ole man and let me give my baby a hug and a squeeze."

"Well Aunt Harriet, I guess this is it."

"Yep. I reckon so."

"I guess with Emancipation, you'll be moving into a new line of work. Its time to let us younger folks see what we can do."

"Chile please. I done already got me a *new* job!"

"Oh yeah?"

"Yeah, starting tommora, I'm going ta be a spy fer da Union army. Working wid some man named General Meade."

"That's incredible. You mean to tell me you're going to provide *reconnaissance* for General George Meade?"

"No baby, just plain ole sense. I aim ta give him a lotta info, ya know; gonna let em know what dem rebs are up to. Dat's fer sho."

Octavius shook his head and gave her another big hug.

∞∞∞∞∞∞∞∞∞∞

The crowd applauded as the men boarded the train. A neighborhood troop of drummers and fifers began to play, as the large crowd cheered until the caboose slowly disappeared from sight. Watching from a third floor window of City Hall, the Mayor shared his thoughts with Boss Conley.

"Do you believe it? That's just what this country needs; a bunch of nigs marching around with rifles and bayonets; wearing the uniform of the United States government! What's this world coming to Connie?"

"I tell ya what Mr. Mayor. If General Wagner ever asked me to wear a uniform and inspect any group of niggers, he'd have my resignation lickety split!"

"Yeah, you're sure as hell right about that. It isn't natural. I don't believe the Almighty ever intended a Negro to be put on a par with the white man."

"You can say that again, Mr. Mayor. You can say that again!"

∞∞∞∞∞∞∞∞∞

Unfortunately, the excitement of Octavius and his men would soon turn to disillusionment. Upon reaching the State Capitol in Harrisburg, Governor Curtin completely reversed his position. Inside the Governor's private office, a heated discussion was in progress.

"Damn it Major Couch, you all didn't tell me they were a *colored* troop! Jesus, Joseph, and Mary, what do I pay you people for? I'll tell you this, as long as I'm Governor, no Negro troops will cross this border. Do I make myself clear?"

"But Governor, they have already been fully mustered and issued orders? What do we do now?"

"Well you better damn well think of something!"

They all paused for a moment of reflection. Then Crouch spoke.

"Well Governor, as Commander of the Susquehanna area, I suppose I can refuse to induct them. It seems to me that there's a loophole here. The Congressional mandate provides for the enlistment of Negroes for not less than three years. This company of coons is technically speaking an emergency militia unit enlisted for limited services of a few months. In effect, the law says that they cannot serve unless we truly need them. You see, we have the legal option to send them all home."

Within a few hours, that is precisely what they did.

∞∞∞∞∞∞∞∞∞

Needless to say, the colored community was outraged by this indignity. A mass rally was held in Franklin Hall to protest the shabby treatment of Octavius and his troops. The rally produced several resolutions and led to a legal appeal that was intended to overturn Major Couch's racist ruling. Meanwhile, Octavius and his men returned to Philadelphia totally rebuffed. They yearned for combat and continued their daily training as members of the First Division of General Louis Wagner's Pennsylvania Reserve Guard that was stationed at Camp William Penn, just eight miles from the city. Their training lasted eight hours a day and six days a week. And despite all indications to the contrary, they remained a patriotic band of ready warriors waiting and hoping for an opportunity to serve.

Colored Troops at Camp William Penn

Their anger and frustration were greatly intensified when they learned about the Massacre at Fort Pillow on April 12, 1864, just north of Memphis, Tennessee. The United States War Department had accused the Confederate Army of deliberately killing over three hundred Negro soldiers at the fort, *after* they had peacefully surrendered.

Yet, when it was all said and done, Octavius' desire to engage in combat would not be fulfilled. Nine months into his training, he was ordered to see General Wagner. He briskly knocked on his door.

"Come in."

"You sent for me sir?"

"At ease Catto. I have some bad news for you. Have a seat."

"Yes sir."

"You know, I have the utmost respect for you and your abilities. The men of the fifth brigade consider you a capable and conscientious officer."

"Thank you sir, but if it's all the same to you, I think I'd rather have that bad news you referred to."

"Well, simply put, it doesn't look like we're going to see any action. I just received orders to permanently disband this entire brigade. There's even talk that the rebels are thinking about surrendering."

"Yes, I've heard that too sir."

"I know you feel snubbed and this is a great disappointment to you; but you have so many other talents. You know, I have never bought into the notion that one's willingness to take another man's life is any proof of his manhood. It seems to me that you could do a world of good for your people right here in Philadelphia. This city is growing like topsy. We are going to need some solid civic leadership or it is bound to blow up like a keg of gunpowder. And, then there's that school you're affiliated with. Surely they must need you."

"Is that all sir?"

"Yes, that's all. Good luck to you."

"You too sir."

∞∞∞∞∞∞∞∞∞∞

Three days later, Octavius moved back home and reported to work at the Institute. Principal Bassett was pleased to have him return to the faculty.

"It's good to have you back Octavius. There's a certain lady in our Preparatory Department who missed you something awful. At least that's what they tell me."

"It's good to be back. How's the school's baseball team doing?"

"Well, they're not as good as the Pythians, but they can hold their own. Say, just in case you haven't heard, I have re-activated the lecture series. We've got some pretty dynamic speakers coming in."

"That's great; some of my fondest memories as a student were of those lectures. Our students need that kind of inspiration and direction."

"Oh, and by the way, a group of us are meeting tonight at seven o'clock in Franklin Hall to talk about political events going on in the city. It would be a good opportunity for you to get caught up on things. Are you up for it?"

"Sure thing. I'll be there."

On March 4, 1865, President Lincoln delivered his second inaugural address. It was a short and somber speech that ended with a heartfelt appeal for national reconciliation and unity.

"...With malice toward none; with charity for all; with firmness in the right, as God gives us to see the right, let us strive on to finish the work we are in; to bind up the nation's wounds; to care for him who shall have borne the battle, and for his widow, and his orphan – to do all which may achieve and cherish a just and a lasting peace, among ourselves, and with all nations."

Victory for the Union Army would be achieved four weeks later. In April 1865, General Robert E. Lee surrendered to General Ulysses S. Grant at a little courthouse in Appomattox, Virginia. The bloody and costly Civil War had come to an end. President Lincoln immediately rallied his administrative cabinet and scores of advisors to help plan for the sweeping reconstruction of the south and the re-unification of a bitterly divided nation.

Then came that horribly unforgettable day. A week later, the country was stunned to hear of President Lincoln's assassination while he was attending a play at Ford's Theater. He was shot in the head by John Wilkes Booth, an apparent southern sympathizer. With an eerie sense of irony and predestination, Philadelphians recalled their beloved President's visit to Independence Hall, four years earlier, on the eve of his first inaugural address. On February 22, 1861, he had eerily told the assembled crowd that he *"would rather be assassinated"* than surrender the principle of liberty for all, which was the foundation of American democracy and the animating spirit of the Declaration of Independence.

∞∞∞∞∞∞∞∞∞

That same year, the Vigilance Committee was disbanded and Negro Philadelphians gratefully observed the emergence of the Pennsylvania Equal Rights League, an organization committed to political and social reform. William Nesbit of Altoona was the League's first President and Octavius was elected to the position of Corresponding Secretary. It was indeed unfortunate that President Lincoln did not have an opportunity to implement his national program for reconstruction. However, the League had plans of its own. At its first meeting, it was decided that they would take the fight for full citizenship to an entirely new level.

At the end of the war in 1865, Philadelphia's colored population still did not have the right to vote or hold public office. And to add insult to injury, the colored population of Philadelphia was denied the use of the city's streetcars that began running in 1858. Bitter racial hostilities persisted and the promise of colored inclusion in the political life of the city was vehemently denied. Thus, "the war to end slavery" was followed by the League's *second war* to win full citizenship rights. William Nesbit was quite adamant on that point.

"Now is the time to put the state and federal authorities to the test. Our boys have fought and died for the Government! President Johnson owes us that much. With the re-unification of the States, the new Union has got to guarantee us the right to fully participate in the democratic process."

Octavius underscored Nesbit's remarks with a specific recommendation of his own.

"Then I suggest that we start in our own backyard. We have some state and city elections coming up and the presidential election in a few years. So we've got to start mobilizing our people right now."

"Well, where do you suppose we should begin?" asked Nesbitt.

"With the Governor himself. Mr. Curtin has cheated us once; we should not let him do it again. We should demand a meeting with him right away."

"Did you say demand, Mr. Catto?"

"Yes, Mr. Nesbit, *demand!* Frederick Douglass said it best; *Power concedes nothing without demand.* Never did, never will!"

37. A Season of Reunions

"So there in the land of Moab, Moses the servant of the Lord died as the Lord had
said; and he was buried in the ravine opposite Beth-peor in the land of Moab, but to
this day, no one knows the place of his burial."

Deuteronomy 34:5

With the end of the Civil War and the victory of the Union forces,
Mr. Still would finally have his season of redemption. He and Uncle
Blue made a pilgrimage to Mount Lebanon Cemetery to unearth his
precious documents. Some of the manuscripts had been lost to mildew
and decomposition. However, most of them had survived and were
quite legible. He estimated that portion to be about seventy-five
percent. With these materials safely secured back in his den, he was
now ready to fulfill the original purpose of his tedious efforts. He
would now go about the task of helping families locate their loved ones
by using the information that he had meticulously collected over the
years.

He began by writing to his countless underground helpers and the
hundreds of passengers whose locations were known to him. He also
enlisted the help of several churches. They were asked to encourage
their parishioners to contact him if there were in search of lost relatives.
After about eighteen months of back and forth correspondence and
cross-referencing, he was finally able to realize the intent of his faithful
record keeping. In total, ninety-seven different families had written to
inform him that thanks to his efforts, they had successfully located their
loved ones.

They all wanted to thank him for his invaluable service. Some even
sent him money as "a finder's fee", all of which he respectfully returned
to them. However, true to his meticulous nature, he retained all of
their letters and re-read them often. Victory was at hand. William Still
had accomplished what he had set out to do. It was indeed a season of
sweet reunions, a time to celebrate a great and long-delayed victory
over the time bandits.

∞∞∞∞∞∞∞∞∞∞

Mr. Still's exhaustive letter-writing campaign had depleted his
supply of ink, so he and Uncle Blue went to Mr. Abram's store for

refills. There they encountered Robert Purvis and Harriett Forten who
had recently returned to Philadelphia and achieved a long-deferred
objective of their own. She and Mr. Purvis informed them that they
that were engaged to be married. As they prepared to leave, Mr.
Abrams reached from behind his counter.

"Wait a minute you two. I have something for you."

He handed Robert a package wrapped in plain brown paper.

"I want you to open it on your wedding day, okay?"

"Sure Mr. Abrams and thank you. Thanks a lot."

"You are so sweet," said Harriet as she kissed him on the cheek
before leaving.

"Say Abrams, how come you gave them a wedding present now?
They aren't going to get hitched until three months from now."

"I know Blue, but tomorrow my friend; I will be celebrating
Simchat Torah."

"Say what?"

"Simchat Torah. It means rejoicing with the Torah, our holy
scripture. In my congregation, we are all called to the altar to read from
Deuteronomy. Then one person reads the last words of that book. He
is called the Bridegroom of the Torah. Then the scroll is rolled back to
the beginning and another person is chosen to read the first words of
the Torah. We call that person the Bridegroom of Genesis. We believe
that as the last and first of the Torah are recited at Simchat Torah, all of
its wonderful stories are summoned into life."

"That's beautiful," said Mr. Still.

"Yes indeed. Our Kabalists say that the Torah existed before the
world was created. Moving backward and forward in time and space,
Torah is the gateway to all the worlds. By the way, Mr. Still, I have
been meaning to ask you something. How are you coming along with
your recorded stories? Any luck getting those families back together?"

"Yes, I was just telling Blue that we've been able to re-unite almost
one hundred families. In fact, I just received a thank you letter from a
reunited husband and wife living in Cincinnati, Ohio. They were so
appreciative that they plan to name their firstborn child after me."

"Yeah, that's all nice," said Uncle Blue. "But I tell you what. If
they name that baby after you Still, it will probably come out with a
quill pen in his hand. Yeah Sol, you had better send a lot of ink to
those folks in Cincinnati. They gonna need it."

"So what are you going to do now with all that information Mr. Still?" "Yeah Still, you gonna keep your house cluttered with all that stuff?"

"Well to tell you the truth Sol, I haven't given it much thought. I suppose they are of little value now."

Mr. Abrams disagreed. He suggested that Mr. Still place those materials back in the old suitcases and bury them *again* in Mount Lebanon Cemetery. With the Emancipation Proclamation enforced and the Union army victorious, the Negro race was entering into a new "promised land" of opportunity and opening up a new chapter in their ongoing American odyssey. Sol likened the Negro's situation to the time when the Jews buried the body of Moses before crossing over into the Promised Land. Mr. Still thought about his recommendation for a few days and decided that it was a good idea. It seemed like an appropriate symbolic gesture and a fitting tribute to those who had led the way to freedom and patiently won such a valiant and hard-fought victory over the *time bandits*.

∞∞∞∞∞∞∞∞∞∞∞∞

That same year, the Catto family would also experience a very special reunion. William and Ellen returned from London and had agreed to reside in the Catto home before moving to a farm in Christiana. Reverend Catto agreed to keep their impending return a secret so that Ellen could have the double pleasure of surprising Octavius on his twenty-sixth birthday.

Returning home from a meeting, Octavius opened the front door and saw the figure of a woman in the parlor, standing alone at the piano, with her back towards him. He walked slowly toward her with anxious curiosity. She turned to him and it was all he could do to keep his composure. So he didn't.

"My God, look at you. My little boy is a man," she whispered with teary eyes and quivering lips.

Her familiar voice and embrace took his breath away. He was choked with emotion and rendered speechless. He desperately wanted to tell her how much he had missed her; how much he thought about her – how glad he was to see her again. But again, words failed him.

Towering over her, his tears landed gently on her soft shoulders as a silent testament to his indescribable and overwhelming joy. Sweet seconds passed and he thought to end their embrace. It was a brief thought that was quickly overtaken by memories of how good it felt to be held in her arms. Time stood still and truth be told, he didn't want to let go of her. So he didn't.

38. Oh, Miss Jackson...

"A little learning, indeed, may be a dangerous thing, but the want of learning is a calamity to any people."

Frederick Douglass

To be sure, 1865 was a major turning point in American history. That year witnessed an end to a costly and bloody war, the assassination of an American president and a very tenuous and nervous peace between the northern and southern states. On a local level, Phialdephia's colored population continued to experience a steady erosion of their civil rights, particularly in the areas of housing, employment and public transportation. In an effort to stem this tide, Octavius and several members of the Equal Rights League began by mounting a citywide campaign to desegregate the city's streetcars. Their tactics included filling up the cars with colored passengers and forcing the drivers to physically remove them. These acts of passive resistance brought public attention to the issue and led to the wide circulation of petitions calling for an end to this blatantly discriminatory practice. These petitions were signed by several colored and white citizens. Nonetheless, the streetcars remained segregated for years to come.

However, 1865 was a memorable year for an entirely different reason. It was the year Miss Fannie Jackson entered their lives. She was to be the newest addition to the Institute's outstanding faculty.

Mr. Cope and Principal Bassett met in the teacher's lounge to discuss plans for the upcoming school year. They looked forward to her arrival with great anticipation.

"I trust thee will agree, I have remained faithful in my promise to secure the highest caliber of instructors available in the country. Thou willst see, Ms. Jackson will be a most valuable asset. We have reviewed her credentials and they are most extraordinary. She is a graduate of Oberlin College and comes to us highly recommended."

"I'm sure she will work out fine. When do I meet her?" said Mr. Bassett.

"She should arrive sometime today. Now if thou will excuse me, I must attend to some pressing business. Good day to thee."

Octavius passed by Mr. Cope in the hallway as he rushed to class.

"Ah Octavius, I have not seen thee in a while. Please drop in on me at thy convenience. I have a few matters to discuss with thee."

"I'll do that sir, take care."

∞∞∞∞∞∞∞∞∞

Octavius' history classes were popular and usually over-enrolled. It was the first day of the school year, and he wondered if he could still fire his students' social imagination and expand their understanding of history. Forty minutes into his lecture, he began to summarize the major points of his first lecture in over six months.

"…Let's not forget that our forefathers and foremothers were the only group of people who came to this country *against their will*. The Atlantic Slave trade was the largest forced migration in the history of mankind. The European settlers subdued the native Indians in an effort to occupy and ultimately lay claim to their land. With regard to the African, they wanted his labor, his *free* labor that is. And, how did they do it? Through that peculiar institution we call slavery. The enslavement of not just the body, but the mind as well. This is a good place to stop as any. We have a few minutes left, so I will entertain a couple of questions. If you have one, I want you to stand and give your name. That way, we can get to know one another. Yes, you in the center?"

"My name is Marcus. Marcus Aurelius Johnson."

Some of the students giggled at the mention of his full name.

"I happen to think that is a fine name. Please proceed Mr. Johnson."

"Professor Catto, how were the European settlers able to subdue the Africans and Indians so easily?"

"Well, that's a complex question worthy of extensive discussion and our time is short. So let me answer it this way. They ruled by sheer force of arms. The Europeans clearly had superior weaponry, which allowed them to take control of the land through military might, fear and physical intimidation. In turn, greed and ambition led them to the mindset that *might makes right*. However, to maintain that control over the past three centuries they also had to create ideological and religious belief systems to justify their subjugation of the colored races. They used these ideas to convince others and themselves that their brutal conquests were somehow morally justified."

"What kind of ideas?"

"Well, for example in the case of the Indians, there was the church doctrine of *Terra Nullis*, a term derived from Latin meaning *no one's land*.

This contrived European doctrine stipulated that all newly discovered lands inhabited by non-Europeans were theirs for the taking because even though people of color obviously inhabited the land, the land was in their view, no one's land. Consider if you will, our nation's history of confiscating the land of the Indian, the countless treaties that were broken and the immense suffering that we visited upon them.

You must understand that these blatant injustices were believed to be entirely justifiable. Again, the settlers adhered to the might is right principle. Some even claimed that these treacherous land acquisitions were sanctioned by the church and encouraged by God himself. On that theological and ideological basis, robbing, pillaging and systematic genocide against the colored peoples of the world was easily justified; at least in their minds."

"I'll take one more question. Yes, the young lady in the blue dress."

"My name is Ida Barrett. Tell me something Professor Catto. That stuff you're talking about happened way back in the past. Why do we have to study it. Shouldn't we be learning learn about the present. Don't we have to live in the *real* world? Shouldn't we focus on what's going on *right now*?"

"Of course we should, but consider this. The past is alive in the present. And this state of affairs that you call *the real world* is merely a collective human creation, brought into being by the thoughts and actions of people. The so-called real world is nothing more than people's attitudes and beliefs that have been agreed to and have, over time been solidified or frozen into habits, laws, policies, customs and social arrangements that are all human creations and thus always open to critical review and change, if need be.

So you see, the study of history can be absolutely liberating. It is a way of helping us understand how the current *real world* came into existence. It is also a way to help us imagine new worlds and better worlds that we might want to create and deliberately *will into being*.

All too often, we fall into the trap of thinking that just because things are a particular way, they will always be a particular way. We lose our sense of *moral oughtness*. We start to believe that just because things are a certain way; they ought to be that way. We lose our vision. And, as it has been noted so many times in sacred and secular literature, when there is no vision, the people perish. It is one thing to tenaciously face facts and recognize reality. But, it is an altogether different thing to accept reality as a collection of unchangeable and inevitable facts and thus fail to seek a better world.

Without historical perspective and without this sense of oughtness, we lack the understanding and the will to be builders and participants in the type of world we want to inhabit and pass on to future generations. We become in effect, unthinking victims of *the tyranny of the present*, when in truth, we are always free to think and do in ways that can bring new realities into being, every day of our lives.

By studying history, we can avoid being passive anvils and become instead, hammers that can help forge new futures. Through historical analysis, we get the chance to exercise our minds in both a forward and backward direction. Then we are no longer prisoners of time, powerless captives of the so-called real world. Let's continue this discussion tomorrow. Class dismissed."

The students began to file out of the classroom and talk amongst themselves. Octavius was packing up his lecture notes and appeared to be unmindful of their conversations.

"What do you think of Professor Catto?" whispered Marcus to Ida Barrett.

"I like him all right, but he sure is long-winded. Either I'm going to have to ask simpler questions or he's going to have to give us shorter answers. I'm not trying to stay here till supper!"

"I heard that!" said Octavius.

"I didn't, ah I…"

"I'll see you all tomorrow," he responded playfully.

∞∞∞∞∞∞∞∞∞

Octavius walked down the hall and knocked on Principal Bassett's door.

"Hello Octavius. How was your first day of class?"

"Well, I'm not really sure."

"What do you mean?"

"Well, let me ask you a frank question. Do you think I'm long-winded? Do you think I talk too much?"

Before Principal Bassett could answer, there was a knock at the door and Octavius went to open it.

"May I help you?"

Octavius did not know the stoic visitor who appeared before him. Although her clothing was wet and her hair matted down, she was noticeably poised and had a dignified air about her. The lilt in her voice and the confidence in her gaze clearly marked her as a women of unmistakable refinement.

"Yes you may. I'm looking for Mr. Bassett, the principal of this school, are you him by any chance?"

"No I'm not. But, you're in the right place. Mr. Bassett, I present to you, Ms... Ms..."

"Ms. Jackson, but you may call me Fannie if you wish."

"Ah, Ms. Jackson! Welcome to the Institute. I'm Ebenezer Bassett and this young man is Octavius Catto who teaches history and philosophy here."

"Please forgive my tardiness Mr. Bassett, but being new to the city, I caught the wrong streetcar. And to make matters worse, the conductor had the insolence to make me sit in the rear, out in the exposed area of the street car, when there were perfectly good seats available inside."

"I'm very sorry you had such an unpleasant introduction to our city," said Mr. Bassett.

"Well you shouldn't have done it. You should have refused to sit out in the rain," said Octavius.

"I beg your pardon?"

"I mean maybe *you* were partially to blame for what happened. Maybe you were complicitous; a co-conspirator in that blatant attempt to humiliate you."

"Oh I see. Mr. Catto isn't it?"

"Yes ma'am."

"Well, Mr. Catto let me tell you this about myself. I believe in punctuality and I believe in good manners. And, whereas as I appreciate that bit of unsolicited opinion, I do believe I was addressing Mr. Bassett."

"I meant no disrespect ma'am."

"I know; it's a pity that you are so unconscious of your rude behavior. But, we can take that up at another time. Now Mr. Bassett, if you will be kind enough to show me the classroom I'll be in tomorrow, I'd be ever so grateful."

"Of course, right this way."

Principal Bassett opened the door for her. He smiled and nudged Octavius as he followed her out of the office. Annoyed by this encounter, Octavius whispered in Mr. Bassett's ear.

"What's her problem?"

Bassett smiled and whispered back to him.

"You know, come to think of it, you *do* talk too much. I'll see you tomorrow."

∞∞∞∞∞∞∞∞∞

Octavius exited the building alone and walked over to Market Street. He stopped in front of the general store where Uncle Blue and Mr. Abrams were sitting on cracker barrels playing chess.

"Hey Uncle Blue. Hey Mr. Abrams."

"How you doing Professor?"

"Just fine, just fine Mr. Abrams."

At that moment, a drunken man, Mr. Courtland approached and offered Octavius a sip from his bottle of rum. Staggering toward Octavius, he slurred a malodorous greeting.

"Lookin' good Professor, lookin' good. Want some?"

"No sir. I don't touch the stuff, but thank you anyway."

"Now ya oughta know better then to offer my boy a drink," snapped Uncle Blue.

"I was jest being friendly Blue."

"Naw, you was jest being a fool! Keep talking and I'll knock you into next Thursday! My boy is going places. He don't need no grog."

"Yeah, you right," said Mr. Courtland. "Sorta like my boy."

"Man you must be crazy! Your boy ain't no more like Octavius then chalk is like cheese."

"Oh, yeah?"

"Yeah! Now get on outta here before I hit you so hard, your grandchildren will come out dizzy!"

Octavius said goodbye to them and continued walking down the street. Two older ladies approached and greeted him.

"Good afternoon Professor. How's your father?"

"Hi, Ms. Sample. He's just fine, thank you."

Octavius moved on and turned in the direction of Wanamaker's clothing store.

"That's a handsome man there," whispered Mrs. Shepard, "I need to introduce him to my Valencia."

"Don't even bother. They say he's sweet on that LeCount girl. They've been keeping company for quite a long while."

"Well, she better treat him right. That one there is a keeper, that's for sure."

∞∞∞∞∞∞∞∞∞∞∞∞

Reverend Catto never offered his son advice regarding affairs of the heart. And Octavius never developed the nerve to discuss male-female relationships with him. It was indeed unfortunate that neither father nor son was comfortable with exploring such an important subject. Uncle Blue, on the other hand, had no such trepidation. He had plenty of advice to give and always found a way to meet and *evaluate* the young women vying for his godson's affection. Uncle Blue first met Caroline one Sunday when he "just happened" to be riding down the street when she and Octavius were coming out of Mother Bethel Church.

"Hey there boy!"

"Hey Uncle Blue. Let me introduce you to someone. Caroline LeCount, this is my Uncle Blue."

"It's a pleasure to meet you sir."

"The pleasure is all mine young lady. I've heard quite a bit about you. Hey boy, I never thought I'd see you coming outta there. How come you're not at your father's new church?"

"I like to move around. Besides, that's all in the past. They have a new pastor and he is positively outstanding. Believe me; Mother Bethel is in good hands; strong and vibrant as ever."

"Yeah, I just hope them folks have learned their lesson."

"What lesson is that?"

"You know boy; that Reverend Reynolds mess. They should have known that you ought not put a man… any man, on a paddy stool.

"You mean, *pedestal.*"

"No kind of stool! It just ain't right. Ain't but one God. That's the way I got it figured out."

"You are so right Uncle Blue," said Caroline. "I see it so many times. People worshipping people. Folks praising creatures instead of the Creator."

"That's exactly what I'm saying pretty lady. Tell this boy of mine. You put a man on a paddy stool and he'll show you his ass every time. Ah, ah...excuse my language Miss LeCount."

"That's quite alright Uncle Blue. You make a valid point."

"See that Octavius, pretty and smart too. But for the life of me, I can't figure out what she sees in you (wink, wink). Listen, I gotta go. It was a pleasure meeting you young lady. And try to teach my boy something, will ya?"

"I'll do my best Uncle Blue, take care."

Uncle Blue continued riding down the street and the strikingly attractive couple resumed their conversation.

"You know something Octavius, I really like him!"

"I *love* him. (pause) Can I walk you home?"

"You may indeed sir."

They walked down Lombard Street together until Caroline came to a complete stop.

"Octavius?"

"Yes?"

"Can I tell you something? I mean ...can you just stop and listen?"

"Yes, absolutely. What is it?"

"Well...what I want to say...I mean... what I mean to say is... well...*I love you*. There I said it! You don't have to respond. You don't have to say anything or do anything. I mean, I...I just needed to tell you that."

They walked another few feet and his silence was deafening.

"Well?"

"Well what?" answered Octavius.

"Well aren't you going to say anything?"

"I thought you said I didn't have to say anything."

"Fine!"

Again, more uncomfortable silence ensued as they walked on. This time, Octavius stopped.

"Caroline?"

"Yes?"

"The feeling is mutual...no it isn't. I suspect I love you even more."

"Well, why on earth did you torture me? Why didn't you just say so?"

"Well...for one thing, it seems like just about everyone I have ever loved has left me in one way or another. I don't think I want to go through that kind of pain again."

"You listen to me Octavius Catto. You needn't worry. I will never, ever leave you."

"Promise?"

"Promise!"

∞∞∞∞∞∞∞∞

It is perhaps one of life's most exhilarating pleasures—the sublime moment when hope meets reality, when dreams unfold in time and in rhythm with one's deepest desires. Theirs was a promise of love in bloom, bearing witness to the mysterious synergy of two lives joined together and creating something new, something sweeter and stronger than the sum of their parts.

They completed one another in ways that were both apparent and unseen. Octavius was brash and outspoken. Caroline bore a passivism that bordered on timidity. Octavius fancied himself as a bold "citizen of the world" and an aspiring politician. Caroline viewed herself as a teacher (first and foremost) and a nurturer of young intellects. She tended to measure her success by the success of her students. Her students would be the proud and strident citizens of a new world; a world that she hoped to cultivate first in their minds. It was her particular (but no less effective) brand of political activism.

For the first time in his adult life, Octavius was experiencing the joy of exploring mature interests and sharing his innermost feelings with a kindred spirit. He was invigorated by their obvious harmony and the distinct possibility that maybe, just maybe, he might have discovered *the* woman meant for him. Caroline was comparatively more certain about their union. She was less burdened by the subtle doubts and insecurities that typically arise when one opens one's heart to another. Like Octavius, she too felt "exposed" and uncomfortably vulnerable to desertion and disappointment. But, her love was intense and reassuring. In that particular regard, she was perhaps the stronger and more confident of the two lovers.

It was a joy to witness how Octavius and Caroline celebrated their love for teaching and their affection for one another. Young folks their age talked a lot about *falling* in love. Uncle Blue often said that it was better to *grow* in love. And that they surely did, with each passing day. They promised to love each other till the end of time. And, for a time, each day was brimming with happiness and the future was pregnant with possibilities.

Although he was less expressive than Caroline, Octavius was not alone in his feelings. That evening, he thought about their budding relationship and received the sudden inspiration to write. That restless evening, he penned a poem that captured his private thoughts and reflected his deepest insecurities. The poem, tentatively entitled, *Confirmation* was not written for public consumption. And true to his well guarded innermost feelings, he had no intention of sharing it with Caroline. Nonetheless, she was very much the source of its inspiration and the subject that weighed heaviest on his mind. Upon completion, he neatly folded it in thirds and placed it in the inside of his suit jacket. There he would carry it close to his heart, where all deep secrets are kept.

Confirmation

The long-silenced lyre resonates with the rumor of love.
The bird of hope is on the wing.
The mind delights in sweet reflection.
The battered soul feels an urge to sing.
Still, the rainbowed heart dispatches steel-gray reason,
in search of confirmation.
But it returned twice in doubt,
with useless information.
'Twas a vain and fruitless mission,
Leaving me nothing left to do,
But move with the rhythm and sing the song,
of your tender love so true.
And so at last, I can no longer imagine,
A world without music,
life without love,
me without you.
By the grace of God—
Merciful rains did gently descend,
To replenish the earth and declare an end,
To a world without music,
live without love,
me without you.

∞∞∞∞∞∞∞∞∞

On the next day, Fannie Jackson met her first class at eight o'clock in the morning. She walked briskly into the classroom and greeted her students with a slight smile that quickly turned into an authoritative scowl of sorts.

"Good Morning, class."

"Good Morning."

"Oh no, that will never do. Let's try that again much louder, shall we? Good morning class."

"Good Morning!"

"Ah, much better! I am Miss Jackson and I will be you teacher in English grammar, Greek and Latin. This year, we will be covering the first six sections of Marable's…"

She was suddenly interrupted by a commotion in the back of the classroom. A girl hit a boy who retaliated by throwing a book at her. They had disrupted Ms. Jackson in mid-sentence and she was none too happy. The class became very silent when Ms. Jackson quickly slammed her textbook on the desk.

"What seems to be the problem back there?"

"Ms. Jackson, he keeps bothering me. All up in my face! He smells, too!"

The class laughed loudly. Ms. Jackson did not.

"Ah, excuse me. Young ladies do not hit young men, especially those young ladies who want to remain in the Institute for Colored Youth. Do I make myself clear?"

"Yes ma'am."

"What is your name?"

"Diana; Diana Shepard."

"And you young man, what is your name?"

"Charles Dorsey."

"Well since the two of you have seen fit to interrupt my class, let me offer you this grammatical correction. If we are going to use words, we must use them in the proper manner. For instance, if we were speaking correctly we would say Ms. Shepard *smells* and Mr. Dorsey *stinks*."

The entire class erupted with laughter.

"I see nothing funny in that!" said Ms. Jackson in a stern tone. "I'm quite serious. You see class, Ms. Shepard is the active subject who has had an olfactory experience. She in fact smells. On the other hand, Mr. Dorsey stinks and has (if we are to believe Ms. Shepard) failed to meet his hygienic responsibilities. In either case, they are both out of order. This of course, brings me to two fundamental rules of my class. You would do well to remember them. Rule number one, we will use words in their proper context. Class repeat after me."

"We will use words in their proper context."

"Very good. And, now rule number two and much louder. We will only use words that we can spell, define and pronounce."

"We will only use words that we can spell, define and pronounce," they echoed.

"Very good. Let us proceed."

∞∞∞∞∞∞∞∞∞∞

The next morning Ms. Jackson was sitting at her desk preparing for her classes in her private office when Principal Bassett stopped by.

"Good morning Ms. Jackson. I hate to interrupt your study period, but Ms. LeCount is not in place to meet her nine o'clock class. Would you be able to cover for her?"

"Well, I'd certainly be able to, but I'm not sure I'm *willing* to do so. I do not believe in teaching without well-conceived lesson plans, which as you can see are not yet complete. If I neglect my class preparation, then my students will be the worse off for it. You do understand, don't you? How long will Miss LeCount be delayed?"

"I really can't say."

"I see, well then I suppose that I can offer assistance, *this time.* However, I certainly wouldn't want to make a habit out of it. Where is Ms. LeCount anyway?"

"I don't know, she's never been late before."

∞∞∞∞∞∞∞∞∞∞

Unbeknownst to Principal Bassett, Caroline LeCount had been unavoidably detained at the corner of 12th and Callowhill Street, where she attempted to board a streetcar. She had just picked up eight new textbooks for her class and was in a rush to get to the Institute.

"You can't come aboard!" yelled the conductor.

"I beg your pardon sir?"

"What are you deaf or something? I said no niggers allowed!"

"You sir, are a cad and I most certainly will ride this trolley. I have very important business to attend to."

"Listen, missy. I'm not moving this thing until you get your black ass off."

"Get off the damn car. We gotta go to work," hollered one of the male passengers.

"You best be getting off and let us decent folks get to work. Who do you think you are?" shouted a female passenger.

As the taunts continued, the conductor lost his patience. He grabbed her by her hair, but she continued to resist and remained seated. Then he wrapped his hairy arms around Caroline's waist and forcefully threw her off the streetcar and onto the sidewalk. Not one of the passengers or nearby pedestrians came to her aid. The streetcar rolled on and Caroline limped away, upset and embarrassingly disheveled. To add insult to injury, the pile of books she was carrying fell into a mud puddle and she was forced to carry them over a distance of two miles to the Institute. When she arrived at the school, she immediately went to Octavius' office. He was of course, outraged by the grim story she told him.

Forced Removal from the Streetcar

∞∞∞∞∞∞∞∞∞

Caroline did not meet any of her classes that day. However, she returned to school on the following day and taught all of her classes, standing on a badly sprained ankle. That afternoon, she attended a special meeting called by Principal Bassett in the faculty lounge. Seeing Ms. Jackson sitting alone, Caroline hobbled over to her and sat down to chat before Mr. Bassett arrived.

"Hello, Ms. Jackson, I want to thank you for taking my class for me yesterday."

"You should know, it was a great inconvenience to me. I hope it doesn't happen again Ms. LeCount."

"Of course. Were there any problems?"

"I should say so. Your students have no self-control whatsoever. It took me five whole minutes just to get them to settle down."

"Well, I usually like to give them a few minutes to talk amongst themselves before I call them to order."

"Why that's totally preposterous. No wonder your class lacks discipline."

"Lacks discipline?"

"Yes, much like their teacher I suppose!"

Caroline was clearly insulted and was about to respond when Mr. Bassett entered the room.

"Good afternoon colleagues. I want to call this faculty meeting to order. We have some pressing matters to discuss, so let us get to them. The first item on our agenda is the proposal to charge a partial tuition for all of our students. As you know, this would be quite a departure for the Institute. Heretofore our Board has managed to keep us financially afloat. However, with increased migration to the city by our brothers and sisters in the South, our enrollment has grown significantly over the past three years and operational costs are escalating. That being the case, the managers have proposed an annual tuition fee of fifty dollars per student, in order to help us meet the escalating cost of running the school. Are there any questions or comments? Yes, Ms. Jackson?"

"I think it is an excellent idea. We should impose such a tuition immediately."

Octavius took offense and bitterly responded.

"Excuse me Ms. Jackson; but you are new to this school. I don't think you understand our children and the types of families they come from."

"Oh really? What is it I don't understand Mr. Catto?"

"Well to begin with, most of our children come from poor, working class families. They simply can't afford tuition."

"Am I to understand that these parents have jobs?"

"Yes, I suppose, most of them do."

"Well then, let them learn the meaning of sacrifice. Let them abandon some pleasure, some comfort or some purchase so that their children might reap the benefits of an education. It is an investment that will serve them and their children for the rest of their lives."

"Well, some of them don't have much to sacrifice already. You know, some of us were not born with a silver spoon in our mouth. We didn't have the benefit of a sophisticated upbringing or the opportunity to go to fine institutions like Oberlin College."

"I want to thank you ever so much for being so keen with the obvious Mr. Catto. But, let me just say that it is my experience that people tend to value something more if a payment is required, rather than receiving it as a charitable gift. Besides, we should avoid dependencies and promote self-help and personal responsibility."

Most of the other teachers disagreed with Ms. Jackson's position. Caroline LeCount listened intently to the debate but offered no opinions of her own.

∞∞∞∞∞∞∞∞∞

About three months had passed since Ms. Jackson joined the faculty. In December, Mr. Cope had his quarterly meeting with Principal Bassett. Ms. Jackson's performance was very much on his mind.

"I've been meaning to ask thee, how is our Ms. Jackson fairing in her duties?"

"Actually, quite well. She's not the most popular woman on the faculty, but her students seem to like her a lot. More importantly, I can see marked improvement in their behavior."

"Really? How so."

"Well, for one thing, their grades are better than the other classes and strangely enough, they seem to be more confident, more sure of themselves. Especially the girls; for some reason they seem to be speaking up more in class. And, unless my ears deceive me, they seem to be speaking more loudly."

"Did thou say, *more loudly*?"

"Yes, it's a most curious thing."

"Indeed so Mr. Bassett."

∞∞∞∞∞∞∞∞∞

By April 1866, the Pennsylvania Equal Rights League had made considerable progress in pressing its claim for full citizenship rights (or so they thought). At their monthly meeting, Mr. Nesbit, President of the League, announced that he was preparing a petition that would *guarantee* the voting rights of Negro citizens in the Commonwealth. However, the petition had to be approved by the Governor and the State legislature. Nesbit viewed their approval of this petition as simply a matter of formality.

"And so gentlemen, if all goes according to plan, it looks like we will be able to vote in the municipal elections next fall."

That proved not to be the case. The League would soon find out that his optimism was unfounded. For the first time, they got a glimpse of Nesbit's political naiveté. Major political battles are rarely won unilaterally or "overnight" and the ongoing debate regarding the Negro's voting rights would surely never be settled by written petitions or rhetorical appeals. The older members of the League's Philadelphia delegation knew that all too well.

Unfortunately, the members would also observe a rather unpleasant exchange of words between Mr. Nesbit and Octavius at the conclusion of the April meeting.

"Now if there is no new business, do I hear a motion to adjourn?"

"Excuse me Mr. President, but there is one additional matter."

"Yes, Mr. Catto by all means."

"I am pleased to report that on May 22nd, the State legislature is expected to pass a bill making it illegal to bar colored people from the streetcars."

Mr. Nesbit was completely caught by surprise. After a loud round of applause, he publicly challenged Octavius in a most disagreeable manner.

"Mr. Catto, I was not aware that we were promoting a bill to desegregate the streetcars. What do you know about it? Why was this body not informed?"

"Well sir, I spoke with Senator Thaddeus Stevens who put me in touch with our State Representatives William Kelly and Morrow Lowry.

I met with them two weeks ago in Harrisburg and we drafted the bill in a matter of days. They have personally secured the necessary votes from their legislative colleagues, so the Bill should sail through without any resistance."

"Let me get this right. You took it upon yourself to contact a powerful member of Congress, met with representatives of the state legislature and participated in the drafting of a bill, all without consulting this organization?"

"Yes Mr. Nesbit, perhaps I should have. But, you see…"

"Perhaps? Listen, I heard about what happened to your girlfriend. But what you did constitutes a gross abuse of your office. You cannot conduct your own private, back-channel crusades. You reached far beyond your authority. You made it personal."

"*It was personal!* And, I did the only thing I could, short of beating to a pulp the man who did it and those men who stood by and watched."

"Now you listen to me. You're way out of line!"

"No, *you're* out of line!" shouted Jacob White. "You all sit up here, week after week, talking about what you're going to do. Octavius did something that should have been done years ago. And you know it!"

"What do you want from me!" shouted Octavius. "The bill will pass and we'll all be better off for it. Sure, I cut a few corners, but if we sat back and let that foot-dragging Mayor of ours handle it, we'd be waiting for years before justice was served. You know that as well as I do!"

"I think we should bring this up with the Executive Committee next week."

"With all due respect Mr. Nesbit, you do what you think you should, as will I. Now if you'll excuse me, I've got someone far more important than you waiting for me!"

Mr. Still clearly understood both sides of the argument. Mr. Nesbit was right. Octavius should have at least consulted with the Executive Committee. Yet he also understood Octavius' point of view. For too long, the Negro's righteous indignation about the segregated streetcar situation always seemed to fall short of direct action. However, he strongly believed that their heated debate should have taken place behind closed doors.

∞∞∞∞∞∞∞∞∞∞

By the spring semester of 1868, Fannie Jackson had established her reputation as an effective and highly dedicated teacher. The students marveled at the excitement and the passion she brought to her teaching. She even managed to make the study of Shakespeare's Julius Caesar interesting and enjoyable to her students. She had the gift of literary interpretation and an amazing ability to show how classic literature was full of meaning for their lives.

"Okay Darryl, then what does Brutus say?"

"I do believe that these applauses are for some new honors that are heaped on Caesar."

"Now Audrey, how does Cassius reply?"

"Why man he doth bestride the narrow world like a Colossus; and we petty men walk under his huge legs and peep about to find ourselves dishonorable graves. Men at some times are masters of their fates: The fault dear Brutus, is not in our stars. But, in ourselves, that we are underlings."

"The fault is in ourselves. Now what do you think Mr. Shakespeare is trying to say to us? Yes, Jerry?"

"He's saying that we shouldn't blame other people for our lives."

"Precisely! You see, Julius Caesar was a great and powerful man, to be sure. But, his greatness was not attributable to some unknown, or uncontrollable forces or the alignment and movements of the stars and the planets. His greatness was in the final analysis, attributable to the fact that he took charge and was the master of his fate (so to speak). So alas, Cassius is correct when he says, "The fault, dear Brutus is not in the stars, but in ourselves." You see children; *the light is within.* Brutus and Cassius must look *within* if they are to …"

Before she could finish her thought, she was interrupted by a loud thud that came from Ms. LeCount's adjacent classroom. She stormed into the noisy classroom and saw a scene of unrestrained bedlam. The students were throwing paper, chasing each other and stomping their feet. Ms. LeCount was in the rear, reprimanding a young boy for having pulled the hair of one of the girls. She was crying hysterically as her tormentor delighted in her distress.

Ms. Jackson entered the room with an angry frown, clenched fists and piercing eyes that seemed to penetrate through their skulls. Without uttering a word, she arched her back and scanned the room. Amazingly, the chaos turned to absolute silence. She then politely asked, Ms. LeCount to join her in the hallway. Before leaving the classroom, she stared back at the students and issued a stern warning,

"And you better stay quiet!"

In the hallway, out of earshot of the students, she proceeded to give Ms. LeCount a brief lesson in classroom management.

"Honestly, Ms. LeCount, how do you expect the rest of us to teach if you cannot contain your students? Look around you. There is learning going on here, everywhere that teachers are able to exert control and command the respect of their students. You must do better!"

"I understand. I do."

"I certainly hope so!"

Ms. Jackson returned to her own classroom and resumed her didactic analysis of Julius Caesar as characterized by Mr. Shakespeare.

"I do apologize for that unfortunate interruption. Now let's see. Where were we? Ah yes, Julius Caesar, a mere man, perceived to be a giant colossus. What a shame. Now I want each of you to tear out a piece of paper and sign your name in your best handwriting. Go on, do it!"

The students complied and started writing and tearing.

"Now I want you to write today's date directly under your signature and pass them in to me."

"What are you going to do with our autographs Ms. Jackson?"

"Why save them of course."

"But why?"

"Well if you must know, Ms. Shepard, they're for me. Call it bragging rights. You see, I'm convinced that some of you will one day be as accomplished as William Shakespeare, Cervantes, and Dumas or maybe even the great Greek and Egyptian philosophers and teachers."

"Yeah, right! I'll believe that when I see it."

"Does that seem so far-fetched to you Mr. Dorsey? I'll have you know that one day, perhaps a day just like today, Plato, a mere mortal, sat down to write his *Republic*. And, as sure as we're here talking, some of you, maybe *many* of you will do the same. You will also reach inside yourself and discover something very beautiful, and very useful to the world—a poem, a song, some piece of literature, perhaps a philosophical treatise or even some needed legislation; some constructive use of language that will stand as a testament to the creative, universal mind, unconstrained by fear and self-doubt."

"Do you *really* think we might Ms. Jackson?"
"Of course *I* do my dear. But a better question is, *do you*?"

39. "We Will Raise No Victims Here!"

"Self-reverence, self-knowledge, self-control,
These three alone lead life to sovereign power."

Alfred Lord Tennyson

At his weekly meeting with Octavius, Principal Bassett shared the most extraordinary news. In recognition of his political, work for the Republican Party, President Ulysses S. Grant had appointed Bassett to the position of United States Ambassador to Haiti.

"You're kidding me. Ambassador to Haiti?"

"It's true Octavius. I received the official letter of appointment from President Grant three days ago."

"I'm speechless. I mean this is a high honor. But, I can't imagine the Institute being without your leadership. When do you start?"

"In thirty days. Octavius, there's something I want to tell you."

"What is it?"

"Well, let me come right out with it. You know I think the world of you. It was always my hope that you would succeed me as principal. And, I made no secret of it. But..."

"But what?"

"But the managers met yesterday and have decided to offer the position to Ms. Jackson."

"You're joking of course. Miss nose-in-the air, Miss cold as ice, Ms. Jackson?"

"I'm afraid so. But whatever you may think of her, she is a very competent teacher."

"This school has had many competent teachers. I for one have served it for nearly ten years. Not that I didn't have other offers and options. As you know, I turned down a principalship in Brooklyn and Washington, D.C, but I stayed because I truly believed in everything this institution stands for. Where is the fairness? And besides, I have been here twice as long as she has. I'll tell you what I think; I think those Quakers simply didn't want to appoint an outspoken colored man with a mind of his own. That's what I think. Hire the woman, she won't make waves, she'll say exactly what they want to hear and do exactly what they want her to do. The audacity! Miss 'high and mighty,' Oberlin College, principal of our school. What a joke!"

"Listen there's no point in getting upset."

"Oh, I'll be alright. It just means that I'll have to go somewhere else."

"I was hoping you wouldn't say that. Why don't you speak to Mr. Cope first?"

"Why should I?"

"Well, because he's always been a fair-minded man. He is committed to this school and he clearly has great respect for you."

"Well maybe I will, maybe I won't. Listen, we've got to celebrate your diplomatic appointment in grand style."

"Well I'm a modest man. But, what did you have in mind?"

"Well, let's see…the Pythians play this Saturday. What say we have a big picnic, invite the whole school; no the whole city! And, if you're lucky, the Pythians just might let you take a few honorary swings."

"You're on!"

∞∞∞∞∞∞∞∞∞∞

After careful consideration, Octavius decided he would confront Mr. Cope. They agreed to meet in Mr. Cope's home on Spring Garden Street. As he was walking north down Broad Street, he spotted Father Kendrick coming in his direction.

"Ah Octavius, just the man I was looking for. Fancy finding you on this side of town."

"Yeah, well I haven't received too many invitations from this side of town Father."

"Now there's a surprise for ya," said Father Kendrick with a chuckle. "Listen, seriously son, I've been hearing some distressing rumors."

"About what?"

" I was in O'Grady's pub last night and I heard your name mentioned in a most unfriendly way. It looks like some of the hooligans in our parish are starting up again. Seems as though you're a marked man. They're talking about retaliation."

"Retaliation for what?"

"Well, that conductor who threw your girlfriend off the streetcar lost his job and was fined $50 to boot. He's a married man, with four mouths to feed. They hold you responsible."

"Well he deserved it and a lot more. We were entirely justified to demand the right to ride the streetcars. We deserve better treatment for ourselves, our women and our elderly."

"Save it son. You're preaching to the choir here."

"Aw Father, you worry too much. No disrespect, but white folks ran all the colored horse and buggy companies out of business. Then they started their own streetcar companies and now they have the nerve not to want us to ride in them. You tell them, if they want trouble, they know where to find me."

"You're not listening to me! I have an awful feeling about this. God knows I've seen it enough times. I can see the war clouds forming. We've gotta do something other than bash each other's heads in."

"Listen, Father, I appreciate your concern but I'm running late for a meeting with Mr. Cope. We'll talk later okay?"

∞∞∞∞∞∞∞∞∞

As the semester rolled on, Caroline LeCount continued to have difficulty in maintaining order in her classroom. It was a beautiful spring day and the children seemed distracted and extremely restless. That morning, a major altercation broke out and some of them responded by throwing books and pencils at one another. This time, Ms. Jackson could hear their unruliness from her private office, which was a considerable distance from Ms. LeCount's classroom. She rose from her desk and walked briskly down the hall and into yet another chaotic scene.

As she moved toward the center of the blackboard, an opened ink bottle was thrown at a student sitting in the front row. It missed its mark and landed squarely on her blouse, spilling ink all over her. In a rare moment of unrestrained anger she shouted,

"At last, Ms. LeCount, we witness the fruits of your teaching methods!"

She hurried out of the classroom and went to her private office to change clothes. There she removed her blouse and silk slip revealing her grotesquely disfigured back. It was entirely covered with thick scar tissue and bulging welts that were the visual remains of several lashings. A few seconds later, Ms. LeCount ran into her office without knocking. She observed Ms. Jackson's naked back and was horrified by the gruesome sight.

"Oh my God, Ms. Jackson. I'm so sorry. I…I…I didn't mean to walk in on you were… Believe me…I just wanted to say I'm sorry for…"

Ms. Jackson interrupted her and quickly put on a new blouse.

"And exactly what are you sorry about? Barging into my office unannounced? Soiling my blouse? Or could it be you're apologizing for what you've just seen. Which is it Ms. LeCount?"

Caroline could not answer. She looked away and then down at the floor.

"Which is it Ms. LeCount?…**Which is it!** Well, permit me to help you. Why don't I accept all your pathetic apologies and excuses here and now? Why don't we bundle them like a bale of cotton, you know, like the cotton I was forced to pick ever since I was old enough to walk. Yes, I shall bundle them all up for you. I'll take yesterday's lame excuses, today's failures and tomorrow's benign lapses and weave them into a splendid quilt for poor Ms. LeCount; one that will cover up every blessed responsibility she has managed to shirk. That is if, and only if, you will kindly leave this office. Now!"

"I can't."

"You mean you won't!"

"No, I mean I can't. Look, I know you don't think much of me as a teacher…maybe you don't care for me as a person either. But, I want you to know, I can keep a secret. You don't have to be ashamed."

" **Ashamed!** You think *I'm* ashamed? No! It is those barbarians who did this to me, not once, but several times who should be ashamed. *The shame is theirs!* My God, I was a mere child when they started it! No Ms. LeCount, it is they who should look away in moral embarrassment. And, as for your ability to keep a secret, it is of no consequence to me!"

"I only meant that, you need not worry about any of this. On my honor, I will never mention this to anyone, not a living soul. You are a lady, a harsh and overbearing lady, but a lady of the first order. And, nothing in your past can ever change that. Listen, I may not rise to your standards as a teacher, but as a woman, a colored woman, I can feel your pain. Yes, and I have even *seen* it. And, you know what?"

"What Ms. LeCount?"

"I respect…no, I love you all the more."

Caroline started crying and headed for the door.

"Ms. LeCount?"

"Yes?"

"Tell me, what do you know about pain? Despite your questionable training, you were a freeborn woman. You and your precious Mr. Catto know nothing about the utter horror of slavery. My parents died in the fields, destitute and beaten down. My Aunt toiled for years just to purchase her freedom. Then she worked for six dollars a month and saved $125 dollars to buy my freedom as well. Do you understand me? That was just about the price of a country mule! You couldn't possibly understand what it was like."

"That may be," responded Caroline. "But we haven't lived charmed lives either. Spit upon, insulted and assaulted every day of our lives. Why? Because of the color of our skin. Tormented by little people, with little minds, with half our education and half our common sense and initiative; insisting all the while that our skin color was a badge of dishonor and a symbol of innate inferiority. It's maddening! But, I still don't understand you."

"What don't you understand?"

"Well for one thing, I would have thought that someone who has experienced such suffering would be more tolerant and would find it easier to relate to the misfortunes of others."

"You must be kidding? What makes you think that I don't relate to people; especially *our* people?"

"I suppose you've become jaded and bitter. It happens you know."

"No Ms. LeCount! Your perceptions reflect a naiveté typical of freeborn Negroes, a benevolent naiveté, but naiveté nonetheless. Oh, I relate all right. Believe me, there was never a time when I rose in my classes at Oberlin College, that I did not feel like I had the entire weight of the African race resting on my shoulders. Every day I had to somehow prove myself as being worthy to be among them.

Every day, I had to demonstrate that a Negro deserved to be in an institution of higher learning. But you see my dear, very few of us come through this world unscathed, unbattered by injustice; and that goes for slaves, free men and women and Cherokee Indians. And it matters not, because the world my dear, doesn't dole out bushels of apologies to those whom it victimizes.

I relate quite well, but not to self-pity. With these children, *especially* those coming out of slavery, I relate all too well. But, I don't cry over what *has* happened to them, I cry over what *will* happen to them if they submit to adversity and self-doubt and stop believing in themselves. I cry over what will happen to them if they don't seize this opportunity to get a good education. I cry when they don't exert themselves. And I'll cry if they don't fully realize their God-given potential."

"But you do it in such an unkind and unfeeling way."

"**No! I do it in a firm way!** There is a difference. I love these children. I would even die for them. You want to protect them, to coddle them, to soothe their wounds. Rubbish! I want to equip them and empower them, and prepare them to live productive lives. You want to pin on them the label of permanent victim. **As God is my witness; we will raise no victims here!"**

∞∞∞∞∞∞∞∞∞∞

Ms. Fannie Jackson was forged in the spiritual fire of redemptive suffering and had emerged with the heart of a saint and the hide of an elephant. Adversity had sorely tested her, but she vowed to conquer it and live her best life – a life of service. And in time, she grew to claim complete victory over the time bandits. She had been ransomed for a pittance but evolved into a woman of incalculable worth. Fannie Jackson was mercifully delivered from bondage, but there were other blessings that marked the design and unfolding of her life.

She had embraced a great Light and it was now the time bandits who bowed to *her* authority. Her only mission in life was to rescue future generations from the clutches of those who would rob them of the fullness of their humanity—those despicable time bandits; the manipulators of minds and the watchful destroyers of hopeful dreams.

Fannie Jackson (Coppin)

40. Redemption

"Let us fall into the hands of the Lord and not into the hands of men. For equal to His majesty is the mercy He shows."

Sirach 2:18

Across town, Octavius was having a poignant episode of his own. Mr. Cope welcomed him into his home with a warm smile and a firm handshake.

"Octavius do come in. I thank thee for thy punctuality. Do be seated."

"Thank you for seeing me Mr. Cope. I realize you are a very busy man."

"Nonsense, I'm never too busy for thee."

"Well sir, I want to speak to you about your decision to pass me over for the principalship of the Institute."

"I see. I have always appreciated thy candor and directness. It is a sign of strong character. I want thee to know it was not an easy decision for the Managers. But, I trust that thou wouldst agree that Ms. Jackson is a most capable teacher."

"And I am not?"

"Of course thou art. Nevertheless, with all of thy political activities and interest in baseball over the past five years, thou hast not kept thyself fresh in all those branches, which are allotted to the station of Principal. But please believe me when I say that we have a high appreciation of thy services to the Institute and would be pleased to do whatever we can to promote thy welfare."

"Then I suppose you leave me no alternative but to resign. I have plans for my life you know."

"I wish thou wouldst reconsider. Tis not wise to make hasty decisions. I am an old man with still much to learn. However, this much I know. There are plans within plans. It may well be that God has a special purpose for thee. If so, He will make provisions for His purposes, but not necessarily for thy plans. Octavius, I feel that thou art at an important crossroad in thy life. I want thee to pray on your decision, will thou do that?"

∞∞∞∞∞∞∞∞∞∞∞

Octavius agreed to give the matter further thought and prayer. However, for the rest of the week, he was preoccupied with planning Principal Bassett's going away celebration in Fairmount Park. It seemed like the whole Seventh Ward turned out to pay tribute to their revered schoolmaster. Most came bearing gifts and small tokens of their great esteem. The younger children from the Institute's Preparatory school prepared special congratulatory cards for him and offered assorted arts and crafts made in his honor. Octavius and the Pythians chipped in to buy him a baseball cap and uniform with the title "Mr. Ambassador" embroidered on the back.

While the Pythians played baseball, several neighborhood musicians gathered to play various brass and percussion instruments that echoed throughout the park. Off to the left of the baseball field, Caroline and Ms. Jackson sat alone under a maple tree.

"So when did he ask you?"

"Yesterday; and I wanted you to be the first to know."

"I am so happy for you Caroline. Octavius is a good man; a very *opinionated* man, but a good man nonetheless. You two will make a great couple. When will the wedding be?

"Well, we haven't set a date yet, but I'll certainly let you know as soon as possible. I want you to be one of my bridesmaids."

"I am touched and honored indeed. You can surely count on me to be there. Listen, we must not appear to be rude. Let's go see what the others are doing over there."

They rose to their feet and walked down a narrow foot path leading to a cluster of weeping willow trees. A group of Institute teachers were telling stories to a large group of elementary school students gathered under the shade.

Ms. Douglass was concluding a story as Caroline and Ms. Jackson joined them. Mr. Still approached the gathering from a different direction and decided to listen in on the lesson.

"…And so the tortoise wins the race! Now what do you think the moral of the story is children?"

"Don't be bragging on yourself or you'll mess around and lose," answered one little girl.

"Well, yes you're somewhat correct Christina. But according to Aesop; the moral of the story is that the race does not always go to the swift."

The children clapped cheerfully. They appeared to like and understand the implicit message of the fable.

"Okay, that's it for me. Who else has a story? Ms. Kearny? I know you have one,"

"No not me, I'm not good at story telling. Maybe Ms. Jackson has one?"

"No thank you. I'll pass."

"Aw, come on Ms. Jackson, I know you have plenty of stories."

The children and other teachers chimed in to coax her on. Caroline pulled her forward and a reluctant Ms. Jackson took center stage.

"Goodness, alright, alright. I suppose I do have one or two to tell you. Well let's see…Once upon a time, there was a little girl playing in the park on a beautiful sunny day."

As usual, the children gave her their undivided attention.

"While walking along, she sees a bird's nest on the ground that had apparently fallen out of the tree. She looked a little closer and behold, what do you think she saw in the nest?"

"Birds!" shouted the children.

"No, not quite. She saw four little bird eggs that had not hatched yet. Then all of a sudden, she noticed the most amazing thing. The little birds were starting to stir inside their eggs."

"Wow!"

"Yes, right before her eyes, they slowly but surely started cracking open their little shells. First, she saw a little claw sticking out and then a tiny head could be seen. The little girl was fascinated as she watched them slowly struggle to free themselves from the eggshells and enter the world. But she also noticed that only three of the eggs showed signs of cracking open. The fourth egg was still, oh so very, very still."

"What was wrong with it?" asked one of the girls.

"Well, I'm going to tell you. You see minutes later, three of the birds completely managed to free themselves from their shells. Once out of their shells, they each stretched their wings, walked around a bit and flew away, high into the sky. The little girl was so excited she jumped for joy. But, then she realized that the fourth egg still didn't show any signs of life."

"Aww!"

"She became worried and do you know what she did?"

"What?"

"She picked up a small stone, and slowly started to crack open the egg and free it from its shell. Sure enough, the little bird started to appear. And, before long, she had completely opened the shell."

"Yaaay!"

"So the little bird started to stretch its wings, walk around and then fly away just as the others had done. She was so happy to see it take flight. She believed that she had done something very good and helpful. Then all of a sudden, halfway up in the sky, the little bird stopped flapping its wings and came crashing down to earth. The little girl ran over to the bird to help it, but there was nothing she could do. The little bird was dead. She was so, so sad."

"Awww."

"She dug a hole and buried the little bird under a tree, just like this one. Later that day she went home and told her father about what happened to the unfortunate little bird. And, do you know what her father said?"

"What?"

"He said it was *her fault* that the little bird died."

"Huh?"

"That's right! He explained to her that the other three little birds had managed to free themselves from their shells by kicking and pushing against the walls of their eggshells. By doing all that kicking and pushing they were strengthening their muscles – making those muscles strong so that they would be able to help the little birds fly away on their own power."

"Oh!"

"Yes, you see the poor little girl really was trying to help that fourth little bird by cracking open his shell for him. But she was wrong. By cracking open that shell, the little bird didn't have a chance to build his muscles. His muscles were too weak. So when it came time to fly away, he couldn't."

The children clapped in appreciation for the story. Mr. Still quietly marveled at Ms. Jackson's uncanny ability to communicate positive and practical lessons to even the youngest of students. Continuing on his stroll, Mr. Still saw Principal Bassett seated at a picnic table with Octavius, John Ansar, Jacob White and Uncle Blue. He joined their conversation just as Principal Bassett was speaking.

"So how's that voting resolution shaping up Octavius?"

"Mr. Nesbit will be presenting a new draft to the League on Monday night. If they ratify it then, we'll send it on to the Governor's office. We've lobbied all the key legislative leaders this time, so we think we have a good chance of it passing."

"Good, I hope you will keep me apprised of your progress while I'm away."

"Yeah, that voting. I'm all for that; teeth to toenails," added Uncle Blue.

Mr. Still joined in by offering Octavius his somewhat biased opinion on the matter.

"Nesbit's a good man. But, I think *you* should be preparing that draft Octavius. You're the best writer in the bunch. Everyone knows that."

"You know something Mr. Still? You're probably right about that," said Jacob White.

"Sho he's right about that! Everybody knows that Nesbit ain't the sharpest knife in the drawer. My boy can out think him, out talk him and out write him any day of the week!"

"Aw, come on Uncle Blue, you embarrass me."

"It's the plain truth. As a matter of fact, my boy ought to be leading that group. And you know something else? I taught him everything he knows. That's right; raised him since he was a pup."

Their festive mood was soon to be dampened by the menacing appearance of a small group of white men on the fringe of the park. They were pointing in the direction of the picnic grove. One of them John recognized as McMullen, one of Boss Conley's men. Some of the others were also a part of the Conley gang, but he didn't know them by name.

"Who's that unsavory-looking character John?"

"Nobody, Mr. Bassett. But I should have killed that nobody while I had the chance."

"I don't know what they're staring at! Those boys ain't nothing but trouble. Got the devil in 'em, that's for sure," added Uncle Blue.

∞∞∞∞∞∞∞∞∞

Two days later, the Monday night meeting of the Pennsylvania Equal Rights League was held. Its agenda was brief and the meeting ended earlier than usual. Mr. Nesbit's resolution was approved with minor revisions. As Secretary, Octavius was asked to make the appropriate revisions and forward the resolution to Harrisburg within three days. As they adjourned, Mr. Still was thinking to himself that they should be guardedly optimistic. *Plan for the best and anticipate the worst,* had become his motto – particularly when it came to those unpredictable bureaucrats in Harrisburg.

When the meeting was adjourned, some of the men lingered and struck up various conversations. Octavius' wagon was being repaired, so Uncle Blue agreed to take him to an evening supper he had scheduled with Caroline and her parents. Octavius went straight to Uncle Blue's familiar wagon. It was a tranquil, moonlit night that was enhanced by gentle breezes blowing across the Delaware River. Caroline had been planning the gathering for weeks and Octavius was looking forward to meeting her entire family. He straightened his neck tie and gleefully climbed aboard.

"Ready to go Uncle Blue? Uncle Blue, you ready?"

When he did not respond, Octavius nudged him with his elbow. Uncle Blue slumped forward. Startled by his stillness and eerie silence, Octavius lifted Blue's head up and discovered that his throat had been slashed. His body was cold and blood was splattered all over his coat.

"Quick! Somebody get a doctor!" he screamed.

He gently shook his body again, hoping to revive him. All of the men came rushing to his assistance. John Ansar was the first to arrive. He frantically examined Uncle Blue for a pulse or any signs of life.

"It's no use; he's gone," whispered John.

The soul-shredding shock of it all was too much for Octavius to bear. He dismounted the wagon and immediately dropped to his knees. His body went into convulsions and he began to vomit uncontrollably in the street. There was simply nothing anyone could do to console him.

John Ansar and Jacob White stayed by his side for nearly two hours until Octavius regained some semblance of composure. Meanwhile, Mr. Still and the other men loaded Uncle Blue's body onto an open wagon and took it to the annex of Mother Bethel Church for funeral preparations. It was all like a horrible nightmare that had come to life.

∞∞∞∞∞∞∞∞∞∞

The murder of Uncle Blue sent shockwaves throughout the Seventh Ward and evoked cries for bloody retaliation. Later that night, John Ansar and a small group of men prepared to ambush Tom

McMullen and three of Boss Conley's thugs who had been seen going into O'Grady's pub. When Reverend Catto heard of this, he pleaded with John not to go forward with his vengeful plan. After a heated and emotionally charged argument, John reluctantly agreed to postpone his strike that particular night. But, he made no promises regarding what he would or would not do in the future. With tensions running so high, no one could predict what was in store. The threat of full-scale retaliatory violence loomed over the city like an ominous cloud.

The next morning, Octavius did not come to school and Caroline began to get worried. He failed to show up for supper the previous night and was absent from his classes. She went to Ms. Jackson's office in total desperation.

"Ms. Jackson, have you seen Octavius?"

"No dear, I haven't. Did you look in the library?"

"I did already. He must be devastated. I have to go to him. I'm going to try the teachers' lounge."

"You do that dear. I heard about Uncle Blue. How could they do something like that to such a sweet, sweet man? If you find out anything please let me know immediately, okay?"

∞∞∞∞∞∞∞∞∞∞

Octavius never made it to school that day. He left the house that morning and walked into Mr. Abrams' store in a trance-like depression. Weighted with grief and choking with anger, he pounded both fists on the counter.

"Give me a bottle of rum."

"I didn't know you drank Professor," said Mr. Abrams.

"Now you do!"

"Listen son; I know you're hurting but this isn't the way to make things right."

"No *you* listen! Are you going to sell it to me or not? I can buy it at another store where I don't have to be interrogated before I make a purchase."

"I'm only looking out for you son."

Slamming two dollars on the counter, Octavius snatched the bottle from his hand.

"Save it for someone else!"

He went home and drank the entire bottle of rum, trying desperately to suppress his boiling emotions. Later that afternoon, he staggered out of the house and went looking for Tom McMullen in Fairmount Park where he was reportedly last seen. But McMullen was nowhere to be found. All he saw was a group of Negro children playing near the Belmont Plateau picnic grove. Some were playing baseball under the watchful eye of Father Kendrick who saw Octavius staggering toward them and reeking of alcohol.

"Octavius, you're drunk!"

"Yeah, I know that. And I know you killed my mother and Uncle Blue too."

"What the hell are you talking about Octavius? Come over here and sit down!"

Father Kendrick reached for Octavius' arm to lead him to a park bench. Octavius reacted violently and shoved him to the ground. Some of the children and adults immediately came to Father Kendrick's aid. Meanwhile, Octavius snatched a baseball bat from one of the children who was near home plate. He then hollered to a startled little boy who was standing on the pitcher's mound.

"Throw me a pa...pa... pitch!"

"No Professor...I can't"

"I said, throw me that damn ball!"

The little boy was afraid and reluctantly tossed a soft pitch over the center of home plate. Octavius swung recklessly at the ball and instantly lost control of the bat. It flew out of his hands and forcefully struck a little colored girl who was playing a few feet away. The extreme velocity and weight of the wooden projectile instantly knocked her to the ground. Parents and children screamed as they rushed to her side. Father Kendrick and a few of the men ran toward Octavius who had collapsed at home plate in an alcoholic stupor.

"I need to check on the girl. You two pick him up and take him to my parish," shouted Father Kendrick. "I don't want his father to see him like that!"

∞∞∞∞∞∞∞∞∞∞∞∞

Later that evening, Octavius regained consciousness in the back room of Father Kendrick's rectory. Father Kendrick placed a wet face cloth on his forehead and Octavius groaned and slowly sat up.

"So you're finally awake. You know you made a total jackass of yourself earlier today. You badly injured a little girl with a baseball bat"

"Oh my God! I did? How is she?"

"She's in the hospital, in a coma; thanks to you. The doctors don't know if she's going to make it. You know, you let a lot of people down, especially the children. They all look up to you. God, what a pitiful spectacle!"

"I don't want to hear that now Father."

"Well you're going to damn well hear it from me Mister!"

"Listen, you don't understand any of this. You white men are all alike, you're all devils," he said, still dazed by the rum.

"Oh yeah? And I suppose that what you did was *inspired by the angels!* You listen to me, you bum! A little innocent girl is fighting for her life because of you. Do you hear me? Because of your stupidity! And as for me, I'll be damned if I ever apologize to you or any other man for the color of my skin; that's for damn sure. Now you shut up and lay there, and get your damned fool self together. That's what you do! … Jake watch him!"

He handed the wet face cloth to Jacob White and left in a fit of anger.

∞∞∞∞∞∞∞∞∞

Hours later, Jake transported Octavius home. And for two full weeks, Reverend Catto tried his best to counsel and care for his guilt-ridden son.

"I brought you some food. You haven't eaten in several days."

"I told you a thousand times dad. I'm not hungry."

"Octavius, you have to eat. You can't just sit up here in this bedroom and wither away."

"Why not? Just leave me alone dad; please leave me alone."

"Son, I know how you feel."

"You couldn't possibly know how I feel."

"Oh really? You're hurt, you're angry and you don't know where to turn or what to do. Did you forget? I know a little something about the subject. I am constantly haunted by the thought that were it not for my work with the Underground, your mother might be alive today. A day doesn't go by that I don't miss her! And, Uncle Blue…well, I loved him like a brother. Believe me; you don't have any monopoly on pain or mourning."

"I never said I did."

"Listen to me son. What happened to that girl was an accident. You know that, we all know that. We just have to pray for her recovery. And, the best thing for you to do is ask for forgiveness from God. Then you've got to forgive yourself."

"But I don't know how."

"Then I've failed you as a father."

"Why can't you understand?"

"I understand alright. I understand you haven't been to the Institute in a long while. I understand those children need you and I understand that you can't sit up here and wallow in self-pity. That's what I understand!"

"Fine, then I'll submit my resignation tomorrow."

"Is that all you can think to do? Listen son, you're not the first man to ever trip over himself. Some of our greatest leaders have fallen down and at some point, lost their way. But you must understand something. There is nothing you have done or are ever going to do, that can separate you from the grace of God and His forgiveness. You think about that."

∞∞∞∞∞∞∞∞∞∞∞∞

In the week that followed, Octavius became more dispirited and refused to return to his duties at the Institute. Later on, Mr. Cope and Ms. Jackson met to discuss an appropriate course of action.

"It's been nearly three weeks Ms. Jackson. I do not think we can keep the position open for Mr. Catto. What happened was a tragedy, but the work of the school must continue."

"I know that Mr. Cope; but there's still hope."

"Thou art an eternal optimist Ms. Jackson."

"Yes, I am. Can't we give him more time?"

"We shall give Mr. Catto till the end of this week. Then I am afraid we must move on. I have a suitable replacement in mind. A Mr. Richard T. Greener has been brought to my attention. He is a native of this city and a recent graduate of Harvard College. I have it on good authority that he is the first of thy race to win that high honor."

"That's good, but we will wait one more week. Agreed?"

"It is done."

∞∞∞∞∞∞∞∞∞∞∞∞

At the end of that week, Reverend Catto knocked on Octavius' bedroom door. Octavius was lying in bed, unwashed, unshaven and looking worn out. The dark crescents beneath his eyes and the thick stubble on his ashen face clearly reflected his restlessness and total withdrawal.

"Come in."

"You've got company son. Better grab a robe."

Without further invitation, Ms. Jackson walked briskly into the bedroom.

"Ah, Mr. Catto. I see you're sleeping in this afternoon. How fortunate for you. The rest of us have work to do and important responsibilities to meet. Nevertheless, you sir, are apparently a gentleman of leisure and have no such obligations. Isn't life grand?"

"Can I help you?"

"Help *me* you say? Oh no, you can't help *me*. But, I thank you ever so much for asking. No sir, I am here for an altogether different purpose. I have been asked to determine your level of interest in a promotion at the Institute. That is all."

"A promotion? Are you crazy? Didn't you get my letter of resignation?"

"As a matter of fact, I did. Well written too; that is, if one has a fondness for melodrama. Yes, I read it and passed it on to Mr. Cope. However, he has refused to accept it and has instead sent me to offer a counter-proposal to you."

"What in the world are you talking about lady?"

"Well it's really quite simple. You are being asked to assume the position of Principal of the Boy's Department while I will oversee the Girl's Department. A reasonable division of labor I must say. But, if you have no interest, I can be relied upon to convey your regrets to Mr. Cope."

"Who do you think you're fooling? Listen, I see right through this."

"Oh you do? Pray tell, what do you see Mr. Catto?"

"It's obvious you're just trying to get me back to work."

"On the contrary Mr. Catto, I am not trying to do any such thing. As I said, I accepted your resignation and have joined in the search for a suitable replacement. And lo and behold, I was made aware of the availability of a young man quite like yourself who is able to step in for you immediately. I do believe Mr. Cope said he was a *Harvard man,* yes, I do believe that's what he said."

"You know something? You're bluffing and you're not very good at it."

"Oh really? Very well then Mr. Catto; suit yourself. I will be sure to let Mr. Cope know of your refusal. Ah, one more thing before I go. There's someone who wants to say hello to you."

She opened the bedroom door and in walked the little girl who was injured by his bat. Her head was still bandaged but her face was rosy and aglow with excitement. She was followed by her mother, Caroline LeCount and Father Kendrick. Octavius dropped to his knees and stared into the little girl's eyes. She flashed him a smile then cupped her tiny hands and sweetly whispered in his ear.

"Please come back to school Professor. Please come back."

Octavius was instantly relieved and overtaken with joy. He hugged her tightly, never saying a word. An excruciating weight had been lifted off his shoulders. Tears streamed down his face like divine rains, washing away the stain of his misbehavior.

41. History Re-Told

"Let our posterity know that we their ancestors, uncultured and unlearned, amid all trials and temptations were men of integrity; recognized with gratefulness their truest friends, dishonored and in peril; were enabled to resist the seductions of ease and the intimidation of power; were true to themselves, the age in which they lived, their abject race, and the cause of man; shrunk not from trial nor from sufferings – but conscious of Responsibility and impelled by Duty, gave themselves up to the vindication of high hopes and the lofty aims of true humanity."

Alexander Crummel

The next Monday, Octavius returned to the Institute rejuvenated and was given the welcomed assignment of teaching history to the Institute's senior students.

"...and so in conclusion, while the study of Homer and Pericicles are useful and important, I would argue that we must place equal emphasis on *our own* history. Beginning with the early Egyptians and extending forward to the Atlantic Slave Trade, the courageous rebellions of Cinque, Nat Turner and Denmark Vesey, including the Herculean work of the abolitionists and the Underground Railroad up to Emancipation in 1863. It is a noble history that we dare not forget. It is a history replete with conflict, struggle and ultimately, triumph. Yes, do you have a question Marcus?"

"But Professor, my father keeps saying that we should not make such a big deal about history; about things that happened so far back in the past?"

"With all due respect to your father, I disagree. The study of the past gives us such great insight into how we arrived at the present. History gives us an understanding of where we stand in the stream of time. It also gives us some ideas about how to plan for the future. We can learn much from the failures and successes of those who came before us. As Dionysius once said, *history is philosophy teaching by example.*"

"Yeah, but he says that we don't need to waste our time trying to memorize all those historical facts and dates and stuff."

"Please understand me Mr. Johnson. I'm not talking about the simple memorization of dates and events in history. I'm talking about a deep understanding of who we are as a people, where we've been and where we're trying to go. I'm talking about a solid and informed appreciation of how we have survived and achieved against great odds to be where we are today, on the threshold of getting the franchise, the pivotal right to vote as full citizens in this country. I'm talking about self-respect and pride; a pride so deep, you will want to drop to your knees and thank God He made you colored!"

∞∞∞∞∞∞∞∞∞

Apparently, the great Civil War did hardly anything to improve race relations in America. Racial hostilities in Philadelphia persisted and increased as the Negro population began to grow and demand the rights of full citizenship. Change had been slow in coming. However, seven years after the Emancipation Proclamation, the federal government seemed prepared to extend voting rights to its Negro citizens. A mighty change did come and it would have a profound impact on the American political landscape. On February 3, 1870, the Congress of the United States ratified the 15th Amendment to the Constitution. The amendment expressly stipulated that:

"The right of the citizens of the United States to vote shall not be denied or abridged by the United States or by any other State on account of race, color, or previous condition of servitude."

It was a great victory for democracy and a crushing defeat for local and state authorities who were determined to deny colored people the right to vote. It had been a long and bitter road. Legally speaking, a major battle had been won. However, the war was still raging. Hardly anyone expected Philadelphia's municipal government to comply with this controversial federal enactment. Thus in April, 1870, Octavius led a march through the city that culminated in a speech made at Horticultural Hall. There, he and Negro voting rights advocates paid homage to the "martyrs and apostles of liberty, among them John Brown and Abraham Lincoln." In order to take full advantage of this opportunity, the Pennsylvania Equal Rights League also launched a statewide campaign to get as many colored people as possible registered to vote in the fall election.

In Philadelphia, the colored population was over 25,000 and constituted the largest urban concentration of potential colored voters outside of the South. Thus, all eyes were on the city as a pivotal battleground for the reform of American electoral politics. Accordingly, the League decided to stage a massive celebration and parade. As planned, the parade route ran through center city and was to end in front of Independence Hall. However, this was not to be. The peaceful parade was violently disrupted by an angry mob of white residents who attacked the paraders with stones, bricks, eggs and rotten vegetables. Police protection was virtually non-existent so the mob succeeded in bringing the procession to an immediate halt.

Later that evening, the League defiantly continued its celebration with a series of speeches delivered at Horticultural Hall. Octavius Catto spoke, along with Robert Purvis, Jacob White and some of the city's leading white and colored citizens. Frederick Douglass capped off the celebration with a stirring speech intended to bolster the determination of Philadelphia's Negro voters. Recognizing the gravity of the historical moment, he declared the 15th Amendment to be a major milestone in the ongoing battle for social equality. His speech was passionate and brimming with hope. In conclusion, he declared,

"As for me, I am no longer a black man. At last! at last! at last! I find myself not only a man, but a man among men. I find myself not a man of color but a citizen."

Yet despite Douglass' bold pronouncement and the optimistic oratory of the evening, the colored turnout in the general election of October 1870 was disappointingly low and not at all what the League had expected. Some of the city's colored voters clearly yielded to the blatant intimidation that infected the polling stations. However, many colored residents of the Fifth and Seventh Wards were undaunted and lined up at four o'clock in the morning to vote. They wanted to be the first in line to avoid attacks and dodge the dangerous gauntlet of bricks, rocks and bottles, commonly referred to as "Irish confetti."

Some speculated that the low turnout was due to the fact that the two contested congressional seats were virtually assured and only two county offices were on the ballot. At any rate, the League declared the elections of 1870 as a "moral victory" and vowed to work even harder to register colored voters and have them fully participate in the upcoming elections of 1871.

In the spring of 1871, the League planned a voter registration rally. A makeshift platform was put together at the construction site for Philadelphia's grandiose City Hall. Construction of this huge edifice began in January 1871 which was to be located at the intersection of Broad and Market Streets. As planned, it was to be nation's largest municipal building. In fact, proud Philadelphians took particular pride in noting that it would reportedly be (upon completion) even larger than the U.S. Capitol Building.

Mr. Still proposed a motion to have Octavius deliver the League's keynote speech at this highly anticipated rally. An overwhelming majority carried the motion, much to the chagrin of Mr. Nesbit. Mr. Still was not just playing favorites. He honestly believed that Octavius' oratorical flair and his widespread popularity throughout the city made him a better representative than their esteemed colleague from Altoona. In fact, few would deny the fact that Octavius' meteoric rise in Philadelphia's educational and political circles made him the ideal spokesperson for a *new generation* of social activists operating in the city and beyond.

His reputation was further enhanced by the achievements of the Pythian Baseball Club and Octavius' role as its shortstop and one of its more prolific batters. For the past five years, the Pythian Club had been traveling throughout the eastern seaboard as Philadelphia's representatives in a burgeoning Negro baseball league. The success of the Pythians in challenging both Negro and white opponents was the source of tremendous civic pride, especially in the Seventh Ward.

Octavius V. Catto

Mr. Still also took it upon himself to invite some of their old friends to the massive rally. Samuel Smith and his wife were delighted to get an invitation. John Miller Dickey came with a small group of students from Lincoln University; and an aging Harriet Tubman interrupted her speaking engagements in New York just so that she could see her "little man" one more time. The mood of the rally was festive and electrifying. Octavius was well prepared to deliver a speech that would be a defining moment in his blossoming political career. Members of the now defunct Vigilance Committee watched young Octavius mount the stage as a charismatic young man of extraordinary persuasion; the pride of the Seventh Ward.

They were reminded of how long their struggle had been. Octavius had not even been born in 1837, when the Pennsylvania Supreme Court literally stole the right to vote from them. They praised God for this miracle; this sacred liberty. As Octavius was delivering his speech, William and Ellen Craft, Frances Harper, Mrs. John Brown and Colonel Wagner beamed with respect. A host of Octavius' colleagues and students from the Institute also looked on with great pride at Philadelphia's increasingly popular "favorite son".

While Octavius was concluding his speech, a group of ruffians gathered on the southeast corner of Broad and Ludlow Streets. They were talking to Boss Conley and occasionally scanning the excited crowd. Unbeknownst to the spectators, Boss Conley had deployed six well-trained marksmen on various rooftops facing the podium. Octavius began his speech totally unaware that he was clearly in the crosshairs of Conley's sharpshooters and exposed from multiple angles.

"...so on this day of celebration, let us remember and never forget a time when our laws failed to protect the less fortunate; days when the law was indeed cruel, days when justice slept. We needed and oh, how we needed, those men and women of strong conviction who were tried and tested by the fires of hatred, oppression and despair. Many of them were former slaves who found their source of hope and faith in the very religion their slave-owners had violated and defiled. They were people of uncommon faith and determination.

They understood the risks involved in this struggle but they were not paralyzed by fear. They understood all too well the words of Benjamin Franklin who warned that those who give up essential liberty to purchase a little temporary safety deserve neither liberty nor safety.

So let the enemies of democracy take heed. The Negro is here to stay. And, let those of you gathered here today take note. Today marks no hollow and colorless victory. On this day, only seven years after Emancipation, we stand on the threshold of full citizenship. After all, it is for the good of the nation that every element of its people, mingled as they are, shall have a true and intelligent conception of the allegiance due to the established powers. Therefore, we dedicate ourselves to being responsible and loyal citizens. But first, let us not delude ourselves. There must come a change! In order to have peace, we must work for justice. We have to…"

BANG, BANG, BANG!

His speech was suddenly interrupted by the sounds of rifles firing into the dense crowd. John Ansar quickly threw Octavius to the ground and covered him with his body. The screaming crowd stampeded and frantically dispersed in all directions. Patrolmen and mounted police converged on the scene brandishing guns and billy clubs.

Octavius lied motionless on the platform, unable to move his arms or legs. His respiration was labored and he felt a sharp compression in his lungs. John Ansar stared at him and saw a very pained expression on his face.

"You alright boy?"

"I can't breathe," gasped Octavius.

"Don't you worry none boy. You just hang in there. I'll get you to the hospital real quick. Trust me; you'll be feeling better in no time."

"John?"

"Yeah boy?"

"You know something?… I'd be feeling a whole lot better if you'd just roll off of me."

John was covering Octavius like a thick carpet that was almost twice his size. He lifted his body off of Octavius, and sure enough, he felt instant relief. Rising to their feet, they both scanned the terrain. Three ambulances had converged on the scene. In total, ten nearby spectators had been injured by the gunfire. They were all taken to Pennsylvania Hospital and subsequently released latter that evening. Octavius' injuries were minimal. He ended the day with bruised ribs and a large knot on the back of his head. All in all, it was an infinitesimally small price to pay for the joy of being alive.

∞∞∞∞∞∞∞∞∞∞

Despite this attack and the threat of future violence, the League's voter registration drive continued without hesitation. Octavius vowed to resume his political activities undaunted by this latest act of terrorism. The following day, he sat alone in the teachers' lounge relaxing before he met his next class. Caroline entered the lounge with a gentleman he had never seen before.

"Oh there you are Octavius. I want to introduce you to a new member of our faculty. Mr. Richard Greener, this is my fiancé, Octavius Catto."

"Welcome aboard Greener. Hmmm…Greener, where have I heard that name before?"

"You remember dearest. Ms. Jackson mentioned him to you a little while ago."

"Oh yes, Richard Greener from Harvard. Hey, wait a minute is there anything I should know?"

"No cause for concern dear," answered Caroline. "The Board of Managers has decided to add a new teaching position due to the increase in enrollment this semester."

"Oh I see. Well then I look forward to working with you Mr. Greener," said Octavius.

"As do I. Look, I had better get moving. I have a number of class preparations to finish. Ms. Jackson made it very clear that we're here to work and everyone's got to paddle their own canoe."

"Well, that's our Ms. Jackson all right," said Caroline. "We'll see you later Richard."

"Okay. It was a pleasure meeting you Octavius."

"Same here."

As he closed the door, Octavius had a sudden revelation.

"I should have known!"

"Known what?" asked Caroline.

"Ms. Jackson wasn't bluffing. There *really was* a Richard Greener from Harvard!"

"No dear, she never bluffs," said Caroline as she kissed him on the cheek. "I thought you knew that."

42. Election Day, 1871

"The right of the citizens of the United States to vote shall not be denied or abridged by the United States or by any other State on account of race, color, or previous condition of servitude."

Fifteenth Amendment of the United States Constitution

The League was undeterred by the attempted assassination of Octavius and death threats directed at the League's most visible leaders. Beginning in June, the League held additional outdoor rallies and public demonstrations that also took place without police protection. Their organizers adhered to a uniform dress code consisting of black coats and hats, white gloves and blue sashes. This officious attire was meant to convey the seriousness and dignity of the voting process. It was the beginning of their efforts to educate and mobilize the colored voters. This was no simple task for a people who were not experienced in electoral politics.

The League's leadership anticipated later that they would have a much better Negro turnout in the election that was scheduled for October 11. This time, they would be ready and would focus less on ceremonial parades and more on political education and community organization. However, the League's consciousness-raising and mobilization campaign would soon be met with an equally vigorous campaign of fear and intimidation designed to keep colored voters away from the polls. Beginning in September, there was a series of terroristic attacks on the colored citizenry. As predicted, the notoriously deceptive and determined incumbents vigorously fanned the flames of ignorance and racial hatred to support their bid for re-election. A month before the big election, Mayor Swift and his political cronies began skillfully to manipulate public opinion by portraying the election as an apocalyptic showdown whereby Negroes were trying to take over "the white man's government".

Their vicious propaganda campaign effectively appealed to the white voters' basest instincts. Its overall message was primitive and grossly distorted. In effect, the campaign was based on the deceptive notion that Negroes threatened to take control of the levers of power and literally "snatch the bread off of the white man's table". In truth, Negro voters constituted less than twenty percent of the electorate. However, the mayor's race was so close that the Negro vote could well determine the outcome of the election. In their view, it was bad enough that Negroes had claimed the right to vote. Now if Negroes turned out to vote and they voted as a bloc; the incumbent Mayor's political party faced certain defeat at the polls.

During the three days before the election, their fear and intimidation campaign reached a fever pitch. Tempers flared and interracial fighting broke out all over the city as lawless rioters took to the streets in search of Negroes and their suspected organizers. No less than twenty Negroes were treated for wounds at Pennsylvania Hospital. One of the League's members, Isaac Chase was shot to death and mutilated with a hatchet on the steps of his home.

As Election Day drew near, it was clear that the mayor had successfully instigated racial animosity to an unprecedented level. In addition, he controlled the newspapers and had ample campaign funds to reward the Irish street gangs and policemen who conspired to suppress the Negro vote. He knew that if the Negro voters of the fourth, fifth, and seventh wards went to the polls, he was doomed. If all went according to his plan, Negro voters in these particular wards would be too afraid to go to the polls. In addition, he was determined that those who did try to vote would soon come to regret their decision. He strongly believed that fear and naked aggression would ultimately determine the outcome of this impending political showdown.

In contrast, his electoral opponent, William Stokes appealed to the citizenry to help him form "a new Philadelphia". He promised to restore law and order to the city by revamping the police department and eliminating the city's volunteer fire companies. Both candidates knew that the election would have far-reaching consequences. In fact, the upcoming election of a Mayor, County Sheriff and the city council would determine who controlled the city and the election machinery itself. Unlike the previous year, the stakes could not have been any higher.

On the eve of Election Day, more fights broke out between Negroes and whites, just two blocks away from the Institute. With tensions running so high, the situation was getting way out of control throughout the Seventh Ward. Two companies of United States Marines were called into the city to help quell the violence in other local "hotspots". Ms. Jackson decided to dismiss the students early as a necessary precaution. Hostilities were so aroused that not even the children were considered to be safe from the violence of the mobs.

When election day arrived, Octavius indicated that he was going to stay at the school and finish some reports before going to vote. While working at his desk, he heard a knock at his office door. Caroline LeCount was preparing to leave the building. The worried look on her face caught his immediate attention.

"I really wish you would leave with the rest of us."

"I can't Caroline. I already told you. I've got some work to finish before I go to the polls. Then I have to report to duty. General Wagner had ordered my brigade to assemble for inspection. Military couriers from Camp Penn were expected to deliver our uniforms and firearms yesterday. I guess they're running late. We're going to help guard the polling sites and maintain order throughout the day. "

"Octavius, listen to me for a minute. Will you?"

"Yes my love. What is it?"

"Do you really plan to go down there to vote?"

"Now that's a silly question. Of course I do."

"I know you don't want to hear this, but I'm afraid. Those white boys have spread it all over the neighborhood, that any colored man who tries to vote is putting his life at risk."

"Oh really?"

"Yes really! And I wish you would take this more seriously."

"Now what exactly is it that you want me to do? Not vote? Not report for duty?"

"Of course not."

"Then what are you saying?"

"I'm saying that I'm scared. Do you hear me? I'm so afraid! "

"Listen Caroline, we can't allow ourselves to be intimidated by those thugs. I'm going to vote and I'm going to get as many of our people as I can down to that polling station. I want our people to vote. I want them to think something of themselves, and I want them to realize that they count."

"But at the cost of your life? What about our commitment to teach these children?"

"Listen, it's going to be alright. I have to do what I have to do. If we let them bully us out of the vote, what do you think will happen? If we don't take a stand now, who knows, it might be decades before we finally achieve full citizenship. Look how long it took us to get the streetcars open to us. Now Caroline; now is the time to make our stand. I want you to go home right away. I'll call on you later tonight, okay?"

"Okay."

Tears rolled down her cheeks as he held her in a long and tender embrace. Caroline reluctantly left his office, no less worried than when she entered it. As she slowly walked out of the building, she saw John Ansar coming toward her.

"Good morning, Ms. LeCount. Where you headed?"

"Good morning John. I have to buy some bread around the corner and take it to my parents. I'm told the stores will be closing early today. Then I'm going straight home."

"Well ma'am, you best be careful. Things are getting crazy. Folks fighting all over the place. They're even talking about bringing in the troops. If you don't mind, I think I should escort you home."

"Oh my God! Thank you John. I'm lucky that you came along."

"Not really luck, ma'am. Truth be told, Octavius asked me to wait out here for you."

Octavius peered out of his window and breathed a sigh of relief as the two of them turned the corner and disappeared from sight. A few minutes later, he finished his work and walked down the empty corridors of the building. There was something strangely unnatural about the quiet and stillness inside. The school seemed cold and barren without its energetic students and faculty going about their business. He locked the front door behind him and walked in the direction of Market Street.

The same eeriness followed him outside. The streets were empty and hauntingly motionless. Shops were closed and shades were drawn in every row house in uniform anticipation of the worst. At the corner of 7th and South Street, Mr. Reid, one of the Seventh Ward's elderly neighborhood watchmen, cautioned him.

"Hey Professor, I'd be careful if I were you. We got trouble on our hands."

"So I hear. Thanks Mr. Reid, now you get in the house, okay."

Minutes later, Octavius arrived at Mr. Abrams' general store. Mr. Abrams was moving his sidewalk wares inside the store as he prepared to close early.

"Hey Professor, you caught me in the nick of time. They say we are in for some fierce rioting. You had better get off the streets yourself. Those Irish fellas have never been too fond of you anyway."

Walking into the store, he asked,

"What do you need?"

"I need a reliable pistol, right away. Mine has not worked properly since I left Camp Penn. I'm going down to the polling station in a few minutes."

"You sure you want to do that son?"

"I'm plenty sure."

"I haven't sold guns in a long time Octavius. But here, take my Colt 45, I haven't used it in years."

"I can't take it. Aren't you afraid you might need it?"

"No, these old eyes have seen a lot. Perhaps too much. I am well past that kind of fear son. Besides, the gun is just a decoy. I keep it under the counter to ward off any stick-up artists. It works fine but it doesn't even have any bullets in it."

"That's okay, I think I have some ammo back at the house; or at least I hope so. Listen, I have to go, but I'll check in on you later. Thanks Mr. Abrams, you be careful."

"You too Professor."

Octavius turned right off of Market Street and reached South Street when a woman came running in his direction. She frantically pulled on his sleeves and blocked his path.

"Don't go down there Professor. They just shot Mr. Fausett."

Octavius politely thanked her and walked her safely to her door before proceeding down the street. He was one block away from his home, on the corner of South and Eighth Street, when he saw three white men briskly coming toward him. Immediately, he reached for the bulletless pistol he had in his coat pocket and prepared to draw it if need be. He then walked to the other side of the street as a defensive maneuver. However, the three men crossed over as well and stood directly in front of him. Octavius clutched the gun hidden in his coat pocket, pushed right through them and took four more steps.

"Watch out Professor he's got a gun!" came a panic-filled voice from one of the row homes. One of the three men pulled out a gun and fired two shots, hitting Octavius in the chest. He staggered away from his assailant and stumbled behind a streetcar in the middle of the street. The assailant then walked briskly forward and shot him two more times, as he lay on the ground. Several eyewitnesses screamed hysterically as the three men fled from the scene in different directions.

"They shot him, they shot the professor. Somebody fetch the police!"

"Forget that! Get a doctor somebody! Don't just leave him there!"

"Oh my Lawd, they done killed em!"

John Ansar and Caroline had just arrived at her door when they heard a horrific chorus of screams. They started running in the direction of the yelling until they came upon a terror-stricken woman wailing in the middle of the street.

"What's wrong?, hollered John, grabbing both of her arms. "What's wrong?" he repeated, shaking her body.

"They shot him... shot Professor Catto... shot him down!"

John and Caroline sprinted in the direction she pointed to. When they reached Octavius, he lay motionless on the ground. Caroline pushed through the crowd of people encircled around him. Mr. Reid was sitting on the ground holding Octavius. He gently passed him to Caroline who lifted Octavius' head and placed it on her lap. Octavius gulped hard and tried to speak but couldn't at first. He was weak and fading fast. Seconds later, he managed to whisper a few words.

"Caroline... my inside pocket...my ballot...I want you to cast my...my vote for me...You do that for me, okay?"

"Yes my love. I'll do it. But we can go together okay? We'll go together," she said, stoking his hair. She reached inside his suit jacket and removed the ballot and a tri-folded piece of paper.

As Caroline cried uncontrollably, Octavius drew a deep breath and desperately tried to speak again.

"Caroline...All this time...I was worried that you might leave me. I never thought...(Gulp)...I would be leaving you... (Gulp)... John?"

"I'm here boy. I ain't going nowhere."

"Tell my father it's gonna be okay...Everything is okay... Maybe now I'll get to see my mother. I've wanted to see her for so long... (gasp)... Caroline, I want you to know I... I....I love you...I will always love you..."

With those faint words, he died in Caroline's arms. As she slowly rocked his listless body, a police paddy wagon arrived on the scene. One policeman got out and ran over to Octavius. A second policeman hastily questioned a few people.

"Did you see who did this?"

"Yeah, he went that way!" yelled Mr. Reid.

"Yeah, I followed him. He went that way into O'Grady's Pub," shouted another man.

The assailant mingled among the patrons gathered in the pub. He took a seat at the bar, trying his best to be inconspicuous. The policeman entered the bar and started interrogating the patrons. No one seemed willing to cooperate. No one saw anything and no one heard anything. As the policeman headed for the door, he was nudged by an elderly woman who discreetly pointed to the assailant sitting at the end of the bar. The policeman walked over to him and drew his gun.

"You, get up! Out this way."

They left together out the rear exit of the pub that led into an alleyway. They were alone and well out of sight.

"Are you the man who shot Catto?"

"Yeah, what of it?"

"Quick, you better get outta here! This way, then turn left on Carpenter Street. It's your best chance to get away. Go!"

As instructed, the assailant sprinted south down the alleyway. The policeman ran north in mock pursuit.

Newspaper Drawing of the Murder of Octavius V. Catto

43. Justice Waits

"Like a cloud, pregnant with terror and destruction, disenfranchisement has spread its wings over our brethren in the South. Like the same dark cloud, industrial prejudice glooms above us in the North. We may not work, save when the new-come foreigner refuses to, and then they, high prized above our sacrificial lives, may shoot us down with impunity."

Paul Laurence Dunbar

The rains returned with a vengeance. On October 16th, Octavius' body lied in state at the Armory of the First Regiment at Broad and Race Streets. Outside, the rains pounded the streets with relentless fury. All city offices were closed in Octavius' honor. Scores of state and municipal representatives and friends joined the three mile long procession down Broad Street. They seemed oblivious to the high winds and driving rains that pelted the city. Jacob White led a group of grief-stricken students and teachers from the Institute who flanked his casket as it rolled down Broad Street. They were followed by General Wagner's regiment and several military units from Washington, Baltimore, and Wilmington. Throngs of Negro and white citizens lined the streets in solemn reverence as the large procession made its way to Mount Lebanon Cemetery, where he was buried with full military honors.

The Philadelphia Daily Ledger reported, **"not since the funeral cortege of President Lincoln has there been a funeral as large and as imposing in the city"**. The Philadelphia Examiner described it as **"one of the most elaborate funerals ever held for a colored man in the nation."**

So ended the career of a young man of splendid talents—a man of rare force of character, whose life was so interwoven with all that, was good and decent about Philadelphia. His very existence was a benediction to the city. His was a life that stood out in bold relief as a guiding star – a brilliant light that was extinguished far too soon.

∞∞∞∞∞∞∞∞∞∞∞∞

Ms. Jackson did not attend the lengthy funeral service nor did she participate in the slow, mournful march to the cemetery. She insisted that Caroline LeCount stay with her at her home so she could keep a close watch over her during this traumatic time. Caroline was devastated beyond words and barely had enough strength to stand up, let alone attend the funeral of her beloved. Her once bright eyes were completely glazed over and she rarely blinked. She had deteriorated into a catatonic state that rendered her devoid of expression. She reclined in bed motionless, clutching the poem that Octavius had written with her in mind. Her characteristically sunny disposition vanished as the rains penetrated to the depths of her very soul.

From her bedroom window facing Broad Street, Ms. Jackson could hear the solemn, staccato cadence of drums beating in slow rhythm with the well-coordinated steps of the ornate military procession. Occasionally, Scottish bagpipes could be heard off at a distance. They too played slowly and spoke of sadness and respectful commemoration of the deceased. But, the sounds of the sorrowful trek offered little in the way of comfort to Ms. Jackson. She slammed her window closed and covered her ears with both hands. Yet, there was nothing that could drown out the mournful sounds and alleviate the unbearable sorrow that she also felt.

Caroline and Octavius had promised to love each other till the end of time. Now, time had been brutally and summarily taken from both of them. The time bandits had snuffed out another bright light. They had claimed another victim and another victory. That afternoon, the city was quiet and remained in mourning. However, there were a few notable exceptions. Across town, the celebration at O'Grady's pub was loud and raucous. A precious life had been taken and in turn, countless other lives had been devastated. But beer at O'Grady's place was cheap and flowed freely from keg to mug. And the time bandits were far too joyful and far too shameless to care.

∞∞∞∞∞∞∞∞∞∞

It did not take long for Ms. Jackson's grief and anguish to turn into anger and indignation. Two days later, she and Jacob White called for a town meeting and an outdoor rally to protest the murder of Octavius V. Catto and pressure the Mayor into bringing the guilty parties to justice. Negro and White citizens turned our in droves and filled Franklin Hall to capacity. The Quaker managers of the Institute added their voices to a growing chorus of citizens who demanded a full investigation into the murder and an immediate end to the anti-Negro violence that was going unchecked in the city. But these protests accomplished nothing. Octavius' murderer, a man later identified as Frank Kelly, managed to avoid arrest with the assistance of several accomplices. City officials and the police department claimed to have no knowledge of his whereabouts. In addition, no one in authority seemed to want to discuss or explain Kelly's sudden disappearance.

The residents of the Seventh Ward were horrified by what was obviously a widespread, conspiratorial cover-up. The students and faculty of the Institute were stunned, as was Reverend Catto who was already in bad health. Upon hearing of Kelly's escape, he died suddenly in his home a week later. The medical cause of death was listed as "double pneumonia". However, Mr. Still knew better. He was sure that his friend had died of a broken heart.

The last entry in Reverend Catto's personal diary revealed a grieving yet resilient man, valiantly coping with the tragic senselessness of it all.

No parent should have to bury a child. But I thank God, for his life and living. Octavius was not shackled to our painful past nor did he fall prey to the many mental slaveries that currently ensnare so many of us. He tried to make the best and highest use of his talents. He had both roots and wings! And I thank you Lord, that he tried and tried again to fly to the Light. I miss him. But alas, Death is our common lot. And it will come soon enough and reveal to us all our lifelong book of accounts.

If I told him once, I told him a thousand times. The world is full of deceivers and deceptions. Their lies and illusions run deep – deeper than most can imagine. They call us all to the pursuit of frivolous goals and petty distractions that mean so little in the big picture and count for nothing at the end of life's journey. The children must not waste their irreplaceable time chasing the wind. Their days are few. And they must spend them wisely. True love abides and only goodness has real value.

Octavius understood this. We simply must guide the children and help them cultivate their gifts, so that can take full advantage of the limited supply of time that they are granted here on earth. And above all things, we must teach them and show them how to love. They must not fail; they must not flounder. Because life is short and the end comes quickly. So with each passing day, we must continue to warn them about the time bandi…

44. The Story Teller

"If you want Negro history, you will have to get it from somebody who wore the shoe and by and by, you will get a book."

Anonymous (Former slave)

In what seemed like an instantaneous flash in time, Mr. Still had to bury three cherished friends: Sarah, Octavius and then Reverend Catto, his dearest friend and most steadfast ally. His heart ached beyond measure and there was no ready relief from the emotional crush of it all. Memories of the Catto family flooded his mind as he tried not to recall the cruel circumstances surrounding their heart-breaking deaths.

Yet the more he tried to suppress those memories, the more they gained in strength and assaulted his mind. Mr. Still had previously buried many friends and several martyrs in his crusade to purge the land of slavery and racial hatred. Their tragic deaths had also taken a heavy toll on him. However, he had always managed to cope with such losses; secured by his faith in the righteousness of their cause and the overarching wisdom of a just and merciful God.

But somehow, the deaths of all three Cattos seemed too much for him to bear; or at least it appeared so on that rainy day in October. His longstanding faith in Divine Providence had been badly shaken and his battered soul yearned for some semblance of understanding. Try as he might, he could not escape the ageless questions that have perplexed humankind from time immemorial. Why does God allow bad things to happen to good people? Why do the wicked go unpunished? And, why is it that the good die young?

The cold and gray day after Reverend Catto's funeral, he paced back and forth in his den, trying to contain the anxiety that had tormented him the previous night and greeted him with the dawn. For some inexplicable reason, he decided to go for a walk and brave the heavy rains that were saturating the city. He left his home and slowly proceeded down South Street without the benefit of an umbrella or any particular destination in mind.

The winds blew relentlessly as his body offered faint resistance to their awesome power. The gusts were reaching gale force as Mr. Still struggled not to be swept off his feet. As an evasive maneuver, he veered onto Eighth Street where there were taller buildings and found himself moving north in the direction of Mount Lebanon Cemetery.

Standing at the gates of the cemetery, he paused for a moment to gaze at the crackling lightening that was illuminating the dark sky with great frequency and ferocity. As the winds began to howl, he experienced a prodding to enter through the gates and walk aimlessly among the tombstones and mausoleums.

He delved further into the cemetery and arrived at a large stone obelisk situated at its center and towering over all of the other gravesites. The obelisk appeared to tilting to the right, but that was most likely an optical illusion caused by the torrential rains diagonally beating down on everything in sight. At any rate, Mr. Still then turned right and within minutes found himself standing in front of the three gravestones of the Catto family, neatly aligned on a grassy mound. An inexplicable force drew him closer to the Catto family plot that was located just a few feet away from the gravesite where he had once buried his tattered records during those dangerous days when the Fugitive Slave Act was the law of the land. Sol Abrams had convinced him to bury those records as a symbolic gesture. And there they remained for the last six few years.

On impulse, Mr. Still slowly knelt in front of Octavius' tombstone and heard a gentle voice beckon to him from the soggy earth. "God does not place on you a burden greater than you can bear. There is still much work to be done." The words were clear and the experience was so undeniably real. It was a brief and unmistakable inspiration that rallied his spirit and filled him with an unexplainable peace. Kneeling at the Catto family plot, he realized an unpaid debt of gratitude that he owed to an even larger family – the faithful and the fallen who had died in the bloody battle for freedom and justice. They too lived and died well. They too were worthy of remembrance.

He dreamt that night and received an even clearer and more directive call to arms. His new task was to write a book. Thus in the morning, a resolute William Still set out on a journey of remembrance. It fell to him and him alone to tell these stories and to rescue from oblivion those souls who had been written out of history, faded from memory and all but forgotten. Even in this final season of his life, he could still see their faces through the mist of time. That was because many of them were his cherished friends. They belonged to an interwoven and ever-expanding family of spiritual warriors who came to rely upon his resourcefulness and the courage and fortitude of one another. In silent reflection, he vividly recalled the gallery of men and women of all races and faiths who gave mightily to his cause – their cause. He would tell these stories as a tribute to the faithful and the fallen – not to romanticize, but to remember those who lovingly and courageously dared to redirect the course of human history. It was time to uncover a hidden past; time to reclaim a vital legacy.

And so it came to pass. One year after Octavius' death, Mr. Still published his book entitled, The Underground Railroad. The book received considerable acclaim throughout the country. After its first publication in 1872, he had it reprinted twice and hired agents to help him market it in several major cities. In recognition of his well-deserved literary success, he was invited to be a guest speaker at the Institute's annual fall convocation named in honor of Octavius V. Catto. On Thursday, October 11, 1876, he spoke briefly about his fond memories of Octavius and reminded the students that while Octavius died at the age of thirty-two, it matters not *how long* you live, but rather *how well* you live.

"Five years ago, Professor Catto was taken from us," he said. "Yes, back then we buried the man. Today, we continue the plan!"

After his brief remarks, Mr. Still introduced the keynote speaker for the occasion. He was none other than Marcus Aurelius Johnson, one of Octavius' former students. Marcus' oratorical flare and rhythmic cadence was eerily reminiscent of his slain teacher. Their striking physical similarities were also hard to ignore. Marcus held the audience in rapt attention for thirty minutes and concluded his remarks by reaching into his vest pocket.

"I carry with me this bullet given to me by my fellow members of the Benjamin Banneker Society. It is an assassin's bullet, taken from Professor Catto's body. It is a small and inglorious object that was used to silence a truly great man. It reminds me of that tragic day in 1871 when he was taken from us. But, it also reminds me of the foolishness of his murderers. Did they really think a bullet could extinguish a flame?

It also reminds me every day of my life, what Professor Catto gave his life for. It bids me to ask you this question: To whom are we more indebted? To our teachers and martyrs or to unworthy, power-seeking leaders who know nothing of true service, courage, devotion and compassion for mankind. Surely, this world of ours needs something better than the destructive results of arrogance, greed and unconstrained power. And, we should demand from ourselves something better than apathy and a passive acceptance of the audacious forward march of evil in this country, trampling on the rights of the many. Mr. Still is right as one can possibly be. Today, we must continue Professor Catto's plan, our plan! So I ask you again, **What are you about?"**

Ms. Jackson looked on approvingly as Marcus graciously received a standing ovation. She was warmed by the fact that he decided to forego a lucrative job in the construction business and opted instead to join the faculty of the Institute's Preparatory Department in the spring. Marcus Aurelius Johnson had summarily rejected the siren song of the *time bandits*. And she would warmly embrace him with open arms as a trusted ally and a stalwart soldier in their battle to win the hearts and minds of Philadelphia's youth.

45. The Trial

"A government which has the power to tax a man in peace and draft him in war should have power to defend his life in his hour of peril. A government which can protect and defend its citizens from wrong and outrage and does not is vicious. A government which would do it and cannot is weak; and where human life is insecure through either weakness or viciousness in the administration of law, there must be a lack of justice and where this is wanting, nothing can make up the deficiency."

Frances Ellen Watkins Harper

The welcomed news came nearly five years and three months latter. On January 17, 1877, Frank Kelly, the man suspected of murdering Octavius, was arrested in Chicago for voting fraud and assault. More importantly, he was being extradited to Philadelphia to stand trial for his cowardly deed. Nearly everyone knew that his extradition did not come about by chance alone. The Mayor realized he needed the vote of the colored community if he was going to win re-election against a very formidable opponent.

Philadelphia's Negro voting population remembered all too well that justice had not been served in the tragic murder of Octavius V. Catto. Mr. Still and other Negro civic leaders hoped that the arrest of Kelly, after all those years, was not just another example of the Mayor's penchant for political gamesmanship. They prayed that the trial would be more than cheap political theater. After all, justice had been delayed for far too long.

∞∞∞∞∞∞∞∞∞

The controversial trial began as scheduled and the courtroom was packed with spectators. Kelly's legal defense team knew of Octavius' outstanding reputation throughout the city. To assail his sterling character would have been fruitless and possibly counterproductive. Instead, they shrewdly developed a defense strategy designed to impugn the "political and racial motives" of the prosecution's witnesses. They were determined to challenge the reliability of several eyewitness accounts based on the fact that over five years had passed and memories had a way of fading over time. Moreover, their defense strategy hinged on the assertion that Octavius drew his pistol first.

Mr. Still was fortunate enough to get a seat on the day that the district attorney and defense attorney delivered their closing arguments. The defense attorney, Mr. Bowman went first. He was strikingly glib and well pleased with the crafty role he had already played in selecting an all-white jury to serve in this high profile case.

"...And yes, ladies and gentlemen of the jury. My client has freely admitted that he fired his weapon at Mr. Catto. But let us not forget some important facts that are pivotal to this case. We have heard striking testimony from his employer, Mr. Conley (a very distinguished businessman of this community) and Mr. Kelly's good friend, Mr. Reddy Devers who have testified under oath that my client was peacefully sitting on a stoop with them when Mr. Catto suddenly and without provocation, charged at them in a fit of rage. So let us remember that my client was in absolute fear for his life.

Now I ask you; who among us would not do the same, if we saw an irate and armed colored man coming in our direction? Since when is *self-defense* a crime in this country?"

The assistant district attorney, Mr. Hagert went next. He was quite confident that the prosecutorial evidence he had presented was more than enough to support a verdict of first-degree murder or at the very least, manslaughter.

"...In conclusion, ladies and gentlemen of the jury, the facts in his case are clear and the evidence is strong and conclusive. The defense attorney, Mr. Bowman, calls it self-defense. *Self-defense? I think not!* You have heard the coroner testify that Professor Catto was shot four times. The first bullet struck him in the back. After that first shot, eyewitnesses tell us that he spun around and threw up both arms and raised them across his body in what we can only assume was a protective reaction. He was then shot a second time and went staggering into the street where he sought cover behind a parked streetcar. He was then followed by Mr. Kelly who proceeded to ruthlessly fire two more shots into Professor Catto's body as he lay defenseless on the ground. And those, ladies and gentlemen, are the simply, incontrovertible facts!

And why was he killed? You have heard vivid testimony that the murder of Professor Catto was but a part of a larger preconceived conspiracy to intimidate and bully the colored voters in the southern section of this city. That fact has been established by several witnesses, both white and colored, who have added their voices to the hundreds of citizens who are demanding that justice be served. There is but one way to end this tragic story; and that is with a verdict of guilty! And, with such a verdict, we can close a chapter in the history of this great city when mobocracy reigned, when street gangs and common thugs were permitted to hold high carnival, and heartless and vicious criminals like Mr. Kelly stalked the streets in the broad light of day. There is but one thing left to say to Mr. Kelly and this court; and that is guilty. **Guilty of murder in the first degree!**"

∞∞∞∞∞∞∞∞∞∞∞

On the morning of May 4, 1877, the lengthy trial of Frank Kelly came to an end. The entire city held its breath in anxious anticipation of the long-awaited verdict. The courtroom was filled to capacity and humming with electric tension. Emotions were excruciatingly high as the bailiff called the court to order and announced Judge Andrews' entry into the courtroom.

The judge took his seat on the bench and was noticeably distracted by an attractive woman who was seated in the first row. In response to her smile, he casually adjusted his robe and combed his wavy hair backwards with the palms of his hands. His gaze then turned to some items on his desk. The courtroom went silent as he perused a few documents, which included the morning newspaper. The over-packed visitors' gallery waited with baited breath for what seemed like an eternity. Finally, he leaned forward in his chair and directed a furtive glance at the defense attorney, Mr. Bowman.

"Ladies and gentlemen, this court has been properly called to order. We are here this morning to conclude the case of the Commonwealth of Pennsylvania versus Frank Kelly who has been charged with the crime of first-degree murder. Has the jury reached a verdict?"

"We have your Honor," answered the jury foreman.

"Members of the jury please stand and face the defendant. Mr. foreman, you may read that verdict."

"We the jury, find the defendant, Frank Kelly, ...**Not guilty**."

Utter pandemonium ensued. The courtroom instantly erupted with raw, pent-up emotion. Friends of Octavius were hysterical and shouted in righteous indignation. Caroline LeCount fainted and had to be carried out of the courtroom. Fannie Jackson stood and stared at the jury in frozen silence; she could scarcely believe her ears. An enraged Father Kendrick stormed out of the courtroom and unapologetically knocked down two newspaper reporters as be bolted out of the building. On the other side of the room, Kelly was congratulated by his lawyer and a large group of friends who were joyously celebrating his acquittal. The controversial and politically charged trial had come to a bizarre and tragic conclusion.

By most accounts, justice had been callously denied. And once again, the ruthless time bandits had gotten away with murder.

Frank Kelly

Three weeks later, Father Kendrick and Ms. Jackson were walking down Bainbridge Street together, alluding puddles of water left by yesterday's rains. It was a bright and sunny day. A gentle breeze was blowing from the east and the cleansing rains had left a welcomed sweetness in the air.

The two of them stopped in front of the Institute as Ms. Jackson took a deep whiff of the honeysuckles that graced the landscaping surrounding the school.

"I want to thank you Father for being this week's guest lecturer."

"The pleasure is all mine I assure you. Ah, by the way Fannie, is there any truth to the rumor that Ms. LeCount is leaving the Institute?"

"Yes indeed Father. The City Council has agreed to build a new elementary school in West Philadelphia. It's to be named after Octavius and she's going to be its first principal."

"That's great. And a fitting tribute I must say."

"Yes it is. But my heart goes out to her. She is so broken up about the verdict. It's hard for her to accept the fact that the man who murdered Octavius in cold blood could be back on the streets again, free as a bird!"

"Oh, I wouldn't bet on that my dear."

"What do you mean Father?"

"Well, I'll let you in on a little secret."

He paused for a moment and flashed her a sheepish grin.

"You see my dear, it just so happened that we paid a visit to Mr. Kelly's favorite watering hole not too long ago..."

∞∞∞∞∞∞∞∞∞

Father Kendrick then proceeded to tell her the story about the plan he had concocted. A week after the verdict, he and Charley O'Rourke went to O'Grady's pub. They sat in a booth drinking large quantities of cheap whiskey and pretending to be drunk. Father Kendrick deliberately started talking loudly in order to attract the attention of Tom McMullen, Frank Kelly and a group of their friends who were carousing in an adjacent booth. As anticipated, they began to subtlety eavesdrop on Father Kendrick's loud conversation. As they discreetly listened in, Father Kendrick became more animated and clumsily knocked over his drink. He immediately ordered another round of whiskey and began to slur his speech even more.

"...Yeah I tell yez what Charley me lad. That Ms. Ogden, she's a card that one! She's got more money and real estate than the Vatican itself. And, let's not talk about diamonds and jewels. Saints alive, she's got a wagonload of 'em."

"Wow Father, where does she keep all that loot – in a federal vault? That's where I would keep it".

"Now that's the kicker. That old woman is insane! Insane I tell ya! Sez she doesn't trust banks. She keeps it right there with her in her bedroom. She sez she likes to keep an eye on all that stuff. Imagine that. It's ridiculous!"

"Father you're joking of course. Please tell me you're joking."

"I kid you not laddie. An old widow like that living alone, surrounded by all that bounty. It doesn't make any sense to me...Anyways, enough about that cuckoo...I gotta annuda joke fer ya. Did ya hear the one about the rabbi, the priest and the farm girl? It's a dilly..."

∞∞∞∞∞∞∞∞∞

The next night, Boss Conley and his new chauffer, Reddy Devers, were sitting in his carriage at the end of a cobblestone path leading to

Ms. Ogden's mansion in the exclusive Chestnut Hill section of the city. They had just dropped off Frank Kelly and Tom McMullen who slowly tiptoed up a winding walkway and stopped on the north side of the mansion. The two men carefully broke a windowpane and nimbly climbed through a decorative bay window.

Once inside, they made their way to the master bedroom where Frank Kelly wrapped the nozzle of his pistol in a towel and fired two muffled shots into a pile of clothes made to appear like Mrs. Ogden soundly asleep in her bed. Then the two would-be burglars were immediately tackled from behind by ten armed policemen who were already inside waiting to arrest them. And that they did, with ready handcuffs and deliberate speed and efficiency.

Meanwhile, Boss Conley and Reddy Devers waited outside and shared a flask of Jamaican rum.

"I want to thank you for giving me this job Boss."

"Don't mention it. I'm always willing to help out a fellow countryman. Just stick with me. Before long, we're going to own this whole city. And I'll tell ya something else Reddy. It looks like Christmas came early for us this year. Like I always say, there's nothing like good inside information. By the way, who gave us the tip on this one?"

"Well Boss, I'm not sure. But, I think McMullen said he accidentally heard it from some priest. I think his name was Father Kender, or was it Kendrick?"

Conley immediately choked and spat out his drink. His face turned beet red as he frantically gasped for air. He instantly realized that it was a trap. Panting heavily, he reached for Reddy's throat just as an additional group of policemen stepped from behind a row of trees and quickly surrounded the carriage. John Ansar and Mr. Abrams watched from behind a tall hedge as Conley and his men were all handcuffed and taken away in a spacious paddy wagon.

∞∞∞∞∞∞∞∞∞∞

Father Kendrick finished telling her the story about the ingenious plan that he and Charley O'Rourke had executed to perfection.

"...so you see, Fannie my dear, it's not likely that Caroline's going to be seeing those characters anytime soon."

"Oh Father, I must say, you're quite a character yourself."

"Well I suppose so. But, you know what Uncle Blue used to say? *Those that bite?*"

"*Shall be bitten!*" she answered.

"*And those that don't bite?*"

"*Shall get et up!*" she replied.

After a bittersweet laugh together, they walked arm-in-arm into the school.

∞∞∞∞∞∞∞∞∞∞

Outside, the sky was a bright crystal blue. Westward winds blew softly across the Delaware River and into countless opened windows throughout the Seventh Ward. The clouds gently parted as the streets below were splashed with the warm rays of a beneficent sun, proclaiming the recurring triumph of light over darkness. Cleansing breezes spread the last remnants of moisture throughout a bustling city preparing itself to receive the bountiful blessings of a new day. Hope, glorious hope reappeared. And once again, the rains had fulfilled their purpose.

Notable Historical Figures Cited in *The Rains*

Absalom Jones (1746-1818)

Richard Allen (1760-1831)

James Forten Sr. (1766-1842)

David Walker (1785-1830)

Lucretia Mott (1793-1880)

Dred Scott (1795-1858)

Levi Coffin (1798-1877)

Nat Turner (1800-1831)

John Brown (1800-1859)

Elijah P. Lovejoy (1802-1837)

Ralph Waldo Emerson (1803-1882)

William Lloyd Garrison (1805-1879)

Robert Purvis (1810-1898)

William T. Catto (1810-187?)

Theodore Parker (1810-1860)

Harriet Beecher Stowe (1811-1896)

Henry Highland Garnet (1815-1882)

Frederick Douglass (1818-1895)

Charles L. Reason (1818-1893)

Harriet Tubman (1820-1913)

William Still (1821-1902)

William Craft (1821-1900)

Frances E. Watkins Harper (1825-1911)

Ellen Craft (1826-1891)

Ebenezer Bassett (1833-1908)

Anthony Burns (1834-1862)

Fannie Jackson [Coppin] (1835-1913)

Jacob C. White Jr. (1837-1902)

Octavius V. Catto (1839-1871)

Richard T. Greener (1844-1922)

Chronology of Key Events in Philadelphia and the Nation
(Cited in *The Rains*)

The Post-Revolutionary War Period

1780   Pennsylvania enacts a law calling for the gradual abolishment of slavery

1787   The United States Constitution adopted on September 17.

       The Reverend Richard Allen et al organize the Free African Society to promote Negro improvement

1793   The United States Congress enacts the first Fugitive Slave Act

1794   The Reverend Richard Allen organizes Mother Bethel Church in Philadelphia

The Antebellum Period

1820   The United States Congress passes the Missouri Compromise

1829   David Walker publishes an anti-slavery treatise entitled *An Appeal to the Colored People of the World*

1830   First National Negro Convention (chaired by the Reverend Richard Allen) meets at Mother Bethel Church in Philadelphia

1831   Nat Turner leads slave revolt in Southampton, VA

       William Lloyd Garrison launches his abolitionist publication, *The Liberator*

1833   Negro and white abolitionists organize the American Anti-Slavery Society in Philadelphia

1833   Philadelphia Female Anti-Slavery Society founded by Charlotte Forten, Maria Stewart and other women of color

1834   Anti-Negro riots escalate. White mobs assault colored citizens in 1835, 1838, 1842 and 1849

1837   Elijah P. Lovejoy killed by anti-abolitionist mob

1838   Pennsylvania Hall burned (May 17)
        Shelter for Colored Orphans burned (May 18)

1842   White mobs attack colored citizens during a Jamaican Independence Day celebration. Anti-Abolitionist and anti-Negro riots occur; African Presbyterian Church burned along with colored homes, businesses and meeting places.

1843   Henry Highland Garnet publishes his, Appeal *to the Slaves* at the National   Convention of Colored Citizens

1847   Frederick Douglass begins publishing his newspaper, the *North Star*

1848   William and Ellen Craft arrive in Philadelphia[2]

1849   Henry "Box" Brown escapes to Philadelphia in a crate

1850   The U.S. Congress passes the Compromise of 1850 including a new Fugitive Slave Act

1851   Christiana Uprising, armed colored farmers resist capture

1852   The Institute for Colored Youth (later named Cheyney University) opens in Philadelphia

        Publication of Harriet Beecher Stowe's controversial book, *Uncle Tom's Cabin*

1854   Ashmun Institute (later named Lincoln University) opens in Oxford, PA

        Anthony Burns arrested, causing protests in Boston, MA (May 24)

        Frances E.W. Harper publishes her, *Poems on Miscellaneous Subjects*

---

[2] For an actual and detailed description of the escape of William and Ellen Craft, see their personal account in *Running a Thousand Miles for Freedom*. This book was originally published in London by William Tweedie (1860) and later published in 1999 by the University of Georgia Press.

1856   U.S. Senator, Charles Sumner beaten (caned) in Congress (May 22)

1857   The U.S. Supreme Court issues its ruling on the Dred Scott case

1858   Philadelphia operates its passenger cars for the first time (January)

1859   John Brown leads revolt at Harper's Ferry, West Virginia

1860   Abraham Lincoln is elected President of the United States

The Civil War Years

1861   Confederate forces fire on Fort Sumter, a federally controlled garrison

President Lincoln calls a special session of Congress to declare war on the Confederate states

1862   The Battle of Antietam, the bloodiest one-day battle of the Civil War

The U.S. Congress authorizes the enlistment of Negroes for military service

1863   President Lincoln issues the Emancipation Proclamation (takes effect January 1)

The Battle of Gettysburg is fought (June)

The Negro 54th Massachusetts Volunteer Regiment leads attack on Fort Wagner (July)

Grand review of colored troops at Camp William Penn near Philadelphia (September 24)

1864   Massacre of Negro troops at Fort Pillow Tennessee (April)

President Lincoln wins re-election (November)

The Reconstruction Era

1865   Confederate states surrender at Appomattox, VA ending the Civil War (April)

President Lincoln is assassinated in Washington, D.C. (April 15)

The Ku Klux Klan is formed

Congress establishes the Freedman's Bureau and passes the 13th Amendment abolishing slavery in the U.S.

1866   Octavius V. Catto leads boycotts protesting racial discrimination on Philadelphia street cars

1868   Fourteenth Amendment is passed stipulating, "No state shall make or enforce any law which shall abridge the privileges or immunities of citizens of the United States; nor shall any State deprive any person of life, liberty or property, without due process of law; nor deprive any person within its jurisdiction the equal protection of the laws".

1870   Fifteenth Amendment is passed, extending voting rights to African Americans

Colored Philadelphians organize a massive parade to Independence Hall to celebrate the Fifteenth Amendment. Angry mobs attack the procession and it is discontinued.

1871   Octavius V. Catto murdered in Philadelphia (October 10)

1876   Rutherford B. Hayes is declared the winner in a controversial presidential election. The Reconstruction era draws to an end.

1877   Frank Kelly is acquitted of murder charges in the death of Octavius V. Catto.

ABOUT THE AUTHOR

Sulayman Clark is a writer, lecturer and fund raising consultant. He is a graduate of Cheyney University of Pennsylvania and Stanford University and subsequently earned his doctoral degree from Harvard University. His appointments include: Vice President for Institutional Advancement at Fisk University and Vice President for Development at Hampton University, Tuskegee University, Lincoln University (PA) and Morehouse College.

∞∞∞∞∞∞∞∞∞∞∞

Visit **www.therains.org** or **www.sulaymanclark.com** to:

- Share your comments about *The Rains*

- Communicate with the author

- Purchase additional copies of the book

- Ask about discounted prices for schools and non-profit organizations

To inquire about having the author speak to your school or organization contact: **sulaymanclarklit@gmail.com**